DANCE OF DESPAIR

THE ILVANNIAN CHRONICLES BOOK TWO

KARA S. WEAVER

DANCE OF DESPAIR

THE ILVANNIAN CHRONICLES BOOK TWO

KARA S. WEAVER

Cover Design by www.originalbookcoverdesigns.com

First Edition: February 2020

DEDICATION

To all the warriors out there, regardless of what battle you're facing.
To Marloes, the wickedest warrior of all.

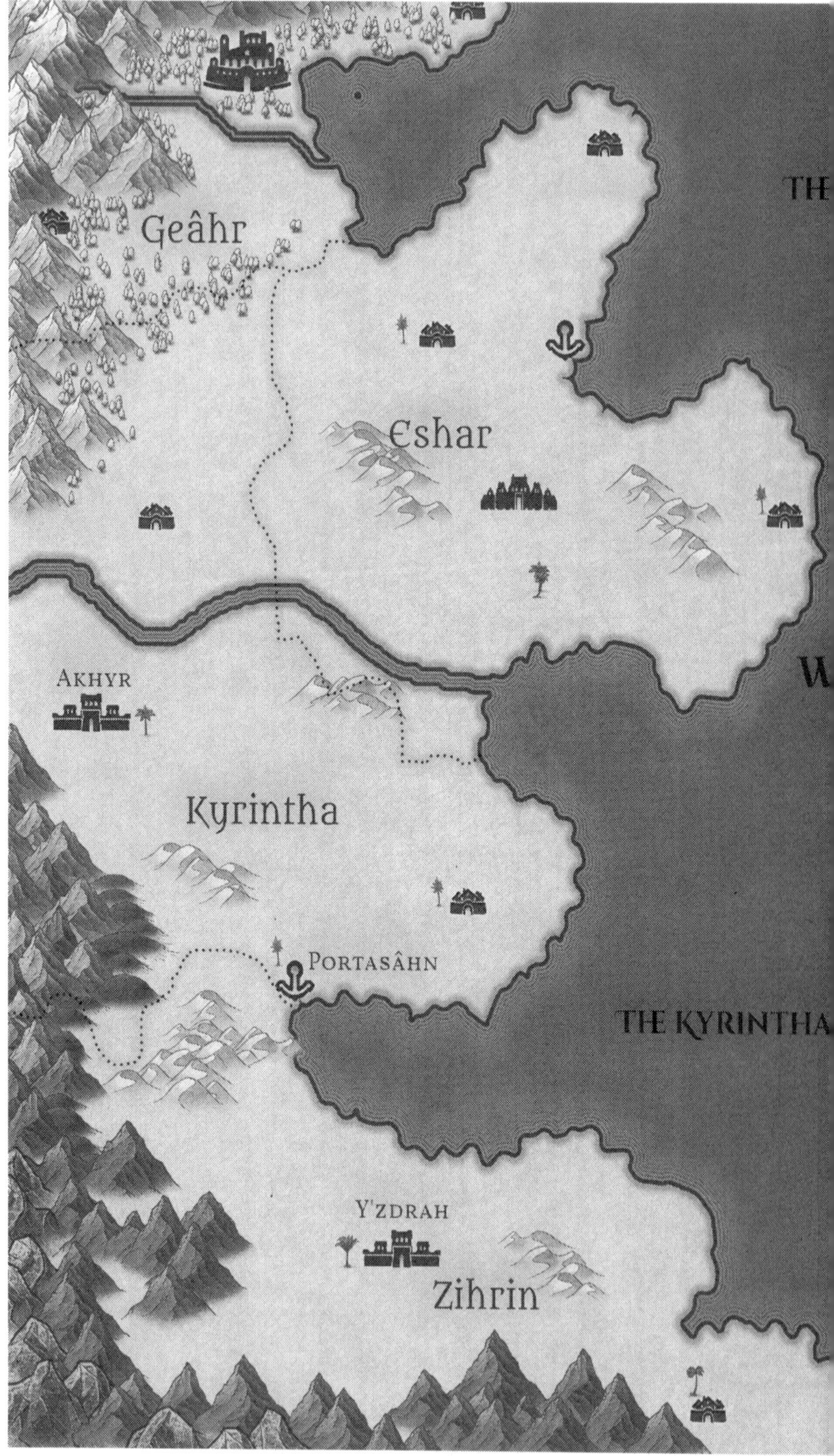

Geâhr
Eshar
Akhyr
Kyrintha
Portasâhn
The Kyrintha
Y'zdrah
Zihrin

SEA
N
E
Ilvanna
Ilvanna
Naehr
Denahryn
Hanyarah
Fayrehnear
Therondia

ORIGIN STORY

Under normal circumstances, I do not bother with the world of mortals, nor do my brothers and sisters. Unfortunately, circumstances haven't been normal for hundreds of years, so we saw fit to make some changes. Minor changes, not enough to disrupt the fabric of the world, but enough to make an impact in the future—and that future, is upon us.

Esahbyen, God of War

PROLOGUE

ESAHBYEN

The world of our children was no longer for us, the Gods, but sometimes I yearned to walk among them, to watch how they made their lives their own and made the mistakes we had so carefully avoided when we still had a presence in their world. But for us to roam it again would mean devastation of the highest order—an apocalypse if you will—so we only deal with them as *Sevaehthaer*, mere projections of our true selves that can only visit their world in very specific places.

Seeing my daughter clearly, no longer a small babe but an adult woman, had been the best part of my last visit. She had had no idea who, or what, I was—which was probably for the better—but she hadn't been scared. In fact, she'd been annoyed, and in that moment had looked so much like her mother—the only mortal with whom I had ever lain—that it broke my heart knowing she would soon lose her.

I had not counted on the ferocity inside of her—the will, the discipline, and the strength to endure what she endured, which was why I sought my brother out.

"Please, Seydeh. Don't do this."

He looked at me, eyes the colour of the great deep ocean

regarding me dispassionately. Seydeh had been of the sea for so long, his personality had begun to match. His moods went from a quiet calm to a ferocious storm in a matter of moments, regardless of what, or who, was in his way.

"I do not control the weather, Brother," Seydeh replied, turning away to look upon the globe through which we witnessed the world. "It comes and goes as it pleases."

"Surely there must be something you can do?"

His eyes changed from the deep green of the sea to a swirling storm of all colours as he turned back to me, tilting his head to the side.

"I thought we had agreed not to interfere with our children's lives?"

Grabbing the rail around the globe tight, I leaned heavily upon my arms, closing my eyes.

"You do not understand, Seydeh," I whispered through clenched teeth. "This is too important to leave to something as mercurial as the weather. Please?"

Hearing footsteps, I looked up to see our eldest sister walking our way. Dressed in a long white gown, silver hair flowing loosely to set off her long, elegant ears, Xiomara looked as impeccable as ever, but there could only be one reason why she would interrupt our conversation.

"Seydeh has the right of it, Brother," she said in her musical lilt. "We cannot interfere. Do you remember the last time we did?"

Her eyes took on a distant look, filled with sadness and remorse, yet it passed quickly.

"Of course I remember," I replied, jaw clenched tight, "although you cannot deny, Sister, the signs of history repeating itself."

Xiomara glided over the floor towards the globe, lips parting as if she were surprised. As the Goddess of Life, nothing much took her off guard, but when she looked at the globe and witnessed why I was begging, her brows shot up and she looked at me.

"Esah," she purred, almost amused. "You would beg for a mortal?"

"I told you," I replied. "She's important to our cause."

"As are all our children," Xiomara said, lifting her chin to look down on me, "but we made a vow all those years ago."

"She's getting stronger." I rose to my full height, staring straight in her eyes. She was tall for a woman. "Can you not feel it?"

Her peaceful façade broke for a few moments, revealing the hurt and anger she kept hidden beneath a mask of perfection.

"Of course I do," she said, her voice like ice. "Do you think I would not love to go and stop this madness myself? We made a pact, Esah, to do what must be done and not interfere again. You are asking Seydeh to break that promise!"

My lips curled up in a snarl. "So you would rather allow *your* sister to bring about eternal darkness to the world of our children than saving one who could stop them?"

"She's your sister too," Xiomara scowled.

"No," I replied, folding my arms across my chest, lips pressed in a thin line. "She forfeited that privilege the moment she attacked us."

"What about him then?" She waved her hand across the globe. "Why not beg for his life too?"

The scenery changed to a room. A young man in the throes of a high fever lay in bed, waist covered in bandages. He appeared to be only a step away from greeting death. Xiomara's eyes, normally light as a summer sky, had darkened to a colour moments away from nightfall.

"She will never forgive you if you do not save his life." Her gaze was drawn to the young *Anahràn* visible in the globe, and I was surprised to see a gentleness in them when she looked back at me.

I straightened, pushing up my sleeves. "He is nothing to me."

She shook her head with a sigh, throwing her hands up in surrender. "I do not wish to fight you, Esah. I merely beseech you to think. You've grown too fond of this girl, and you are risking everything by doing so."

"I am not, and I promise that before the end, you will see the right of it."

Xiomara relented with a shake of her head and took a step back to bow in my direction. Seydeh watched us with an unreadable expression on his face.

"There is a price for what you ask," Seydeh said. "It is the way of the world—our way. Nobody is exempt."

I nodded. "And I am willing to pay it, Brother."

He inclined his head and made a sweeping gesture towards the globe. From the corner of my eyes, I saw him go out of focus and before long, he was gone. I gripped the bars around the globe and peered inside. It was a dark, swirling mess with a speck of white in the middle sinking slowly into the darkness, white hair floating like a banner of peace as if she had surrendered.

"He's too late," I whispered in disbelief.

"Seydeh is never late, Brother," Xiomara murmured. "You do know what price he will demand, no?"

I shrugged. "No price is too high to pay for *her* life."

CHAPTER 1

TALNOVAR

Accompanied by a thousand voices raised in an eerie lament, flames danced against the dark backdrop of the night, licking up the pyre in their hungry conquest for more. As the haunting melody reached a crescendo, goosebumps rippled across my arms and slithered down my back, leaving feelings of awe and desolation in its wake. My thoughts were a whirl of whys and ifs chasing each other in an endless loop of despair.

Hollowness established at the top of my head as blood slowly drained from it. A slow buzzing began in my ears, turning into a ringing that reverberated deep inside of my skull. A sharp pain pierced my eyes at the same time as a strangling sensation wrapped around my throat. My mouth turned dry, halting a wail of anguish on the tip of my tongue. The ache in my chest was bad enough it made me want to carve it out—with a blunt knife if I had to. No amount of pain would ever come close to what I was feeling now. Every fibre of my being fought the gut reaction my body had to the undeniable truth in front of my eyes.

No matter how hard I tried to envision it, I couldn't imagine how she could have survived.

It was impossible.

My gaze swept up the burning pyre as it succumbed to the unrelenting flames. Unable to hold back my grief, I howled into the night air in an almost otherworldly cry. The part of me that still struggled with this new reality was at war with the side that wanted to give in to the grief and deal with it on its own terms.

I didn't care much for those terms.

Despite knowing the body on the pyre wasn't Shal's, my legs gave way from under me. The grass underneath my hands and knees was wet and instantly returned my thoughts to Shal's demise.

I could only hope she had died quickly.

A hand on my shoulder returned my attention to the present, and looking up, I found the *Tari* looking down on me, hard eyes hiding a deeper sadness. Rurin hovered just behind, his gaze never leaving her. Ever since she'd fallen ill months ago, before they had taken Shal, he'd been her silent shadow.

"Rise, *Anahràn*," she said, not unkindly. "Your knees are no place to be on in front of Ilvanna."

I swallowed hard and gritted my teeth.

Ilvanna be damned.

Even so, I rose to my feet, reining in my emotions until they were neither visible nor tangible. Within the space of a few heartbeats I returned to the husk of a person I'd become since hearing the news of Shal's death. *Tari* Arayda watched me, her eyes normally dulled by pain now twinkling with curiosity. They were so much like *hers* my chest constricted, so I looked away. Her hand on my cheek brought my gaze back to the *Tari*, only to find her standing close and on her tiptoes.

She was so much shorter than her daughter. How had I never noticed before?

"Your grief for her is admirable, Talnovar," she said, "but do not let it consume you. She wouldn't want that."

"Yeah well," I muttered, tugging at my bracers. "I doubt she wanted to die, yet here we are."

Something flickered in the *Tari's* eyes—something akin to anger, but not quite. Her jaw set in the typical *an Ilvan* manner and pulling back her hand, she straightened herself to her full height. Even though the top of her head barely reached my shoulders, I would never mistake her lack of height for lack of authority.

She had plenty of that.

"Talnovar Imradien." The tone of her voice brooked no argument, which was emphasised by the hands on her hips.

I folded my arms, looking down at her, my anger matching hers. In my peripheral vision, I noticed movement and realised Evanyan had come closer. Between Rurin and him, they could easily wrestle me to the ground if they thought I was a danger to her, but not in a million years would I consider attacking my *Tari*.

We both exhaled at the same time.

"My apologies," I mumbled, jerking a hand through my hair. "It's just... hard."

"I know."

We needed no more words.

A glance at the pyre revealed it had crumbled entirely. The body had been burnt to ashes. Whoever it had been, their family had been well-compensated by a rite most could only dream of. It sickened me that this had been done in order to close off a life I couldn't let go of.

"Arayda," Rurin murmured to her, fondness in his voice. "You should get inside. It's getting too cold."

He draped his cloak around her frail shoulders, drowning her in the sheer size of it. Like myself, Rurin was a tall man, although his build was lean rather than muscular. He dwarfed the *Tari* without even trying. A gentle smile ghosted on her lips when she turned her face up to watch him.

"Please excuse me," I said in a strained voice, stepping back with a stiff bow.

Without waiting for her approval, I hightailed it away from the field and back up to the palace, taking the stairs two steps at a time. People jumped aside as I paid no heed to where I was going.

I knew the route by heart.

THE TIGHTNESS in my chest returned as I ran my fingers across the silk of the last dress she'd ever worn. In the twelve moons since she'd been gone, nobody had really bothered tidying up her room. Everyone else had treated her disappearance as a minor nuisance, expecting her to return all backtalk and sarcasm within a matter of weeks. Yet as time passed and there was no sign of her, rumours had begun to spread—rumours I'd done my best to ignore.

Imagine the shock when Soren appeared a little over a moon ago with the news the *Tarien* had perished at sea. Whether he had escaped or was set free was still a mystery—he hadn't been forthcoming with that information, but aside from looking tired, he had looked well. Whatever the reason for his return, it had been to deliver this news at the least. At first, I had denied all plausibility of her death, claiming she could've somehow gotten out on a rowboat. Surely, whoever had paid good money for her would have been careful with a prize like that.

That was until stories returned of the terrible storm that had raged over the Kyrinthan Gulf and had even made landfall on the shores of Therondia. Villages had vanished without a trace —people had not had any time to escape. Eyewitnesses claimed the wind had blown so hard it had been visible, spinning and churning in an awful maw of destruction, tearing apart everything it came into contact with.

If the news hadn't come from sources in the form of spies and refugees, I would not have believed it. As it was, all that was left of her was in this room, scattered about like cheap items, while in truth they'd become priceless antiquities to her family —to me. Without conscious thought, I picked up the dress and brought it to my face, inhaling the faint scent of oranges, vanilla, and wood—her scent. Even now it stirred emotions I should have kept buried. Father had been right all along—falling in love with her had gotten her killed, while I was supposed to have protected her.

She's dead because of me.

A sob caught in the back of my throat in an inarticulate growl. My hands clenched the fabric in an attempt to hold on to what little I had left of her.

It was all I had.

"Hey lover boy, Mother wants to see you."

Haerlyon stood lounging against the doorpost, looking his usual smooth self while chewing on something. To anyone who knew him, it was clear he was anything but himself. His eyes, usually full of mischief, were hard and cold, and the everlasting smile on his face never quite reached them. Upon hearing the news of his sister's death, he hadn't even flinched. In fact, he had looked relieved. He hadn't even bothered to show up to her burial.

He blamed her for Tiroy's death at *Hanyarah* and now she'd received due payment in his eyes.

I wanted to punch him.

"Coming," I muttered, draping the dress over the back of the chair where I'd found it.

With a last look at her room, I followed Haerlyon into the corridors, keeping a safe distance so I wouldn't be tempted to make him trip or walk into a column by accident.

"Why does the *Tari* want to see me at this ungodly hour?" I asked.

Haerlyon shrugged. "Beats me. Ask her. I'm just your average errand boy."

Average my ass.

I decided it was in my best interest not to speak my mind and huffed instead, regarding him quietly.

Not only Tiroy had died that night.

Tari Arayda sat in front of the fire, a cup of tea in her hands, a blanket enveloping her small frame. She looked up the moment I entered. A smile was on her lips, although that might very well have been the light of the fire playing across her features.

"Come." Her voice was soft, feeble. "Sit with me."

It was as much a request as it was a command, so I took the chair next to her, stretching my legs.

"There's tea if you want any," she said. "Forgive me for not pouring it for you."

"Nor should you, *Tari*," I replied, my lips quirking up at the corners. "After all, I'm but a servant in your army. A *Tari* has no business waiting upon the likes of me."

She snorted. "You're too much like your father at times."

My brows shot up in surprise until I remembered they were of the same age and had most likely grown up knowing each other.

"Mother used to wish I was more like him," I replied with a shrug, settling back in the chair.

Tari Arayda smiled kindly, a hint of remembrance in those mysterious eyes. She'd known my mother too, but where it brought a smile to her face, it only brought misery to mine, adding to the guilt I'd felt since the news of Shalitha's death.

"She was a remarkable woman indeed," the *Tari* murmured.

Pinching the bridge of my nose, I closed my eyes, suddenly exhausted with the world and everyone in it.

"Why did you want to see me, *Tari?*"

She stared at the fire, warm eyes suddenly hard, the set of her jaw promising determination if nothing else.

"Tell me truthfully, Talnovar," she began, turning to face me. "Do you believe my daughter is dead?"

I arched a brow. "You've heard the news, *Tari*. She has to be."

"Don't be coy with me, *Anahràn*," she said icily. "Answer my question."

It required me to dig deeper into my feelings than I honestly cared for right then, but one didn't deny the *Tari* a request unless it was at one's own peril. I was of half a mind to say I thought she was, but deep down inside, in that part where emotions and beliefs are stashed for safekeeping against a cruel world, I knew I didn't quite believe it.

Not until somebody presented me with her body.

"I don't think so," I replied at length.

"Think so," she began, "or know so?"

Rubbing my jaw, I observed her quietly. Despite her illness, she looked as strong as ever, but I knew it was a lie. Underneath the blanket, she was trembling, and it could hardly be from the cold. The room was so stifling hot I regretted not having taken off my leather armour.

"With none of the search parties having returned, we don't know for sure," I answered with a shrug, "unless we send out a more covert mission."

A smile instantly pulled her lips up at the corners, lighting up her entire face, mischief included.

"Good, you're catching on."

I stared at her. "I'm not su—"

"I need you to go find my daughter, Tal." *Tari* Arayda spoke softly, glancing around the room as if she were afraid to be overheard.

"Excuse me?"

She rolled her eyes. If it hadn't been for the situation, the gesture would have been comical, knocking at least a hundred years off her age.

"I don't believe my daughter perished at sea," Arayda said, her eyes boring into mine. "Call it a gut feeling, or wishful thinking, I don't care. Whatever happened out there, Shalitha survived. I just know it, and I need you to find her."

My jaw dropped.

"And how do you propose I do that, *Tari*? We just sent her off with a grand ceremony. If I leave now, people will think I've gone insane."

"Good."

If at all possible, my jaw dropped even further. As it was, I could do no more than stare at her and wonder if she'd gone entirely mad. Something on my face made hers relax, and she smiled.

"You're not a *khirr*, Tal," she said, her voice hoarse. "The madder they think you are, the better."

"Why, *Tari*? Why now?"

The look of compassion and anguish on her face nearly undid me.

"I'm dying, Tal," she whispered, shaking her head softly. "When I do, if Shal has not been reinstated, my sister can lay claim to the throne, and trust me when I tell you that she will."

My blood ran cold at the mention of Azra. There was something about that woman that set my teeth on edge and made me wish I was anywhere but near her.

"Judging by the look on your face, I trust that's a bad idea."

She merely nodded, pressing a handkerchief against her lips. When she started coughing, blood soon stained the fabric in her hand, becoming worse with each hack until she was doubled over and wheezing. It shocked me to see her like this.

"*Tari*?"

Gently, I helped her sit up to return air to her lungs. Her

features were suddenly wan and haggard, and blood trickled down the corners of her lips.

"You should rest," I murmured, looking at her.

Without preamble, I lifted her in my arms, receiving the second shock in a matter of minutes at how little she weighed. The *Tari* snorted at my insolence but didn't argue the matter.

"Tal," she murmured as I laid her in bed, drawing the sheets over her. "Promise me you'll find her."

I rubbed the back of my neck, feeling troubled. "How, *Tari*? With Shal gone, and you soon, I am but an army *Anahràn*. Leaving will be seen as deserting."

"Make it look like a desperate man's attempt."

CHAPTER 2

SHALITHA

The buzzing in my ears thumped to the steady beating of my heart, drowning out all noise while I focused on my quarry as he sauntered across the market, the look on his face that of a carefree man who expected to be left well enough alone. Copper skin shimmered in the sunlight. His face was graced with high cheekbones and an angular jaw. My eyes travelled up his jawline to elongated ears ending in a perfect tip, and back to the huge smile showing a row of perfect white teeth as he greeted one of the vendors. Flexing my fingers, I inhaled to the count of ten and exhaled in the same slow process. My eyes never left him as I tucked my white hair underneath the *hijrath* and affixed the veil—a necessity around these parts as my ivory skin stood out—across my face whilst stepping out from my hiding place.

Keeping my eyes downcast, I hurried in his direction, deliberately pretending not to pay attention to where I was going. I had one chance and one chance alone. Messing it up would mean I'd get into trouble, and my back was still sore from the last time I did.

One chance, so I had to make it count.

Just pretend it's training. You can do it.

I risked a glance up and as I did, I realised I was much closer than I thought I'd be. Only a few more steps.

Collide. Grab what you came for, apologise and leave.

How hard could it be?

Steadying my breathing, I did exactly as I was instructed. The moment of impact was precisely what I had expected and in the confusion of our collision, I swiped the pouch from his belt and hid it in the sleeve of my blouse.

"My apologies!" I gasped, looking up with wide eyes.

I wasn't prepared for what stared back at me.

Emerald eyes—a colour which I believed I'd never see again—stared back at me from a face they had no business belonging to. The colour looked wrong surrounded by dark skin, but they were so much like Tal's, I had a hard time looking away.

"My apologies," the copper-skinned stranger said, his lips curling up in a gentle smile. "Are you all right?"

I nodded, willing my frantic heart to take it down a notch.

"I...I am," I stammered, looking away. "A...apologies, *mishan*. I...I wasn't looking where I was going."

His head tilted to the left as his quizzical gaze bored into me, almost as if he was trying to look into my soul and lay it bare. My window of escape was closing. I had to go now or he would surely find out what I'd done.

"Not a problem, *amisha*. Please, don't let me hold you up."

To my surprise, he stepped out of my way with a flourishing bow, a playful smile tugging at his lips, adding to the mischief in his eyes.

Something's wrong.

Forcing my feet to take one step in front of the other, I murmured a thanks as I passed him, keeping my eyes cast down. I'd bolt as soon as I was out of the way.

"Before you go," he mused. "Can I have my money back?"

Nohro!

I was running before I had consciously decided to do so, dodging people and stalls in a mad dash to avoid capture. Shouts behind me were enough proof that guards were in pursuit. Cursing myself in silence, I realised I had to get out of sight. Easy enough if you knew the streets of Y'zdrah like the back of your hand, but unfortunately, I still had a way to go in that regard. Had this been Ilvanna, I would have shaken off my pursuers in a matter of minutes.

As it was, I had a hard time staying out of reach.

Although this city was run by the *Akynshan*, Prince of thieves, smugglers and other petty criminals, theft was frowned upon and the penalty for it was the loss of one's hand—or both. The *Gemsha's* instructions had been clear—rob and leave without being detected.

I'd be on my own if I got caught.

I cursed again.

My eyes darted left and right as I ducked through stalls, dodged people, and clambered up and over crates, wares and carts, all in an attempt not to get apprehended. I settled my gaze on a beam lodged between two buildings up ahead. Veering left, I jumped onto a pile of heavy crates and used the momentum to propel myself upwards.

I barely caught the beam.

The guards were close—their shouts and clamours reaching me within the space of three heartbeats. Risking a glance over my shoulder, I noticed them at the beginning of the alley only a few steps away.

Nohro!

My shoulder burned painfully in memory of the old injury as I hoisted myself up. Down below, the guards stood watching and cursing me in their own tongue, but none of them attempted to follow me up here. My eyes were drawn to a solitary figure at the end of the alley—to the man I had robbed, arms folded lazily as he watched me. Catching my gaze, his lips quirked up.

I quickly clambered onto one of the buildings and disappeared out of sight.

After skipping over several rooftops, I dropped to my knees on one and pulled away the veil, catching my breath which now came in desperate wheezes as I sucked in air. That had been too close. My mind returned to the altercation with the stranger. He'd looked like someone with money, but not like anyone important, yet the guards had done his bidding instantly.

And he knew I'd robbed him.

If it hadn't been for his eyes, none of this would have happened. I wouldn't have faltered. I wouldn't have hesitated. I would have grabbed the pouch, apologised, and continued on my merry way.

Who is he?

Pushing myself to my feet, I looked for a way off the roof, glad to find there were stairs running down the building. People looked at me curiously as I made my way to ground level, placing the veil back across my face. It was the one thing I always kept up while I was out and about.

Time to get back.

Keeping to the shadows, I returned to the *Gemsha's* establishment, my stomach coiling into a tight knot the closer I got.

He would not be happy with my tardiness.

NOT HAPPY WAS an understatement the likes of which I'd never seen before. Red in the face from anger, the *Gemsha* was awaiting my arrival personally, his rotund form blocking the entrance quite formidably. His hand shot out, wrapping around my upper arm in a vice-like grip. My self-restraint was pushed beyond limits I didn't know I had.

"What took you so long?" he hissed, spittle flying into my ear.

"I had to take a detour," I replied. "Some people don't take kindly to being robbed."

If possible, he turned even redder. "He found out?!"

"Obviously." I shrugged, retrieving the pouch from its hiding place. "But he didn't catch me."

I tossed the *Gemsha* the goods and while he was busy catching it, ducked inside and passed him, moving swiftly so he couldn't seize me. The clinking of coins told me he was too preoccupied, so I made my way to the stairs in the back, ready to slink up, until his voice halted me.

"Siora," he boomed. "Stay."

Hugging my arms to my body, I took a few steps down and flopped on one of the benches usually reserved for customers. At this time of day, there were none. I watched as the *Gemsha* waddled closer, his slippers clapping on the carpeted floor in heavy thuds. If fate had a way of coming for me, I was sure it would sound like that.

"You do realise I must punish you for getting caught?"

"But I didn't."

He took a deep breath and held it. "You said he found out?"

"Semantics. He found out, but he didn't catch me."

"Does he know who you are?"

"How can he?" I snorted. "All he could see of me were my eyes, and they're heavily kohled."

He pressed his fat lips together, his expression one of bemusement.

"You're becoming cocky, Siora," he murmured, taking a step closer, "and I'm not sure I care much for that attitude."

You have no idea.

As much as I knew I should, I didn't apologise. Not this time. He could take his precious flogger to my back for all I cared—I was done grovelling before him. Khazmira and I were biding our time, hoarding what little money we could pilfer from this man so we could escape.

"As for your punishment," he drawled, stepping close enough that every inch between myself and him was occupied by his bulk. "I think twenty lashes should be enough?"

I stiffened.

"To be given to Khazmira," he added.

"No!" I roared. "Khaz has done nothing wrong! You can flog the skin off of *my* back, but you will leave her alone, or I swear on Laros, I *will* end you."

"You dare threaten me?!" he asked, his voice rising in pitch and volume. "You're threatening *me?*"

He turned a deep shade of purple which I'd come to learn preceded a wicked display of fury the likes of which would even put Eamryel to shame. I flinched and curled in on myself almost immediately, preparing for what was to come next as my eyes followed the path of his hand rising into the air, ready to strike.

A gentle cough from the door halted his progress.

The *Gemsha* twirled around, fury contorting the chubby flabs of skin he called his face right to the tips of his pointed ears.

He stiffened, blanched and bowed as deep as his paunch allowed him.

"*A...Akynshan*," he stammered. "I did not expect you here today."

Curious as to who the infamous *Akynshan* was, whose title I had heard drop many times before but to whom I could put neither name nor face, I peeked around the *Gemsha*.

My heart stopped.

Strolling into the establishment was the copper-skinned stranger from the market—the one I'd robbed. His eyes shifted from the *Gemsha* to me, and even in the dim light I saw his brows quirk up in surprise. Quickly, I pulled the veil back in place and hid behind the *Gemsha's* massive form.

"*Gemsha*," the *Akynshan* said in that pleasant honeyed voice. "I'm not interrupting anything, am I?"

"Oh, no! Of course not, of course not, your Grace."

Your Grace. Huh.

Seeing this man grovel was a grim satisfaction in light of what he had put me through in the past three moons; better would be to see him punished for his outbursts, but I could hardly expect that to happen.

"What can I do for you, *Akynshan*?"

The stranger made himself comfortable on the bench next to mine, keeping his eyes on the *Gemsha*.

"A drink would be good," he said, glancing at me.

"Of course." The *Gemsha* stared at me as well.

I stared back.

"Now. Please. Siora."

One day.

Dragging out the moment, I rose to my feet, glaring at the *Gemsha* with ill-concealed contempt. My eyes locked with the *Akynshan's* for a moment, and I could swear the amusement I'd seen in the market was still there. A smile ghosted on his lips, but I could tell he was making an effort not to show it.

"What do you want to drink?" I asked, refraining from the niceties on purpose.

The stranger's brows shot up. "Tea, thank you."

I groaned.

Out loud.

"Siora!" The *Gemsha* all but shrieked. "Go! Get the *Akynshan* his tea. Don't dawdle."

Despite myself, I rolled my eyes at him before disappearing into the kitchen where I made a show out of preparing tea by creating as much noise as possible. It would annoy the *Gemsha* on any day, so I figured it would add to the fury already boiling inside of him.

Let him explode in front of the Akynshan. Let him explain that away.

The low hum of voices reached me in the kitchen. If I remembered anything from my lessons back home, it was that knowledge was good to have in any shape or form. The water would take a while to boil anyway, so I snuck towards them, sticking to the shadows. The *Gemsha* was seated with his back towards me—the *Akynshan* sat facing the opening to the kitchen, arms resting on the back of the bench. At a distance, his features were even more astounding than they'd been in the marketplace, where I'd been too busy staring at his eyes. He was handsome, by every account of the word, made more so by his startling gaze and playful smile. The dozen or so small golden hoops in his ears added a certain villainous demeanour to him, although he didn't look evil.

He rather looked like he owned the place.

Maybe he does.

"What can I do for you, your Grace?" The *Gemsha* asked, his voice back to its usual slickness.

Shivers crept down my spine.

"I was just doing my rounds," he replied, his voice even. "Checking in on my people."

"Ah yes, of course."

The *Gemsha's* shoulders bunched and rolled, and judging by the way he smacked his lips, I guessed him to be nervous. It was good to see someone having that effect on him.

"Forgive me, your Grace," he said at length, "but isn't it a bit early for your visits?"

The *Akynshan's* lips curled up in a pleasant smile that lit his entire face, and as it did, his eyes flicked to the shadows where I was hiding. It was so fast a movement, however, I wasn't sure if I'd seen it, or imagined it.

"You caught me." He laughed, relaxing back into the pillows. "I'm actually here to extend an invitation."

I wanted to hear more, but I knew I'd been gone too long already, and the *Gemsha* would flog the skin off my back if I didn't return with tea soon. Not that I needed to have worried about not catching the conversation—the *Gemsha* was quite loud in his delight. As quickly as I could, I poured tea into a pot, grabbed a cup, placed both on a tray and carried it back to them.

Their conversation halted the moment I stepped inside, as if they'd been discussing something private.

"Your tea," I said, keeping myself from dropping the tray onto the table in front of the *Akynshan*.

Grinding my teeth, I put in the effort of pouring him a cup but was so clumsy about it that some of it splashed over the rim and onto my hand. I hissed and would have dropped the pot had the *Akynshan* not taken it from my hand.

"Are you all right?" he asked, taking my injured hand in both of his.

Please don't look too closely.

Him opening his hands revealed the *Araîth* snaking over my fingers and disappearing into my sleeve. His eyes flicked up and narrowed, but that moment passed and he smiled again, placing a gentle kiss on my hand. I quickly pulled it away and hid it behind my back, glancing at the *Gemsha* to see how much he'd noticed. Judging by the vacant expression in his eyes, probably not much. It did make me wonder why he was grinning like a madman though. Stepping back, my eyes returned to the *Akynshan,* who was watching me with newly kindled interest, head tilted in much the same way as he had back at the market.

I looked away, suddenly uncomfortable.

"*Gemsha?*" the stranger mused.

The *Gemsha* looked up startled. "Yes, your Grace?"

"Bring her tonight," the *Akynshan* ordered with a nod in my direction.

"Y...your Grace?" the *Gemsha* stammered. "Surely I can bring a girl, but...her? Do you not want one of the others?"

The stranger grinned, revealing a set of perfect white teeth. "No. I want her."

He picked up his tea, eyes on the *Gemsha* as if to challenge him again. Without breaking contact, he blew his tea, making it look more elegant than he had a right to. Taking a careful sip, his gaze fell on me and his lips pulled up in a lopsided smile.

How could he still look charming that way?

The *Gemsha* sputtered an incoherent response, but the *Akynshan* had already lost interest. He rose to his feet, picked up the cup and downed the tea in one go.

"My thanks for the tea, *amisha*," he said, awarding me with a light bow before he sauntered out of the establishment.

Before the *Gemsha* could turn on me, I made a mad dash up the stairs towards my room, locking it behind me the moment I closed the door. Khazmira sat up bleary eyed, not looking amused at being woken up.

"What's wrong?" she murmured.

"I stole from the *Akynshan*."

CHAPTER 3

TALNOVAR

My military training kicked in as soon as I heard the creaking of the door and even softer footsteps padding over to where I lay, pretending to be asleep. My fingers curled around the hilt of my dagger, holding on tight, waiting for whoever had come in to be at my side. The knife was at their throat, drawing blood, the moment they touched my shoulder.

"*Nohro ahrae*," Evan cursed.

The pressure against the blade left as Evan stepped back.

"Apologies," I muttered, sitting up on the bed. "Old habits die hard."

"But I don't," he replied vexed.

"Why are you here anyway?"

Evan's grim expression, made visible by what few moonbeams passed through the curtains, fell and made way for one of anguish.

"It's Mother," he croaked and swallowed, running a hand through his hair. "You need to come."

You should've started with that, khirr.

Not bothering with shoes, I followed Evan out of the room

—Shal's room—and to the *Tari's*. After her request, I'd taken up doing whatever necessary to appear as the grieving lover, going the extra mile to make it believable. Sleeping in her bed was one of those things—burying my face into her clothing and her pillows to inhale her scent, another.

Anything to have her close.

Although the *Tari* had given me a purpose, something to do with myself, I knew it was a fool's mission. The chance of me succeeding would be slim indeed. I knew if I'd propose the idea to either Evan or Haerlyon, they would talk me out of it, arguing how futile an attempt at finding her would be. Yet I had to agree with the *Tari*—deep down inside, I knew she wasn't gone.

It didn't make any of this easier.

However I felt about the *Tarien's* disappearance paled in comparison to the heart-wrenching scene I witnessed while entering the *Tari's* bedroom. A small figure on the bed, she looked paler than usual, her skin almost translucent to the point where it had a moonlike glow to it. Her breathing came in laborious bursts. Blood tinged her lips and trickled down her chin. Her movements were so feeble it was clear she focused all her strength on staying alive.

Haerlyon had curled up on her left side. Evanyan did the same on the other. She was barely able to pull her sons to her for one last hug. The lump in my throat grew bigger by the moment, stealing my breath from me.

I'd bear it, for her.

"I'm sorry, *mey shareye*," she whispered. "I'm sorry I have to leave you behind in such a mess."

Haerlyon caught a sob in his throat, burying his face in her hair. Evan managed to keep his wits about him slightly longer.

"Don't worry about it, Mother," he replied, gingerly wiping the blood from her mouth and chin. "We will handle it."

She nodded, but faintly. "Look after each other while I'm gone?"

Somehow, she made it sound as if she was going on a journey for a couple of months rather than dying, and I had to give her credit for her strength and courage. If only my mother had had an ounce of her will, she would have managed.

She would have still been alive then.

Movement from the corner of my eyes caught my attention. Rurin slipped inside the bedroom, giving me a curt nod. His eyes were red-rimmed, evidence to the fact he had been crying. I couldn't blame him.

"Rurin?" her voice was barely audible.

He was at her side in a few strides. Evan moved out of the way as gracefully as a cat while looking as forlorn as a mewling kitten. Placing my hand on his shoulder was all I could do to comfort him.

"Please hold me, like you did that day?"

Without having to ask which day she meant, he slipped onto the bed and ever so gently lifted her into his lap, cradling her. Resting her head against his shoulder, she looked up at him. He gazed down at her.

All that existed in the world was the two of them.

Her breathing, laborious at first, became slower, quieter, until she drew the last one and relaxed within his embrace. Rurin hugged her to his chest, tears rolling down his cheeks in silent defiance to his tough exterior. Haerlyon stood next to the bed looking for all the world like a lost little boy, arms dropped alongside his body, a look of disbelief etched onto his face.

Only Evan managed to keep his decorum through what looked like sheer effort of will.

Ruesta, mey Tari. Your fight is done.

The lack of tears surprised me. Instead, seething anger coursed through my veins on a path of vengeance.

Shal should have been here.

"Finally," a honeyed voice, all lilt and seduction, sounded from behind me. "It took her long enough."

A deep, guttural growl escaped my lips, but before I had a chance to act upon it, Rurin whisked past me and pushed Azra up against the wall, arm on her throat.

How did he get from under Arayda so fast?

"*You* did this," he hissed. "*You* killed her, like you killed Shaleira."

Azra smirked. "Is this how you treat your *Tari*? I should have you arrested."

With a derisive snort and an extra push, he let her go and stepped back, a look of murderous intent written on his face as plain as day.

"You're not my *Tari*." He spat in front of her feet, his lips curled up in a snarl. "Nor will you ever be. I know it was you. You've done it before."

"Well now," she all but purred. "That makes this situation rather problematic then, don't you think?"

My hands balled at my sides for want of anything better to do. Would I have had a weapon, she'd be at the end of it. As it was, there was nothing we could do. With both Arayda and Shalitha dead, she was in fact the rightful heir to the throne. Even if we had had any hope of keeping this under wraps, it would only have bought us days.

I needed months.

"Do us one courtesy?" It was Haerlyon, his voice surprisingly level.

We all turned to look at him.

Azra cocked her head to the side. "Anything for my favourite nephew."

"Give us the chance to say goodbye," he said. "The proper way."

A mix of emotions crossed her delicate features as she regarded Haerlyon. Watching her, I realised how closely she resembled Arayda. Logical, considering the fact they were sisters, but where Arayda had been pretty, Azra was beautiful in a lethal kind of way. It was that malignancy, however, that made her ooze danger from every pore.

My skin prickled in a less than pleasant way at the notion.

"But of course!" she replied in feigned shock. "What kind of *Tari* do you think I am?"

"The kind that leaves a trail of bodies in her wake," Rurin growled.

Dark eyes snapped to him, flashing furiously in their pursuit of directing anger at the intended target. Rurin didn't flinch. Whatever was going on between them went back a century, if not more. I glanced at Evanyan, who looked as lost as I felt, and even risked a glance at Haerlyon, whose jaws were set so tight I feared he'd never be able to unlock them again.

"You can have your burial." Azra waved her hand dismissively. "I'm fairly certain her people would want it too, but it's the one and only courtesy I'll do you."

She pivoted on her heel and left the room without even a backwards glance.

"*Hehzèh!*" Rurin yelled at her retreating back, slamming the door shut.

He slid down against it, burying his face in his hands. I was at a complete loss, and from the looks of it, so was Evan.

"Who's Shaleira?"

The question came from Haerlyon, whose face had returned to the emotionless state it had been in over the past year. Rurin looked up through his fingers, old pain resurfacing.

"I shouldn't be telling you this," he said, voice cracking. "I vowed not to, as did your father, Talnovar," —he looked at me, eyes full of hurt— "but none of that matters now that she ascends the throne anyway. All has been for naught."

"Don't say that," Evan replied in a strangled voice. "We can figure this out."

"Why bother?" He rubbed his temples and shook his head. "Azra's well within her rights. Arayda is dead. The *Tarien* is dead. She's won."

"It's grief talking," Evan said.

It took me everything to remain quiet and not offer him even a whisper of hope that Arayda did not believe in her daughter's demise, and that she'd sent me on a mission to find the *Tarien,* wherever she may be. Admitting as much even to him would be dangerous. With Azra ready to take over the country, I had to leave as soon as I could, even though I wanted to wait for Arayda's official burial.

Maybe—possibly—I could find an ally in Evanyan, if grief didn't strike him too hard.

Promise me one thing, Tal? Don't tell anyone. As soon as you do, Azra will know and she will do whatever it takes to stop you.

I let out a deep sigh, pushing my hair from my face.

"Who is Shaleira, Rurin?" Haerlyon asked again, more impatient this time.

"Azra's dead twin-sister."

All air was sucked out of the room at his statement, and I felt certain if I looked at the other two men, I'd find my shock echoed on their faces. Clearly, this was a part of the brothers' history even they hadn't known.

"Another sister?" Evan asked, incredulity marking his face. "Why hasn't Mother ever mentioned her?"

Rurin shook his head. "Because she wanted to protect you."

"Protect us from what?" Haerlyon scoffed. "A dead aunt? I'm fairly certain she's a good deal better to be around than the one still alive."

"Haer!" Evan gasped, staring at his brother. "Mind your tongue."

"Or what?"

"You'll lose it." Rurin replied. "And she won't be nice about it."

"She'll have to hear me first," Haerlyon offered, folding his arms. "And I don't see her here."

"Just because she's not here doesn't mean she can't hear you," Evan muttered, dragging a hand through his hair.

Haerlyon snorted. I was glad to see at least one of them had an ounce of common sense left, considering the circumstances.

"What happened to Shaleira?" I asked tentatively.

The fact my father had vowed to remain silent about her—and had in fact never mentioned her—spoke louder than words. Even so, I wanted to know what had happened to her, if only to ease the dreadful feeling settling in my gut. Rurin watched me—no, beyond me—as if he was seeing something happening there, judging by the distant look in his eyes. A deep shudder went through him.

"Azra killed her," he said at length, his voice husky. "I,"—he fell silent, blinked and focused on me— "I brought her to the infirmary that day, but it was already too late. She died moments after. The injury was the size of a hunting knife. Gaervin, he—"

"Father?" Haerlyon piped up, every bit of boredom gone from his face. "Why was father there?"

"Let him finish." Evan sounded strained.

"Gaervin accused Azra of having killed Shaleira, but it took a trick on Cerindil's part to make her confess. *Tari* Xeramaer made us vow never to speak of this to anyone, so it was hushed up and passed on. Shaleira had, to everyone's sorrow, died on the battlefield that day, like so many others."

I pressed my lips together, letting the information sink in while trying to make sense of it. Evan flopped down in a chair, rubbing his temples. Haerlyon paced the room, rapping his fingers on his arm.

"Why did he accuse her?" I asked. "Gaervin, I mean."

"Because he was the one who told her how to do it."

Had he spoken in a different language, the result would still have been the same. Haerlyon stopped dead in his tracks, turning around slowly as if the movement pained him.

Rather as if he's about to pounce on Rurin.

Evan looked properly sick.

"Azra and Gaervin," Rurin began, "had something going on. As it turned out, he was promised to Shaleira—neither of the sisters knew. Azra, who already disliked her, took it a step further."

"She killed her own twin out of jealousy?" Evan asked incredulously.

"No." Rurin exhaled, his throat bobbing. "She did it out of pure hatred. I've never seen anyone as crazy as her."

"Why wasn't she executed?"

Haerlyon had never been about subtlety when he wanted answers, and although I appreciated his honesty on any day, I wished he went a little easier on Rurin. The man looked like he was moments away from a nervous breakdown.

"She was supposed to be," he replied with a heavy sigh, "but she escaped. Rumours had it she had help."

"From whom?" Haerlyon again.

Rurin shrugged, but from the way he clenched his jaw, I knew he was lying through his teeth when next he spoke. "We don't know. Whoever did it, they covered their tracks well."

Haerlyon harrumphed but left well enough alone, turning to his mother. He was at war with himself—the expressions on his face alternating between sad and angry telling me as much. The moment he noticed his shoulders slumped, he pulled them straight again. He was trying to put on a brave face while he most likely wanted to crawl back in the bed with his mother and grieve.

"I'll go get Soren," I said eventually. "He needs to be made aware. I'll have servants come take care of her."

"No." Rurin's voice was gruff, raspy. "I'll do that."

"I'll help." It was Haerlyon who offered, much to my surprise.

Before I left, everybody had something to take care of. In truth, I just wanted to bolt. I had other preparations to make, and none of them concerned Soren. I had to get out of Ilvanna before Azra became *Tari*—before she decided to keep a close watch on any of us. If she was capable of murdering her own sisters, I believed she was capable of just about anything else. Besides, if what Soren had shown me was true, Azra was behind Shalitha's disappearance as well, even though she'd gone through a lot of trouble of hiding her hand in it.

As far as I was concerned, Yllinar had taken her, and he would pay for it.

With his life.

CHAPTER 4

SHALITHA

According to the *Gemsha*, being invited to one of the *Akynshan's* many parties was quite the honour, and he couldn't believe his luck that night. Decked out in his best attire, he eagerly waddled over to the gates of the palace, keeping up a distinctive monologue about the *Akynshan* and his many wives.

I had stopped paying attention to it minutes after we left.

Unlike him, I didn't feel excited at all—I felt scared, and justifiably so. I kept picking at the dress I was wearing, unaccustomed to the freedom of movement underneath the skirt, and kept checking the *hijrath* and veil to make sure my face and hair were still covered. Swallowing hard, I tried not to dwell on my feelings for too long. Back at the *Gemsha's* establishment, the *Akynshan* had known perfectly well I'd been the one who had robbed him, and he had only extended the invitation to me because of it. I could see no other reason. Tonight, in front of everyone, he would punish me for stealing. There was no other explanation.

After all, I was but a lowly thief here in Zihrin.

When we passed the gate, my gut coiled into a knot and my chest tightened for the first time in many moons. Swallowing hard, I tried to fight the oncoming panic attack, but try though I might, I didn't succeed. The closer we walked, the more laborious my breathing became. Despite the crisp night, my palms were sweaty and no amount of rubbing them onto my dress made it any better. By the time we reached the stairs, I could barely put one foot in front of the other and air was hard to come by. As I dropped to my knees, sure I was about to faint, the *Gemsha* in his ignorance puffed up the stairs to personally greet the *Akynshan*, leaving me behind.

My ears were buzzing, and my vision was swimming.

"You sure know how to keep a man's interest." The *Akynshan's* sounded from close by.

Glancing up from under my lashes, I found him kneeling in front of me, a worried expression on his face.

"What?" I asked confused, trying to get air into my lungs.

He smiled. "You look like you're having a hard time. Anything I can do to help you?"

I stared at him dumbfounded. To my surprise, the worst of the attack ebbed away, and I was able to gulp in air, quieting my frazzled nerves.

"Come," he said, helping me to my feet. "Let's get inside."

Confused by what was happening, I allowed the *Akynshan* to guide me indoors while doing my best not to pay attention to the people gawking at us, including the *Gemsha*. He didn't look pleased.

"Please," I murmured. "I do not want to impose."

The *Akynshan* chuckled. "On the contrary, *amisha*. I'd love to have your company tonight."

"Mine?" I asked incredulously. "So… you're not going to punish me for stealing from you?"

"Do you want me to?"

"No," I replied. "I'm quite attached to my hands, thank you very much."

"And such intriguing hands they are."

Something told me it wasn't necessarily my hands he found intriguing, but I decided not to comment on it lest I gave away more than I wanted. He was already too nosy for my taste.

"Can I get you something to drink?" he asked, guiding me into a ballroom twice the size of the one at home.

Except that the decorations outdid ours.

Red and gold gauze curtains hung from rings from the ceilings and fanned out to the walls, draped elegantly to the white tiled floor. At the end of the room was a dais, and the throne on it—I couldn't call it anything else—was gilded and sparkling. Compared to this, Mother's throne—*mine*—looked like a common chair. To make matters worse, there wasn't just one, but two, and the second was occupied by a beautiful dark-haired woman who looked anything but pleased when her eyes settled on me.

When she rose to her feet, the *Akynshan* groaned low under his breath.

"Excuse me," he murmured.

My eyes followed him as he made his way over to the woman, his hands up in surrender. When she folded her arms, I could tell she wasn't amused.

"What in Laros's name do you think you're doing?" the *Gemsha* hissed from my side, his hand digging painfully into my arm.

I squeaked in surprise. From up ahead, the *Akynshan* glanced my way, eyes narrowing.

"Let me go," I said under my breath. "I'm not doing anything."

"Do not lie to me, *zrayeth*," he growled. "Why is he interested in *you*?"

His jowls were quivering—a clear indication he was fighting to keep his temper under control.

"Your guess is as good as mine," I replied. "Please, let me go. You're hurting me."

What's happening to me?

Back home, I wouldn't have tolerated anyone touching me like this, not after Yllinar and Eamryel, but perhaps that was the problem—I wasn't home. Out here, I was nobody, and I had to remind myself of that every single day. It made me painfully aware of the respect I'd been treated with back in Ilvanna, even if I hadn't liked my status.

"Don't pull any stunts, or I promise you won't be able to sit for a week."

Do that, and I'll make sure you won't wake up next morning.

"*Gemsha*?" The *Akynshan's* lazy drawl sounded close by.

I'd missed him coming back.

The vice-like grip around my arm disappeared almost instantly, and to my side, the fat *grissin* started grovelling, bowing deeply while shuffling away.

I tipped my head to the side with a close-lipped smile.

"Can I have this dance?"

I narrowed my eyes at the *Akynshan*, not sure what to make of him and his gentle disposition towards me.

At least he wouldn't be taking off my hand.

"There's no music."

He grinned, and with an eloquent gesture, he ordered the musicians to play.

"What about that woman?"

"Do you question everything?" he asked, guiding me to the dance floor.

"Not everything," I replied. "Just everyone."

He laughed. "That sounds fair."

The music was not something I was familiar with, nor were the steps, but the *Akynshan* guided me through them expertly, making me stumble only twice before I got the hang of it and followed the rhythm of odd flutes and stringed-instruments.

"What's your name?" he asked.

"Siora." It didn't sit right with me to lie to him.

He flashed me a lopsided smile. "Your real name?"

"Are you calling me a liar?" I asked before he spun me around.

"Not a liar," he replied. "But I know it's not the truth either."

My brows shot up in surprise. "What makes you say that?"

"All those questions," he whispered in my ear as he leaned forward, "amongst other things."

"Amongst other things?"

"Let's just say an aura of intrigue surrounds you, *amisha*," he said, "and I love a good puzzle."

The music stopped and I pulled back my hands, my jaw clenched. "Good luck puzzling then."

As I turned to walk away, his hand wrapped around my wrist. I was surprised at the gentleness of it.

"Please," he began softly. "I meant when I said I'd love your company tonight."

"Will you lay off the questions?"

"If you walk with me."

I was of half a mind to decline, until my eyes fell on the *Gemsha's* scrutinising gaze upon me, sending chills down my spine. Steeling my resolve, I nodded at the *Akynshan* and accepted his offer for a walk. An uncomfortable feeling settled in my neck as we passed people's curious gazes—the *Akynshan* didn't look bothered at all. Only when we were out of sight did I start to relax. He had taken me to an outdoor enclosure reminding me of the smaller gardens back at the Ilvannian palace, except that out here, there were hardly any flowers. Like its surroundings, it was a harsh place with harsher plants. Even the ones that looked beautiful had thorns.

"How did you end up with the *Gemsha*?" the *Akynshan* asked after a while.

"Fate's a *heh*—monster."

He looked quietly amused. "I can tell you're not from around Zihrin."

I shrugged. "I never pretended to be."

"Yet you hide behind a veil in fear of what people will see."

"Who says it's in fear?"

A soft chuckle escaped his lips. When he sat down, he patted the bench beside him as an invitation for me to do the same. Normally, I would have declined, and I knew I should have, but as intriguing as he found me, it occurred to me I bore him a similar interest.

"Does he know?" the *Akynshan* asked, turning to look at me. "Who you really are?"

I shrugged. "That man cannot tell his left from his right, let alone see what's right in front of him."

"You underestimate him."

"Perhaps," I replied, "but I don't think so. He's just like any other power hungry fool."

His lips curled up in a smile, and I realised I might have dragged him into the bargain of fools. I blushed.

"Go on," he offered.

"He only cares about that which makes him money. As long as I provide him with that, he doesn't care what's under the veil."

A vein pulsed in the *Akynshan's* neck. "Does he… sell your services?"

I was surprised at the hidden note of anger in his voice, as if the mere idea was a personal affront to him.

"No. Not like that."

"He makes you steal?"

"Amongst other things."

When he turned to face me, bringing up his hand, I scooted to the side, watching him warily. Despite my outward confidence, I felt very little of it. I was alone with a man whose name I hadn't yet caught, and I had no idea what he was capable of. For all I knew, he decided he'd want my services and take them from me. Instead, he ran his hand over his black short-cropped hair, setting the golden hoops in his long ears jingling. From this distance, it was plain to see they were slightly shorter than my own. His eyes, now dark, betrayed the thoughts going on inside his head.

"Why are you staying with him?"

"Because I have no choice," I replied, looking at him curiously. "It's either that or live on the streets."

"What if you did have a choice?"

I snorted. "People like me aren't given choices out of the kindness of someone's heart."

"I'm serious."

"So am I," I snapped, turning to him, balling my fists at my side. "But for the sake of argument, let's assume I do have a choice. Let's assume I would have gathered enough money, I'd leave that place in a heartbeat, taking Khazmira with me, and go ho—elsewhere."

He nodded, brows knitted together in thought as he contemplated my words. At least, I assumed he was—the alternative could be anything.

"Who is Khazmira?"

"I thought you'd lay off the questions?"

He let out a breathy laugh and shook his head. "You're right. My apologies. As said, I love a good puzzle, and you, *amisha,* are an enigma."

"I'm glad that I'm cause for your entertainment," I muttered, glancing sideways at him.

"I meant no offense."

I exhaled deeply. "It's fine."

"So...Siora." My false name sounded foreign on his tongue. "What made you decide to rob me?"

I stilled, barely daring to draw in a breath. Hiding my trembling hands, I looked anywhere but at him.

"I didn't know who you were," I replied at length. "You looked like any one of the rich guys I've robbed."

He chuckled softly. "How many have you parted from their coin and valuables?"

Silence stretched out between us until it became unbearable.

"A dozen," I mumbled.

"A dozen!"

"In the last week…"

Somehow I had expected him to get mad at me, to start yelling at me like the *Gemsha* would, but instead he flashed me a wide, amused smile.

"You're resourceful," he commented. "I like that."

I looked away. "I'm rather surprised you haven't called your guards yet."

"Why would I do that?"

Wringing my hands nervously, thankful they were still attached, I looked at him, brows furrowed. "Rumour has it the mighty *Akynshan* doesn't stand for theft in his city, that he will punish anyone who is either caught or tickle his fancy. They're made an example of."

He snorted. "And you believe in rumours?"

"I've learned even rumours have a heart of truth."

Amusement twinkled in his eyes. "I suppose there is, and you're not entirely wrong either. Admittedly, you have put me in a tricky situation."

"Why is that?"

"Because by law and your admission," he began, eyes searching mine, "I should indeed punish you for thievery. However, I feel that if I do, I'll be committing a crime worse than stealing."

I frowned. "And why would that be?"

"Because I still don't believe you are who you say you are."

CHAPTER 5

TALNOVAR

Love, when answered, is sweeter than *ithri,* more powerful than hate, and deadlier than any weapon known to our kind. Unanswered, it is as painful as having your heart ripped out and watch it beat and bleed until it shrivels into nothing. To love unconditionally without being allowed to act upon it in fear of endangering one's life, yet staying close to the object of affection was the hardest thing in the world. It is no surprise that watching such a love die, while you can do nothing about it, is sure to break anyone.

From the way they lay together—one arm underneath her head, the other across her waist, his face buried in her hair—one would think they were merely asleep. The crimson stain beneath them, however, told an entirely different tale. All these years they had made it work through adversity, until adversity turned on her and took her away from him.

Ruesta mey mahnèh. May you and Arayda find your peace in the otherworld.

Whatever had driven Rurin to take his own life, I could only assume it had been love. The way he had looked the day before, mad with grief and completely and utterly lost, had been enough to make me forget my own misery for a while.

I couldn't blame him.

It had been my first thought upon learning Shalitha was dead.

"He must have loved her deeply," Evan said from my side, looking wan and stricken.

All I could do was nod.

He swallowed. "We cannot leave them here, but somehow it feels wrong to disturb their peace."

"Then don't," Haerlyon said, looking grim. "Let them have this moment until we no longer have a choice."

"They're dead, Haer," Evan muttered. "They won't know the difference."

Haerlyon's voice was strained when he spoke. "But we will."

Pivoting on his heel, he awarded his brother a dagger-like stare only he was capable of and disappeared from the room. Evan dragged his hand through his hair, his face falling.

"I can't seem to do anything right by him these days."

I snorted. "Don't beat yourself up over it. Nobody can."

"Some days," he began, sighing deeply, "I wish I could turn back time, turn it all the way back to when we were barely in our teens and we had not a care in the world. I know it's wishful thinking, but sometimes…"

"I know."

Although my own sentiments didn't go quite as far as all that, my teenage years not having been my best, I too wished I could go back and change things. First of all, I'd have kissed Shal a lot sooner, disregarding my father's useless warning. Knowing what I know now, I would have made sure to have watched the signs better, to have seen the hints she left.

I should have seen her desperation. Should have seen her fear.

Hanyarah. The name alone brought nightmares to those

who'd seen the carnage. My personal one had been reliving the moment the sword went clean through me, and Yllinar's sneer as he looked down upon me while I slumped to my knees, disbelief suffusing every fibre in my body. I had watched as they'd taken her away, but before she was even out of sight, my world had tilted and holding onto my bearings had taken up all my energy.

Although we heal fast, the six moons of recuperation had been hard—harder than I'd ever thought possible.

One inch to the right, and I would have died straightaway.

A shudder travelled down my spine and I breathed in deeply to gather my wits. Although the memory still struck fear in me, I couldn't let it overpower me. Not now.

"Would you do it?"

I rolled my neck and sighed. "Maybe. Would you?"

Evan's thoughts showed on his face while contemplating a question he had no ready answer to. It was like watching his mind at work in a distressed kind of way, ultimately turning his features into a caricature semblance of its original.

"I don't know," he said at length. "But I don't think that's ever a question I need to answer."

The expression on his face turned sour instantly. I didn't need to ask him what he meant. His betrothal to Nathaïr hadn't exactly gone smoothly over the past few moons, especially not with her father and brother having gone up in smoke. It made her the only member of her family to be held accountable for their actions, even though Arayda had assured her she would never do that.

She had been a better woman for it.

"Perhaps there won't be a wedding anymore," I murmured. "I doubt Azra feels like competition."

Desperation crept into Evan's eyes, giving the impression of a startled deer.

"We need to talk," he murmured. "Not here though."

"SHE'S *WHAT*?!"

Pacing up and down the confines of the secluded garden, I ran my hands through my hair, grappling with the news Evan had dumped on me the moment we arrived.

"Pregnant," Evan murmured, rubbing his jaw.

"How?" The moment the question left my lips, I realised the error of my words, dismissing it with a wave of my hand.

"Surely—," Evan began.

"Yes, yes, I know *how*," I muttered, glaring at him. "But seriously, Ev, this couldn't have happened at a worst time!"

"Yeah well, we didn't exactly take Azra's ascending into account. We figured we'd be married by now."

As they should have.

His words deflated my anger like a punctured sack of air, but it didn't take away my concern for her safety. While Nathaïr and I weren't friends by any measure, her child had done neither me nor mine any harm. It was innocent in all this. A nagging feeling persisted in the back of my mind, trying to claw its way to the surface as if I were supposed to remember something. With a shake of my head, I dispelled the sensation. Rubbing my temples, I regarded Evan, who looked for all the world like a lost little puppy.

"Now what?"

He rubbed the back of his neck. "I don't know, Tal. I was kind of hoping you would have one of your brilliant ideas."

"You put a great deal of faith in me, *mahnèh*."

"Not really." Evan flashed me a wry smile. "But you're the only one I dare tell in these crazy times. Mother knew, of course. I couldn't let her go without telling her as much, but now that she's..."

"I know."

Patting his shoulder for comfort, I turned away from him, feeling like the worst friend ever. Here I was planning on escaping Ilvanna as soon as I could to go on a mission sanctioned by our dead *Tari,* leaving behind the two people who'd welcomed me with open arms after father dragged me to the palace, but the choice between the royal brothers and their sister was an easy one to make.

I was *her Anahràn* after all, not theirs.

"You should leave the palace," I said, turning back to him. "Take Nath, go anywhere that's not Ilvanna. Find sanctuary in Naehr for what it's worth, but leave this place and don't look back."

He stared at me as if I'd gone insane.

"You know it makes sense," I argued. "There's nothing left for you here."

"Except everything," he said in a strangled voice. "My life's here, Tal. Everything I've ever known is *here*. How can I leave it behind? This is the place where"—his throat bobbed and he ran a hand through his hair, looking away— "the place where I've met everyone and everything I've ever loved. Knowing it has fallen into the hands of that...that...*woman*. I can't leave. There must be something I can do."

"Leave."

We'd never been proficient at staring contests so neither of us gave it a shot for longer than three heartbeats before giving up. Judging by the look on his face, his mind was at war with his heart. The decision I put before him wasn't an easy one to make —I knew from experience, but it was one he had to seriously consider if he wanted Nathaïr to have a chance.

"What if she bears a daughter, Ev?" I asked.

I watched the implications of my words settle on him, turning him several shades paler in the process as the meaning behind them dawned on him.

"Azra wouldn't..." he said on an exhale, running both his hands through his hair, his eyes widening in shock.

"She's done it to her own sisters if we're to believe Rurin."

She's done it to your sister, you khirr.

The *Tari* had believed her daughter wasn't dead, but the brothers had appeared to believe every single word they'd been fed. To them, I had no doubt, their sister was gone. Forever. On top of that, they hadn't seen the note Soren had given me on the night of his return—the note Shal had mentioned at *Hanyarah*. It turned out to be nothing more than a piece of parchment written in Xaresh's elegant handwriting. It had been barely eligible, but I'd been able to make out names.

The conspiracy ran deeper than any one of us suspected.

I'd been wondering ever since how much Shalitha had known, and if that knowledge had been the reason for the abduction, or if they'd planned it all along. Her being the sole heir to the throne had made her a target for sure. Piecing together the information Rurin had given us, and whatever my father hadn't been willing to speak about, I deducted it had to be the same matter.

"There's something I need to tell you," I said at length, kicking a pebble out of the way.

Evan looked at me quizzically. "Which is?"

Hope suffused his features, lighting a twinkle in his eyes I'd not seen in quite some time. I clenched my jaw and looked away, trying to ignore the sour taste in my mouth. I hadn't wanted to give him hope.

"After Soren returned," I began, my voice barely above a whisper, as if I were afraid that if I spoke too loud it would become true, "he showed me something given to him by your sister before she was taken away."

Evan tensed.

"It was a list of names—names of people who were in some

way related to the conspiracy against your mother, against your sister."

"Go on." The strain in his voice was testimony to his strength and will power.

I'd almost hit Soren after revealing this news.

"It should come as no surprise Azra's name was on it, or Yllinar's for that matter." Hatred laced my voice as I spoke. "But there were more..."

Glancing at Evan, I racked my brain to come up with the right words to soften the next blow, only to realise there was no soft way to go about it.

"Queran's name was on there, but so were Nathaïr's... and Rurin's..."

He turned a deadly shade of white.

"What are you saying?"

I sagged against the wall, shaking my head. "I don't know, Ev. There was too little information to go on, but if Xaresh was right about Rurin..."

"Xaresh?"

I nodded. "He'd been compiling the list, before he got murdered."

His eyes narrowed, lips setting in a thin line. "Seems like there's a lot you've been withholding from us, *Imradien*."

"Get over it," I muttered. "I knew as much as you did until Soren's return. If you want to blame anyone, blame your aunt, or your sister, or even your mother if it makes you feel any better, but don't shove it onto me."

Despite the fact I had my eyes on him, I had not taken into account he would physically assault me. We went down in a flurry of blows as colourful expletives my vocabulary hadn't seen in a while left my lips. His fist connected with my jaw at the same time as mine did with his, leaving us sitting in stunned silence, regarding each other warily. Moving my jaw to check if it was still functioning, I scooted out of his reach, resting my back against a wall.

"Gotten it out of your system?" I asked.

Evan rubbed his jaw, glaring at me.

"Good," I muttered. "Now think, keeping in mind what you know of Rurin, do you truly think he'd have joined the conspiracy?"

"No," he replied after a while, pulling up his knees, wrapping his arms around them.

"Neither do I," I replied, trying to make sense of the thoughts scattered through my mind.

"What are you implying?"

I shook my head. "I'm not sure. It's just a thought—a hunch. What if he was part of it, because your mother wanted him to?"

"Like a spy?"

The idea had formed based on something my father had said a long time ago about how Rurin came to be *Anahràn* while he had been a spy in his younger years. Arayda must have known about it and deployed that old skill to her own advantage.

"He used to be one," I murmured. "A long time ago."

Evan's brows shot up. "How do you know?"

"Father told me," I replied. "Perhaps not intentionally, and I'm sure he thought I'd forget, except that I didn't."

"If that's true," Evan mused, a frown on his face. "Wouldn't Azra have known about it? Why would she have allowed him to join?"

I shrugged. "That's the question, isn't it?"

"Do you think he was..."

Evan didn't need to finish his sentence for me to catch the gist of what he was thinking. It had been on my mind since finding him.

What if he was killed too?

"I don't know." A deep sigh escaped my lips. "What I do

know is that whatever is going on—whatever this conspiracy is, it's big, and we've only just seen the beginning of it."

"What do you propose we do?"

Find your sister before all else.

I responded with a shrug and a shake of my head. "I don't know, Ev. I truly don't know."

CHAPTER 6

SHALITHA

Despite the veiled warning the *Akynshan* had given the *Gemsha*, the moment we returned to his wretched place, he took out his anger on me with his cane. He'd drawn out a yelp of pain only once—never since, and especially not that night. Seven lashes landed on my back before one of the other girls talked him into a semblance of control, taking the cane from him like she would from her drunk father in case he decided to take it out on her. One of the more matronly women had taken me upstairs, the look on her face one of contempt. I wasn't sure if it had been directed at him, or at me.

I ignored the incessant ache as I crouched in my hide-out the next day, eyes on a wealthy young woman too ignorant to deserve her wealth.

Like you, qira?

My inner voice had taken up the habit of scolding me whenever I accused someone of being like me—the past version of me, even though I'd never flaunted my status the way she was doing now. If I'd learned anything, she was an accident waiting to happen, and if I didn't move fast, somebody else would. Fastening the veil across my face, I stepped out of my hideout and moved into the direction of my target. She was chatting amiably with a woman of similar interest, dressed in expensive silks and even more expensive jewellery. For a brief moment I considered robbing them both, but I didn't want to push my luck, so I settled for the first choice instead, or more specifically, the bracelet she was wearing.

The *Gemsha* was opposed to the idea of stealing such valuables because they could be traced back to the owners, but I had other plans with it.

All I had to do was slip it off her wrist.

"I wouldn't do that if I were you," a familiar voice spoke from behind me.

Whirling around, I stood face to face with the *Akynshan,* who was leaning against the wall and inspecting his fingernails as if there was a blemish to be found on them.

"Or what, you'll cut off my hand?"

He smirked. "No, I won't..."

"But?"

Nodding in the direction of the women, he dropped his hands and pushed himself off the wall.

"Those two women are my wives," he whispered conspiratorially, "and they'll want more than just your hand if you rob them of their precious jewels."

I stared at him. "Wives? Plural?"

"I'm almost offended at your shock," he said, but the twinkle in his eyes told me otherwise.

He was enjoying this.

My eyes narrowed. "How many wives do you have?"

You would have known had you listened to the Gemsha.

"Exactly or approximately?"

I turned away with a derisive snort, deciding he wasn't worth my time. Instead I scanned the crowd for other victims, but unfortunately, being in the *Akynshan's* proximity had drawn quite a lot of attention—many eyes were on us. A disgusted sound escaped my lips, and I turned back to him.

"I hope you're happy now," I muttered.

"Very much so," he replied, "although I doubt it's for the reason you're implying."

With a deep growl rumbling in the back of my throat, I moved away from him, striding into the alley I'd used as my hide-out, desperate to put some distance between myself and that righteous son of a *hehzèh*.

"Siora, wait!"

Rather than doing what he asked, I picked up speed until I was jogging, but when I glanced over my shoulder, I saw that he was pursuing me.

What's wrong with him?

When I started running, he accelerated too and just before I managed to slip into another alley where I could disappear from sight, he caught up with me and halted me with a hand on my shoulder.

I flinched and hissed, causing him to let go immediately.

"Apologies, did I hurt you?"

Rolling my shoulder, I shook my head and turned to face him, annoyance building up. "No, it's fine, although I don't much care for you stalking me."

"Stalking you?"

I rolled my eyes. "Is there something I can do for you? I have places to be, stuff to do."

"Like robbing people?"

"Yes." I pressed my lips together.

"Why do you keep doing it?"

Folding my arms to make sure I wouldn't take my annoyance out on him, I regarded him dispassionately.

"I told you why."

"And I remember asking what you would do if you had a choice," he replied, doing his best to hang on to his sanity judging by the look in his eyes.

"Yes, well, I don't recall having been given one," I snapped. "Excuse me."

As I tried to push past him, he encaged my wrist in his hand, somehow managing to be surprisingly gentle.

"What if I tell you I can give you one?"

My heart skipped a beat as I considered his words, because it could mean a way home. I turned on him so fast he let go of my wrist, taking a startled step back.

"And then what?" I asked with a sneer. "Add me to your collection of wives?"

He offered a bemused smile. "That's an option too."

"You're insane," I muttered and turned away again. "Let me know when you've come up with a better offer."

"Siora..."

"What?" I whirled on him with an exasperated sigh. "Just... let me go, all right? The chances of me succeeding today are close to non-existent and I'm already dreading going back to that snake pit. Please, just... leave me alone."

Turning away from him, I did my best not to huddle in on myself—to show him that dread didn't even begin to describe how much I loathed the place. If it hadn't been for Khaz, I would have taken him up on the offer, but she was ill and she needed me, just like I had needed her after she'd found me on that beach over ten moons ago. If not for her, I'd surely have died, even after surviving that shipwreck.

"Why?"

Such a simple question. I wished the answer would be as simple, but I couldn't tell him without imparting delicate information that could get myself and Khaz in trouble.

"Please, let it go." I exhaled, all fight leaving me. "It's kind of you to offer, but you don't know me and I just... I cannot take you up on it."

He was about to ask why again, so I answered before it could leave his lips. "That too is something I cannot tell you. Let it go, *Akynshan,* I am not the woman for you."

His face fell, but I wasn't sure if it was because of my denial of his advances, or because he couldn't work out the puzzle he'd been dead set on solving. With a small wave, I stepped out of the alley and soon disappeared into the throng of citizens going about their business. On my way to the *Gemsha's* establishment, I managed to filch a few coppers from people, but I knew it wasn't enough to keep his wrath at bay.

I'd pay for my failure, one way or another.

THE DOOR to the bedroom I shared with Khaz creaked as I pushed it open, wincing at the strain it put on my shoulders and arms. She shifted in the bed as the door clicked shut behind me, her wan face taking on a look of worry.

"What's wrong?" she asked in a feeble voice, pushing herself up to a sitting position.

"It's nothing," I replied, gritting my teeth as I made my way over to the other side of the bed.

Sitting down without grunting in pain was a monumental task I'd rather have foregone, but I didn't want to concern Khazmira any more than I had to. I didn't want to add to her guilt. This was my burden to bear—not hers.

"He hit you again, didn't he?" It was as much a statement as it was a question.

I shrugged and winced.

"I swear I'll gut him like a f"

"You won't do anything," I interjected in a calm, collected voice. "His time will come. First, you have to get better. How are you feeling?"

"I still haven't stopped vomiting," she replied. "Every scent, every bit of food, it either makes me nauseous or makes me toss everything up again. I can barely keep water down."

"You need to see a healer."

We both knew what seeing a healer would mean. Most of the money we'd saved—if not all—would go toward paying him, which meant our escape would be delayed. Before today, we'd spoken of it, but not with as much sincerity as I did now.

Khaz needed a healer, sooner rather than later.

If only Soren were here.

"Maybe I can talk to the *Gemsha*," I murmured, "maybe he will pay."

She snorted from behind me. "You know he won't. As far as he's concerned, we're only as good as the money we bring in, which means right now, my life is worth next to nothing to him."

"Don't say that."

"You know it to be true," she replied, undoing my hair from its confinement.

It fell in black rivulets over my shoulder, and without looking into the mirror, I knew it highlighted my porcelain skin even more. Before we left her hometown, Khazmira had urged me to dye my hair, considering how much more I'd stand out if I didn't do it. That day, and every day since I'd seen the reason for it.

I hated every moment.

The veil was as much a disguise for the outside world as it was for myself. I didn't want anyone to see my face, nor did I want to catch my reflection anywhere either. The woman I had once been was a far cry from what would look back at me, and I wasn't sure I was ready to face her yet.

"I have to try," I said, rising to my feet. "If he refuses, we can always get one ourselves."

Before I could make another move, Khaz grabbed my wrist firmly—she was trembling.

"Don't ask him," she said in a small voice. "Please."

I turned to her with a deep frown. "Why not?"

"I..." She looked crestfallen and insecure, as if whatever she was about to tell me would betray her.

"I know what's wrong," she whispered so softly I barely heard her. "I..."

Without making any move—I was sure I didn't even blink—I watched her as she came to terms with herself.

"I'm pregnant," she said at length.

"W...what?"

I sat back on the bed, wincing at the loud creak of the strain it put on its frame. Too much noise, and someone would be banging on our door soon. *Be seen, not heard.* At home, it had been similar, although the thought had translated to *don't do anything that can endanger your life*. Mother would have a heart attack if she saw me now, stealing from the rich, clambering up and down buildings to my heart's content, risking my life every single day just to survive.

"I'm sorry," Khazmira murmured, sitting down next to me. "I didn't want to bring it up because... because I know how important escaping is to you."

My gaze settled on her and I tried for a smile. "How long?"

Khaz frowned. "What?"

"How far along are you?"

"I'm not sure." She folded her hands in her lap, looking anywhere but at me. "A... are you mad?"

"Why would I be?" I asked surprised.

"Because I didn't tell you."

I flashed her a faint smile, taking her hand in mine. "I'm not mad at you Khaz. I could never be, but... there is something I'd like to know, and please, don't get mad at me for asking?"

She nodded mutely.

"Do you want to keep it?"

Khaz was silent for such a long time, I thought she had fallen asleep. Instead, I found tears rolling down her cheeks and silent sobs racking her body. Without a second thought, I wrapped my arms around her and pulled her close. We sat like that for a long time, because by the time we let go, it was already dark. Without speaking, I set to lighting the candles, listening without judgement as Khazmira threw up what little she must have left inside of her.

"I don't know if I want to keep it," she said after she'd snuggled back under the covers. "A part of me does, and a part of me does not."

"Do you know the father?"

In the dim light of the candles, I saw her jaw tense and her eyes flash furiously. It was only brief.

"Yes." Her voice trembled. "And so do you."

CHAPTER 7

TALNOVAR

The only place in the capital that catered to what I needed for my journey was also the last place in this world where I wanted to go. Security at the palace had been upgraded by at least four score guards, if not more, and going out was as much a challenge as coming in.

Azra hadn't wasted any time, despite not yet being crowned.

A curfew had been set in place for every Ilvannian living in the city. Anyone out beyond dusk was breaking the law and would be dealt with accordingly, if caught. It was only one of the many decrees she had announced on the first day after the *Tari's* death, and there was no doubt more to come. To pass these through, however, she needed to be *Tari* and as far as I knew, Evan was working hard to postpone the coronation.

He wanted his mother's death rite done first.

As much as I wanted to be there, I couldn't. My window of escape was closing; I was already late getting these last supplies because I hadn't been able to leave the palace any sooner. Today I'd managed by the skin of my teeth, and if Azra found out, I'd pay quite a price for it. The rumble of footsteps marching up the street told me of a squadron heading in my direction. I had to disappear fast if I didn't want to get caught. Pulling the hood farther over my face to hide my features, a sudden sense of *cirtae* overwhelmed me, except that it wasn't me hiding my face, but Shal.

She always did that when she tried to outrun us.

Don't go there.

"Halt!" a deep voice bellowed from behind me.

Nohro, they've seen me.

My eyes swept over the dozen men marching in my direction, faces grim, weapons not yet within their grasp. Maybe I could come up with a viable excuse for being outside, yet the moment the thought entered my mind, I realised there was no reason whatsoever for me being here other than the truth, and I wasn't about to let them in on that.

They'll be with me soon.

Casting a furtive glance over my shoulder, I started walking away from them, huddling deeper into my cloak. The ringing of steel as swords were unsheathed echoed off the streets, sending a warning chill down my spine.

They were serious.

So am I.

In no small amount thanks to my days spent catching up to the *Tarien*, I knew a few routes I could take to disappear. With night settling over the city, hiding wouldn't be a problem, but I still had to make sure they would be totally lost, so they wouldn't catch my trail later. Some of them, I knew, had never patrolled this city before, so escaping them shouldn't be much of a problem.

My heart rate elevated at the thought of a chase, and despite myself, I grinned.

This would be good.

Taking a sharp turn to the left, I picked up speed until I was running, weaving my way through narrow streets, ducking under low hanging flowerpots while dodging benches and stools left out by their respective owners. The hardest part was circumventing the lanterns which were placed or hung nonsensically throughout the streets. The sound of footsteps pounding rapidly on the cobblestones told me they were in pursuit—or at least some of them were. A shout indicated they had seen me.

Nohro. Run, old man.

Running faster meant I'd lose control taking corners, risking the chance of losing speed as I took them, but it was one I had to take. I did not want to end up in *her* claws. Exhilaration coursed through me and for the first time in my life I understood how Shal must have felt every time she led us through the city in a merry catch-me-if-you-can game. If I ever found her and returned her home, I'd let her run through the streets as much as she wanted—and I'd chase her.

I owed her that much at least.

It's one big if, mahnèh.

Caught up in my thoughts, I missed the alley I had wanted to take. Doubling back wasn't an option, so I continued ahead. They were on my tail all right and much closer than I cared for. I took another turn and found myself on a small square with five different exits. In this part of the city, such exits often meant dead-ends and one had to know which one to take to get to another part of the city.

Out here, I knew exactly which ones to choose to stay alive.

My heart thundered to the rhythmic beat of my pursuers' footsteps. My breathing came in ragged bursts. Because of my severe injury, I was sorely out of shape, but I didn't let it stop me. Although I knew which street to go into, this pursuit was going to take forever if I didn't make a choice, and as much as I enjoyed leading them on this merry chase, I had business to attend to.

Without them.

Inhaling deeply a few times, ignoring the sharp stabs in my chest, I glanced over my shoulder, waiting, watching. They had to see me disappear into the alley, even though it meant they'd get awfully close.

If she can do it. You can, too.

Assumptions were deadly on their own, but add to that a confidence I wasn't quite feeling and it made for an awkward bed-partner. Everything rode on this decision. My escape. Leaving the city. Finding her.

Don't stuff it up, Imradien.

One chance.

Shouts echoed off the houses. There was my cue. Without looking back, I bolted to the street across from me. One try. One shot. And I'd better get it right. When I heard their footsteps behind me in the alley, I pushed deeper, withdrawing a strength from within I didn't know I possessed. A wall too high to scale in one go loomed before me.

There was only one way across.

I swerved to the side, took a few long strides and jumped up on the stone bench. In the same motion, I pushed myself off it, vaulting up to the wall. I grunted as the impact knocked all the air out of my lungs, and I was barely in time to throw my arms over it. As I began hoisting myself up, someone grabbed at my ankle, his fingers latching onto my boot.

Nohro ahrae!

I kicked him with my free foot, satisfied when I heard a crunch and a curse, and the pressure on my leg momentarily lifted. As quickly as I could, I hoisted myself up on the ledge, waiting to catch my breath and gather my wits. Below me, half a dozen men stood panting, their faces contorted in annoyance and rage.

I flashed them a grin, swung my leg over the other side, and dropped myself to the ground. That had been close. Too close.

"Get him!" someone roared from behind the wall.

It would take them some time to find a way around to this alley. Less concerned, I trotted down the street. Although I heard nobody close, I kept an eye out for trouble. It would be a shame if I ran into the rest of them after having deceived the first group, especially now that I was close to where I needed to be.

DECEPTION IS ONE THING.

Betrayal quite another.

When I rounded the corner to the tavern I wanted to visit, I stopped dead in my tracks. As did my heart. Two squadrons were hauling people outside and lining them up on the other side of the street. I would have thought nothing of it, had the squadrons not been led by a white-haired *Zheràn* I had always considered my friend.

Haerlyon.

His eyes lit up the moment he saw me, his lips curling up into that lazy smile he usually reserved for his enemies.

"There you are," he mused. "I've been waiting for you."

"Haer," I gasped, trying to catch my breath. "I… what?"

A thousand questions raced through my mind but none of them seemed like the right one to ask. My eyes halted on the people sitting in one row, looks of misery and hurt on their faces. Only one pair of eyes, set in a face as lovely as I remembered it, were blazing furiously. Cehyan, the owner of the tavern and the person I was supposed to meet, stood with her hands on her hips, refusing to sit down. None of the guards made her kneel like they did the others.

My attention returned to Haerlyon as he came sauntering up to me, thumbs hooked in his kidney belt. He looked every bit the royal son he'd always scoffed at.

Why now?

"Under the first act of the royal decree signed by *Tari* Azra an Ilvan," Haerlyon said loud enough for everyone to hear, his gaze sweeping from Cehyan, to the people, only to rest on me. "You are hereby under arrest for breaking the law."

"Law?" I asked. "What's gotten into you, Haer?"

"It's *Zheràn* an Ilvan for you, *Anahràn* Imradien." His posture was stiff, and the corners of his lips were turned down. "You'd do well to remember that."

Nothing I had expected came remotely close to this. I watched as guards hauled the men and women to their feet, adding shackles to their wrists and ankles so they couldn't run. Cehyan, feisty as ever, didn't comply. She shrieked and raged until Haerlyon took it upon himself to silence her by knocking her over the head. As she slumped into his arms, disgust crept over his features. He quickly handed her over to one of his guards.

When he turned to me, his eyes were devoid of emotion.

"Haerlyon, please." I held up my hands defensively. "Why are you doing this?"

His fist shot out and connected with my jaw, sending me staggering back. I stared at him dumbfounded, testing my jaw to find if he'd broken or merely bruised it. I knew Tiroy's death had hit him hard, and losing both his sister and mother within a moon had to have been difficult, but surely not like *this*. Never had he done anything he didn't want to do—Haerlyon didn't operate that way. Everything he did was a calculated move on his part to further a cause.

He always had a game plan.

Judging by the insanity in his eyes, I wasn't sure he had one now. Pleading with him obviously didn't work, and I doubted returning the favour to smack some sense into him would either. His lips lifted in a wicked grin as he regarded me.

"Didn't see that one coming, did you?" he asked. "If not for that list, a whole lot more damage could have been done. Oh well, it is what it is... it's all working out better than expected in the end. It's a shame Mother had to die over it, but I'm kind of glad Shal's gone… I got tired of looking after her, didn't you?"

"You don't mean that." My voice shook, as did my hands.

I wanted to hit him—wanted to hit something.

He chuckled. "No, of course you wouldn't. You loved her too much to see everything that was wrong with her. She never was able to rule her emotions—let alone an entire country. Who knows what language we'd end up speaking. Therondian would be the most obvious, but for all we know, it could be Ghaeran or Kyrinthan. By the Gods, it could even be Zihrin we'd speak!"

Anger coursed through me, adding power to my limbs, getting ready to fight or flee.

"Has anyone ever mentioned that you talk too much?" I growled.

"I've heard it said in passing." He waved his hand dismissively. "Now, let's get back to the palace, shall we? I'm fairly certain the *Tari* would love to hear why you are disobeying her orders."

"The *Tari's* dead," I hissed.

It earned me another backhand.

My heart sank when Haerlyon marched me up to Arayda's chambers, his hands firm on the shackles around my wrists. The room we stepped into was a far cry from its previous appearance. Sparse in furniture and decoration, it looked more like a dungeon than anything else, but judging by the look on Azra's face, she appeared perfectly happy with the arrangements. I couldn't help risk a glance at the bed, which was obviously completely empty save new sheets and pillows.

Nothing hinted at the tragedy that occurred here less than a week ago.

A kick to the back of my knee sent me measuring my length

against the floor. An agonising jolt spread through my elbows, and settled in my shoulders. It had been the only way to catch myself. With a grunt, I pushed myself to my knees, but before I could do anything, Haerlyon added a new set of shackles to my wrists before taking off the other ones. To my surprise, these were attached by a chain to a ring in the floor.

"*Grissin*!" I yelled, pulling at the chains.

It wasn't even three feet long.

My eyes snapped from Haerlyon to Azra, who looked immaculate in every possible way. The resemblance to Arayda and Shal was uncanny. Nobody could deny her heritage. Dark eyes flashed above a pleasant smile, but I knew that smile wasn't directed at me.

"Thank you, Haerlyon," she purred. "I knew you'd pull through."

He bowed. "He's all yours, *Tari*."

"*Verathràh!*"

Haerlyon grimaced at my accusation of him being a traitor, pivoted on his heel and stepped out of my peripherals. The click of the door announced his departure—I was completely alone with the one woman I'd love to strangle with my bare hands. Unfortunately, that wasn't an option. My eyes never left her as she walked towards me, hips swaying seductively. I was sure it would work on any other man.

"Have you been a bad boy, *Anahràn?*"

Cold shivers slithered down my back, nestling in my gut like restless snakes waiting to be fed. I almost wished I could be, and the thought made me recoil in horror. Before now, I would never have contemplated cold-blooded murder—for her, it would be too good an ending.

I pressed my lips together, refusing to answer a question like that.

She ran a talon along my jaw where Haerlyon had slugged

me, pushing lightly into the bruised flesh. I suppressed a wince, fixing my gaze dead ahead.

"According to my guards, you gave them the slip," she began, "even though they asked you to halt. Did my niece teach you a trick or two, huh?"

Exhaling with a loud huff, I turned my head to glare at her rather than replying. She was trying to get under my skin, and she would succeed if I allowed her.

"The real question is," she continued as she lowered to be at eye-level with me, running her hand down to my chest, "why you were out after curfew set in? With severe punishment as penalty for leaving the palace after dusk, one would think it's enough to keep you indoors, so either you are stupid, or desperate, and I never pegged you as the first."

I gritted my teeth so hard my jaw ached. A delighted laugh escaped her lips as she rose to her feet. Azra walked around me, assessing me, keeping one hand on my body at all times.

"It would be such a shame," she murmured more to herself than to me.

I tensed when her hand slid underneath my tunic, and I swallowed the bile in my throat.

"What do you want, Azra?" I growled.

She dug her nails in between my shoulder blades, drawing out a hiss. "First of all, you will address me as *Tari*. Second, there's many a thing I want, but I'm still trying to decide what I want from you exactly. The possibilities are endless..."

It was her words as much as it was the tone in which she said them that turned my blood cold and made me want to escape at the first opportunity. Not only did I hear the longing in it, but the malice too. A part of me wanted to know what I'd done to ruffle her feathers until I realised crazy people didn't need a reason—the justification for their actions stemmed from within a deep-rooted conviction of their own right.

Azra didn't need any validation.

This was her justice—her version of how things should be, and whoever she had to kill to get there was a minor inconvenience. The thought she could not tell right from wrong bothered me, because as much as it was her reality, it was ours now too, if only by circumstance.

I need to get out of here. Fast.

Haerlyon might be a lost cause, but I could at least try to get the others out. I bore no illusions Azra would not target them as well—differently perhaps, but she would, one way or another.

"As for your punishment." The tone in her voice was one of excitement as she turned to me, lips a bare inch from mine. "I think ten lashes will do for your insubordination?"

Without permission, she kissed me. I pulled my head away with a grunt, licking my lips. A strange taste lingered in my mouth, but it was so short-lived I forgot it almost immediately.

Azra laughed in delight and patted my cheek. "Oh Tal—can I call you Tal? You'll be so much fun to play with. Piece by piece I'll make you mine, until your father no longer recognises you."

"My father?" I asked surprised. "What does he have to do with this?"

Her eyes flashed furiously at my question. "He's got *everything* to do with this. Everything! And I am going to repay him, starting with you."

I bit the inside of my cheek until I could taste blood and was seeing stars in my vision. I needed the pain to divert my thoughts from the words she'd just spoken. Yet no matter how hard I tried to keep from speaking, I couldn't help myself.

"You're doing this out of spite?" I asked, shocked.

She pulled her lips up in a sneer, dark eyes crackling with unbridled fury. Whatever he had done, she hated his guts for it.

"Not spite, *shareye*," she hissed. "Vengeance."

CHAPTER 8

SHALITHA

Sometimes I wondered what would have happened if Khazmira hadn't found me on that beach, or what would have become of me had she left me there instead? Chances were considerable I'd have died shortly after washing ashore, either from dehydration or drowning, who was to tell? Yet she'd rescued me. She'd taken me in, shared with me everything she had, until there was neither enough food nor money to sustain us. Her people, superstitious by nature, cast us out on the streets, driving her from home and hearth after accusing her of having welcomed evil into her house. I was that evil in their eyes. She'd suffered through the hatred and torment without ever laying blame at my doorstep.

Now, it was my turn to help her.

Sticking to the shadows, I crept down the stairs of the *Gemsha's* establishment and slipped into the kitchens, hopefully without being seen by either him or one of his patrons. Some still clamoured for my services after too many drinks, and I was awaiting the day he would allow it with a growing sense of dread. Goosebumps raced across my skin, leaving shivers in their wake. If I got caught sneaking out now, there was no telling what would happen.

But Khaz needed help and time was running out.

The kitchen window, no more than a square affair barely big enough to squeeze a sack of flour through—let alone me—was my only escape, and I had to be smart about it, or get stuck.

Thankfully, it's not my first escape.

I placed a crate upside down underneath the window and tested whether it would hold my weight by putting my foot on it and shifting back and forth in slow, deliberate movements. It creaked once, sending my heart into a fluttering frenzy. Certain it had alerted the *Gemsha* and his men, I listened for shouts that never came while slipping first one leg through the window, followed by my body, my head and then the rest. Thanks be the Gods nobody had considered taking away the crates I'd stacked against the back of the building earlier that day, or my escape would have been much more painful.

As soon as I was clear of the crates, I dashed out the back alley and into the cover of night, for once glad I was getting to know the streets of Y'zdrah.

Looks like running away from the palace is showing its benefits.

Despite my outings in Ilvanna, life here was quite different and a lot more dangerous, so I had adapted and learned. My hand wandered to the dagger strapped to my back to reassure myself everything would be all right. The mission was relatively straightforward—go to the market, buy the herbs, return home.

How hard could it be?

As it turned out, a lot harder than I'd expected. In my efforts to plan this outing, I'd forgotten about the *ygr'eth* happening tonight. My only saving grace was the fact this party was only for the common people, so the chance of me running into the

Akynshan—whom I realised I hadn't seen in almost a week—were slim.

Making sure my veil was still in place, I moved out of the shadows and into the throng of people enjoying their night. It would be easy to rob them on a night like this, but when I started depriving the denizens of Y'zdrah from their money, I made a vow to never rob from the less fortunate. Despite my own situation and status in life these days, I didn't consider myself poor—unfortunate, yes, but not poor. I shrugged it off like a coat and focused on the task at hand. All I had to get was some herbs, and I couldn't help but snort at the irony.

Herbs had gotten me into trouble before.

Even at this time of night, with the *ygr'eth* in full swing, the market was still in place and people were still selling their wares. Y'zdrah didn't sleep, and this time, I was grateful for it. The stall I was looking for was tucked away in an alley off the side of the market square, hidden from view by a stall selling silks and chiffons. Out of habit, I cast a furtive glance over my shoulder to make sure I wasn't being followed before ducking out of sight.

The saleswoman—an old lady whose skin was as dry and wrinkled as often used parchment—stared at me so profoundly, I wondered if she was even open for business.

"Apologies, *amisha*," I said. "I'm looking for Vanya?"

"I'm her," the old lady said in a voice belying her frail appearance. "What do you want?"

I looked around to make sure nobody could overhear us. "I… am looking for herbs that can end a pre—"

"Hush."

"But I—"

"Quiet."

"You—"

With more strength than I'd given her credit for, she clamped a hand over my mouth and pulled me deeper into the alley. Once we were well out of sight, she released me, glaring up at me.

"Listen here," she said in a sharp tone. "When I tell you to hush, you hush, understood? No questions, or no business."

I rubbed my chin. "But I—"

"I know what you need." She cut me off again. "But you cannot come asking for these kinds of things without precaution, unless you want to be picked up by the guards that is."

I blinked rapidly. "Why?"

She tilted her head, regarding me through narrowed eyes. "You're not from around here, are you?"

"Not exactly."

A heavy sigh escaped her lips. "Oh, *Fayra* keep me. Listen here, *amisha.* Such a thing as what you ask for is considered contraband here in Y'zdrah. These herbs have been expressly forbidden by the *Akynshan* considering the fact that so few children are born these days."

"What?"

Rage flared inside me like a newly kindled fire at the revelation of the old woman, and I resolved to give the *Akynshan* a piece of my mind if I ever ran into him again. How dare he decide what a woman could or could not do with her body! Seething, I turned my attention back to Vanya.

"Do you have it though? I have good money."

She looked at me for a while longer, no doubt sizing me up. With a headache-inducing eye roll, I pulled forth a heavy pouch from my side and jingled it once. A bright smile lit up her wrinkled visage as she seemed to decide I was worth her business. Within moments, she was at least ten silver pieces richer, and all I had to show for was a small pouch.

Its scent was almost unbearable.

"Do not ingest it straight away." Vanya fixed me with a hard stare. "You must boil the leaves for tea and drink it no more than three times within a day."

I nodded mutely.

"Be prepared for pain," she added, shaking her head, "the likes of which you've never experienced before."

Deciding it wasn't worth the trouble of telling her I doubted it, I inclined my head, thanked her for her time and left the alley, tucking the little parcel in my shirt. If anyone decided to pat me down, they'd have a hard time finding it.

"You keep interesting company, *amisha*," the one person I had hoped not to encounter said from behind me.

"I don't see how it's any of your business," I replied, walking away from him.

"Here in Y'zdrah, everything is my business." His nonchalance oozed from every syllable. "But I do hope it's not for you..."

Fuming, I stopped and turned to him, fists balled at my side. "Why do you even *care*? And besides, when did you think it was ever right to decide over a woman's body!"

He blinked at me as if I'd spoken in a different language, so I went over what I'd said in my mind, but I'd spoken *Zihrin*.

"What are you talking about?"

"Play the innocent." I rolled my eyes, and started walking away from him, resolving he wasn't worth my time.

Unfortunately, the *Akynshan* was like a dog with a bone and he went in pursuit. Again.

He's getting on my nerves.

"You're quite... something," I said after a while, "and I don't even know your name so I can curse you properly for creeping up on me every time."

"Most people refer to me as *Akynshan*," he offered.

The smug smile on his face fuelled my fury, so I bit my tongue and turned away with a noise of disgust.

"Elay," he added hastily. "You can call me Elay."

Something in the way he said it made me stop and turn to him. My anger deflated and resignation settled deep within me.

Elay was leaning casually against the wall, one ankle hooked over the other, arms folded in front of his chest. His easy smile lit up eyes that called up memories I'd tried to bury for more than ten moons. At that moment, I was failing miserably, and Tal's face came to mind, roguish smile and all.

I'd have preferred a punch to the gut.

"Listen, Elay," I said, clasping my hands firmly together, looking for words. "I don't know what made you come and find me at this time of night, but I need to go back. If the *Gemsha* finds me missing..."

"Why do you fear him so much?"

I clenched my jaw and looked up. "I do not fear him, not for my sake anyway, but his temper is one to be reckoned with, and I do not care to be on the receiving end of it... again."

Elay frowned. "Why do you stay?"

"I told you before." I ground my teeth. "I have no choice."

"I gave you one."

He said it so casually I could only stare at him. Pinching the bridge of my nose, I shook my head slowly to dispel what he'd just said—how he'd said it—as if nothing else mattered.

"And I told you I don't want to be one of your wives."

He smirked. "You never did let me finish my proposal..."

Folding my arms in front of me, I watched him. "Fine, let's hear it then."

"Come live with me," he said. "You can continue whatever you're doing now, except that you have my protection rather than my wrath."

"What about my friend?"

He shrugged. "Is she useful?"

"When she's not ill, yes."

"Ill?" he echoed, tilting his head. "How come she's ill?"

While I thought up a way to tell him without incriminating Khazmira and the *Gemsha*, realisation dawned on him—it was ugly.

"The herbs," he murmured. "They're for her?"

I nodded, my voice choked with emotion when next I spoke. "They are."

Fury crossed his face as fast as compassion and indignation did, only to settle on resignation and a look of concern.

"Bring her to the *K'ynshan*," he said. "Tonight. Do not give her the herbs."

"She's too sick to be moved."

Elay regarded me quietly. "Tonight, or the offer is for you alone."

"Fine."

I stormed away without looking back, refusing to even acknowledge him with a glance over my shoulder. Just before I turned the corner, I saw he was where I'd left him, but it was too dark to make out the look on his face. The moment he was out of sight, a stone settled in my stomach.

He'd given us a way out, but I had to find a way to bring Khaz to him.

Short of carrying her out the front door, I did not know how we'd circumvent running into the *Gemsha* and explain we'd been given a better offer. I doubted he'd take kindly to being left like that after paying for us.

Worries for later. I'd best get back inside before he realises I've been out and about.

MERCIFULLY, getting back inside was easier than I'd anticipated. Nobody had moved the crates on either side of the window, and nobody was in the kitchen at this time of night. Most likely, the *Gemsha* was too busy entertaining guests of his own to have many customers around. The middle day of the week was always slow for business, and peeking into the main area, I saw today was no exception.

As expected, only a few men were present.

Sneaking up the stairs, I was grateful they'd been made of stone rather than from wooden boards. One creak, and I'd be begging on my knees—again. Unfortunately, the upstairs floor was made of wood though—I had turned into an acrobat navigating these planks to avoid noise and was thankful for it this time.

Once in front of our door, I dared breathe again.

As soon as I stepped inside, however, I knew something was amiss. The scent in the room was wrong—coppery, or perhaps more like iron, but it was a smell I knew only too well.

Blood.

With my heart hammering in my chest, I lit a few candles, only to find my suspicions confirmed. Khazmira lay dead on the bed, eyes wide in terror, her belly cut open from top to bottom. A sudden wave of nausea hit me and I turned away, adding the contents of my stomach to the floor. The smell was enough to make me gag again. Burying my nose in the crook of my arm, I backed out of the room, bumping into something soft.

"Isn't it sad," the *Gemsha* spoke up from behind me.

He circled his arm around my shoulders, pulling me against him while placing a blade against my throat. Heedless of the knife that could kill me, I twisted out of his arms and attacked as a haze of blind fury washed over me.

He'd killed Khazmira.

And for what?

Another memory resurfaced and for a moment I returned to the library back home, my eyes fixed on Elara as the assassin cut her throat. My mind slipped into survival mode and my body followed suit.

My foot connected with the *Gemsha's* knee, eliciting a howl of pain, moments before I clipped him underneath his jaw. His attention wavered for a second and in that little window of time, I kicked the blade from his hand. I never noticed how it cut me—how blood trickled down my neck. All my attention was on him. There was no rhyme or reason to my assault—I hit, kicked, scratched, as long as my hands or feet connected with something, it was fine.

Fear permeated him like a heavy cloud of cologne—it was in the way his jowls shook, in how his eyes bulged with disbelief at my audacity. It was in the way he pressed himself against the wall. Whatever he saw in my eyes was enough to start him shaking. My lips curled into a wicked grin as I slipped the knife from my back into my hand. In a desperate attempt, probably hoping to catch me off guard, the *Gemsha* lunged at me. Unfortunately for him, I was ready and ducked out of his reach. As he blundered into the opposite wall, I stepped behind him and slipped the knife between his ribs, right where his heart was.

If he had one.

He staggered back, trying to reach the injury, but his fat arms wouldn't allow him. As he turned around, his expression blanched and paled as his mouth went slack.

I remembered that look from Xaresh.

"Murderer!" His voice, strong despite dark blood bubbling on his lips, echoed through the halls.

It was now or never.

I plunged the knife deep into his throat and left it there. Doors opened. Women screamed.

Without thought, without telling Khazmira goodbye, I fled down the stairs, into the establishment and out the front door.

"Murderer! Get her!"

I ran.

CHAPTER 9

TALNOVAR

If past events were any indication, I should have expected the show Azra would make of my punishment. As it was, surprise and disgust rolled over me in rapid succession as guards wrestled me into a throne room filled to the brim with spectators. It was a relief to find that the first faces I locked gazes with looked as sick and horrified as I felt.

Allies.

Try though I might to remember the faces, the more of them I saw, the more they blurred into one until none of them were distinguishable from another. It reminded me entirely too much of a night spent indulging in *sehvelle,* but I was fairly certain I hadn't taken any.

Perhaps it was the ridiculous situation.

As the crowd thinned out, my gaze fell on Soren and Mehrean, their faces perfectly composed. Evan, his arm circled protectively around Nathaïr's shoulders, did a poor job of concealing his anger, his eyes flashing the moment they met mine. A light shake of my head was all the warning I could give him before my jailers yanked me towards the dais and pushed me to my knees. I bit my cheek to keep from making a sound as pain shot through my legs upon impact.

Despite trying not to, my eyes were drawn to the woman on the dais, travelling up at such a snail's pace I began to wonder what was wrong with me. Her dress revealed more skin than the garments of all the women in this room put together, especially at the front and on her hips. The neckline plunged so low, I felt certain we would see more than our fair share should she bend forward.

As my gaze continued its way up to settle on her face, an inkling of a thought bubbled to the surface—one I couldn't quite grasp. There was something off about her, and it wasn't just her personality. Blood red lips curled into a predatory smile as our eyes locked, and the way she licked her lips didn't leave much to the imagination. She was enjoying this. A cold feeling of dread slithered down my back as she tore her gaze from mine, sweeping over the crowd behind me.

"*Irìn. Irà.*" Her voice rang strong and clear through the throne room.

Everyone fell silent.

"It is with deep sorrow and great pleasure that I welcome you inside our walls. A tragedy befell us less than a week ago when our *Tari* died after a long and debilitating illness, and this so soon after the news of our *Tarien's* untimely demise. Mark my words. We will find who is responsible for this deed!"

Only a few people cheered.

If there had been absolutely nothing at stake, I would have opened my mouth then and there and outed her, but instead I glowered at her, cowering like a child behind his mother's skirts. Self-loathing had become quite the bed-friend in the past twelve moons, and today was no exception.

If I hadn't failed…

If she hadn't agreed to his *terms and would have fought…*

Forcing my thoughts away from the dark abyss looming just ahead, I returned my focus to Azra.

Right now, she was the one I had to worry about.

"As you may have noticed," she said, as eyes twinkling with mischievous delight swept over the crowd, "things have changed and will continue changing around here. First of all, nobody is allowed outside after curfew. Sadly, some seemed under the impression this rule did not apply to them,"—her eyes settled on me— "which is why he will serve as a reminder of what happens should you disobey. Guards?"

Before I knew what was happening, they hauled me to my feet and wrestled me over to a wooden pole that had been set up to my right.

How could I have missed it?

Fighting their hold, I tried to get free, but they were strong—much stronger than I was on my own, and I realised not only my sight was affected as if I'd used *sehvelle*, but my body felt much the same way. I had the feeling as if I were on a boat, the sea rocking beneath me in arrhythmic waves, tossing me left and right in a vain attempt to throw me overboard, and when they tied me to the whipping post, I held on for dear life.

The sensation was unnerving.

Azra's cackle sounded distorted.

"What's wrong, *Anahràn*?" she asked for my ears alone as she moved into view. "Drunk a little too much in that bar?"

I frowned. "I never..."

"No," she whispered, stepping close enough to run her knuckles down my cheek. "You wouldn't, would you? Always so prim and proper. So dull..."—a playful grin spread across her lips— "but I'll get that out of you too. You'll be begging for more. Soon."

"Never," I replied, the feeble sound of my voice surprising me.

What has she done to me?

She laughed. "You cannot even figure out what's wrong with you. Do you really think you can best me?"

Spitting her in the face was the only worthy response I could think of.

Azra wiped it away, a cold smirk settling on her lips. A flash of metal perceived out of the corner of my eyes made me flinch, drawing out a chuckle from her. I clenched my jaw, expecting the knife to end up somewhere between my ribs. Instead, she sliced the shirt from my back, and I shivered as the cold air suddenly hit my naked skin. One hand ran from my lower back upwards, pausing on the scar left by the injury I'd sustained at *Hanyarah*, her fingers tracing the shape of my muscles as they bunched beneath her touch.

I refrained from making any sound, but I couldn't help the goosebumps following in the wake of her caresses.

"Get on with it already," I hissed. "Hasn't your mother taught you it's not ladylike to play with your food?"

She laughed delightedly. "Ah, but nobody would mistake me for a lady, would they?"

"I suppose," I replied as nonchalantly as I could make it sound. "I know I wouldn't."

"Such a shame," she purred, lifting my chin so I couldn't look anywhere but at her. "Not that it matters though. You're mine, and you will learn what it means to be so."

I smirked but didn't feel the certainty I went for. "Sure. You keep those delusional ideas. Know that I will make it impossible for you every step of the way."

Without preamble, she yanked my head back and turned it so Soren, Mehrean, Evan and Nathaïr were in my vision.

"Are you sure?" she asked softly. "Because from the way I see it, you've got quite a few reasons for complying, unless you want me to kill them now?"

She made a move to command her guards.

"No!"

The grin on her face turned my blood to ice. "I knew you'd come around."

When she stepped out of sight, I expected the first lash to hit straight away. It didn't. Azra was playing a game, but without having the rules to it, it was hard to play along and fight her.

If this is how Shal had to play it, no wonder she felt one step behind every single time.

Coiled tight with pent up anger and frustration, the first lash to kiss the skin of my back felt like a hot poker searing my flesh. The next hit barely registered—it merely sent another flare of agony through my body. I clutched the pole as if it were a lifeline and I needed saving. Perhaps I did, but I wasn't going to ask for it. I'd gotten myself into this mess—I would get myself out of it.

The third through the eighth lash were teasing licks compared to the first one, what with my body on fire as it was—the last two were my undoing. Aimed for my shoulder rather than my back, the sensation shooting through me was indescribable. It was pain in all its glorious, malevolent forms while at the same time it was a blessed relief.

The punishment was over.

My knees buckled under the last lash but by some act of mercy, I didn't sink to them. She had had her pleasure—she had enacted her punishment, but she hadn't broken me.

Yet.

The thought struck more fear into me than Azra's threats had, and it nearly did make my legs give way.

"The punishment has been exacted," Azra called out. "His misdeeds have been paid for. Let it be a warning to you all! Ten lashes today might be twenty tomorrow."

Murmurs arose amongst the crowd, not of consent, but of fear and shocked disapproval. I didn't need to see their faces to know this to be true, because the alternative didn't bear thinking about. The shudder coursing through me sent new waves of pain assaulting my body, and it took every ounce of will I possessed not to faint.

She'd enjoy it too much, and I was afraid of where I'd wake up.

"Now, before you all leave." The tone in Azra's voice caught my attention straight away. "There is something we need to take care of first."

I craned my neck to watch her from my position, but all I could see was the left side of her back, and only if I stretched myself to the point where the pain sent stars into my vision.

"Tomorrow, we shall say our farewells to my sister," she continued, her voice level but strained, "and the day after will see my coronation. Before then, I need to know who I am to invite."

I frowned at that statement.

Since when are invitations personalised?

"Therefore, I will give you the chance to swear your allegiance to me now."

The statement in and of itself wasn't out of the ordinary—in fact, I'd say it was two days early—it was in the way she said those words. I almost expected a counteroffer in case people didn't, but Azra wasn't forthcoming. Instead, she stepped back on the dais and assumed her place on the throne. My eyes met hers, and the evil grin she flashed me instantly froze me to the spot.

She's up to something.

"Untie *Anahràn* Imradien, please," she said in a delicate purr. "He doesn't need any more agony than he is in now."

Oh, the irony.

As soon as my wrists were released from the ropes, I slid to my knees, no longer able to keep myself up. The chuckle escaping her lips riled me up enough to rise to my feet, ignoring the stabbing warning my body flared into my consciousness.

She will not have me on my knees.

Turning to meet the crowd I inclined my head, arranging my face into an emotionless mask—it didn't come as easily as it used to. My eyes slid over the assembly and rested on a pair of wide violet ones, sending me back to a time when a friend bore those eyes. Xaresh. I'd never realised how much Samehya—his sister—looked like him. Not until now. Defiance was written all over those young, ignorant features, so I shook my head ever so slightly, hoping against hope she wouldn't be her usual feisty self.

It would get her killed.

"*Irìn. Irà,*" Azra called out. "To swear your fealty to me, take a knee, it's as simple as that."

Confused looks passed between people. Some—those either too afraid or already loyal—took a knee and bowed their head, but they comprised less than half of the crowd. My eyes surveyed the room and rested on Evan. His gaze snapped to mine almost instantly. A shrug and a shake of his head was all the communication I needed to know he had no idea what was going on either.

"Haerlyon, if you please?" Azra asked politely—too politely.

Appearing from behind the crowd, Haerlyon, along with several other guards, grabbed people still on their feet and hauled them forwards. Amongst them was Samehya, all fur and teeth as she fought Haerlyon's hold, cursing him with enough colourful expressions to make Xaresh turn in his grave.

If he had one.

Suffice to say, it probably was a good thing he couldn't hear his younger sister right now.

The guards kept hold of a dozen people facing Azra. Most of them held on to their defiance—some were shaking. I couldn't blame them. I returned to look at Samehya, arms restrained by Haerlyon's vice-like grip around her wrists, which he held uncomfortably above her head. Her eyes were blazing furiously.

Azra, ever the woman of dramatics, rose to her feet elegantly and stepped down the dais, moving in such a way all eyes were on her. I had to hand it to her—she knew how to play a crowd. I followed her movements as she stopped in front of a minor *Irìn*, lifting his chin with one finger so he had to look at her.

He seemed about to soil himself.

"Out of the goodness of my heart, I'm giving you one more chance." Azra smiled benevolently as if she knew the meaning of the word. "Do you swear fealty to me, your *Tari*?"

Finding his courage, the *Irìn* spat her in the face. "You're not *my Tari*."

I fought a bitter tang in my mouth when his head toppled backwards, throat slit from ear to ear, blood gushing from the injury like a tiny waterfall. Shrieks of fear and cries of pain echoed through the throne room—his family was here too. Pressing my fist to my lips, my gaze swept across the assembly, finding my disgust echoed on many faces. Despite their feelings, more people sank to their knees, bowing their head in deference to our new sovereign. Glancing at Evan, I noticed the tight set in his jaw and the balled fists at his side.

At least none of them had gone to their knees.

"Will you swear fealty to me?" Azra's voice cut through my reverie.

The *Irà* at the other end of the dagger inclined her head and sank into a curtsy, followed by five more in their line. Two men and Samehya were still on their feet, their eyes shouting their defiance to the world. I willed Samehya to look at me, but no matter what I did, her eyes were focused on the tyrant coming closer with every breath she took.

She had to be afraid.

Neither of the men swore their allegiance to Azra and found their demise at her feet, except she was less merciful to them. Instead of killing them almost straight away, she injured them to the point where a healer would be too late. Their gurgles and whimpers were the only sound in the throne room.

They died a slow death.

In my peripheral vision, I noticed more people going down to one knee.

Still not everyone.

My attention snapped back at a yelp from Samehya. Azra had her hand wound into her hair, yanking her head back with force. Haerlyon had let go of her wrists. Our eyes met briefly, and I could swear there was loathing in his—fear even, until his lips lifted into a lazy smirk and whatever friendly contact I'd believed was there, disappeared in the blink of an eye.

"Such a devious little thing," Azra chuckled, tilting Samehya's head a little farther, resting a small knife I knew I'd seen before against her throat.

Shal's knife. Hehzèh!

"You resemble that oaf of a brother quite a lot. Same eyes. Same scruffy appearance." Her voice dripped with disgust. "But at least you seem to be smarter. And prettier."

Samehya shrieked and fought her restraints. "Let me go! You foul good-for-nothing *hehzèh*!"

A part of me wanted to smack her upside the head—the other part applauded her courage while simultaneously putting me to shame. Here was a girl half my age showing more balls than I did in the last weeks.

"*Tari*," I said through clenched teeth, taking a step forward.

The pain intensified in a split second—how could I have forgotten about it? I blamed the atrocity going on before my eyes.

"What?" Azra snapped, turning to me, fury oozing from her.

"She's a promising talent in fighting. I'm certain she'll be to your liking as *Arathri* should you be inclined to have them like your sister did, and your Mother before you."

Azra lifted her chin, her eyes narrowing to half slits as she watched me. I could see her brain working around the words I'd offered her.

"No!" Samehya yelled. "I will *not* work for *her*! I promised my allegiance to the *Tarien*, like my brother, and I will stand by it, even if she's gone."

Azra backhanded her, turning on her so fast I was sure she'd slit Samehya's throat without a second thought. From the corner of my eyes, I noticed Haerlyon start forward too, but he quickly caught himself. My eyes narrowed.

What are you *playing at?*

"Well then," Azra said loud enough for everyone to hear. "You've put me in quite the position, *shareye*. I really don't think I can allow you to live after such a declaration."

An involuntary gasp escaped my lips, but I forced myself to stay where I was. Azra turned to me with a wicked grin.

"But I shall be merciful this time," she purred. "You get to see another day, but one toe out of line, and I will have your life."

"I don't care," Samehya replied, softer this time. "Kill me if it makes you happy."

A sob escaped from someone in the crowd—her mother was here. My gaze snapped to Azra whose lips curled up into a wide smile. With just a nod of her head, she commanded her guards, and all too soon, one of them dragged Kalyani forward. Tears were streaming down her face as she watched her daughter. Samehya's courage faltered, and a soft whimper escaped her lips. Azra, cruel as she was, gave another command and before anyone could make a move, there was a dagger at Kalyani's throat.

"Let me make myself perfectly clear," she told Samehya. "You will behave, or I will kill her instead of you. Understood?"

Samehya nodded mutely.

Azra smiled and let go of her. The guard released Kalyani, who crawled to her daughter on hands and knees, careless of how it must look. My eyes locked with Azra's as she turned and made her way back to the throne. I didn't care for the look in them.

She wasn't done yet.

Turning to the crowd, her eyes surveying the room, her lips set in a thin line. I followed her gaze and realised some people were still standing. An ominous feeling settled in my gut.

I should be standing with them.

Whatever prompted the thought soon disappeared as Azra raised her hand, eyes hard, voice booming when she spoke. "While I commend your tenacious efforts of holding onto something which is no longer among us, I call you fools. Guards!"

Although I'd heard about the depravity this woman was capable of, I was in no way prepared to witness it with my own eyes. One by one or in pairs, those still on their feet crumpled to their knees, blood gushing from mortal wounds. The throne room erupted into mayhem; screams of fear mingled with shrieks of pain until it all turned into a cacophonous blur of anguished cries. I watched in horror as people fought to escape the throne room, pushing towards the closed double doors. Azra stood watching the chaos in glee, the look on her face of a woman close to reaching her climax.

Not glee, but ecstasy.

My eyes sought out Evan, who looked as shocked as I felt, and Soren, who had turned a few shades paler. Nathaïr was hiding behind Evan. Everyone was looking away—everyone except for Mehrean, who was watching Azra with a mix of curiosity and interest.

Azra only had eyes for the carnage in front of her.

When the doors opened, people streamed out, pushing and jostling each other to get away first. Nobody cared for the person they had been standing next to moments ago. I doubted they cared about their own family at that point. All they were concerned about was their own survival.

I cannot blame them.

The result of Azra's game became evident when the throne

room had emptied out. The dead and dying lay scattered across the floor by the dozens. My eyes swept over them until they landed on Samehya and her mother sitting huddled over a body. From this distance, I couldn't recognise it, until I realised it was because her face was trampled. Xaresh's and Samehya's youngest sister had not made it out alive.

Fury burned white hot inside of me and without conscious thought, ignoring the protests of my body, I charged Azra.

Weak from pain and blood loss, I was no match for her, and I was on my knees and gasping for air while she stood over me, hand fisted into my hair, small dagger at my throat. The amused expression on her face fuelled my anger, but all I could do was fight her inside my head. Panting, I watched her, hissing at the fiery jolts flaring through my body.

"What did you think of doing, *Anahràn*?" she spat, yanking my head back. "You're barely worth a copper. Did you really think you could fight me?"

"I'll try," I hissed through my teeth. "Every. Single. Time."

"Good," she replied. "I don't expect anything less."

Her lips curved into a wicked smile as she ran her knuckles over my cheek. Without warning, she suddenly pressed a finger into one of the welts, sending the world into a spinning frenzy. My stomach lurched and the floor rose up to meet me.

Don't forget, Anahràn. I know the rules of this game.

CHAPTER 10

SHALITHA

My lungs were on fire, my legs cramped up, and my heart was thundering so hard I couldn't hear beyond the roaring of blood in my ears. Doubling over, I tried to catch my breath, a voice on the edge of my perception tugging at memories of training.

Stand up. Get air into your lungs.

Stretching was the last thing on my mind, but I did as ordered, only to realise it was no order at all but a figment of my imagination. My eyes searched for a way out while my brain tried to come up with a hiding place where I'd be safe. My pursuers were close—I could hear their voices and footsteps in the alleys down below.

Time was running out.

Breathing in deeply one last time, I pushed myself to my feet and propelled forward, forcing one foot in front of the other without any clear path to take. No matter where I ran, they'd find me. Nowhere in Y'zdrah was safe, and going out into the desert at night, without food, drink, or shelter was suicide.

It was why Khazmira and I hadn't escaped yet.

My stomach tightened at the memory of Khaz, lying dead in

our bed, belly cut open as if the culprit had wanted to take out the baby.

Maybe he did.

The sudden thought made my stomach lurch, and I was barely in time to stop myself from throwing up on the roof I was on. Clutching my abdomen, I waited until the sick feeling subsided. It didn't. I had to move forward though. Staggering on, I made my way across the roofs where it was safest, no longer going for jumping the ones that were more than seven feet apart. I'd done it before and had succeeded, but I'd been fed, healthy and not been running for the past few hours, dodging guards at every intersection.

I had to find a safe place.

Up ahead, highlighted by the moon against the dark background of the endless sands behind it lay the *Akynshan's* palace.

Perhaps.

Although my mind was waging a battle of wits, my feet didn't take as long to decide, and before I knew it, I was climbing down the walls of a building closest to the palace to get back to the ground. Mercifully, the *ygr'eth* was still going strong despite the time of night, so after ensuring my veil was still in place, I made my way through the crowd, desperately keeping my head down and trying to avoid bumping into people.

I needed to get through this unseen.

Arriving at the garden walls, I thought my luck had turned. Nobody had followed me here—or so I believed. The moment I started running to gain momentum to scale the garden wall, shouts sounded behind me, and much closer than I'd anticipated them to be. Without looking back, I ran as fast as my feet would carry me. My heart beat frantically, and I couldn't help but wonder when it would give out.

It had to happen sometime soon.

Pushing all thoughts of dying aside, I focused on the here

and now, and more importantly, the task ahead. I had to get up that wall or my life would be forfeit.

Stop the morbidity. Focus!

The wall was looming closer now. Only a few more steps. All I had to do was time my jump correctly, run up the wall and grab the ledge. Then I could haul myself up and be out of trouble—or so I hoped.

Focus, Shal. Come on.

I jumped precisely on time and managed to run up high enough, but just as I grabbed the ledge, someone got a hold of my ankle. A string of expletives burst forth from my mouth, and I realised too late they weren't in Zihrin.

"Get her! Pull her down!"

Not going down without a fight, I kicked hard and repeatedly against whatever my foot connected with. As soon as the pressure on my leg lifted, I scrambled up. Shouts and curses—these were in Zihrin—followed me up. I threw myself over the ledge and onto the roof where I lay spread-eagled, my vision swimming as my lungs fought to get some air.

That had been close.

"Warn the *Akynshan!* Get into the gardens! Find her!"

Nohro.

Reluctantly, I rolled onto my hands and knees and crawled over to the edge of the building I was on. Although hard to distinguish in the moonlight, I could just make out the bushes down below. Unfortunately, there was no way of telling what kind of bushes they were until I dropped myself down and landed amongst them.

There was no other way.

Assembling the last of my courage, I wriggled over the edge until I was hanging from my hands, and without second-guessing myself, I dropped down. Branches tore at my clothing and skin, but I was thankful the plants weren't of the thorny kind. That would have brought on a whole new set of problems I wasn't ready to face.

Staying low, I listened for the guards I knew had to be perusing the perimeter. Shouts and commands sounded in the distance, but they were too far for me to worry about. First, I needed to find a place where I could hide—inside. I remembered the garden the *Akynshan* had shown me the week before, but I had no idea in which direction it lay. Besides, I wasn't sure I had any strength left to haul myself across another wall. At this point, if hiding wouldn't be easy, I would rather turn myself in. Staying there was a bad idea regardless, so I snuck out of my hiding place while sticking to the shadows, and made my way over to the other side.

There had to be a way in.

To my delight, candles were burning in a room just above ground level. I had to pull myself up on a balcony, but I was confident I could do so without much of a fuss. Voices drifted closer from around the corner, and were preceded by a bulb of light cast by a torch. Looking around, I realised this was happening on both sides. They were scouring the garden quite thoroughly.

I had to go now if I had any hope of survival.

Having no time to second guess my decision, I pelted from the garden wall over to the balcony, flattening myself against the cold structure to catch my breath. I cast furtive glances left and right to check where the guards were, then surveyed the balcony, relieved to find it was easily accessible and empty, and that it had enough hand and footholds to get up. I scrambled up and over before the circles of light came close enough to catch me, and was glad for the solid structure against my back, grateful there was no way for them to see me unless I rose to my feet, or they climbed over.

Surely they won't do that, will they?

I listened quietly as they passed, huddling closer to the wall as their light washed over me. I flinched the moment it did, even though they couldn't see me. In any case, I had to find a better hiding spot than this—all it took was one smart guy to decide to climb over and all would be for naught.

If there was one thing I was even more grateful for than the architecture of the building, it was the fact the Zihrin weren't particular about closing doors or windows like we were in Ilvanna. Granted, we'd freeze to death if we didn't make use of them, unlike here in Zihrin where it was sweltering hot every moment of the day, and even the nights were too warm to sleep comfortably.

I understood why they kept everything open, and I was happy I could use it to my advantage.

On hands and knees, I made my way inside, steering clear of what little light the candles gave off. There were many things that could go wrong from here on out, and it all depended on who was inside the room. Not until then did it occur to me that I counted on Elay finding me, and I realised I'd risked it all on a fool's hope.

I wasn't even sure Elay was the one who'd find me, let alone help me.

Qira!

Despite my doubts, I crawled into the shadows farthest from the door and balcony and pulled up my knees, praying to the Gods and Goddesses he'd be intrigued enough in my offer not to have my head separated from my body.

It all depended on the whims of a man I barely knew.

A SOUND at the door jolted me back to awareness. I must have dozed off. Pushing myself deeper into the shadows—if that were even possible—I peered towards the entrance, my eyes adjusting to the light of only two candles. The rest had burnt down. My gaze settled on a tall figure, but I didn't need any light to tell me it was Elay. From his posture alone, I knew it was him.

He stopped halfway towards his desk, tilting his head.

"I know you're in here."

My heart skipped several beats at his words. Regardless, I remained in my hide out.

"I can smell the blood from here," he continued as if he were having a regular conversation. "I'm certain you didn't come here just to hide?"

He turned to me so fast, an involuntary yelp escaped my lips. A soft chuckle came from him.

"If I'd wanted you dead, I'd have sent my guards in here hours ago."

"You knew?" My voice was hoarse when I spoke.

"I had my suspicions," he replied, moving closer. "A girl lay dead in a room, and the *Gemsha* dead in his establishment. His girls described how you killed him and ran."

"How did you know I was here?"

His teeth flashed white, despite what little light there was. "Because it's where I would have gone had I been in your position. Will you step out of the shadows please? I feel like I'm talking to myself here."

I huffed. "I had no idea you were so vain."

"If only you knew."

Despite my reservations towards him, this kind of banter put me enough at ease to uncoil myself from my cramped position and rise to my feet. I stumbled when I did, a sudden spell of dizziness overwhelming me, and I would have dropped to my knees had Elay not steadied me at the elbows.

"I'm not accustomed to women falling into my arms," he commented dryly, guiding me to a chair.

"I wouldn't get used to it if I were you."

Being so close, I could feel the rumble of a laugh starting in his chest. It had been a while since I'd felt something like this, and although I harboured no feelings for Elay whatsoever, it stirred memories I'd buried in the deepest recesses of my brain.

I couldn't fall apart now.

After he made sure I was seated and wouldn't topple over a second time, Elay set to lighting more candles around the room. I flinched at the sudden brightness and flung my hands over my eyes, keeping them shut.

"Light sensitive eyes?" he asked, faintly amused.

"Been in darkness for too long," I muttered. "Would you mind getting them out of sight?"

"What if I say I would?"

"I'm not above begging at this point," I replied with a heavy sigh. "It's not as if I've got anything left to lose anyway."

"Indeed?"

Not only did he sound amused—he sounded intrigued, just like I had hoped.

"You said you didn't want me dead," I continued, lowering my hands and slowly opening my eyes. "Why?"

Thankfully, he'd taken away the candles that had been straight in my vision and had instead placed them off to the side. He stood leaning against his desk, arms folded in front of him, eyes slightly narrowed as he regarded me.

"Are we doing this again?" he asked.

I shook my head. "No. I'm done with tiptoeing around each other. I'm here to make you an offer."

He perked up. "An offer even? And why do you think I'd entertain the idea of an offer after you refused me so many times already?"

I was too tired to play this game—too tired, and really not feeling that well at all.

"I thought we weren't playing games anymore," I said.

His lips pulled up into a smirk, eyes twinkling in mischief, briefly reminding me of my brother, Haerlyon.

It felt like a stab to the chest all over again and I had to look away.

"But I do love our banter," he all but purred, pushing himself away from the desk. "As for your question—I do not want you dead, because I do not think you deserve it."

My head snapped up. "What?"

Elay moved closer, emerald eyes—Tal's eyes—boring into mine. "I'd say that fat bastard had it coming."

My eyes widened, and I frowned. "Were you waiting for this to happen?"

He shrugged, but his lips had curled up into that mischievous smile again. I was torn between wanting to strangle him and hitting him.

Neither was a good option.

"So, this offer," he said. "What is it?"

I gulped. It was now or never, and if my offer wasn't good enough, never was the likeliest of outcomes.

"In return for your protection." I sat up straight. "I'll reveal my identity to you."

He perked up. "And why would that interest me?"

"Because I'm worth as much alive as I am dead, depending on which party you decide to do business with."

Not only had I piqued his interest, I'd interested the businessman in him—I could tell from the hungry look that appeared in his eyes.

"Go on," he said slowly.

I rose to my feet, leaning against the chair to remain steady. "It's up to you what you decide for me, although I do hope you'll stick to your desire of not killing me."

Elay merely nodded, his eyes never leaving me.

"For now," he said, "I'll stick to that promise. From the sounds of it, this could be fun."

I snorted. "You have a strange definition of fun."

“Maybe.” He shrugged. “But I also know a good offer when I see one, and right now, I feel like I’m about to get rich.”

“Don’t get your hopes up,” I replied, clutching the chair to keep from falling over. “Will you agree to my terms?”

“I will,” he replied, “but by doing so, you will also agree to mine.”

I worried at my lower lip with my teeth, hesitation coiling uncomfortably in my gut. It was one thing to ask a man I hardly knew for protection on my terms—quite another to agree to his terms without knowing them.

It was all I had.

“I will,” I said.

“Allow me,” he murmured and closed the distance between us.

Without saying anything, he removed the veil from my face—his eyes widened just slightly. It was when he started removing the hijrath from my head that his lips curled up in a grin wider than any I’d seen on him. Although black hair tumbled from under the fabric, it was the porcelain skin that gave me away. He didn’t speak when he pushed up my sleeve to reveal the *Araîth* coiling up my lower arm, disappearing under the fabric he couldn’t push up.

He watched me in wonder.

I half expected him to exclaim in pure delight, judging by the look on his face. Instead, he readjusted the hijrath and put the veil back over my face.

“Come with me.”

CHAPTER 11

TALNOVAR

When I woke up, a persistent throbbing behind my temples evolved into a headache I was sure would split my skull, but the pain in my back was nowhere near what I expected. It was a dull ache reminding me of soreness in the morning after having spent a day out on the fields training rookies and *Arathrien* alike rather than having the skin flogged off of my back. I did remember a feeling of light and warmth instead of fiery agony the night before, but I couldn't explain the absence of agonizing pain now. When I opened my eyes, a second surprise awaited me—I was neither in the infirmary nor my own room, or Shal's for that matter.

"Son of a *hehzèh*!"

I sat up with a start, cursing as a flare of pain rolled across my back. There it was. Sudden disgust washed over me when I confirmed my suspicions by looking around.

Azra's room.

"Finally awake, are you?" Her honeyed voice sounded from my left.

Turning on my side, I found her reclining next to me on the bed, wearing nothing but a robe, revealing more—much more—

than I cared to witness. Nevertheless, my eyes were drawn to her naked skin, more specifically to the side where there should have been an *Araîth.*

Nohro!

Despite myself, my eyes travelled south, down her legs, confirming what I hadn't been able to figure out the day before. Barring the starting lines on her calf and foot, Azra's skin was flawless—her *Araîth* had never been finished, which meant that by law, she couldn't be crowned.

Yet.

All she had to do was find an *Araîtiste* and force her to ink her, but that could take weeks—weeks we could use to set up anything to keep her from becoming *Tari.* A spark of hope ignited in my chest, but I didn't dare kindle it until I'd spoken to Evan. If anybody knew the law, it would be him.

"Like what you're seeing?" she purred.

I realised my eyes were still on her, even though I wasn't actively watching. In fact, I'd been staring without seeing, triggering a feeling of fear she might figure out what I'd been looking at.

"I'd rather gouge my eyes out," I said through clenched teeth. "What am I doing here?"

"Sleeping. Resting. Healing." She slid off the bed and sashayed over to a cabinet set with food.

Even from here, I could smell it was breakfast.

"How long have I been out?"

She turned to face me, a wicked gleam in her eyes. "Long enough for me to enjoy watching that body in all its glory."

Goosebumps rippled across my arms and it took everything I had to slip out of bed with my dignity intact, wrapping a sheet around my hips. One survey around the room showed me we were alone. I assumed guards would be posted at the door, but they'd be too late if—I only had one chance. Raking a hand through my hair, I stretched slowly, wincing at the fierce ache it caused in my back, but it allowed me to look around the room to find something—anything—with which I could hurt her.

There weren't any weapons at hand, but there was cutlery.

I wanted nothing more than to bolt out of the room and continue running until my heart gave out, but I would disappoint a whole lot of people if I didn't at least try, so I swallowed my pride and sank back on the bed, rubbing my face. Azra walked around and offered me a cup of tea, a curious look stealing over her face before her eyes travelled south. The moment just before she splayed her hand against my chest, I caught her wrist, my lips pulling up in a one-sided snarl.

She chuckled. "I love it when they put up a fight."

I released my grip with a heavy eye-roll and took the cup of tea from her, deciding no answer was the best answer in this case. She strolled over to the cabinet, and started piling a plate with bread, cheese and foreign edibles I couldn't put a name to. I half expected her to hand me the plate, but instead she made herself comfortable on the bed, balancing the plate on her legs.

"Feel free to get some breakfast yourself," she purred, popping a grape into her mouth.

I downed my tea in one go, disregarding the fierce ache in my throat as it burned its way down. I knew tea was supposed to be hot, but I didn't know it was usually this spicy.

With one hand on the bedsheet to keep it from slipping down my waist, I sauntered towards the cabinet, Azra's eyes boring into me as I piled my plate with grapes and added a bowl of *diresh* —porridge, in the common tongue, but tastier. I slipped a knife into my right hand, keeping it flat against my lower arm, and picked up my plate with the same one to keep the hilt hidden.

For this to work, I had to make myself comfortable on the bed as well, like two lovers enjoying their breakfast after a good night. A deep shudder ran through me at the thought, and I quickly sat down on the bed, resting my back against the headboard. The bedsheet slipped down a little until it was less than an inch above my private parts, and out of the corner of my eye, I saw a hungry look flicker in Azra's eyes.

I doubted it was for whatever she had on her plate.

My breathing sounded loud in my ears, so I exhaled slowly to calm my nerves and steel my resolve. If I wanted a chance, I would have to play along, so I plastered a smirk on my lips and looked at her, tucking a lock of hair behind my long ear before I popped a grape into my mouth, making sure to flex my muscles as I did.

I had her attention.

"I'd have thought you'd have me locked in the dungeons," I said casually, willing my beating heart to steady.

"Oh, I considered it," she replied, her voice deep and husky, "but it meant I'd have to miss all of this."

I slipped her a forced smile. "I'm a lucky man then."

She squinted. "And why is that?"

"Because you've managed to restrain yourself," I replied, "rather than jump me."

"And how can you be so sure?"

I offered her a half-shrug and a lazy grin. "You're sizing me up like a piece of meat. You wouldn't have done that if you'd already had me."

In response, she ran a finger down my arm, leaning closer to me. It took me every bit of self-restraint I had not to stiffen under her touch and keep the bemused look on my face. She inched closer, until her thigh was touching mine through the sheet, and her hand lay once more on my chest. Only the erratic beating of my heart could give me away, but Azra seemed more intent on something else.

Tucking the knife underneath my thigh, I breathed as shallowly as possible as her hands began to wander. Just in case, I placed the bowl and plate on the bedside cabinet, if only because I didn't want to entertain the idea of having *diresh* spilled in my lap.

"I thought you'd be a lot harder to get," Azra purred as she straddled me.

I grunted, willing my disobedient body to cool off.

"Turns out," she said in a husky voice, lips brushing mine. "You're just like the rest of them—thinking with the wrong head."

My lips quirked up into a lopsided smirk. "What can I say..."

I drew the knife from beneath my leg and plunged it into her neck. A scream of pain escaped her lips, and her eyes widened in disbelief as she brought up a hand tentatively. Without waiting for anything, I pushed her off of me and slipped out of the bed, careless of my state of undress. My heart hammered away in my chest as I watched blood seep into the bedclothes beneath her, but rather than gasping for air as her life seeped out of her, she pushed herself up, pulling the knife from her neck slowly.

I staggered back. "What the..."

Azra giggled—a young girl kind of giggle that was completely at odds with the scene in front of me. As soon as the knife left her skin, the blood slowly stopped trickling, leaving only a nasty injury that should, by all accounts, have killed her. She got off the bed and in slow, sensuous movements glided my way, a wicked smile ghosting on her lips. I backed away towards the door step-by-step, getting ready to bolt.

"You should be dead," I whispered, watching her.

She tilted her head, pursing her lips in thought. "I should be, yes, and it would have made you a murderer—or a hero, depending on who you'd ask, but as it is, I'm quite obviously not dead."

I backed up against the wall and flinched as stone grated sensitive skin while inching sideways to find the door handle, my eyes never leaving her. My hand found the knob, but before

I could turn it and flee, she was upon me, pinning me against the door. I was hyperaware of the places where our naked skin touched.

"What…are you?"

She chuckled. "Something out of your nightmares, *shareye.*"

With one hand, she cupped my cheek, running a thumb over my lips. I pressed them together, swallowing hard. She pushed herself flush against me, leaving nothing to the imagination. Standing on tiptoe, she ran her hand to the back of my neck, and pulled me to her so my lips were brushing hers. Her tongue flicked over my lips.

"You tried to kill me, Tal," she murmured, a wicked gleam in her eyes. "For that alone I should kill you…"

I tensed.

"But," she continued, "I think I'll keep you."

I twisted my mouth and closed my eyes. "To what end?"

She giggled again, a sound so at odds with whatever, or whoever, she was, it made my skin crawl.

"I want to see you squirm," she breathed against my lips, "and one day, I will have you."

With that said, she stepped away from me, giving me a good look before she waved her hand in dismissal.

"Now go," she ordered. "before I do decide to jump you."

The doorknob seemed to turn off its own accord, or my hand was faster than my brain—either way, I left the room in a mad dash, ignoring the surprised looks and catcalls as I made a beeline for Shal's room.

It was closest.

Short of kicking the door open, I entered the room and slammed the door shut behind me, locking it before I sank down. I ignored the stabs of pain my back sent off in warning, raking trembling hands through my hair. Cold from the floor seeped into my body, but I hardly noticed as my mind replayed the event of my killing Azra, and her not dying. No matter how hard I tried, I could not come up with a viable explanation as to why she wasn't dead.

The tea. It had to be the tea.

Pushing myself to my feet, I stumbled forward, convincing myself she had drugged me somehow, and it had all been a delirious dream—one that had felt much too real. As I started pulling clothing from the chest at the end of Shal's bed, I noticed the blood splatters on my hands and realised with infinite horror that I *had* tried to kill her.

And she hadn't died.

My hands began to shake as I slumped to the bed, bewilderment setting in. I couldn't stop trembling. I had tried—and failed. The blood had stopped trickling, and she had barely been injured. I had a hard time wrapping my mind around the truth, convinced this couldn't have happened. Perhaps the blood was from something else. Maybe I had injured myself with the knife —that had to be it. I'd been careless, cut myself, and it splattered all over my hands. What I'd seen was just *wrong*.

The tremors slowly subsided, leaving me a weak and aching mess, but I had to get up. I had to do something normal. I picked up my trousers from the floor and jerked them on, followed by my boots, trying not to look at the blood on my hands. A knock on the door halted the process of my struggling into a tunic, finding that despite the pain in my back not being too overwhelming, my arms and shoulders were stiff, and lifting anything over my head was a good deal more challenging than I'd thought.

"Who's there?" I called out, my voice muffled by the fabric.

"Soren."

That guy's got timing.

I discarded the tunic on a chair as I made my way to unlock the door. The moment I did, surprise shook me for a third time that morning—*or afternoon*—merely by seeing Soren. Bloodshot eyes and a tired smile were my first sight of him, and as he stepped inside, I noticed the heavy fall of his feet, as well as the sagging of his shoulders.

"What happened to you, *mahnèh?*"

Closing and locking the door, I watched him as he sat down, moving as stiffly as I felt—perhaps even more so—ignoring the question I'd posed him. I'd almost swear he was the one who got punished instead of me.

"You look terrible," I offered, deciding I didn't want to see my own visage anytime soon.

"So do you," he replied, tilting his head slightly. "What possessed you to run naked through the corridors?" His eyes lowered to my hands, the frown on his face deepening. "And why is there blood on your hands?"

"You wouldn't believe me if I told you," I muttered, hiding them behind my back. "I'm not sure I do."

Soren looked at me a moment longer—I couldn't tell if he wanted to know or not—before exhaling deeply, shaking his head. "How's your back?"

"Better than expected. I thought it would be much worse considering the pain I was in yesterday."

He flashed me a tired smile. "They did a poor job of it to be honest, barely broke your skin."

Something told me he was lying, but I wasn't going to argue with the man who most likely saved my life, especially not with him looking like that. Dark circles under his eyes stood in stark contrast to his ivory skin.

"When is the last time you slept?" I asked, picking up my tunic.

"Oh, I slept," Soren replied. "Just not very well, and not very long, not after…"

I merely nodded. He didn't need to finish what he was thinking of. The memory of what happened in the throne room was imprinted on my mind, and I was certain it would never go away.

Nor would what had happened that morning—if it had happened.

"We need to do something," I said after a while, struggling into the garment, and succeeding. "Anything."

"What can we do?"

I shrugged. "Your guess is as good as mine. After yesterday, I won't put anything past her."

For some reason, as much as I trusted Soren, I didn't want to drag him into anything just yet. I had to tell someone about the missing *Araîth*, and as much as I wanted to tell someone about the fact Azra couldn't be killed, I doubted they'd believe me. I wasn't even sure I believed it myself. I needed to talk to Evan most of all, although I was rather reluctant to pull him in considering the baby he had on the way. A thought suddenly struck me.

"I take it Azra doesn't know about Nath yet?"

Soren shook his head. "No, not yet, which is exactly why we have to do something."

Jerking a jittery hand through his short-cropped hair, rubbing his long ears, he stared at the floor as if the answer to our predicament was written there.

"We need to get her out of here," he said at length. "The moment she starts showing, she's in danger."

"Yeah, I said as much to Evan, but he refuses to leave." I sighed. "And a part of me can understand why, but unless we kneel to Azra and her ambitions, none of us will get out of this alive. The moment we've served our purpose, she'll kill us."

"She seems pretty infatuated with you."

I snorted. "Hardly. It's full out vengeance on my father."

Rubbing the back of my neck, I watched Soren's expression go from surprise to something akin to amusement.

"Vengeance? What in Aeson's name did your father do to her?"

"I'd tell you if I knew." I flopped down in a chair with a

heavy sigh, rubbing my temples. "But he's always been tight-lipped about a certain time in his life. According to Rurin, it's because they made a promise to the previous *Tari*—Arayda's mother—not to speak of what happened, and he mentioned something about Father tricking her. I've no idea what he meant."

Soren nodded. "She'll kill you too."

"Not for a while," I replied with confidence, even though I was feeling none of it.

I was about to say more when a knock on the door sounded moments before it was thrown open and Haerlyon strode in, two guards in tow.

"The *Tari* expects you."

"I highly doubt that," I said, "considering she's *dead*."

His jaw tensed, and his hands rolled into fists at his side. I was sure he'd punch me, until I remembered that was not his style. A dagger to the back was more likely to happen.

"Move," he said through clenched teeth, "or I'll make you."

My lips pulled up into a smirk, but before I could antagonise him further, I strolled out of the room. Haerlyon motioned Soren to get to his feet, who did so reluctantly and with a look in his eyes that spelled murder.

"What does she need me for this time?" I asked casually.

"You'll see," Haerlyon replied, his voice cold enough to freeze the Ilvan Mountains.

"I remember you being a lot chattier."

"I remember you being less so." Haerlyon turned on me with a growl. "Will you shut up? Please."

"Look at that," I scoffed. "He remembers how to say please."

I was barely in time to dodge the punch I had expected. I grabbed his wrist and in the same motion pulled him off balance and into a headlock.

"I don't care what she's promised you," I hissed, "or threatened you with, or even if you're doing this of your own volition, but you're making a big mistake, *an Ilvan*. You'll end up losing everything."

He snorted, trying to break free. "I already have."

Without responding, I let him go. His words were a punch to the gut I hadn't expected, but looking at him—at the furious yet pained expression in his eyes—it occurred to me we were more alike than I thought. It made me take a step back and shake my head, mourning the loss of a friend I knew I'd not get back—not yet, anyway. Soren looked at me with sympathy, giving a light shake of his head as we continued on our way.

"It's as if he's not there anymore," I murmured.

"Oh, he's there all right," Soren whispered, "but don't discard the trauma he's been through as something easily forgotten—or forgiven."

"I…" I rubbed my jaw. "I just don't get why he's so mad at his sister."

Soren looked at me, faintly amused. "Have you forgiven Yllinar yet?"

I stiffened, glaring at him.

"I didn't think so."

Releasing my breath slowly, my gaze returned to Haerlyon's back. It was clear he was tense, as if he expected another attack.

"I'm not sure I can forgive him for picking her side though," I said after a while, my voice audible for Soren alone. "Azra killed his mother… kidnapped his sister… in the end, she was behind Tiroy's death. How can he work for her?"

Soren lifted his shoulders in a half-hearted shrug. "I don't know, Tal. You'd have to ask him."

I snorted. "Yeah, that will go down well. How do you propose I do that?"

Soren didn't respond.

His eyes, wide with shock, had been drawn to something behind me, and I realised we'd made it out the main gate and into the square in front of the palace. Turning to see what he was looking at, it occurred to me we weren't alone. The Main Street was filled with people from every walk of life—most looked horrified, a lot were crying, and some looked so shell-shocked I was sure a breeze of wind would knock them over. I wondered what made them respond like that until I turned around, my gaze fixed on the palace walls.

My breath caught in my throat.

My heart stopped.

No. No. No. No. No!

CHAPTER 12

SHALITHA

The farther Elay guided me into his domain, the more I realised how much trouble I would have been in had I not ended up in his study. Mother's palace had twists and turns, and staircases up and down that could lead a person into a maze of corridors so they'd end up lost—Elay's place was much the same, except there were more twists and turns to remember, and by the time we'd passed the twentieth, I had no idea where we were.

Certain Elay was bringing me to his dungeons, I resigned myself to being a prisoner yet again. Clearly, that was what my life had come down to, so the fact it actually hurt surprised me. I'd given him the benefit of the doubt—a deal I knew he would accept because of the kind of man he was. Although I knew it would come with rules and agreements, the fact we hadn't even discussed them made me uneasy, especially since I had no idea where he was taking me.

Thankfully, nobody but us seemed to be awake at this time of night.

"In here." Elay invited me into a dark room heavy with the scent of lavender and other herbs I couldn't quite place.

This is it. He'll kill me in this nice smelling dark place.

"Stay here," he murmured. "I'd rather not have you break your neck."

Not killing then.

Confused, I stared into the direction his voice had come from, trying to decide what to make of this. One by one, candles flared to life, their light dancing across glittering tiles. The more he lit, the more the room we were in took shape, and to my shock and delight, it wasn't a dungeon, but a bathing room somehow reminding me of the hot spring at *Hanyarah*. Even at this time of night, steam billowed from the water.

"What are we doing here?" I asked in a raspy voice.

"I thought you might like a bath," he replied, sounding a little confused. "Unless you'd rather stay in those blood-soaked rags?"

I shuddered at the thought. "No, thank you."

He grinned, white teeth flashing in the little light we had. "Good. Feel free."

With one hand, he gestured to the bath to invite me in. Reluctance made my moves slow, but it was the release of fear and the feeling of remote safety that made my hands tremble.

I could barely unclasp the veil, let alone do the rest.

"Here, let me," Elay said surprisingly gently.

Dropping my hands to my sides, I allowed him to unclasp the veil and take off the *hijrath*, relishing in the feeling of my hair tumbling down my back. Without a word, he stepped behind me, undoing the single button that kept the garment around my neck. The gentleness with which he did this surprised me, but then I didn't have any comparative material on how this should be done.

Our dresses didn't involve any tenderness—neither in the dressing nor the taking them off.

"Such tension," he said, resting his hands on my shoulders. "Relax, Siora. I'm not going to hurt you."

"I've heard that before," I replied softly, "and they never meant it."

Elay stilled behind me. "I gave you my promise. I might be a Prince of Thieves, but when I give my word, I keep it. On my honour."

I merely nodded and proceeded to shrug off the coat I was wearing, followed by lifting the shirt over my head. My shoulder locked halfway, leaving me stuck in the garment that was now half over my head. An indrawn gasp sounded from behind me, and a second later, fingers trailed the *Araîth* on my back.

"I knew it," Elay whispered in awe. "You're… *her*. You're the missing Ilvannian princess."

"I'm hardly missing, am I?" I quipped. "Instead of touching me and staring at me, which isn't awkward at all, could you please help me?"

Mercifully, he wasn't asking any questions… yet. As soon as my shirt had gone, I wrapped my arms around myself to cover up the vulnerable parts. He might have saved my life, but it didn't give him any access to anything. Casting a furtive look over my shoulder, I realised he was watching me, eyes hard as they fixed on my back. A second later, his fingers traced the scars Eamryel had left.

"Someone hated you."

It was an observation rather than a question, and it made me feel more vulnerable than my state of undress did.

"He said he loved me."

"What an odd way to express it."

He ran his fingers from my shoulder to my lower back, following the lacerations left by the *Gemsha*, sending shivers travelling down my spine.

"Did the *Gemsha* do this?"

I clenched my jaw. "Yes."

His hand stilled. A sharp intake of breath was all the

response he gave to my words. Instead, his fingers continued their sojourn across the *Araîth,* up and down as if I were a painting or mosaic he was desperate to unravel. I didn't like where this was going. A disgusted sound escaped my lips as I looked at him, brows furrowed.

"Do you mind?"

"Hm? What?"

"Looking away?"

A lazy smile spread across his lips. "I was just admiring the view, or what little I can see of it."

I bit the inside of my cheek and exhaled slowly through my nose.

"What happened to that bath you offered?"

"It's right there," he replied, nodding in its direction. "I'm not stopping you."

"Not literally…"

A soft laugh escaped his lips and when I looked, he was shaking his head, his eyes twinkling in the candlelight—or perhaps it was just a trick.

"I had no idea you were so prudish," he mused, "after having lived where you did for three moons."

"Yes, well," I began. "It wasn't by choice and I didn't much care for the sounds at night either, but I'm not stupid. I just…"

Don't want you to see me at my most vulnerable.

"Never mind," I finished out loud and dropped my arms along my sides to start undoing the knot that kept my trousers from sliding down my waist. With a deep sigh, I let go of the bonds, shivering as the fabric pooled around my feet.

When I made my way over to the water and slipped inside, I noticed Elay was looking away.

I smiled.

The water was blissfully warm and after only a few moments in, I felt my muscles starting to relax.

"Whatever you do," Elay said, gathering my clothing from the floor, "don't go anywhere. Stay here until I'm back."

"What are you going to do?"

He chuckled softly. "Getting rid of the evidence and find you something to wear, unless you would like to walk around in nothing but that? Not that I mind, but I might keep you to the confines of my bedroom then."

I growled under my breath.

His laughter echoed through the room long after he was gone. Folding my arms on the side of the pool, resting my head on top, I closed my eyes and let my mind wander over the deal I'd offered Elay, and how he hadn't asked anything in return—yet. He'd taken it all in easy stride, as if he had expected this to happen and had merely been waiting for me to come crawling his way. It was almost as if he had known. A dark, ugly thought was forming in my mind as I contemplated the evening. What if he…

No, he's a schemer and a thief, but surely he wouldn't…

As much as I didn't like to entertain the idea of him having ordered Khaz's death, I had to take into account this man most likely had a hidden agenda.

As do I.

My thoughts drifted back to Khaz, to how she'd been when I first met her—full of life, twinkling eyes and a penchant for mischief much like myself. After we'd been captured, it hadn't changed, until they started doling out punishments. She'd become more silent, more careful, and much more afraid. Despite the short time they'd kept us as slaves, it definitely left a mark on her, and the time we spent with the *Gemsha* hadn't made it better.

His getting her pregnant had been the last straw.

A SPLASH from close by startled me back to awareness, and I realised I'd dozed off. Most of the pain and stiffness had gone from my body, except the ache in my neck.

"You look comfortable," Elay said.

Opening one eye, I found him in the water and in close proximity—too close, so I scooted back a little, gazing warily upon him. His lips curled into one of those smiles reserved to ease skittish animals. I'd seen it on Haer often enough when he was dealing with a particularly frightened horse.

I would have felt offended if I didn't at least partially feel that way.

"You really have nothing to fear from me," he said. "If I'd wanted to harm you, don't you think I'd have done something by now?"

"I guess..."

"Let me treat the injury in your neck," he offered. "I'm not keen on explaining blood in the water come morning."

I blinked. "Injury?"

Gentle fingers touched the place on my neck where the pain hadn't gone away, drawing a hiss from my lips. Again, Elay was invading my personal space, made even more awkward by the fact there didn't appear to be a shred of fabric between us.

"It's nothing big," Elay murmured, lifting my chin to have a better look, "but you'll want it taken care of, trust me."

"Just another scar for the collection," I murmured under my breath.

My body is full of them.

The way Elay set about taking care of the wound reminded me of Soren—solemn, focused and quiet while doing this task. His hands were equally gentle, and by the time he finished, I was in that blissful in between state of sleep and awake.

"Before you doze off," Elay said, his tone one of amusement, "I suggest we work out the details of our... arrangement."

His words pulled me back to awareness with a start, earning him a reproachful growl.

"I also don't recommend falling asleep here," he continued. "Unless you can breathe underwater."

I snorted. "If only."

"Well then." He grinned, leaning back on the side of the pool. "Let's get to business."

"This is an awkward place for business," I muttered, suddenly conscious of my state of undress.

He ignored the comment.

"You asked for my protection." His eyes had lost all their twinkle and were instead dark and solemn. "And I will give it to you, under one condition…"

"Which is?"

"You help me with a problem I'm having."

I bit the inside of my lip. "What kind of problem?"

"One that could get both of us into serious trouble if we fail," he replied, a wry smile on his face. "If I don't try though…"

"I'll help," I replied.

If I wanted his protection, I really had no choice but to agree to the condition he posed me, even though I didn't like the idea of getting into trouble if it went wrong. Not that it mattered—my life was an accumulation of things going wrong at this point. Sooner or later, I was bound to run out of luck, but I already had the feeling I was living on borrowed time as it was.

I should have died in that storm.

Or that night after Eamryel hunted me, or after the fight at Hanyarah.

The thoughts triggered the memory of the night of the storm, taking me back to the moment a wave swept me off the deck and into the dark abyss of the sea. My lungs had ached and burned, desperate for air, until my limbs grew heavy and my thoughts foggy. I remembered hearing a voice—strangely familiar yet haunting, notes of desperation and determination in it. It had spoken in the old tongue, but I had understood.

It's not yet your time, dochtaer. Live to fight another day.

Beyond that point, I didn't remember anything at all until Khaz found me on that beach.

"Siora?"

I focused again on Elay, who was watching me with a mix of amusement and annoyance.

"Apologies," I murmured. "I was just thinking."

He chuckled. "I noticed when you didn't reply to my question."

"What question?"

"If you'd be my wife."

I stared at him dumbfounded, trying to look at that rationally rather than give in to the anger rising up inside of me. This man had balls!

He raised his hands in a placating manner. "You asked for my protection, and that is the only way I can ensure it."

I opened my mouth, and closed it again, trying to wrap my brain around what he was trying to tell me. It made sense, I couldn't deny that—my head couldn't anyway, but my heart was an entirely different matter. Despite the conviction Tal was dead, my heart still belonged to him.

"I..." I shook my head, not knowing how to respond.

"Most women reply with yes," he offered, a bemused smile on his lips.

I glared at him, biting back the retort that was on my lips. Running a hand through my hair, I winced at the tug in my neck. As I brought up my hand to feel the injury, Elay caught it in his, and shook his head. My heart fluttered at the sudden gentle touch.

"Don't, you'll undo my handiwork."

Nodding mutely, I looked anywhere but into his eyes—eyes that could make the decision a whole lot easier had they not been so similar to Tal's. A shiver crawled down my back, sending goosebumps trailing over my skin.

Elay must have felt it through my hand and smiled.

"I know it's awkward," he said in a soft voice, "but consider the alternative. As a servant, there is no way I can protect you—they have little to no rights and someone would only have to dislike you for no reason at all to get you into trouble. As a guard I'm sure you would be effective, but you would look too much like you did when you were prowling my streets, so the only thing that is left to you… is being my wife."

"You make it sound so easy," I muttered. "Easy and logical."

"It is."

With a shake of my head, I withdrew my hand from his, wading through the water for want of something better to do. Elay watched me quietly as I went over the implications of his words, trying to come to my own conclusion.

Sadly, but not surprisingly, he was right.

"I'll be a target though," I said at length, looking up at him. "As would you."

He laughed softly. "*Amisha,* in my line of work, there is always a target on my back. In your case, I expect it was a birthright."

I snorted and felt one side of my lips pull up in a smile. He wasn't wrong there.

"What about your other wives?"

"They'll just have to deal with it."

"How do you explain my sudden appearance?"

At that question, a thoughtful expression appeared on Elay's face, and I could swear he even looked somewhat nervous.

"I've considered that…" he began, looking mischievous. "How good are you at pretending?"

"Not at all."

He laughed. "Well then, this should be fun."

"Something tells me your vision on fun is warped," I replied, looking none too pleased.

"Perhaps, but it sure will be entertaining."

A groan escaped my lips. "You're making me regret my decision."

"Don't worry, *Mìthri*," he said, suddenly pulling me close.

I was glad to find he wasn't entirely naked.

"We both have our role to play," he murmured, "and I promise you I won't make it hard."

"Make what hard?"

He grinned and stepped back.

"Falling in love with me," he whispered, kissing both my hands.

CHAPTER 13

TALNOVAR

The entire wall on either side of the gate was lined with bodies strung up by ropes around their necks. My eyes moved over them excruciatingly slowly, taking in every little detail. These people had been killed because they had not bent their knee to a tyrant. They had died standing up for what they believed in, and here I stood watching them like a fool dancing to the piper's tunes. Bile rose in my throat as anger coursed through my veins. Then my gaze settled on two bodies in the middle. I staggered back, pressing a fist against my mouth while folding an arm against my stomach.

She'd promised.

I followed the flow of the dark *araîth* coiling up her arm, her shoulder and her face, marking her of the house an Ilvan. Arayda had been hung amongst her loyal followers, together with Rurin, all on full display as if they had been criminals of the highest order. Her once well-tended hair was whipped into a tangled mess by the wind. Rurin's eyes bulged as if he couldn't quite believe their fate. The only solace lay in knowing all of them had died before they'd been hung.

The warrior inside of me roared to life, vowing his silent

vengeance to the Gods.

Azra had promised the brothers a decent burial for their mother, and she'd taken that away from them without any consideration. If I'd been dead set on thwarting her before, it was nothing compared to what I would be willing to do now. Neither Arayda nor Rurin deserved this—none of them did, but if nothing would be done, this was our future.

No matter the cost, Azra had to be stopped, even if she couldn't die.

"Doesn't she look perfect up there," Azra purred right next to me, sliding an arm around my waist as if we were lovers.

I stepped out of her embrace.

"I'm fairly certain the meaning of perfect is different from what you think it to be," I replied, forcing my voice to stay neutral. "You promised the brothers a proper burial, Azra."

From the way she stiffened, I knew there would be another punishment in the near future. If it hadn't been for my promise to Arayda, I'd have antagonised her until the end of my days. As it was, I needed to find a way out of here.

Fast.

"I have promised a lot of things," she cooed at length, "but I've never been known to keep them."

"No wonder they didn't want you on the throne."

She backhanded me hard enough to rattle my teeth, but it only served to steel my resolve. I knew getting on her bad side wouldn't help my case, but it was easy.

And oh so satisfying.

"Don't get cheeky with me," she hissed.

"Or what? You'll punish me? Take your vengeance on my father out on me? By all means, go ahead, I've lost everything anyway. Why would you think I care? Death would be a welcome relief."

A desperate man's attempt.

Her lips quirked up into a wicked smile. "Who says I'll allow you to die?"

While her words sent goosebumps chasing along my skin, they also confirmed my suspicions. No matter what line I crossed, she wouldn't have me killed for it, which meant the odds of escaping had gone up a bit, if only because there was the slight chance of trying a second time if the first one failed, provided she didn't lock me up.

"Be a good *Anahràn*," she said, patting my biceps, "and do your job. Scowl if you must, but keep the people at bay."

"I'm not your *Anahràn*."

"Oh dear." Playful shock registered on her face, her lips parting in a delicate 'o'. "Did I forget to tell you?"

I narrowed my eyes, getting fed up with her antics. "Tell me what?"

"You *are* my *Anahràn*," she purred. "So do your job."

"What if I refuse?"

"I'd reconsider that thought," she said, nodding at somewhere behind me. "Unless you want *her* body to hang up there?"

Following the direction in which she nodded, my eyes settled on Cehyan. Her clothing was torn, her lips cracked, the bruise on her cheekbone evidence of the beating she must have gone through.

"She's told me quite some interesting things," Azra continued. "About you, in fact. Who knew…"

I stilled. "*Hehzèh*."

Her laugh rang out loud and clear across the square, drawing the attention of everyone within hearing distance. Stepping forward, she gave me no choice but to obey, so I squared my shoulders and kept my hands tight behind my back, face set in the perpetual scowl I'd always worn with Shal.

This time, I didn't have to pretend.

Silence rippled over the crowd as Azra raised her hand. My gaze swept over their heads, spotting guards positioned on the side lines at even intervals. Some looked as queasy as the rest of us—most looked positively bored. Those that were close enough for me to survey had their hands hovering over the hilts of their swords, as if awaiting an order.

This will be the throne room all over again.

"As you can see," Azra said, her voice ringing clearly across the square, "your precious *Tari* has been hung as a common traitor, because that is what she was! Many years ago, she took the throne from me through lies and deceit, turning Mother and the man I loved against me. After she killed our beloved sister, my *twin-sister,* she framed me and would have had me killed had a benevolent benefactor not helped me escape..."

Gasps sounded around us—people in the first row were looking wide-eyed, looks of shock and disbelief registering on their faces.

It nearly made me vomit.

"I learned something from that experience," she continued, straightening her shoulders.

What are you up to?

"Nobody can be trusted," she said, "but above all, nobody is worth it. Guards!"

The unsheathing of weapons echoed across the square and down the main street in a deathly staccato. With guards on either side and people pressed tight together, the gathering had turned into a death trap, and Azra was using it to her advantage. Screams of terror filled the air along with cries for help and pleas for mercy, but even from here I could see mercy wasn't given.

I was running before my mind had fully caught up with my plan. Having nothing but my fists, I barrelled into the first guard I came upon, careless of which side they were on. It wasn't hard to wrestle the weapon from his hands, and just before I was about to knock him out, I realised whom I was facing.

"Caerleyan?" I gasped. "What in Esahbyen's name..."

He'd been one of the *Arathrien* under my command before the *Tarien* was kidnapped and had always been a loyal man. Judging by the horrified look on his face, he didn't like what he was forced to do either.

"Help me!" I yelled over the cries.

"What's the point?" Caerleyan looked at me defeated. "She's already won."

"Only if we stop fighting," I retorted, pushing the sword back into his hands. "You think Shal would have wanted this? Or the *Tari* for that matter? We vowed to lay down our lives to save hers—if not her, then her country!"

Something in the crowd around us shifted, and not just in the crowd, but in some of the guards as well. Instead of fear permeating the atmosphere, a sense of determination rolled over those closest to us. Instead of trying to flee, they prepared themselves, and out of nowhere, an anonymous cry rose from around us, echoed by dozens of others.

"For the rightful *Tari!* For Ilvanna!"

Caerleyan and I were swept up in a mob of angry citizens and together we fought the guards and helped those in need. My focus became singular, my mind tuned out everything around me that wasn't important enough to pay attention to. As tranquillity stole over me, my senses heightened—at least I liked to think they did. Somehow, it seemed as if movements were slower, giving me enough time to block a blow or dodge a punch. It allowed me to shut down everything I didn't need.

Although our numbers grew, fear prevailed, and our enemies had more weapons between them than we did. On top of that, most fighting alongside us hardly had any practice in a mock battle, let alone a real one. It was a massacre, even worse than the one at *Hanyarah*, and there was no way we were going to win this.

As our support dwindled, I'd lost sight of Caerleyan and found myself surrounded by a dozen guards pointing their swords at me, Haerlyon among them. The angry grimace on his face was at odds with the look in his eyes.

He is afraid.

It was gone in the blink of an eye, replaced by a more calculated demeanour which was more like the Haerlyon I knew, but about as cold as a pack of snow down my shirt.

I shivered.

"Bring him to the *Tari,*" Haerlyon ordered. "Round up the rest of the rebels!"

Rebels, huh?

"Do you enjoy being her lapdog, Haer?"

I'd expected a punch—not the big grin spreading across his lips. "I'm afraid you've failed to notice your own status, Imradien. Have you not heard the rumours?"

I tensed, forcing a lazy smile to my face. "You know what they say about rumours, *mahnèh*—they're nothing but fodder for the wicked and the jealous. I care nothing for them."

"You should," he replied. "Rumours damage a reputation faster than anything else, and right now, yours is about to keel over like a drunkard after too much *ithri*—or should I say an addict after too much *sehvelle.*"

"Don't go there," I growled, taking a step closer to him. "That is long in the past."

Haerlyon grinned and leaned closer, his voice barely a whisper. "Perhaps for you, but for the *Tari,* it's a treasure trove of knowledge, and you *mahnèh,* are about to find out how far she's willing to go to discover the truth behind it."

If I didn't know any better, I could have sworn it was a warning, but Haerlyon was known for his riddles and his games. Besides, why would he warn me? He hated my guts, just as I did his. With a nod of his head, two guards grabbed my arms and propelled me forwards.

In the corner of my eye, a discarded doll stained with blood caught my attention. A little farther, it was two hands holding tight. Next, a pair of sightless eyes staring up at the ridiculously cheerful sky. Blood ran in rivulets amongst the cobblestones, staining the street red. The closer we walked to the palace, to Azra, the more the results of today became clear.

The death toll was sky-high. Nothing we did had helped. In fact, I was sure whatever we had done had made things worse. I had instigated a rebellion without it being my intention—I had just wanted to remind Caerleyan of his duties—but others had picked it up, had seen it as an act of revenge, an act of honour, and most if not all had lost their lives over it.

I didn't even know if he was still alive.

Azra was where I'd left her, a delighted smile playing around her lips as she surveyed the havoc she had wreaked. My chest tightened as my gaze fell on Caerleyan, his white hair red from the blood pooling underneath. Someone had gotten to him much sooner than I thought.

"If it isn't our little rebel leader," Azra tutted. "Such a waste of time..."

I straightened my shoulders underneath her scrutinising gaze, unwilling to give in to her. Somehow, whenever I laid my eyes on her, logic went out the window and instinct took over, but as it did, so did fear, knowing she couldn't be killed. This woman was as bad as they came. Nothing of what had happened seemed to trouble her—if anything, it excited her, judging by the sheer look of delight crossing her face.

"I really hoped those lashes would have served as a lesson," she said, tilting her head, "but I see I was wrong. Do you enjoy pain, *Anahràn*? Because if that is the case, I'm sure I can give it to you in much more... pleasurable circumstances."

I dry-heaved at the thought. "No, thank you. I'm good."

Her lips curled up in a mischievous smile. "Shame. You have no idea what you're missing."

"I have a vivid imagination," I replied.

The girlish giggle escaping her lips was so wrong under

these circumstances, it made my skin crawl. When she stepped closer, I tried to step back, but found my way blocked by the guards behind me. Azra cupped my cheek in one hand, brushing her thumb over my lips.

"The problem," she murmured, "is that I'm going to have to punish you right here, so that the stragglers don't get any ideas, but you've made it quite... interesting with your refusal to submit even after the lashes. I can give you more, but you will only rise to the occasion and keep on doing this, unless I kill you, right?"

I pressed my lips together, staring dead ahead.

"I thought as much." Her voice held a tone of wicked glee. "Thankfully, your little friend has given me some insight into... you."

My gaze cut over to where I'd seen Cehyan last, finding her on her knees with Soren next to her in a similar position, and Evan standing off to the side, guards flanking him. Both Soren and Cehyan had a sword resting against their neck. I had no doubt Evan was kept in check as well. Any action on my part would get them killed.

"She told me you'll fight for your friends," Azra murmured, her breath warm against my neck, "and you must remember me telling you I would kill her if you disobeyed me again?"

I nodded stiffly, and in my peripheral vision, I saw her raise her hand for the command.

"No, please," I said. "Don't kill them."

"And why would I oblige you?" she purred.

I shifted my weight. "Because I'll promise to behave."

Her response was sudden and unexpected. Out of nowhere, her arms snaked around my neck and her lips were on mine, hard, unyielding, her tongue forcing my lips apart. The fingers digging into the back of my skull were a warning.

Refuse now, and one of them will die.

I opened my mouth and answered her kiss.

She pulled back breathlessly, a grin on her lips, and took a step back. The look in her eyes promised nothing good.

"Well done, *shareye*!" she said loud enough for everyone to hear. "Such a great idea to make them think they could rebel. I knew I could count on you."

My stomach clenched and lurched but by some miracle I managed to keep everything inside. Her words turned me cold to the bone. When I returned inside, it took all the self-control I had to keep my head up high and not scamper off into the first room I came across.

She will not break me. Two can play this game.

Despite repeating these words like a mantra, by the time I slipped into my bedroom, I was ready to punch something, or kill myself, whichever came easiest. Instead I sank to my knees, feeling empty, as if she'd hollowed me from the inside out and I was nothing but a husk. The knock on the door didn't even register, but the closing of it did. When I looked up, I expected Azra to stand there and gloat, but it was Cehyan, looking bewildered and afraid.

She was on the ground and in my arms before I'd fully grasped the situation.

"I'm sorry," she cried. "I'm so sorry."

"It's not your fault," I murmured into her hair. "It's fine."

For the first time in over a year, despite everything that had just happened, I felt at ease and safe, if only a little. Of its own volition, my hand snaked into her hair, my lips brushing her forehead, her nose, until they found her lips. I was careful as not to spook her, but she answered eagerly—almost too eagerly—but in that moment, it didn't matter and I didn't care.

I knew what was coming, and it was exactly what I needed.

I'm sorry.

CHAPTER 14

SHALITHA

Releasing my breath in slow steady counts, I closed my eyes, relaxed my knees and adopted the initial position, my arms limp alongside my body. On an inhale, I pulled my arms up slowly until they were slightly above my shoulders and lowered them again on the exhale. I repeated these moves three more times before turning my foot out, twisting my upper body gently to the right while bringing my hands closer together, sensing the energy flowing between my opened palms.

After Elay had taken me from the baths, he had told me I needed to stay out of sight from the rest of the palace until he returned. To my horror, my hiding place was his bedroom which, to his delight, was the only place nobody could or would enter uninvited. With him out of the palace, there was no reason for anyone to be here. He had failed to mention servants would come in to dust and mop the tiled floors until they looked like mirrors rather than stone.

I had hidden underneath the bed every time, scuttling out of the way of mops and brooms. Two days in, I learned they never reached for the perfect middle of the bed, which is where I'd go whenever servants came in. Every morning, afternoon and night, food and drinks were brought in, as if they knew someone was staying here.

Or as if they'd been told to do so. He could've told me.

Six days had passed, and there was still no news of Elay.

What if something has happened?

If that were the case, I was free to go wherever I wanted, but getting out of Y'zdrah would prove somewhat of a challenge.

You've managed for this long; you'll find a way.

Once upon a time, I'd wanted to go out on adventures, see new countries, meet new people, and come home with the most marvellous stories and gifts. I'd gotten what I wished for, albeit not the way I'd had in mind, and I doubted the stories I'd come home with—if I ever got home that was—would be worth telling. Besides, I had no way of knowing if there would be anyone alive to tell it to. *Perhaps he knows*… I dismissed the thought as soon as it came to mind—Elay wouldn't know a thing.

Voices at the door arrested my next move.

I all but slid over to the door, pressing myself to the wall and straining my ears in an effort to hear who they were and what they were discussing. To my relief, it was Elay on the other side, and he appeared to be arguing with a woman. I wondered if it was the same one from the party. Secure in the knowledge it would be him walking through that door soon, I moved away and sat down on one of the many couches, picking up the book I'd been trying to read over the past several days to keep the boredom at bay.

I didn't do too badly considering it was written in Zihrin.

"I see you've made yourself comfortable," Elay commented.

I looked up to find him strolling my way with an amused expression on his face. A grunt escaped my lips as I put the book down, sitting up cross-legged on the couch.

"If you consider crawling under a bed as comfortable, then yes, I am."

His eyes moved from me sitting on the couch to the space underneath the bed, confusion knitting his brows together.

"Why were you under the bed?"

"To avoid your servants."

He opened his mouth, most likely to ask another question, when comprehension dawned on him, and an apologetic smile wavered on his lips.

"My apologies, *Mìthri,*" he said. "In my haste to make these arrangements, I forgot to let you know where to stay when they came."

I rolled my eyes and waved my hand in dismissal, my gaze drawn to the foreign package—foreign to him—in his hands. Whatever was inside was wrapped in paper in the Ilvannian style, and such packages usually held either a dress for a woman or a tunic for a man.

My eyes narrowed. "What have you got there?"

"A gift," he replied, offering it with a bow. "For you."

Leaning forward, I took the package from him, feeling heat rising to my cheeks. Why in Xiomara's name would he bring me a gift? Out of the corner of my eye, I watched him settle down in one of the chairs, moving like a man who had slept little and had sat on horseback for a long time.

I unknotted the cords of the package and opened it.

Although I was right in guessing what was inside, seeing an Ilvannian dress after such a long time came as a shock. Memories flooded me and tears brimmed my eyes. It had been over a year since I'd worn one—a gift from Haerlyon for an occasion I'd never forget, no matter how much I tried. Swallowing the lump in my throat and ignoring the tightness coiling in my chest, I rose to my feet, holding up the dress to get a better view of it.

I frowned. "Elay, why is it covered in blood?"

"It's part of the plan."

"What plan?"

Rubbing his jaw, he regarded me, still looking entertained, but I sensed something deeper rippling underneath, as if he was hiding something—his ulterior motives, most likely.

"Sit down," he said, leaning forward, his hands between his knees. "Remember me asking you how good you were at pretending?"

"Vaguely," I replied, carefully sitting down with the bloodied dress in my hands.

Something told me this pretending involved it.

"Do you trust me?"

I shrugged. "About as far as I can throw you."

"Yeah, we'll work on that." He flashed me a wicked grin before sobering up. "The walls have ears but prepare for a ride tonight. I'll leave you something warm to wear."

"Elay?"

"Yes…"

"Why are you going through so much trouble?" I asked with a frown. "Surely there's an easier way?"

"In your case," he answered. "I'm not so sure about that."

I tilted my head. "How so?"

He grinned and leaned back. "You're not the only one with trust issues, *Tarien*. You know Y'zdrah, you know its denizens—they will take almost everything at face value, but they smell a lie from miles away. And then there are my wives…"

"Ah yes," I murmured. "Plural."

His lips curled up in a smile. "Yes, all twenty-three of them."

"Twenty-three!"

"You're actually the twenty-seventh…"

I stared at him wide-eyed and slack-jawed. "You're joking?"

"Not at all…"

"No wonder they're grumpy," I snorted. "How do you please them all?"

Elay laughed, shaking his head. "I'll show you if you allow me."

"Not a chance."

"We'll see." He chuckled. "We'll see."

He stifled a yawn and rose to his feet, swaying a second or two before straightening himself out.

"If you don't mind, I'll catch up on some sleep. We ride out after nightfall."

I just nodded, resuming my cross-legged position on the couch, the dress still in my lap, contemplating everything he hadn't said as I watched him drop face-down on the bed, barely able to crawl in. As he grabbed a pillow and hugged it to his chest, I was reminded of Tal and the morning I'd woken up next to him. He had looked so at ease then. I wondered if Elay looked the same, but I wasn't so curious as to get up and have a look.

There would be enough time for that in the future I suspected.

ELAY HADN'T BEEN KIDDING when he told me to add as many layers as I could without losing mobility. Cold air bit what little skin I hadn't been able to cover. My eyes had started watering the moment the *camelles* started moving and hadn't stopped since. By then, I'd given up trying to wipe them away.

The only thing that kept me even a little warm was Elay at my back. Of all the things I'd learned while living in Zihrin, riding *camelles* wasn't one of them. I learned quickly that Elay wasn't a man to pepper with excuses and pleas once he had made up his mind, which is how I ended up on the same beast of burden as him.

"How much longer?" I asked through chattering teeth.

"Not far now."

"You said that hours ago." My voice sounded whiny even to my own ears.

I felt Elay's laugh rumble in his chest rather than hearing it.

"Not used to the cold, princess?"

I huffed. "On the contrary, I grew up at the foot of the Ilvan Mountains. We have snow and storms about three quarters of a year and summer lasts about one to two moons, but at least I knew what to expect!"

"Don't underestimate the desert," he said. "Going out at night without proper preparation will most likely see you dead come morning."

"I know. It's why I didn't escape the *Gemsha*." I refrained from snapping at him. "Why the warning?"

"Just a word of advice."

I couldn't help but snort. "Sure."

We rode on in silence. My thoughts turned inwards to the bloodstained dress I was wearing underneath all these layers, and the words Elay had spoken upon our secret departure. I had to play my role well, or everything would fall apart. It would have been nice to know his version of everything, but so far he hadn't been very forthcoming with his plan, so it was anyone's guess what was going to happen next.

It involves blood, I'm sure.

In the distance, dark shadows against the darker backdrop of the night hulked like monsters ready to devour its prey. There was no doubt in my mind this was where we were headed, because it was the only thing for miles around. Getting closer, I could see torches at what looked like an entrance of sorts.

"What's that?" I asked.

"You'll see," Elay replied.

His voice sounded tense. Come to think of it, I'd noticed the shift in his body miles ago, tension running through the arm around my waist. He'd straightened up as well, although I felt it rather than saw it. Nevertheless, his words did nothing to ease me. The closer we got, the more it felt as if a giant trap was waiting to catch me. I had the sudden urge to jump off the *camelle* and sprint back to Y'zdrah, never mind the warning Elay had given me earlier.

"This place feels wrong," I murmured, pulling the hood closer over my head. "Like bad stuff waiting to happen."

Elay chuckled softly. "You've got quite the imagination."

"It's the only thing that kept me sane." I shrugged. "You try being cooped up in a palace for almost three hundred years."

He was silent for a while before he spoke. "They kept you locked up?"

I shook my head. "No, not quite as bad as that, but I wasn't allowed to go outside on my own. There were always guards... so I ran."

"Is that where you learned to jump up and down from buildings?" He was amused.

"No, Khaz taught me that."

"Convenient."

Convenient for whom?

More than once I'd landed badly, messing up my leg just a bit more, but I wasn't going to tell him that. Even though he had agreed to help me, which was to his own benefit as much as to mine, he was still on a need to know basis—he didn't need to know.

"We're here."

Even without Elay's announcement, it would have been clear we'd arrived, although I still couldn't tell what it was exactly. Stepping away from the *camelle* that had conveniently lain down, I stared at my surroundings in wonder and fear. Torches were placed on either side of an entrance into what looked like a cave, reminding me of the narrow entrance into *Hanyarah* and the beauty that had lain beyond.

It hadn't ended well.

Trepidation coursed through my body as Elay laid his hand on the small of my back, guiding me forward. The closer we came, the heavier the pressure on my chest became until I was breathing as if I'd run here.

"Siora?" Elay halted, looking at me with worry. "Is everything all right?"

I nodded. "Enclosed spaces have never been my favourite."

While it wasn't exactly a lie, it was quite a stretch from the truth as well, but this was another thing he didn't need to know —I still suffered from panic attacks, even though they'd been far and few between in the last few moons. But this place reminded me so much of *Hanyarah*, of what I'd found and lost there, that it triggered a fear I thought I'd overcome.

How mistaken I'd been.

"You need to lose the warm clothing." The tone of his voice was apologetic.

"Why?"

"Because we need them to believe I rescued you," he replied, helping me out of my warm coat.

"Hence the blood," I said through chattering teeth, taking off my gloves reluctantly.

He nodded, tucking a lock of hair behind my ear. Now that I was dressed as an Ilvannian noble, there had been no need for the *hijrath* and the veil, and it made me feel naked—vulnerable.

I hated feeling vulnerable.

"Come," he said. "We're losing precious time as it is."

The tightness in my chest didn't ease as we passed the torches, and my breathing didn't return to normal either, but I had to make do. Elay was pressed to go farther, and fast, although the reason was beyond me, until we passed through the tunnel into a clearing. This place *was* like *Hanyarah*, but much less beautiful and tranquillity was a word they'd never heard of. Make-shift huts lined the walls of the rock formation in a haphazardly strewn about way. I didn't have to look inside to know who were inside these huts.

"A slave camp," I whispered. "Elay, why are we here?"

"Not a slave camp, *Mìthri*," he chuckled. "Although definitely a camp. We're here, because I need Rhana to train you."

"Train me? For what?"

I sounded exasperated, annoyed even, only because I couldn't make sense of why he would drag me out to the middle of nowhere in the middle of the night while it was cold enough to freeze my assets off. Tucking my hands under my arms, I scowled at him.

"If this is your idea of helping..."

He chuckled softly. "If you want to survive at *my* court, *Mìthri*, Rhana is your best chance."

"Well," I said, looking around. "If it's not a slave camp, what is it then?"

"Welcome to *Vas Ihn*," a woman said from behind me. "My name is Rhana. You must be Siora."

I inclined my head and glanced at Elay, who just stood there with a grin on his face, watching the exchange between us.

"*Vas Ihn* is a camp where I train women to be more than what they appear," Rhana said, encompassing the whole camp with a sweeping gesture. "Here, women learn how to fight, how to protect themselves, how to gather information, and if so desired, how to obtain... items."

"They learn how to steal you mean?" I asked, one brow raised.

"Elay tells me you're quite adept at that."

Heat flushed my cheeks.

"So far, she's the only one who managed to rob me of my money," Elay chuckled, looking at me.

I squared my shoulders and stared right back at him. "I'm not going to apologise for that."

"Good," he said. "I don't want you to."

I frowned. "Then what do you want me to do?"

"Master the skills Rhana will teach you as fast as you can," he replied, "and return to Y'zdrah—to me."

"And wouldn't that raise any suspicions? How are you going to explain me away?"

He had the audacity to tap me on the nose as if I were a small child asking stupid questions. Maybe I was, but that didn't give him the right to belittle me.

"I bought you," he remarked simply. "At a slave market."

I stilled and closed my eyes as his words returned me to the slave market where the *Gemsha* had bought me, and everything that had happened since. His hand cupping my cheek startled me back to awareness.

"I'm not him," he whispered. "It's just a ruse so that people won't start asking strange questions."

I swallowed hard and nodded. "I understand."

"Good," he murmured, his thumb stroking my jaw gently. "Go with Rhana. She will send word when you are ready, and I will come pick you up. Can you agree to that?"

"I can," I replied, biting my lip.

"But?"

"I wish you would have just told me your plans," I said, looking at him. "Instead of going about it all secretly."

"I apologise for that, *Mìthri*, but I promise you this secrecy has a reason, and it's not because I don't trust you—it's because I trust nobody else."

Other than the fact he had no reason to trust me, nor did I have any business trusting him, his words calmed me enough to step back and watch him leave without going into a full-blown panic attack. When Rhana laid a hand on my shoulder, I tensed.

"Come, I'll show you where you can sleep. Training starts at dawn."

"It's almost dawn," I observed.

"Good thing you're on time then," Rhana quipped. "I don't take kindly to stragglers."

CHAPTER 15

TALNOVAR

My services had been in high demand over the past week, sending me from training the rookies—those who were still alive, too scared or actually loyal—to serve as *Anahràn* to the tyrant *Tari.* At night, at least, I found solace in Cehyan's arms, although never without a persistent feeling of guilt rolling around in my gut.

I had pushed it to the background.

Breathing in deeply, I knocked on Evan's door. When he stuck his head out, hair tousled, eyes half-open, I felt more than a little guilty for waking him up in the dead of night.

"Tal? What are you doing here?" he murmured, rubbing his eyes.

"We need to talk."

"Now?"

I rolled my eyes. "Six days ago, but I didn't have any time. Please, it's important."

A grunt escaped his lips, but rather than slamming the door in my face, he stepped outside, pulling his robe closed and folding his arms across his chest. I guided him to a secluded area in the royal wing and sat down on a bench in one of the niches. Evan followed my example, stretching his long legs to the side, resting his head against the wall.

"What's so important that you had to wake me up in the middle of the night?"

"Azra's *araîth* was never finished," I blurted. "She cannot be crowned before it's finished, right?"

He sat up straight away, wide-awake. "Yes, but... it doesn't really matter, does it? Who else do we have in place?"

I shrugged. "That was the next step. I'm just trying to figure out ways to thwart her for as long as possible, at least until—"

Stopping myself short, I looked anywhere but at Ev. I'd already said too much.

"Until what?" he asked suspiciously.

I shook my head. "Never mind. I know it probably won't do much, but I thought... seeing as you're still trying to keep her from that crown..." I shrugged, running a hand through my hair. "We have to do something..."

Ev stared at me. "Like indulging her the way you do?"

"I'm no—," I began vehemently, clenching my hands into fists, continuing in a more level tone of voice. "I'm not indulging her. She's... she's insane, Ev."

"Could have fooled me," he muttered, lips pressed in a thin line. "Still doesn't explain why you do everything for her."

"Because she's got me by the balls, *mahnèh*. One toe out of line, and she kills any one of you."

He stiffened. "Why?"

Pinching the bridge of my nose, I sat back, closing my eyes. Once upon a time, I would have divulged every secret to Evan, or Haerlyon, perhaps to Xaresh, but now, I wasn't so sure. Haerlyon had already betrayed us, and I didn't know to what lengths Ev would go to keep his unborn child safe. Selling me out was amongst the possibilities.

"Because she's crazy." I sighed. "Utterly insane without

remorse. You saw what she did in the throne room, and out on the square…"

"You had a hand in that too," he retorted. "Or did we not hear her correctly?"

I stilled. As much as I wanted to yell at him how wrong he was—how she had played the situation and turned it to her own advantage, I didn't have the heart nor the energy to get into a fight with him. Pressing my lips together, I rose to my feet, glaring at Ev.

"Do with the information what you want," I said through clenched teeth, "and be careful you do not choose the wrong side of history."

"Likewise, *mahnèh*." Sarcasm dripped from the word as if it had been coated with it, which was so unlike Evan it made it all the more painful.

Without replying, I walked away, trying to keep my dignity as much as I could and not hit a wall on my way to my bedroom. Forcing my annoyance down, I opened the door and closed it without waking Cehyan. Resting my back against the door, I watched her in what little light the moon offered. She'd thrown most of the sheets off of her, despite the chill in the room, allowing for my gaze to travel up her long legs and farther.

It was a good thing I was wearing something more comfortable.

When she turned in her sleep, the sheet slid off of her completely, exposing her in her full naked glory. I didn't even hesitate—didn't even falter as I stalked to the bed and rid myself of the fabric covering me. Lying down next to her, my hand slid up her leg and over her hip as I nestled behind her, burying my face into her neck. I breathed in, half-drunk on her scent while my hand slid down her stomach and between her legs.

A soft moan escaped her lips and her eyelids fluttered, but she didn't wake up.

Need settled itself in my loins and moving her leg aside, I slid inside of her, a soft groan escaping my lips. I moved slowly, deliberately, fighting against the urge to have my way with her without any consideration for her. It wouldn't have been the first time. When she pressed herself against me, I looked up, staring into a pair of languid eyes.

"I missed this," she whispered in a husky voice. "Don't stop now."

I placed my hand just above the apex between her legs and thrust again, harder this time, more purposeful. If I was being honest with myself, I needed this as much for relief as to get the anger out of my system. Picking up on my urgency, Cehyan turned on her stomach, lifting her hips.

A deep growl escaped my lips, and I settled myself behind her.

"Don't hold back," she whispered breathlessly. "Please."

She didn't need to tell me twice. A deep moan escaped her lips when I entered her. I was as relentless as she was willing—it had always been like this between us, which was probably why it hadn't worked out. That, and the fact my father had forbidden me to ever see her again. I slid my hands around her chest and pulled her up against me.

"By Nava, I missed you," she gasped, trembling underneath my touch.

I didn't respond other than sliding in and out of her, focusing on that—on releasing my anger—more than on her. Her breathing picked up, and it became increasingly more difficult for her to keep quiet. The soft squeals and delicate yaps leaving her lips whenever I entered deep urged me on, and I could feel it wouldn't take long for either of us. She was shuddering against my chest, breathing irregularly. Deep groans escaped my lips, and I thrust until we found our release almost simultaneously. Disengaging Cehyan from my embrace, I lowered her gently to the bed and got out of it myself, pacing restlessly through the room.

"What's wrong?" Cehyan asked.

I glanced up at her and shrugged. "I don't know."

Evan's snide comments had hurt more than I thought, if only because I'd believed I still had an ally in him. How wrong I'd been. First Haerlyon, now Evan—whatever Azra was trying to accomplish seemed to be working. A bit more of that and I'd have no friends left. Anger flared up at the sudden realisation, and I caught myself just in time before hitting a wall. Breathing in sharply, I tried to regain a sense of self, a sense of calm.

Azra was getting under my skin, and I was allowing her.

"Come to bed," Cehyan murmured. "I'll help you relax."

I gave her an arched stare which I was sure she couldn't see in the poor light. "It didn't do me a lot of good just now…"

"I'm not talking about that…"

Breathing in sharply, I turned to her, my head warring with a longing I hadn't considered in a long time. With a shake of my head, I turned away from her and picked up my clothing from the ground, slipping into my trousers and blouse.

"No," I said, steeling my resolve. "I won't get back to *that*."

"Just a little," she said, wrapping her arms around me from behind.

I hadn't noticed her stepping from the bed. When she rested her head against my back, I closed my eyes, willing my body not to respond. I knew, as did she, she could have me in the bed in a heartbeat. She left it at this, not moving at all.

"Is it her?"

"Who?"

"The *Tari?*" she asked, moving so she was standing in front of me, arms still around me.

I looked down at her. "Maybe, I don't know."

"She seems to have it in for you," she murmured. "More so than with others."

"Hm, well, you're the only one who seems to believe so," I muttered. "Nobody else does."

"Then they're blind and stupid."

A faint smile tugged at my lips, but I didn't respond to her words. Instead, I placed a kiss on her forehead.

"Get some sleep. It's still the middle of the night."

"You should get some sleep too," she countered, taking my hand in hers. "Come to bed with me."

I shook my head. "I'm not tired."

"Suit yourself."

Letting go of my hand, she sashayed back to the bed and slid in seductively. Had I been in another mood, I would have gone for it. Instead, I put on my boots, grabbed my leather coat and a cloak, and walked out of the bedroom without looking back.

It wasn't cold outside—it was freezing, and the moment I stepped into the garden, I regretted my decision of not bringing more items to keep me warm. Grabbing the edges of my cloak, I pulled it tight about me and made my way over to a more secluded area where I'd at least be out of the wind, although the thought of letting myself freeze was a welcome distraction from my current reality.

Stop the morbidity, Imradien. What's wrong with you?

When I rounded the corner to my destination, I was surprised to find I wasn't the only night owl around. Huddled under a heavy blanket, Mehrean appeared to be asleep, but the moment I walked closer, she opened her eyes.

"Can't sleep?" she asked in a soft, melodious voice.

"No, I'm sleepwalking," I replied, perhaps a bit too sarcastically.

She chuckled and patted the bench, lifting the blanket. I'd be stupid if I declined an offer like that, and she at least didn't seem disgusted by my presence. A sigh of relief escaped my lips the moment warmth enveloped me, and I slid deeper underneath it.

"How are you holding up?" she asked after a while.

I shrugged. "As well as anyone, I guess."

"Hmhmm."

"What's that supposed to mean?" I looked sideways at her.

"I know when you're lying," she replied. "And that was through your teeth."

I snorted, clenching my hands together underneath the blanket. Mehrean and I had always been more of acquaintances. She'd been Shal's best friend and confidante at court, and probably knew more than I'd like her to know, but she'd never been unfriendly. Resting my head against the wall, I watched the night sky, marvelling at the thousands upon thousands of stars. For a moment, I wished I still had the faith of a child and believed our departed loved ones were amongst them.

I wouldn't have felt so alone then.

"Do you believe I'm helping Azra?"

"No."

"You sound so confident." I sighed. "She's clearly fooling everyone else."

"People see what they want to see," she replied sagely. "Right now, people are terrified of what's happening. Most have lost someone and are grieving, so it's easy to put blame where it doesn't belong."

I scowled at her. "I suppose, but it feels as if..."

As if one by one I am losing everyone I've ever cared about, and I don't think I can do this alone.

Mehrean was watching me with her head slightly tilted, reminding me of a cute little bird. I exhaled deeply, focusing on the brightest star.

"It feels as if it's all pointless," I said at length, glancing at her. "It doesn't matter what we do—she wins either way."

"Perhaps," Mehrean mused, "but perhaps it's a longer game we're intended to play, and not one any of us can end."

"Who then?"

"The rightful heiress to the throne."

I frowned at her. "She's dead."

Mehrean laughed and turned to me. "Don't lie to me, Tal. I thought we had agreed on that much at least."

I arched a brow. "Fine. How much do you know? Really?"

"Enough," she replied.

"If we're going to be honest with each other," I said, my lips pulling up in a smirk. "You might as well start too."

She looked at me in amusement. "And where exactly do you want me to start, Talnovar? With the fact I don't believe for one minute Shal died, or with the fact I know about the mission our dying *Tari* sent you on."

I opened my mouth to retort something and snapped it shut, realising I had no proper comeback for that.

"I'm not sure I want to know anymore." I groaned. "You're… unusual."

"So I've been told."

My brows shot up in surprise at her response, followed by a feeling of regret for my words. "Sorry."

"It's quite all right," she replied.

Whether it was or wasn't, I could not tell. We sat in silence for a long time after, revelling in each other's warmth. A thousand questions raced through my mind, and I wanted to ask them all, but I didn't even know where to begin. Mehrean seemed to know a lot more than she was letting on, but I doubted she'd divulge her secrets just like that.

"How did you know?" I asked at length, looking at her.

"The *Tari* told me," she answered with a smile. "Don't forget, I wasn't just Shal's confidante."

"That must have been a difficult position to be in."

She chuckled softly. "Sometimes. There were moments I'd

loved to have smacked them both over the head and tell them to talk to each other, but both of them were so gods-be-damned stubborn. Pardon my language."

I grinned. "Stubborn doesn't even come close to describing the *Tari* and her daughter."

At that, she burst out laughing, shaking her head from side to side slowly as if to deny the truth. I smiled faintly.

"I'm not sure which of the two was worse." Mehrean chuckled. "The *Tari* or—"

"Shal," we said simultaneously.

"I hope she's all right," she said wistfully, looking up at the stars. "Wherever she is."

"You and me both," I murmured.

Silence stretched out between us. I wasn't sure if I should say something, and just as I was about to take my leave, Mehrean spoke up, looking at me.

"Tal?"

"Yes?"

"Don't go for her yet," she said. "Now is not the time."

I rubbed my brow and turned to look at her. "When *is* the time?"

Shaking her head, she turned to face me completely, her eyes dark with solemnity. I could tell this wasn't easy for her either, although I had no idea why.

"I don't know," she whispered. "But something tells me it has to get worse before it gets better, and you need to be there for it."

I growled and rose to my feet, instantly regretting the move as the freezing cold air hit me full force, sending shivers down my spine.

"Terrific. Sure. Let all the bad stuff happen to me so none of you have to go through it."

She shook her head, looking up at me with solemn eyes.

"That's not what I meant. Tal. I'm serious. Without you, whatever needs to happen will fail."

"And how would you know?" I yelled at her, a sudden flare of anger overtaking me.

"I wish I could tell you," she replied in a pained voice. "Please believe me. Please, don't go try to find her. You will know when…"

With a disgusted sound, I turned and walked away from her, fuming on the inside. By the time I entered the palace, my fury had cooled off, and instead I was trying hard to keep my teeth from chattering while making my way to my bedroom.

Cehyan yelped in her sleep when I crawled in next to her, stealing her body heat.

If only you were her.

CHAPTER 16

SHALITHA

As promised, training started at dawn every day without exception, and although I had muttered about it the night Elay brought me to *Vas Ihn*, it gave me a sense of serenity I hadn't felt since before Xaresh was killed and there was still a semblance of order in my life. Rhana was as relentless in training as Talnovar—maybe even more so, but it got my head back into the game. Whatever Elay was up to, whatever plan he had concocted, I was in the middle of it and I had a part to play.

I had to play it well—for my own benefit as much as for his.

Caught up in my thoughts, I almost missed the attack coming from above, but I parried, stepped in, and struck my opponent on the hands with my staff.

She dropped it.

Aside from Rhana and myself, twelve other women currently resided at *Vas Ihn*, all of whom came from different walks of life. Some had arrived by accident, but most had been brought here either by Elay or one of his men. He was clearly running a business, and Rhana made sure it was run well.

"All right ladies!" Rhana called out. "Time for a break. Get something to eat. We'll continue after breakfast."

Breakfast was something the Zihrin called *ch'iti*, a dish similar to *diresh*—porridge—but tasted of absolutely nothing, and looked even less appetising. The only upside was its nourishment.

"Look at that," one of the women sneered as she sat down opposite me with some others. "Her skin's the colour of my breakfast. I bet she's just as bland."

I pretended I hadn't heard it and scooped a spoonful into my mouth, ignoring the shudder of disgust snaking down my spine.

"I bet she's as frigid as she looks," another one said.

Her comment was followed by a round of laughs. Others chimed in, but by that point, I had stopped listening. They could have their laughs at my expense—I didn't care. From the corner of my eyes, I saw one of the women move, but didn't pay much attention to it. Not until the moment I felt lukewarm *ch'iti* drip down my head and back did I wish I had.

The women howled with laughter.

"See! You can't even tell the difference!"

I looked up, wiped the worst of it from my hair, and returned to my breakfast. My eyes never left them. None of them dared come close again, so they continued being nasty until they realised they weren't getting a rise out of me. When they switched their conversation to something else, I let my attention wander.

"I'd expected you to jump them," Rhana said from my left.

I watched as she settled herself next to me, a bowl in her hand.

"Not worth the trouble," I replied with a shrug. "It means they're scared of me and haven't found a better way to deal with me yet."

"Don't underestimate them. They've been here training for months."

My lips quirked up into a lopsided grin. "And they're still here? Must be going well then..."

Rhana looked at me as if I'd personally offended her. "Why would you say that?"

"If they've been here for months," I replied, glancing in their direction, "I would have expected them to be stronger, considering your rigorous training schedule, yet none of them barely have any muscles to speak of. Two of them don't know how to hold their weapon properly, and the rest are more concerned with their looks than they are by staying alive. Ergo, either they don't care and don't put in the effort they should, or they're not who you claim them to be."

"There's something else than strength," Rhana commented. "All these women have their own skills."

"Weren't you training them to be skilled and resourceful in just about anything?" I asked, glancing sideways.

"Not everybody can be."

"But Elay wants me to be?"

"Yes."

After rubbing my cheek, I ran my hand through my hair, grimacing as my fingers touched upon cold food, and leaned back against the rock. I wiped my hand on my trousers while staring up at the clear blue sky. The Zihrin days were as hot as the nights were cold, which was why Rhana made us do the heavy training in the morning. During the afternoons, she drilled us in other parts.

"Come," Rhana said after a while, rising to her feet. "I've a job for you."

Before walking away, she ordered the rest of the women to continue their training, putting one of them in command to oversee it. The woman looked as surprised as I felt, but when I asked Rhana about it, she just shrugged and invited me into her hut. It was the only proper hut in the vicinity, and the moment I stepped inside, I was assaulted by different scents and nearly stumbled back out again. I was fairly certain I smelled sage, some rosemary, and something heavier—something I couldn't place, but it was heady and made me feel drowsy.

"Have a seat," Rhana said, sounding a little tired and strained.

I watched her as she pulled forth parchment, ink and a pen from a small cabinet hidden away in a corner. She placed all of it in front of me on the table.

"I want you to write a letter," she said, "in Ilvannian."

"Why?"

She flashed me a smile. "Because you're going to have to learn to lie."

I blinked. "Excuse me? Who is this letter to?"

"You can start by writing, in your own language, of course… *Dear Yllinar*," she instructed, sitting back in a chair opposite mine.

I stopped the process of retrieving the pen halfway and stared at her wide-eyed, feeling as if she'd just slapped me across the cheek.

"Sorry?" I whispered, barely noticing my trembling hand.

Rhana narrowed her eyes at me. "Do you know him?"

"Know him?" I breathed in deeply and exhaled slowly. "I want to kill him."

"Good," she said. "Now let go of that anger, and write down what I dictate."

"Why are you sending letters to him?" I asked suspiciously.

If Rhana was working with Yllinar, I had to get away from here as fast as possible, because if she was, maybe Elay was too. My heart picked up speed and my hands turned clammy, but rather than allowing the panic attack to consume me, I calmed myself down by counting from twenty to one in Ilvannian.

"One of Elay's men intercepted a messenger many moons ago," Rhana explained, looking at me. "He was on his way to a Zihrin noble who was willing to pledge men to Yllinar's cause. Judging by the content of the letter, we assumed it was the first one, so we've been in contact ever since."

"Does he know it's not this Zihrin noble?" I asked.

She shook her head. "No. He has no reason to believe it's not."

"He's a highly suspicious man," I said, picking up the pen. "He'll figure it out at some point."

"Perhaps," she replied, "but he's also vain, and very sensitive to offers of power, which is exactly what we're going to give him."

I blinked. "How?"

"Just do as I say," she replied, leaning back with a lazy grin. "Dear Yllinar…"

Putting pen to paper, I wrote the first two words to the letter, my stomach churning at the thought I was writing to the man who was responsible for my situation and for Tal's death. As quickly as my anger flared, I pushed it away again, needing my focus to listen to Rhana dictate the letter.

Mercifully, my tutor had seen fit to teach me this skill.

He'd seen fit to teach me a lot of things I thought useless at the time, and I finally began to understand why Mother had always been upset when I ditched my lessons with the old man.

"Everything is going exactly according to plan," Rhana intoned, her attention on the letter she was holding. "Soon I will have enough men and women to send in your direction in order to help keep *Tari* Azra on the throne."

Although I had suspected it, hearing it confirmed was a blow to the face, and it took me all effort of will to continue writing in a neat, steady hand.

"The good news is," Rhana continued, her eyes suddenly on me. "That word has reached me that the *Tarien* is currently held captive in one of the slave camps. She won't be able to cause any problems."

She knows who I am.

As the thought kept circling through my mind, I started to

feel sick. If Rhana knew who I was—really was—she'd have the price in her hand I had offered Elay for my safety.

Then he shouldn't have left you here.

Breathing in deeply, I snapped back to attention, hoping that my nerves would hold out a little longer than this.

"However, I beseech you to give us more than three moons to get ready," Rhana said. "While I will have sufficient forces to aid you in your endeavour, we will not be able to get them to Therondia on such short notice. Please allow for at least six moons to be ready."

I snorted but said nothing else.

"Per your request, I have looked into a Zihrin citizenship and am happy to inform there will be no trouble for you whatsoever. Please let me know when you expect to arrive. Was signed, Idrihn am Ihrn."

By the time I finished writing the letter for her, my hands were shaking and perspiration trickled down my temples as if I'd run for my life. With delicate precision, she picked up the letter I'd written, reading over it with her lips pulled up at the corners.

Somehow, the smile did not put me at ease.

She's a force unto her own.

It was in the way she uncurled from her seat, like a giant cat stretching its paws just before it's ready to pounce—in the way she rose to her feet and swayed over to the door, exuding confidence that reminded me of Nathaïr. I watched as she handed the letter to someone waiting outside, whispering clear instructions to him in Zihrin. When she returned, I expected her to send me back to training. Instead, she sat down in her chair facing me, the look on her face one of business.

"Now that we've got that out of the way," she spoke in accented Ilvannian, "let's get down to business."

I blinked. "What?"

"Stop the charades, princess," she said, a wicked smile on her lips. "I have just saved your life—well, Elay did, but that's not the point, is it?"

I rubbed my temples in an attempt to fight the headache building behind my eyes, glancing at her from under my lashes.

"You figured it out, huh?"

A chuckle left her lips. "No, Elay told me before you arrived, but the rest here are too ignorant to know better. You weren't wrong in saying they should be doing better, which is probably why Elay hasn't given them a position yet."

"It'll be a matter of time before they find out who I am though," I replied, sitting back with my eyes closed. "You might as well have given Yllinar my coordinates for all that it's worth."

"Elay made you a promise," she said. "And he will keep it, despite the massive bounty on your head."

I shuddered. "I'd better not disappoint then…"

At that, Rhana's face split into the widest grin, as if she'd just opened a package containing the biggest gift anyone could ever have given her. I felt at such a loss, I could only stare at her. Whatever Elay's plan was, it involved her and me, and she clearly enjoyed the thought.

I wasn't so sure.

"What do you know of the *Akynshan's* wives?" she asked, sitting back.

"That there are quite a few of them," I replied, annoyance seeping through in my voice. "I think he gave me a number, but I forgot."

"Twenty-three who are still alive. You'll be the twenty-seventh."

Her words were spoken in such a matter-of-fact manner it made me wonder what had happened to three of them, but as soon as that thought came to mind, I decided I was better off not knowing.

"He said you were going to train me." I frowned. "What will

you teach me exactly? He wouldn't have sent me here for fighting practise."

Rhana grinned. "No, indeed he wouldn't. You'll learn everything I can teach you when it comes to politics, spying and gathering information. The *Akynshan's* palace is a cutthroat place where every woman fends for herself, and you *amisha,* can certainly do with some help."

I pressed my lips tight together. "I was raised at court..."

"...and see where you ended up," she replied in an off-hand manner.

Looking away from her, I balled my hands into fists in my lap, breathing in to the count of ten, and out again. Rhana sighed.

"Listen," she began, sounding apologetic. "I know you were raised at court, and I understand you can hold your own perfectly fine, but Ilvanna's court is not like Elay's, so from where I'm sitting, you have two choices. Either you take your chances and find a knife in your back the first day after you're married, or you suffer through this and come out on top and maybe, if you ever get to return home, face that woman on your throne."

"I take it you don't like her either," I commented drily. "Although I'm surprised you know of her."

"Everyone in Zihrin knows of her," Rhana replied darkly. "She's been a Kyrinthan Queen for years and didn't much care about borders."

"What?"

"Oh yes, caused quite the scandal too. She had an illegitimate son by the King, then tried to overthrow him, but failed and blamed one of his sons for it."

Her words triggered a memory, a story rather—one I had pushed away to the recesses of my brain, chalking it up to one of her many adventure stories.

"Son of a *hehzèh*," I muttered. "She told us this story when she returned."

"Did she also tell you the end?"

I shrugged. "Perhaps, but… I can't remember. Was he killed?"

"They sure tried to," Rhana replied and rose to her feet, "but he wasn't as quick to catch as all that and fled. Nobody's seen him since."

"Convenient."

"It is that. Now come, we have work to do and I will not have anyone sneaking up on us."

Rising to my feet, I furrowed my brow, seeking support because of the sudden dizzy spell. "Where are we going?"

"You'll see."

Where I had expected her to lead me out of the hut, she led me deeper into it, through a curtain and into a tunnel. I figured they'd either hewn the tunnel, or easier, built the hut in front of it. Rhana picked up a torch and lighted our way deeper inside.

"Stay here."

The sudden sound of her voice made me jump, but I caught my startled gasp just in time. I didn't want Rhana to think I was afraid, even though this place was giving me the creeps. It reminded me of the words I'd spoken to Elay—it felt like bad things were about to happen here. One by one, she lit candles all around the cavern, exposing a large ring in the centre. It was as if we'd arrived at some kind of underground fighting pit.

I'd heard of those during my time as a slave, and none of the stories ever ended well.

"Where are we?" I asked, blinking away the fairy lights in my vision.

"A safe place," she replied, adding her torch to a wall sconce.

"And why would we need a safe place?"

"You really do ask an awful lot of questions, don't you?"

I shrugged. "It's what you get when people betray you from every side."

Rhana snorted and shook her head, then motioned me to follow her. At the back of the cavern, inside a smaller cave, several beds took up space. At the end of each bed stood a chest, and it was here she was taking me. I wanted to ask what this was, thought the better of it and closed my mind.

"There's basic attire in the chest. Put on some clean clothes and meet me in the middle of the cavern."

"What for?"

Rhana just smiled. "If you just do as I tell you, all of this will go a lot faster."

I would have loved something to wash with, but if nothing else, Rhana had made a point—I needed to move fast. Perhaps not for Elay, but from the sounds of it, for my people.

I had to get home.

The clothing was nothing more than a pair of trousers and a blouse. Barring an overcoat, it was exactly what I'd worn the past year. If I ever did get to sit on Mother's throne, I'd do so in something similar to this—propriety be damned.

A smile tugged at my lips at those thoughts. I used to speak them out loud whenever Tal—or anyone else for that matter—began talking about things being improper. I'd never cared much for it then, and I didn't contemplate beginning it now. While strapping bands around my sleeves to keep them from billowing, I made my way to the middle of the cavern where Rhana was waiting, quarterstaffs in hand.

I frowned. "How is this supposed to help me navigate Elay's court?"

"It won't." She grinned. "But I've seen you fight, and although not bad with a quarterstaff, I can teach you a trick or two. Besides, something tells me you need to get rid of your anger, and in my opinion there's no better way to do so than fighting."

She threw me one of the staffs. I'd barely caught it when she charged, giving me no time to respond except but hold up the weapon to block her. The sound of wood on wood echoed through the cavern. My training had truly started, whatever that was supposed to mean.

Let's hope Elay keeps his promises.

CHAPTER 17

TALNOVAR

With my arms behind my back, feet parallel with my shoulders, I made an effort to keep my face in check while my eyes followed Azra's endless sojourn through the council room. She'd taken to keeping me at her side as much as possible—I guessed she was afraid I would run somewhere. After Mehrean's words, my desire to find Shal was still paramount, but her warning kept me here, restless and on edge. Three weeks later and her words still sent shivers down my spine, so I tried not to dwell on it too much. These days, I tried not to dwell on anything too much lest it drive me insane or rebellious.

My gaze focused on Azra pacing up and down the council chamber hugging herself with one arm, while chewing nails on the other hand. She was nervous. Of all the things I'd attributed to her, being nervous wasn't one of them. Insane, wicked, deceitful, all of those in a heartbeat, but never nervous.

I couldn't keep the smirk from my lips.

"Something funny, *Anahràn?*" she hissed, glancing up at me.

"Enough things," I replied, forcing my face into something

more neutral. "None of which have anything to do with what's going on here."

She glared at me, but for once wasn't at my throat straight away. Her mind had been solely focused on the hunt for Ione, the *Araîtiste,* who had disappeared somewhere during the night shortly after my revelation to Evan. As had Mehrean. Upon finding out, Azra had been more than furious and had lashed out at everyone in close vicinity. I'd been one of the lucky ones, but I'd taken her lashing with pride, knowing my information had been used wisely. She and I both knew that without her *Araîth,* she would never have full claim to the throne and despite everything else Azra disregarded, she did seem to hold this law in high regard.

Either that or she really just wants to see it finished.

For every Ilvannian, whether common born or noble, receiving the *Araîth* was a milestone in their lives. Not only did it indicate a certain rite of passage, a certain place amongst peers, it also served as a testament of one's bloodline. I suspected this was more a thing with aristocracy than commoners, but it was something every youngster looked forward to, despite knowing full well the pain it would bring.

Azra had been deprived of that, whether by her own machinations or her mother's.

A part of me—a very small part—felt sorry for her, but the other was elated we could postpone the coronation. If only Mehrean's sign would come so I could look for the *Tarien,* life would actually be looking up for the first time in moons.

"Why are they so *nohro* slow!"

"She could be anywhere by now. It has been three weeks already."

A low growl left her lips, but she kept up her endless pacing.

I'd rather have her volatile and predictable than like this—brooding, calculating, looking as if she's about to solve the world's problems in a heartbeat. The knowledge of what she could do was unnerving at best.

The doors to the council chamber banged open and in strode the remainder of the Council, and with them none other than Yllinar, marching in as if he owned the place. A daze settled over me and I was only vaguely aware of what I was doing. I was on top of him before anyone knew what was going on. My fist connected with his nose hard enough to hear it crack and my other fist connected with his jaw before he could begin to defend himself. I got a punch into his ribs and his sternum too before I was hauled off of him.

Breathing hard, I struggled against the hold on my arms.

Yllinar, now sporting a bloodied nose, which was already swelling to the size of a grapefruit, spit blood on the floor and slowly rose to his feet, needing the support of a chair to steady himself. It was oddly satisfying to watch. I managed to pull one arm free and lunged for him again, but this time he was quick enough stepping out of my way.

"Restrain that beast, will you!" he growled.

Someone twisted my arm behind my back, pushing it up farther than it should normally be able to go. I hissed. Touching a kerchief to his nose, Yllinar dabbed the blood, cold, calculating eyes looking me up and down in disdain.

"I had hoped that sword to the gut would have finished you off," he muttered. "Guess I was wrong."

"And I'll make sure you keep wishing it had," I answered in a growl.

The guard twisted my arm farther. I grimaced.

"You don't look in any shape or form to be making any threats," Yllinar replied, sounding stuffed.

My blood roared in my ears. "As if I care. *You* took her from me. *Grissin.*"

"My poor boy, still hurting over the loss of your little love. How cute."

Smirking, I grabbed my own fist to double my strength while I pushed the guard's arm down, startling him. I stomped on his foot and brought my free arm around to grab his head and hold his arm at bay so he couldn't punch me in the stomach. Next he knew, his arm was locked between mine and he had nowhere to go. With a grunt, I pushed him into his comrades and went for my main target. Yllinar wasn't fast enough stepping out of my way. Both my hands snaked around his throat, and I squeezed as hard as I could.

"Her death is on your hands," I hissed, "but yours will be on mine, and I will enjoy every single moment."

Yllinar gasped, his hands clawing at my fingers to seek release, but he knew—I could see it in his eyes—I was the stronger of us, and there was no way he would get out of this. Not without help anyway, because I would not let him go until he'd drawn his last breath.

"That's enough!" Azra roared. "Let him go, or I *will* kill your father."

"Spare me your false threats, *hehzèh*," I growled without looking at her. "You don't have him."

"Tal..."

My father's voice brought me up short like a slap to the face, and I instantly released Yllinar from my grip. The red marks around his throat were quite satisfactory to see. I turned to his voice—my father's voice.

I was not prepared for the sight of him.

Blue, purple and yellow bruises covered most of his face and an ugly cut ran from his temple down to his jaw. Even from here I could tell his nose was broken, and I wouldn't be surprised if they'd broken more than just that.

"Let him go, Azra," I said through clenched teeth. "You have me. Am I not good enough for your vengeance?"

Her lips curled into a mischievous smile while raking her talons across my father's chest, drawing a loud hiss from him.

Perspiration beaded his forehead as if he'd ran here, but something told me he was spiking a fever, if nothing else.

"Oh, you are," she purred, "but what could be better than using you against each other? If you don't do as I say, your father will pay the price and vice versa. Isn't that delightful?"

Her voice hitched on the last words and she all but clapped in glee. Father looked positively sick, and I had to admit I wasn't feeling too well myself. Of all the scenarios I could have come up with for her to punish me with, this one had been the furthest from my mind. Father didn't even look surprised. Instead, resignation was written all over his face, which only served to fuel my anger.

Do not give in, khirr.

"What do you want from us?" I asked with a heavy sigh.

"I told you," she said. "That hasn't changed, but now it looks like I have the best deal of all. Are you going to behave?"

I clenched my jaw and inclined my head. "Yes."

"Yes, what?"

"Yes, *Tari*."

She looked positively delighted at my words, and with a single nod ordered the guards to release their hold on him. He fell to his knees almost immediately.

"Father!"

I sprang forwards to catch him but was held back by two guards. Azra looked amused—Yllinar anything but, yet he didn't make a move towards me. He was too busy tending to his broken nose.

"Before I allow you to take care of him," Azra said, her eyes on me. "There's something I need you to do, but first"—she turned to the Council and smiled— "*Irà* and *Irìn*, please take a seat."

All of them did, although most looked sceptical, some worried, and only one looked absolutely terrified—Nya. I'd never much liked the woman, but for once I couldn't agree with her more. If Azra had summoned the Council, there had to be an excellent reason, and my gut told me it wasn't going to be pretty.

"As you all well know," Azra said, "I have made my claim to the throne abundantly clear, and everyone in this room knows I am well within my right to ascend. Yet you deem yourself above me, and have been thwarting my efforts every step of the way."

A shiver ran down my back in anticipation of what was to come. My eyes surveyed the room, and I realised behind every Council member stood a guard. I didn't have to guess where their hands were resting. I could see it out of the corner of my eyes. Bile rose to my throat, coating the inside of my mouth.

Not here. Not now.

"You will understand when I tell you I cannot tolerate this kind of insubordination," Azra continued, pacing up and down, hands folded delicately in front of her. "At first, I thought you were only doing your job, and that it wasn't because of me, but then"—she turned on them fast, a wicked grin on her face— "the real problem occurred to me. You *were* doing your job. Now, everyone here knows that a position on the Council is for life due to the nature of what is discussed here..."

The Council members turned pale—much paler than should be possible considering their ivory skin—upon the implication of Azra's words.

Nobody would leave this room alive.

Some members' eyes turned wide, others began to sob quietly. Only a few, Chazelle amongst them, remained stoic. Although the dislike between Chazelle and myself was mutual, she didn't deserve this—none of them did.

Except Yllinar.

Yet Yllinar had taken a position behind Azra, the tell-tale Arolvyen sneer on his face as he watched his former colleagues.

Someone has slept his way up.

I'd half-expected a riot because of the time that passed, but in truth, between her words and her command, it wasn't even to the count of fifty. The sound of swords being unsheathed echoed through the council chamber, followed by surprised gasps as the weapons hit home. I watched in horror as one Council member after the other slumped in their chair, their last breath drawn.

"Ruesta mey mahnèh," I murmured.

"Anahràn." Azra's voice drew my prayers up short.

She presented a dagger to me, a wicked gleam in her eyes. I looked from her to the table and realised the only one still alive was Chazelle sitting straight-backed in her chair. When her eyes met mine, she gave me a curt nod.

"Do it, *Anahràn*," she said in a soft, steady voice. "Please, don't let me be a part of this charade for much longer."

Despite her words, my stomach coiled tight when I took the dagger. I halted momentarily, my eyes resting on my father. I could protest—could not do this, but he would pay the price. Holding the dagger tight, I made my way over to Chazelle, my pulse quickening.

"I'm sorry." I placed the dagger against her throat, and slit it in one fluent motion.

As warm blood seeped through my fingers, I forced myself to look at Chazelle while she died.

Ruesta, Irà.

Resisting the urge to throw the dagger at either Azra or Yllinar, I let it clatter to the floor and walked to my father, manoeuvring him so that I could support him.

"Excuse us."

Without waiting for permission, I supported him out of the council room, deciding Soren would be the best place for him to go.

"You look terrible," Father muttered, and coughed.

Blood trickled down his lips.

"I take it you haven't looked into a mirror lately?" My lips quirked up in a faint smile.

He shook his head.

SOREN WAS EXACTLY where I expected him to be, moving about the infirmary with purpose, going from one patient to the next. I'd never seen it this busy, not even after *Hanyarah*. He looked up when I entered, a deep frown creasing his brow.

"Because I wasn't busy enough," he remarked drily, waving us over. "Who did you bring?"

"My father," I grunted as I helped him lay down on the examination table.

Soren's brows shot up in surprise, a questioning look in his eyes. I shook my head, mouthing a 'not here'. Thankfully, he obliged and set to tending to him.

"What's your name?" he asked.

"Cerindil," Father said with a grimace. "Cerindil Imradien. *Ohzheràn* of *T... Tari* Arayda an Ilvan and h... her daughter."

"At least he's got his priorities straight," Soren said, glancing at me.

"Loyal to a fault."

He flashed me a grin. "Like father like son?"

"Shut up."

"I take it Azra got to him?" Soren asked, serious this time.

I nodded, raking my hand through my hair, but when I was about to reply, my father got ahead of me.

"N... not Azra. Y...Yllinar."

"Oh?" Soren sounded surprised, though not amused. "That *grissin's* found his way back here then?"

"Unfortunately, yes," I replied, rubbing my jaw. "But I think he might be regretting that decision right about now."

Soren frowned. "Why?"

"Because I broke his nose." I shrugged. "And would have strangled the life out of him had Azra not brought my father in."

"Sometimes," he replied with a soft chuckle, "I swear to the Gods someone needs to do something about those anger issues."

"He almost killed me," I growled. "And he took Shal, *and* you! Surely you can't blame me?"

"Not at all. I merely wish I'd been there to see it."

"T… the l… look on… on his face was p… priceless," my father gasped, ending up in a coughing fit.

When his hands came back with blood spatters, Soren's look went promptly from amused to dark and he all but shooed me out of the infirmary.

"We'll deal with this," he said. "I'll send someone to get you when we're done. I'm sure you're expected elsewhere."

He said the last words with enough sarcasm for me to know he was still on my side, which meant more than I'd ever let him know. With one last look at my father, who had turned even paler under the colourful array of bruises on his face, I left the infirmary. Looking about, trying to wrap my head around everything that had happened, I tried to decide where to go and found my thoughts returning to the Council room instead.

I'd killed before, but never in cold blood.

Out of nowhere, memories—images, sounds and scents—assaulted me from every direction. Pressing my hands over my ears, as if that would help against it, I staggered through the corridors, bumping into people as I went, mumbling apologies as I tried to find my way to my room. Cries of pain reverberated inside my skull as if it was happening right next to me—the coppery scent of blood stuck inside my nose, never coming out again, and the clatter of steel on steel echoed in the distance as if a war was raging outside the palace.

Perhaps there is.

I all but crashed inside my room, kicking the door shut hard enough to make it rattle on its hinges. My hands were jittery when I pulled them away from my ears, and my steps faltered as I made my way to the bed. I needed to calm down—somehow. Sitting down, my eyes fell on the leather sling bag on the single chair in my room, and without a second thought, I picked it up.

Cehyan must have left it.

Trembling, I pulled out a pipe, a small leather pouch and flint and steel. Somehow, I managed to add the dry leaves to the pipe, put it to my lips and light it. The moment I inhaled, other memories—memories of good friends and good times—resurfaced, pushing the nightmarish ones away. Settling back on the bed, I inhaled again, letting the *sehvelle* do its work, taking away the edges of the pain and troubles plaguing my mind.

It had been over a hundred and fifty years since I'd last used.

CHAPTER 18

SHALITHA

"Try again," Rhana said patiently, watching me from where she sat perched on a ledge, cleaning her nails with a dagger.

I awarded her a flat stare, unamused by the fact she kept putting me through making this tea for the thousandth time despite my endless complaints. She joked I'd make a horrible wife, and I had stuck with the notion.

Perhaps I would.

In my defence, I'd never been trained to be a wife—I'd been trained to be *Tari,* and as far as I knew, they did not make tea. Breathing in deeply, I settled myself on my knees in front of the fire and rearranged the pouches of spices lying next to me. Not that the order threw me off—the amount needed for each spice did. One by one, I added them—cinnamon, cardamom, peppercorns and cloves, inhaling as the warm fire freed their scent.

The first time, I had added so much cinnamon, it burnt our throats on its way down. The second time, there was hardly any in there, but the pepper was too powerful. Preparing the perfect cup of tea, or so Rhana made me believe, lay in adding just the right amount of herbs and spices. She made it sound simple.

It was anything but.

I shook the pan to make sure the spices didn't stick to the bottom and carefully added water and ginger. All I had to do was make sure the water simmered.

"Don't boil it!" Rhana had screamed a few days prior.

After I believed it had simmered enough, I took the pan off the fire and set it to the side, adding tea leaves in what I hoped to be was the right amount, covering it with muslin. The process was strenuous at best, and I often compared it to torture. Rhana had scoffed and asked if I'd ever gone through any real torture.

I never replied.

"Don't let it sit for too long," Rhana offered, slipping off the ledge. "I'm sure you don't want to repeat it again."

I growled low in response. She laughed.

With practiced care—I'd done this a million times by now—I tied the cloth to the pan so it wouldn't fall off when I turned it over. In some ingenious way, the muslin served to sieve the tea, making sure the cinnamon and pepper wouldn't end up in the kettle.

"Here goes," I muttered, pouring the tea into it.

Rhana was watching me intently, more so than she'd done before, which didn't help the nerves. She'd assured me Elay's wives would be much worse and even more picky than she was.

It hadn't helped. At all.

Picking up the tray with the teapot and two cups, I made my way over to where Rhana had made herself comfortable and knelt in front of her. At least pouring tea had been part of my education, even though I'd never paid much attention to it, so I'd been glad to find I had not forgotten it entirely.

"Here you are, *amisha*," I said, offering her a cup.

Rhana smiled brightly. "Why, thank you."

I watched as she took a sip, scrunching up her nose as if she'd smelled something foul. The thoughtful expression on her face could mean anything, and with a heavy sigh I resigned myself to the fact I would have to do it again.

"Not bad," she said. "You're almost there."

I flopped back spread-eagled with a loud groan, staring up at the ceiling with imminent despair lodging in my chest.

"Please don't make me go through that again," I muttered. "I'll beg you on my knees if I have to."

Rhana laughed, a high-clear laugh that echoed through the cavern. "Don't worry, I'll let up for today. There's training to be done."

Finally, something I can do.

NOT ONLY WAS Rhana relentless in developing my tea making skills, she was harping even harder on my fighting skills today—more so than usual. She kept hammering in on me, barely giving me quarter. Her breath came in hard puffs as she exhaled on every thrust and blow. I parried and dodged but didn't get a jab in edgewise.

She was master of the quarterstaff for sure.

"You need to trust your instincts more," a deep, melodious voice sounded behind me.Rhana yelped, twirling in the direction of the voice I knew I'd heard before, but not anytime recently. I'd heard it in the deep dark of the sea, and before then in an uncomfortably hot cave. Back then, I'd put it down to hallucinations, and in the sea I'd been dying. Now, I did not have any viable reason to believe this wasn't real.

Breathing in deeply, I turned to him with a scowl.

"Really, and what would you know about it?" I muttered.

"I am minded to give you a demonstration, but that would not be fair," he replied, trying to sound offended despite the amused look on his face. "You would be on your ass within three heartbeats."

"Bluff."

Not even two beats later, I was contemplating my challenge to him from the flat of my back, glaring up the length of his sword. His dark eyes twinkled in mischief. Long white hair was tied back in a high ponytail, pronouncing long, elegant ears. For the first time, I noticed one of them looked like a bit had been taken out of it. He was dressed differently than last time—gone were the long flowing robes. Instead, he was wearing armour the likes of which I'd never seen before. A combination of leather and metal it looked lethal on its own, and I doubted any weapon could get through it.

"Again?"

I grunted. "You've made your point, but it still doesn't answer my question. What would you know about it?"

"Surely you remember who I am?" he asked, brows squished together, offering me a hand.

"You claim to be a God," I replied. "Anyone can claim that..."

He looked amused. "Has a man done that to you before?"

"Not the point."

"No? I wonder"—he began, tossing the sword up— "what would it take to make you accept"—it disappeared into thin air — "that not everything is what you were brought up to believe, and sometimes we are who we say we are."

I gawped at him, blinking like a full-blown *qira,* opening and closing my mouth like a fish out of water. Throughout all this, Rhana remained quiet and looking at her, I realised she was looking as flabbergasted as I was.

"Did you see that?" I asked her.

"I think so." She glanced from me, at Esahbyen, and back again. "Shalitha, who is this?"

"Allow me to introduce myself," Esahbyen replied with a deep flourishing bow. "Esahbyen, God of War, well, in the Ilvannian tongue at least. You may call me—"

"Laros," they said simultaneously.

Rhana looked unimpressed. "A God? They haven't walked this world for thousands of years. Why should I believe you?"

"Because I would not advise to test my patience," Esahbyen replied, lips curling up in a mischievous smile. "Now, please be a dear, and leave us alone? The *Tarien* and I need to have a serious conversation."

She opened her mouth, judging by the look on her face to protest. Before she could, he made her disappear with a flick of his hand.

Like the sword.

"Where were we?" he mused. "Ah, yes. Have you ever wondered why you did not drown that night?"

"Every day since," I replied with a deep sigh, flopping down on one of the many pillows strewn about. "Why? Are you telling me you had a hand in that too?"

"Not me directly..."

I snorted and shook my head. "I need to wake up. This is all ridiculous."

"And yet," Esahbyen commented drily, "you are still here, meaning you must believe some of this is true."

Knuckling my eyes until stars appeared in my vision, I contemplated his words. By now, I should have died twice, which was an impossibility all on its own, yet I'd come back—somehow. He'd admitted to saving me the night after I escaped Eamryel, and now he more or less did the same with the shipwreck. A deep shudder went through me, raising goosebumps everywhere on my body. Swallowing hard, I looked at him.

"For the sake of argument." I breathed in deeply. "Let's assume what you are telling me is true. Why are you here?"

His lips curled up in a wicked grin and he clapped his hands. "Now we are getting somewhere."

I rolled my eyes and slumped back into the pile of pillows, regarding him with apprehension. His twinkling eyes never left mine as he stalked closer, reminding me of a predator. To my surprise, he dropped himself onto the pillows next to me, folded his arms behind his head and stretched his legs, making himself comfortable. He was close—too close.

"Let's assume all of this is real," he said, "then you are a damsel in distress, and that would make me your knight in shining armour."

I raised an eyebrow.

"Do you know what is currently going on in Ilvanna, *Tarien*?"

I winced as the title rolled of his tongue with a particularly distinguished Ilvannian accent. Looking away, I shook my head.

"Do you want to know?"

His question took me by surprise. On the one hand, a part of me desperately wanted to, but knowing meant I'd have to live with it, and I wasn't sure I could handle the truth. On the other hand, not knowing wasn't doing me any favours either—nightmares and the constant fear of being found were ever present companions. My nerves were frayed and my sanity was wearing thin.

I wasn't sure how much longer I could hold on.

"Remember what you asked of me at *Hanyarah, dochtaer*?"

"The wisdom to know what to do once I was *Tari*," I replied, looking at him with a wry smile. "As you can see, I'm a long way off of that path."

One side of his lips quirked up. "What if I tell you, you are exactly where you are supposed to be?"

"I'd say you're dafter than I initially thought." I shook my head and pulled up my knees. "Look where I am… a cavern in the middle of nowhere of Zihrin, hundreds of miles away from Ilvanna. How is this being where I'm supposed to be? If you ask me, I'm supposed to be six feet under. The Gods know Azra gave it a fair try."

Esahbyen watched me for a long time after, his face a perfectly composed mask, not even his eyes betraying anything.

His scrutiny made me uncomfortable and I started fidgeting, looking anywhere but at him, until he took my hands in his, halting my progress of pulling apart a pillow.

"How do you expect to defeat Azra once you return?"

I looked up sharply. All I'd been concerned about was getting back somehow—I'd never actually considered what I would do once I came face to face with my aunt. With me gone, her claim to the throne was legitimate. Once I returned—if I returned—I would undoubtedly have to fight her for it. Cold dread settled itself in my gut and I slowly shook my head.

"I… I don't know."

"This is why I am here," he replied with a heavy sigh, rubbing his jaw. "Your aunt must be stopped, whatever it takes…"

"But?"

He sounded as if there was a but coming. The apologetic look he gave me was not what I expected.

"You are the only one who can."

I stared at him, trying to make sense of what he was telling me. On top of everything he'd said already, this was just another surprise I could have done without, although his words made sense in that strange way where you know something to be truth, yet you can't explain why. Running my hands through my hair, I regarded him in silence for some time, trying to put one and one together.

My ability for calculus had left me.

"Why only me?"

"That, *dochtaer,* is an answer I am afraid I cannot give you." Sadness stole over him, but only for a little while.

Folding my arms in front of me, I watched him through narrowed eyes. "So you come here under the pretence of helping me, telling me I'm exactly where I'm supposed to be, although I need to get back to stop my aunt from whatever antics she's up to because I'm the only one who can, yet you cannot tell me why?"

"Exactly."

I grunted. "And this is exactly why I do not put much stock in you so-called Gods. If you want to help me… help me. Otherwise, please leave me alone."

"And why would I do that?"

Annoyance turned into full-blown anger as I turned on him, ready to pick a fight. He was already on his feet, a mischievous smirk on his lips, eyes twinkling in wicked delight.

"There she is," he purred. "Come on then, you know you want to."

With no sense to what I was doing, I jumped to my feet and attacked him, trying to get in punches from every direction, but Esahbyen was fast and seemed to know what I was going to do before even I did. To my chagrin, he didn't fight back—he merely deflected my punches by stepping out of the way or catching my fists.

"I love your fighting spirit," he said, "but you need to control that temper."

His words took the fight out of me and gasping, I watched him, annoyance still burning inside of me.

"What's wrong with my temper?"

"Really?" He looked me up and down, brows knitted together. "First of all, it makes you attack like a wild animal. Second, you project your moves without even knowing that you do. By me, what *did* that *Anahràn* teach you."

A low, guttural growl started in the back of my throat. "Leave him out of this."

"Fine," he said, folding his arms, "if you start acting like a proper adult and heed some advice."

I threw up my hands and stalked off. Deep down, I knew he was right. I was behaving like a petulant child, but I wanted answers and I wanted them now. Every fibre of my being rebelled against the notion of Gods existing and walking the world, let alone being here with me, ready to teach me things.

Despite my wariness of him, I had no reason to believe he'd lie to me.

"Very well," I said at length, turning to him. "I'll play your game... on one condition."

"Which is?"

"Don't save me again."

He stared at me, unblinking like an owl, lips pressed in a tight line. His eyes flashed once, but then he inclined his head.

"As you wish, *dochtaer*."

"And stop calling me that," I muttered. "I'm not your daughter."

He grinned but didn't comment. Instead he walked over to one of the beds, kicked off his boots and made himself comfortable as if he owned the place. I followed more reluctantly, still peeved.

"Where did Rhana go?" I asked as I sat down on another bed. "Where did she disappear to?"

"Right where she ought to be."

"You really need to work on your answers."

"I will," he said with a chuckle, "if you work on that temper of yours. Deal?"

Just in time, I prevented myself from tossing a pillow in his direction, and I caught myself smiling despite my feelings towards him. With it came a wave of sadness as it reminded me of Tal.

"He's still alive, you know," Esahbyen murmured from the other side. "Unhappy, but alive."

A sob caught in my throat and I pressed my face into the pillow. I didn't want him to hear me cry.

He's alive. Tal's alive!

CHAPTER 19

TALNOVAR

After another week penned up inside the palace, the necessity to get out was high—high enough to disregard Azra's summons and sneak out instead. I knew I was taking a risk with my father as her prisoner, but I had to get some fresh air, if only for a little while. The walls inside had gotten a life of their own and I was convinced they had it in for me too. No doubt one of Azra's cronies would find me soon and take me back—until then, I'd enjoy my freedom, such as it was.

The cobblestones were still coated in dried blood—the people in the streets were subdued, keeping eyes downcast, shoulders hunched, as if a heavy burden lay upon them. A few cast me curious looks, some furtive glances, but most downright scowled when I passed them. Guilt washed over me every time it happened until I could take no more and fled to the one place where I hoped I could get a clear head.

Shal's hiding place.

As far as hiding places went, sitting on top of the city walls was a sure-fire way for people to watch me, but being out of reach made their reproachful glares easier to deal with. Resting my head against the wall, I closed my eyes, contemplating my situation and Ilvanna's. If Arayda were still alive…

None of this would ever have happened, khirr.

Rubbing my temples, I wondered where it had all gone wrong. Why, if Arayda had known about her sister's ambitions, had she not done anything about it before now? Why had she let it come this far? Surely she'd never considered her daughter going missing, or her country falling under the tyranny of a monster? I couldn't help but wonder how well she'd known her sister, and how much she suspected could, or would happen.

Maybe not even she knew the depths of her sister's depravity?

If I were to believe Rurin, Azra hadn't been above killing her twin, so it came as no surprise to me she would orchestrate a genocide of her own people. The question was, to what end, unless she wanted to rule over the dead. In that case, she was well on her way. The thought turned me cold on the inside.

Now is a good time for that sign of yours, Mehr.

I hoped she was well on her way smuggling Ione out of the country. As far as anyone knew, she was the only *Araîtiste* far and wide who was sanctioned to ink the royal *Araîth,* so whoever held her had the upper hand.

At the moment, that was us.

Or so I thought.

The clatter of hooves alerted me from my silent song of woe to a group of horsemen riding through the gate at high speed. Their leader, white hair shaved on one side, stood up in the stirrups and yelled for people to get out of the way. An ominous feeling settled itself in my gut.

If Haerlyon had returned, it could only mean one thing.

"*Nohro ahrae*!"

By the time I arrived at the palace, everything and everyone was in an uproar. Servants were rushing around as if in preparation of something, and the guards had been tripled in the time I'd been out. Dazed, I walked inside, my head swivelling left and right to make sense of this sudden change of atmosphere.

I decided I needed to find out what had prompted this when the one voice I absolutely did not want to hear hailed me.

"*Anahràn*!" Azra called out, walking towards me. "I'm so glad you decided to return. I was almost afraid I'd have to take it out on your father again."

I gritted my teeth. "You made my predicament abundantly clear."

"Good," she purred, hooking her arm through mine, continuing her way in the same direction I was going.

I tensed underneath her touch but didn't pull away from her. Before, I would have tried anything to keep my reputation intact. As it was, that reputation was damaged and blemished and quite honestly, I was too tired to fight it. If this made her happy, so be it. Not until then did I realise she actually was happy, which set my teeth on edge and my hair on end.

What are you up to, hehzèh?

"Come, there's something I need to show you." She smiled brightly. "Today will be the best day yet."

When it came to her, I'd learned a best day could be anything from carnage to a wedding, although I doubted she was marriage material. Perhaps once, but certainly not now. Besides, I didn't even want to think about whom she would marry—the thought was sickening. The reason for her abundant happiness became clear the moment we stepped into the throne room.

Up on the dais stood the one person we'd been trying to hide from her.

Ione.

A string of expletives escaped my lips in both the old- and the new tongue, earning a highly amused look from Azra.

"Didn't expect that, did you?" she mused. "Come."

"I don't need to see this," I said through clenched teeth. "I thought this was a sacred ceremony?"

Azra cackled. "It was... until I had *Hanyarah* levelled to the ground, Laelle killed, and with Mehrean now gone too, the Sisterhood is leaderless."

I stilled.

What do you mean, gone? Hehzèh.

"Leaderless?" My voice came out in barely a whisper.

"Didn't you know?" she asked, straightening herself. "Mehrean was Laelle's successor. The moment that woman died, she became head of *Hanyarah*."

Digging her nails into my arm, she escorted me farther into the throne room, keeping up her monologue.

"Here's the funny thing," she continued. "At first, I did not understand why Evan and the council brought up the problem of my *Araîth.* After all, none other than Yllinar knew about it. And then, all of a sudden, about a moon ago, Mehrean fled the palace with Ione, the only woman in this realm who could finish it. I knew Yllinar wouldn't have told anyone—he pinky promised, you know? And then I realised"—she tutted and patted my arm gingerly— "there has only been one other person who could have seen it. Guess who?"

I didn't respond, knowing full well who that was.

"Imagine how hurt I felt when I realised it was you," she said in a low, husky voice. "I had such plans for us, you know?"

"I'm not interested," I replied, fighting to keep my voice level. "In case you hadn't noticed."

She giggled. "Not yet. Anyway, you really hurt my feelings, *Anahràn,* and seeing how ineffective my torture methods have been thus far—you still do not obey me—I've had to come up with something more creative..."

Despite myself, I swallowed hard. Whatever creative way she had come up with couldn't be anything good. Risking a glance at her, I found her watching me with a wicked grin on her face.

"I won't spoil the surprise," she said, "you'll see. But just in case you decide to disobey me again"—she nodded to our right where my father was tied to the whipping post I'd previously occupied— "after I've flogged the skin off his back, I'll kill him… slowly, and I'll make you watch."

No curse words I could think of sufficed to express my feelings. Whichever way I turned, Azra had me by the balls—again —and it was starting to get on my nerves.

"You have my word."

She patted my arm. "Good boy."

Taking no chances, she guided me up the dais and released her grip on my arm, clearly expecting me to take up my position as her *Anahràn*. I never used to have a problem standing where everyone could see me, but now it made me feel like the biggest *verathràh* of Ilvanna. Clasping my hands behind my back, I squared my shoulders and pressed my lips into a thin line, composing my features into an impassive mask. It was all I had to keep the wave of guilt at bay.

My eyes settled on my father looking so broken and desperate that it hurt. Never before had I seen him like this. Despite our differences in the past—and there had been many— I'd always looked up to him, always sought his approval. Not that he never gave it. He did when it was deserved, but for a very long time, I hadn't been deserving of it. Whatever he did in the past to make Azra hate him so much—he'd more than made up for it straightening me out.

I hope I get to tell him that before…

I couldn't finish the thought and looked away, guilt coiling itself around my heart, squeezing it until it became painful to breathe. I tried to swallow it away, but the heaviness on my chest remained. My gaze returned to Azra, whose speech I mostly seemed to have missed.

It was probably more of her tyrannical propaganda I could do without.

My eyes drifted to Ione, taking in her countenance. When first we'd met, she'd been a skittish woman, eyes always downcast, shoulders slumped forward as if all fight had gone out of her. Over the course of months, I'd seen her bloom into radiance until she wore a smile as if it was her favourite dress. Although I hadn't spent much time talking to her, she had told me of her time with the *Tarien* while I recuperated in the infirmary, and how sad she'd been upon learning she had been kidnapped. There had been more to that, but I hadn't been able to figure it out, and she hadn't been very forthcoming.

Ione had taken the news of Shalitha's death hard—harder than I'd thought she would.

We hadn't spoken since.

Now, Ione looked stronger than ever, shoulders squared, lips pressed in a thin line, defiance blazing from her eyes. I wanted to tell her to calm down, keep a neutral look, but there was no way of drawing her attention other than calling out to her, and I doubted that would go over well with Azra.

I watched as she turned her back to the crowd, her eyes finding mine. The gleam in them didn't spell anything good and had me rooted to the spot. Too stubborn to look away first, I scowled at her in the hopes she would, but all it elicited was a smirk from her as she lay down on the table.

Ione didn't even wait for her to make herself comfortable before she started tapping the first ink into the skin just above her ankle, continuing where the previous *Araîtiste* had left off. The grimace stealing over Azra's face was a poor substitute for vengeance, but it would do, for now. People clapped automatically, as if someone had cued them to do so and fell silent just as fast.

The first and the last day were the worst, or so I was told, because everyone who was someone had to be present during both days until the royal heir could take no more and the *Araîtiste* had to stop. Ione had told me Shalitha had managed for quite a long time—longer than anyone she'd ever inked, although she'd attributed it to stubbornness more than stamina.

It had sounded like Shal all right.

By the time Ione stopped, day had turned into night, and a lot of people were fighting to keep their eyes open—me included. Azra was sweating profusely and breathing laboriously. From the looks of her, she'd gone on much longer than she had been capable of. Her eyes were brimming with tears, but there was a determined look on her face.

"Continue," she hissed to Ione. "I want this done as soon as possible."

"With all due respect, *Tari*," Ione replied, "your body isn't capable of handling more. Your skin is bleeding continuously, which makes it hard to tap even a straight line, let alone the design you requested."

Azra pressed her lips together, narrowing her eyes, but where I'd expected her to command Ione again, she breathed out with a grunt.

"Fine," she muttered. "I'll have the guards bring you to my quarters at sunrise, so prepare for a long day. I suggest you rest up."

It wasn't a suggestion at all. Guards came up and guided both Ione and my father out of the throne room—I assumed to the prison cells. Without elaboration, Azra sent everyone on their merry way, missing the grateful looks on their faces as they hastened to their beds. I wished I could follow them, but Azra fixed me with a glare.

"Take me to my room," she ordered, pain suffusing her features.

I arched a brow, waiting for her to get off the table. When

she didn't, I realised she was in too much pain to do so, and I couldn't help the snigger escaping my lips.

"Laugh all you want." She grimaced. "But you're next."

Her words stopped me dead in my tracks. Her eyes lit up with mischief at my response to her words.

"What's wrong, *Anahràn*?" she purred. "You look like you've seen a ghost."

"You can't," I began.

She can, and she will.

My mouth went dry, and I crossed my arms over my chest as if to protect myself. Azra's delighted laughter seemed to come from far away. Breathing in deeply through my nose, I calmed my nerves and steadied myself. A voice in the back of my mind told me I should have seen this coming—it had been obvious from the moment Ione had returned.

I was her *Anahràn* after all.

"Let's get you to your room," I managed in a steady voice as I picked her up, drawing out a deep hiss from her.

My lips curled up in a satisfactory smile, but I felt none of it.

Once we arrived in her room, I dropped her on the bed unceremoniously and made to leave when she called me by name. I turned back torturously slowly, trying to get a handle on my mood and my temper.

"You know this could all be a lot easier if you stopped fighting?" she mused, displaying herself on the bed.

"Over my dead body."

CHAPTER 20

SHALITHA

Perspiration ran in steady rivulets down my back and forehead, plastering what hair had come undone from my braid to my face. The moment I wiped my brow, Esahbyen struck, but having expected it, I moved out of the way before his fist connected with my jaw. It would have been painful considering the still healing bruise marring the left side of my face. He attacked in a flurry of movements, almost too fast to see. Having Godly powers made him a *nohro* nuisance to fight against, but I had to admit that in the time I'd spent with him, I'd honed my skills to a level I had never thought I could reach. Not only could I follow his movements, I managed to deflect them more than I collected them, earning praise from the God of War.

I had to say, that was quite a feat.

"Keep your arms up," Esahbyen muttered, "or I will be able to add some more colours to that hideous face."

"Who are you calling hideous?" I growled.

He grinned. "Mind that temper. Anger does not get you anywhere."

I scowled at him, but I knew he was right. Even Tal had

observed so often I did better when I didn't let my emotions control my movements. Tal. At the sheer memory of him—of the knowledge that he was still alive, my heart soared.

The distraction was all Esahbyen needed to sweep me off my feet.

The back of my head connected with the floor hard, pulling me into a dense darkness where sound and sight were non-existent. Drifting into nothingness, a feeling of tranquillity enveloped me, as if dragging me to sleep. It triggered an innate fear—a feeling of pressure on my chest, my lungs burning, my body fighting for air. I regained consciousness with a gasp, blinking against the sudden brightness of the candles.

"Get up," Esahbyen said, nudging me with his foot. "We are not finished."

"My head hurts," I mumbled, rubbing the back of my head.

My fingers touched a warm and sticky substance and came back bloodied. I blinked, staring at ten fingers, of which five looked a little hazy.

"Get. Up."

"I... I'm not su—," I began.

"Get up!" he roared and attacked.

I was barely able to roll out of the way and onto my feet, swaying where I stood. I blinked against the double vision, bringing my arms up just in time to block a punch aimed for my nose. Something told me getting hit in the face now could just be the end of me.

"Attack!"

"I can't," I gasped, trying to focus on him. "There's two of you."

"Pick one," he offered snidely and attacked again.

His foot connected with my ribs, sending me flying to my back a few feet away. A grunt escaped my lips when I landed, my hands grasping my ribs while doubling over in pain. Anger built up inside of me, starting like a rumble deep down while slowly rising to a crescendo. Stars burst into view and the dual vision turned the world lopsided. My arms and legs were trembling as if they could barely keep me upright, but I knew it wouldn't matter if I could or couldn't. He'd attack, again and again and again, until I learned whatever lesson he was trying to teach me.

Weighing my options, I knew that as soon as I rose, he'd either sweep me off my feet, or get me into some kind of lock. I had to surprise him, but how did you surprise the God of War while there were two of them? I wasn't even sure which one to target.

Trust your instincts.

How often had Tal not told me that? How often had he not harped on me to listen to my gut rather than trust my eyes? Esahbyen had said something similar but in much less words. Without a second thought, I rose and kicked my leg upwards, going for the groin. Esahbyen caught my foot and twisted it, forcing me down to the ground, drawing out a yelp of pain.

"Get up," he ordered.

There was nothing left of the amiable God with his mischievous grins and twinkling eyes.

Well, what did you expect from the God of War?

Pushing myself to hands and knees, I grimaced at the pain flaring in my ankle. Somehow, I still managed to keep my temper in check, but it wouldn't be long before I gave in—or out. Any time now, I was sure I'd fall over and not get up. A sudden pain bloomed in my stomach and I fell over, staring up wide-eyed at Esahbyen as he placed his foot on my chest, lips set in a thin line.

"You are dead."

"I wish I was," I grunted and grimaced.

"Is this a joke to you?"

"It stopped being a joke a long time ago," I muttered. "I can't go on. My head's spinning and my vision's unfocused. Why did you make me go on?"

He squatted next to me, hands folded in his lap. "Why do you think?"

"Because the enemy won't stop either," I replied. "They'll keep going until I'm dead."

"Exactly." A smile tugged at his lips. "I am glad to see someone got some sense into you."

I snorted in derision, glaring at him. "How long will this be going on for? And what is the point if I'm going to be added to Elay's collection anyway?"

Esahbyen just smiled, getting that faraway look he always did when he wasn't allowed to answer something.

Allowed or just doesn't want to?

"You know what would be great right about now?" I muttered, rubbing my chest. "A hot bath."

"Who says we are finished?"

I groaned aloud. "But I can hardly stand on my feet!"

"You are making assumptions, *Tarien*," he said with a lazy grin, rising to his feet. "Fighting is not the only thing I do."

"Could have fooled me."

He helped me to my feet, quite carefully too, and guided me to a seat farther down the cave. The biggest surprise of all came when Esahbyen went to prepare tea over the fire, much in the same way I had days before. I took the moment to observe him. In favour of fighting, he'd taken off his overcoat, and was now dressed in a simple tunic and pants common in these parts of Zihrin, looking as if he'd just stepped out of his bedroom—all refreshed. Unlike mine, his shirt didn't cling to his body, and his hair appeared as dry as when he'd started.

Must be terrific being a God.

The thought stopped me short. After my encounter with him at *Hanyarah*, I'd believed him a figment of my imagination, but now, after having spent more time with him than was normal for a mortal—of that I was sure—I had finally started to believe he was who he claimed to be. In hindsight, I had to admit that the things that had happened, the things he had claimed to have done and prevented, were outside any range of normality.

A shiver went through me.

"Here." Esahbyen offered me a steaming cup of tea as he sat down next to me. "Looks like you can do with some."

"Thank you," I murmured, taking it.

We sat in companionable silence for a while, sipping tea that was absolutely spot on. Rhana would have loved it. Her disappearance bothered me, but I knew he wouldn't answer the question of where she was—I'd tried before and he had outright ignored me, so instead I focused on my tea, trying to memorise the flavours in the faint hope of being able to recreate it when the time came.

"How long will we stay here?"

He shrugged. "That depends on your definition of time."

I frowned at him over the rim of my cup. "Why do you never give straight answers?"

"Because your narrow mind would not comprehend."

I grumbled. "First you call me ugly, and now you call me dumb? Friendliness wasn't part of the job description?"

A deep timbre sound echoed off the walls when he laughed, and the mischievous twinkle was back in his eyes. I exhaled deeply, closed my eyes and counted to ten.

"You're neither ugly nor stupid," he said after a while, "but I told you there are things beyond your comprehension, and some things I simply cannot divulge."

"Yes, yes, Godly agreements and all that," I replied, waving my hand in dismissal. "Fine. When am I getting back to wherever I was?"

"You are not."

I frowned. "You've found a way to drop me off in Ilvanna?"

At that, he snorted. "If it were as easy as all that, do you not think I would have whisked away your aunt?"

"Now that would be helpful." My lips tugged up in a faint smile, remembering Rhana's words. "Is it true Azra has been a Kyrinthan Queen?"

Esahbyen nodded. "Yes, but it is something you need to find out on your own."

A sound of disgust escaped my lips. "I thought you were supposed to help me?"

"Help you, not do it for you."

I sighed and rubbed my temples, wincing at the pain in my face. "You're not making it any easier though. Why don't you just let me go back to Elay and let me figure it out myself? I was doing quite well until you showed up."

"You call thieving doing quite well?" His brows shot up in surprise. "Interesting."

"Fine," I muttered. "I was doing quite well considering the circumstances until that *grissin* murdered my friend."

"He had it coming," Esahbyen remarked drily, "and you did what you had to, which brings me to our next lesson."

I groaned, watching him through bleary eyes. "I'm not sure I have a head for more lessons right now."

"Tough luck. We are running out of time as it is and I am not yet done." He sounded irritated, but I wasn't sure if it was because of me or despite me.

"Fine."

Esahbyen rose to his feet, the rustle of his robe catching my attention. When had he gotten dressed? With a firm shake of my head, I dispelled the thought, remembering he had made a sword and a woman disappear into thin air. Redressing without me noticing was probably the easiest trick in his book.

"One of the things you are going to have to get well at in a short amount of time," he began, looking at me, "is how to play 'the game'."

He used his fingers to emphasise the last two words.

"What game?"

I had an idea of what he was talking about, but he had been so vague in his answers before, I wondered if I could get a clear one out of him now.

He grinned. "The one game you have always hated, *dochtaer*, but one I believe you will be highly proficient at if you put your mind to it."

"Stop calling me that." I scowled at him.

My words fell on deaf ears—Esahbyen continued as if he hadn't heard me. Before, this would have riled me up—now, it only made me roll my eyes. All I had to do was practise this with everything that got under my skin.

"Why do you think I'd be so proficient at it?" I asked.

He flashed me one of those mysterious smiles. "Because it is in your blood, whether you like it or not."

I knew that was all the answer he was going to give me on that. Considering his words about the game, I knew he was right. Rhana had said something to similar effect—I'd have to navigate a court I knew nothing about, and deal with people—women—who'd most likely put a knife in my back before befriending me. On top of that, my aunt was obviously a skilled schemer, so if I hoped to take my throne back one day, I had to outsmart her.

"I'm listening," I said at length, making myself comfortable.

"Finally."

WHEN HE BEGAN SPEAKING, I focused on his words, but I soon found that the tone of his voice along with the cadence of his speech lulled me into that state where I wasn't sure whether I was awake or dreaming. All I knew was that my answers were either so automatic they didn't register, or I'd lost my ability to speak entirely. Either way, Esahbyen went on, weaving a scene with his words that made me feel as if I were there.

"Watch," he said, his voice distant, commanding. "Listen."

My eyes were drawn to two women navigating corridors I didn't recognise, but their richly colourful dresses marked them as Zihrin, without a doubt. One of them was a younger woman I thought I'd seen before, the other—her face still as smooth as a baby's—was older, and they moved with purpose. Their words came to me from a distance—heavy and distorted, as if I were under water, but I could make out what they were talking about.

"He's not been himself for weeks, Jahla," the younger woman said. "He has spent all this time locked up in his office, not allowing anyone in or out. Can you believe he's refused me to share his bed?"

"Really?" the other woman asked. "I had no idea..."

"Don't listen to their words alone." Esahbyen's voice came from far away. *"Listen to the intonation, the lilt and drop of their voices. Listen to what they're not saying and always, always watch their body language."*

My eyes drifted over to the older woman.

"I feel like I've done something wrong," the young woman said with a sigh. "It feels like I'm losing him."

"Of course you're not," Jahla replied, her voice even, uncaring. "He's just a busy man, that's all."

The older woman didn't even make a move to comfort the younger one, who looked genuinely distressed at the thought of this man not paying attention. I had the vague sensation I knew who they were talking about, but I pushed the thought away quickly.

"If you'll excuse me," Jahla said, posture rigid. "I have some things to attend to."

As the younger woman nodded, the scene around us shifted and focused as the older woman turned down a different corridor. When she was halfway, a shadow disconnected itself from the walls, turning into a short, wiry man. His shoulders were hunched as if he was carrying a heavy burden.

"I need you to do something for me," the older lady said, voice cold and full of hatred.

"Anything, *amisha*." The man's voice was oily—slick, obviously used to grovelling before someone higher in rank.

I'd heard it often enough myself, but I'd never paid attention to it then. I'd simply ignored it.

"I need you to poison that girl," she said in an off-hand manner. "Slowly, of course. He cannot suspect anything."

The man bowed deeply. "Of course, *amisha*. Anything you desire."

When he scuttled away, the scene swirled and slowly dissipated, making way for the cavern and Esahbyen. I gasped as if I came up for air and blinked against the sudden lack of bright light.

"This happens everywhere," Esahbyen said, his voice coming from right next to me. "In every court all over the world. People will do anything to gain or keep power."

"She," I began, running a hand through my hair. "She sounded so… heartless."

"How do you think powerful people keep their power?" he asked, looking at me.

"By being relentless?"

He gave me a pointed stare. "Was your mother relentless?"

"No, I don't th—," I began and fell silent. "What do you mean, was?"

"She passed away, *dochtaer*," he said with remorse. "A few weeks ago."

I swallowed hard. "All right…"

Esahbyen watched me, a sorrowful expression in his eyes. He looked like he was about to say more, thought the better of it, and shook his head.

"Your mother was not relentless," he said, "but she did what had to be done."

"Then why didn't she kill my aunt before it all got out of hand?" I asked, anger lacing my words.

Biting my lip, I watched him. Mother was dead because of Azra. I was stranded here in the middle of a *nohro* desert because of her, and Ilvanna was under the rule of a woman I now knew did not have them at heart.

He kept his lips firmly shut. Another question he couldn't, or wasn't allowed to answer.

"Why did Azra do it?" I asked at length. "Why did she want the throne so badly?"

"Because—" He fell silent, brows furrowing in thought. "Because it was her birthright after their eldest sister died."

I blinked. "What eldest sister?"

"That, *dochtaer,* is a piece of history you will have to learn by yourself," he said, a faint smile on his lips. "Not because I do not want to tell you, but because you would not believe me if I did. Find out the truth for yourself, and in it, find what you need to defeat your aunt."

I pinched the bridge of my nose. "And how do you propose I do that?"

A distant look stole over him as I asked my question, almost as if his attention was elsewhere. When he snapped back, he looked at me, sadness crossing his eyes.

"Our time is almost up," he said after a while. "I have taught you as much as I can. The rest is up to you."

I just nodded, draining my cup.

"So, what will happen next?" I asked.

"I do not know."

A part of me was desperate to ask why, but judging by the dark look on his face, I knew I wasn't going to get answers—no straight ones anyway. When he rose to his feet, so did I and all of a sudden, my nerves strung tight like a coil. There was a finality in the way he stood that told me the end had come a lot sooner than I'd expected.

"We will meet again, Shalitha," he said, the tender smile on his face at odds with everything that he was. "Until then, try to stay alive?"

I snorted. "But of course..."

The moment he disappeared, so did everything else and I blacked out. There was a sense of falling, as if I'd been dropped out of the sky, but not a stop—not one I expected anyway.

CHAPTER 21

TALNOVAR

Much to Azra's displeasure, Ione took well over three weeks to finish her *Araîth,* and she was unapologetic about it, even when Azra threatened to have her killed. Every time, Ione had looked at her as if the threat was a mere insult—or she just didn't care. I hadn't been able to figure that out yet.

Every day since that day in the throne room, I'd been forced to watch Ione work, and every night, Azra made me take her to her bed. I felt dirty—dirtier than I could put into words, but if I didn't comply, she'd hurt Father. According to Soren, the damage he had sustained put him at great risk already. Any more severe damage, and Father wouldn't live through it. I suspected Azra knew this because she kept hinting at what a shame it would be if I'd lose him too.

One day.

"Are you ready?" Ione asked.

The hard wood of the table prodded in my hip uncomfortably and I was nowhere near ready, but this was happening, whether I liked it or not. It wasn't the first time an *Araîtiste* worked on my body, but it would be the last time. The fact it would be Azra's design on there instead of Shal's hurt more than Ione's needle did the first time she tapped into my skin.

I grimaced, but no more.

Under normal circumstances, this would have been done during the *Araîthin,* a party in celebration of the *Tarien* presumed ready to take the throne. But these circumstances weren't normal, and this *Tarien* was well past the age of a party like that. My gaze shifted to where she was seated in the windowsill, knees drawn up, eyes on something outside. Her dark red hair cascaded over her shoulder like a river of blood, setting off the ivory of her skin. I'd never much cared for women dyeing their hair, but the an Ilvan family had a way of pulling it off.

A hiss escaped my lips when Ione tapped into a particularly nasty spot on my hip, sending an involuntary jolt through me.

"Lie still," she murmured. "Else you'll have some sketchy lines."

"They'll be sketchy no matter what," I muttered. "No offense, but I will never love this piece you're creating."

"We'll see," she mused quietly, a secretive smile playing around her lips.

I grimaced, but thought it wiser not to comment. Closing my eyes, I focused on anything but the persistent sting in my body. From experience, I knew it was only going to get worse. Surprisingly, the rhythmic sound of Ione's craft almost lulled me to sleep, and a part of me wanted to give in.

The Gods knew I could do with some.

Between Cehyan and *sehvelle,* falling asleep wasn't the problem, but every time I closed my eyes, nightmares awaited to pull me into their dark abyss of pain and loss and guilt. Each night, I woke bathing in sweat. Each night, I experienced the moment that sword went through me.

I couldn't fall asleep now.

So instead I focused my eyes on Azra, allowing hatred to

course through me—allowed it to fuel my anger, my loathing for that woman. Perhaps she had won this match, but she couldn't win all of them. As if on cue, she turned and looked straight at me, dark eyes swirling with hurt and sadness.

I stilled.

They were emotions I'd never seen on her, and for a brief moment, I felt sorry for her, until I remembered what she had done, and all compassion scattered in the four directions of the wind. Looking away, I focused on Ione instead, watching her brow furrow in thought as she bent over her handiwork, dabbing away blood and ink with a cloth. When our eyes met, she smiled, excitement flashing in her eyes.

I had no idea what she could possibly be excited about.

"How are you holding up?" she asked as she continued. "Not too much pain?"

"No, it's fine."

"Good."

Even our conversation felt forced. A rustle drew my attention, and casting a furtive glance at the window, I found Azra had left her perch. She was close now, standing next to Ione to watch her progress. My eyes trailed the *Araîth* coiling delicately from her neck, over her jaw, disappearing into her hairline. It gradually went from the darkest black in her neck, to a light grey just above her elongated ear.

If anything, Ione knew her craft.

"Keep up the good work," Azra said, her eyes roving over me. "I have some matters of state to attend to. There are guards at the door, so don't even think about doing anything funny."

We both nodded and watched her leave in trepidation. The moment the door closed behind her, we both exhaled deeply, as if we'd been holding our breath.

"Finally," Ione muttered. "I thought she'd never leave."

"I'm surprised she did."

"I can do with a break," she said, sitting back. "Do you mind?"

I shook my head. "No, not at all. I can't say I'm very comfortable here either."

"I can imagine."

Stiffly, I slid off the table and stretched my back, wincing at the stinging sensation in my side. Ione sat down in her chair, closing her eyes.

"What happened?" I asked at length.

"What do you mean?"

"When they caught you," I said. "What happened?"

Ione opened both her eyes, and stifled a yawn, rubbing her temples. The look on her face turned stony.

"They caught up with us much sooner than expected," she said, "much sooner than they should have. Almost as if"—she shook her head as if in denial— "as if they knew that we'd gone and where we had gone."

I frowned but said nothing.

"They'd been ordered to kill Mehrean," she continued, her voice soft, strained, "and return me to the palace."

"What happened to her?"

She shook her head, looking up apologetically. "I don't know. Haerlyon took her away from the rest of us. When he returned..."

Ione stuck her hands between her knees, rocking back and forth, tears brimming her eyes. When next she spoke, her voice was constricted with unshed tears.

"When he returned," she whispered, "he was covered in blood. The grin on his face... I'm sorry, Tal."

I tensed upon her words, trying to reconcile the image she was painting with the Haerlyon I knew, and coming up empty. Despite my efforts, I couldn't. No matter how I twisted or turned it in my mind, I could not believe Haerlyon was capable of something like that. He may have had his shortcomings, but I doubted he'd kill a long-time friend like that.

"I'm sorry," I said, meaning it.

I didn't know what else to say.

Ione shook her head and looked up, tears gone, determination set on her face. "Let's continue before that *hehzèh* returns."

After I'd taken my place on the table, Ione continued her work, tapping relentlessly into my skin until it became too much and she had to stop. While I struggled to pull my shirt over my head, Ione set to cleaning her materials.

Neither of us spoke.

"It's not your fault," I said at length, looking at her.

"I know."

Her tone of voice told me something else, but seeing the look on her face, I didn't push it.

"Same time tomorrow?" I asked.

"I guess."

Although Azra hadn't yet returned, I left the room, not wishing to be there any longer than I had to. Looking down at my hands, I noticed a severe tremble, and my nerves were strung tight—too tight. My body screamed for release, for a time out, so when I slipped into my room and found Cehyan lounging on the bed, taking a long drag from the *sehvelle* pipe, all thoughts and worries ceased to exist.

At least for the time being.

"SHE DOES KNOW what she's doing," Cehyan murmured, trailing her fingers over the abrasions on my hip and side. "It looks amazing."

Shivers chased each other down my spine until I could take no more and grabbed her hand, kissing her knuckles gently.

"Shame it's Azra's design." My words came out in a guttural growl that made Cehyan wince.

"I'm sorry." I pulled her close and nuzzled her neck. "I didn't mean to growl at you."

"It's all right," she replied, a faint smile ghosting on her lips. "I know it wasn't meant for me. There's just somet—"

She snapped her mouth shut and looked away.

"What?"

"Nothing," she replied. "It's nothing."

I raised an eyebrow. "That didn't sound like nothing."

"Sorry," she said, placing a kiss on my lips. "I lost my train of thought—that's why I stopped. Honestly, it was nothing."

The urgency in her next kiss melted my resolve, and I wrapped my arms around her, pulling her in for a deeper kiss, nestling my leg between hers. She hooked her foot behind my calf and pulled herself flush against me. My breath hitched, and I growled against her lips this time for entirely different reasons. This round, we were gentler with each other, savouring each kiss, each touch, until we were both completely oblivious.

EACH MORNING, I was expected to report to Azra's room where Ione would be waiting. Azra would sit with us for an hour, maybe two, before she decided she had had enough. Before she left, she'd cast a cursory glance at Ione's progress, nod to herself, and leave with the announcement she'd be back in a few hours. Most of the time, Ione made sure she was finished well before then, even if I could still go on a while longer. To my surprise, Azra didn't seem to care at all that she did, or that I'd left her room by the time she returned.

In those nine days, she never once commented on it.

"What aren't you telling me?" I asked at some point on the tenth day, grimacing as Ione hit a spot just on my shoulder.

I was glad for the chance of sitting up.

"I'm not sure I follow," Ione replied.

"Don't take me for a *khirr*, Ione," I muttered. "You've been stopping much sooner than necessary lately, making sure we're finished well before she returns. Why?"

She tapped into my skin—hard. I bit back a yelp, certain she'd done it on purpose. My glowering at her didn't perturb her at all.

"You'll see why when I finish," she said after a while. "The less you know, the better."

I frowned. "I hate being kept in the dark."

"That's your problem."

When did she get this cheeky?

"How long do you think you need?" I asked, honestly interested.

She looked at me then, a thoughtful expression on her face as if deciding whether she should tell me or not. A dark look appeared in her eyes, but it was gone quickly enough for me to start doubting my own sanity.

"Two, maybe three days." Her voice was soft when she spoke.

It sounded as if there was more to it, but I chalked it up to concentration and decided to leave it be for now.

As time wore on, I noticed the slight tremor in my body, and I cursed myself silently. Ione noticed it too—I could tell from her annoyed sighs as one ran through me.

"Do I need to stop?" she asked. "If those tremors get more severe..."

"It's fine," I hissed through my teeth. "Just an annoying spot you're working on."

It was clear she didn't believe me if the look on her face was any indication, but she didn't push the issue. At least, not until a heavy tremor went through me again, and she tapped her needle in far deeper than she should have. I cursed. She cursed and whacked me on the back of my head with the flat of her hand.

"*Khirr!*" she shouted, hitting me on the shoulder for good measure before pulling the needle out of my upper arm.

"Apologies, *Irà*," I muttered, wincing.

"Ugh, don't *Irà* me." She scowled, inspecting the skin on my arm where the needle had gone in. "I should've stopped after that first tremor."

With a shake of her head, she pushed and prodded the skin until blood appeared from the injury. I ground my teeth. The previous time, I'd been given a full on explanation what could happen if ink went in too deep, which was why I had to sit very still and tell the *Araîtiste* when to stop. Mine hadn't been Ione—she was reserved for the royal family—but a man whose name I couldn't remember. He'd been less gentle than Ione had been—less skilled too in my opinion, but he had gotten the job done. My *Araîth* didn't look bad at all, but Ione certainly did a better job of it.

"All right, well." She sighed. "That's our session for today. If you experience sudden high fever, sweats, chills or shaking, go see Soren and tell him what happened. I'll pray to the Gods and Goddesses you got lucky, or I won't be able to finish it within the next two to three days."

I nodded as I rose to my feet, snatching my shirt from the back of the chair. While struggling into it, I made my way out of the room and back to my bedroom. The craving was enough to push all rationale aside, but not the feelings. I loathed myself for everything I was doing—to myself, to others. Guilt ate me from the inside, but now that I had started again, I found it was a lot harder to stop than before.

Cehyan wasn't in my room when I returned, but she'd mercifully left me enough *sehvelle* to get me through the rest of the day and night. Disgust nestled in my gut as I sat down on the bed and started preparing the pipe. If Father found out…

Don't let him find out.

The moment I settled on the bed, a sound alerted me.

"Old habits die hard, I see," a familiar voice I couldn't quite place said. "Cehyan told me you were back at it."

I groaned. "What are you doing here, Ruvaen?"

CHAPTER 22

SHALITHA

By the time I came around, my throat was parched beyond a dryness I wasn't sure even water could solve. Holding my hand over my eyes, I blinked against the dark red of the sunrise staring me in the face, trying to make out my surroundings. As far as the eye could see, there was nothing. Nothing except the vast expanse of the desert stretching in every direction. Sand dervishes danced across the empty space as if they owned the place, and I realised with a sinking feeling I was completely and utterly lost.

Trust your instincts.

The voice echoed in my mind like a memory, yet I couldn't shake the feeling of being watched. Wherever Esahbyen had gone, he was no longer in this realm, but he still felt close.

Finally, a believer, are you?

I wasn't sure if that was him, or just my inner voice, but it wasn't wrong. Esahbyen was real, and if he was, I had no doubt the other Gods and Goddesses were too. Rising to my feet, I wrapped my arms around myself, and spun around and around to find any marker, any indication of where I was. Hopelessness settled within me when I realised I had no idea where to go.

I was going to die out here.

"No, you're not," I chided myself. "You didn't survive a shipwreck just to die out here in this *nohro* sandbox. Pick up your feet, choose a direction and move that sweet ass a little faster."

I tried to imitate Tal's voice on the last words, but they didn't come close to the real deal. It did make me chuckle. He would have said it like that and probably admired the view once I got on my way.

Huh, no wonder he liked walking behind me.

The thought was ridiculous, but it served as a distraction to keep my mind off the horrible truth of Elay's warning the night he had brought me to the training camp. If one got caught in the desert at night without proper equipment, one would die. I didn't have any equipment on me, although it wasn't yet night.

Stop thinking that way. Stop thinking at all.

I put one foot in front of the other and started moving in the direction of the rising sun. It was as good a place to go as any.

After hours on my feet, I needed a rest. My body was still aching from the beating Esahbyen had given me, and the need for water was high. Every step had turned into agony until I could bear it no more and sank to my knees where I stood. I watched the sun's progress through the sky, willing my tired body to get up, to place one foot in front of the other and move, but my limbs were unwilling to cooperate. Silent tears trickled down my cheeks.

Try to stay alive.

And I had made him promise not to try to save me again.

Pulling from deep within, I managed to get myself to my feet and start walking. If I stayed down, I would surely die, and I wasn't ready to give up. Not yet. I turned my thoughts to Tal, to our training sessions back at the palace, trying to remember what he would tell me whenever I was ready to give up. Right now, trudging through sand, I missed him more than ever. My chest tightened as my stomach twisted itself into a knot. If I had

had any left, tears would've brimmed my eyes, but I was too dehydrated for that. All I wanted was him to tell me everything would be fine. All I wanted was to feel his arms around me, inhale his scent, hear his heartbeat, and know everything was all right with the world.

He won't always be there. You will be entirely alone at times, and then what? Trust in yourself, and you'll get there.

If it was my inner voice talking to me, I commended it for its wisdom, but cursed it for its lack of encouragement.

By the time the sun was well on its way to disappearing on the horizon, the pain in my legs was so intense I wasn't even sure they were still attached. Cramps had seized my calves a long time ago, and every step was a challenge not to collapse to the ground. Inhaling felt like sucking in air through a reed, and my throat was the equivalent of sandpaper. Tremors had overtaken my body miles ago, and I knew I was on the brink of shutting down.

Up ahead, in the dim light of the setting sun the outline of buildings—black against the vivid orange palette of the sky—became visible and my heart soared. If I could see it from here, it meant I could get there. All I had to do was put one foot in front of the other and keep on pushing. It sounded easy enough, until the world began to spin and went off-kilter.

The last thing I remembered was a mouth full of sand before I passed out.

"Over here!"

The voice came to me through a fog. It sounded strange—foreign, and it took me a while to grasp that whoever it was had spoken in Zihrin.

I tried to open my eyes, but they were kept shut by something. When I tried to move, my body protested. Speaking wasn't amongst my abilities either. Just when I thought it couldn't get any worse, spasms ran through my body.

"*Mìthri*!"

This voice *was* familiar, and it couldn't have come at a better time.

"Elay?"

My voice was a croak, no more, and I doubted he'd even heard me. Something warm was wrapped around me as somebody settled behind me, keeping me upright so I didn't have to do it myself. A cup was placed against my lips.

"Take a few sips, no more," Elay ordered, his voice close to my ear. "You'll get sick otherwise."

I obeyed, but only because I was too tired to do anything else. The first sip came out almost immediately, trickling down the corners of my mouth and onto my neck. The second sip fared better, but it was barely enough to coat the inside of my mouth when the cup was taken away again.

"More, please?" my voice was barely a whisper.

"Not yet," Elay murmured, wrapping his arms around me. "Let's get you to safety first."

Weightless, as if I were floating in water—that's how I felt when I was lifted from the ground. Voices murmured overhead, but they were too soft and too fast for me to follow, tired as I was. I was shifted from one person to the next, and Elay's scent wrapped around my senses almost immediately. He held me close to him, resting my head against his shoulder. I heard the click of his tongue, felt the jolt and lurch underneath me, and then the gentle sway I knew belonged to a *camelle*.

"Let's get you home, *mìthri*." His voice held notes of worry. "I'll keep you safe."

It occurred to me he had promised that before, and he'd taken me to that camp anyway. My mind chased one thought with the other, but they were gone before I could grasp them. My feelings were a jumbled mess, tumbling over one another to be recognised, but the only one that prevailed was a feeling of safety. Whatever else happened, I was safe—for now.

"Where have you been?"

Elay kept repeating the question, but more to himself than to me. I wasn't able to string two words together, let alone an entire sentence. I don't think he expected me to answer. To my surprise, he pulled me closer to his chest, keeping his protective arms around me. It was almost as if he actually cared about me.

I pried my eyes open, wincing at the sudden light. Elay was watching me, concern etched on his handsome face, lines creasing his brow and eyes. His lips lifted into a gentle smile when I managed to keep one eye open.

"Hello there," he murmured. "Take it easy."

I nodded carefully and quickly stopped when my vision began to swim and the world began to lurch sideways. Elay tensed beneath me.

"We'll get you back on your feet," he said, again more to himself than to me, "and then we'll have to see about our arrangements."

"You promised to protect me," I murmured.

He stilled first, then shifted his weight a little, and I felt muscles bunch beneath me. Heat crept up my neck and nestled on my cheeks.

"I did promise," he said in a tense voice. "And I failed you. I'm sorry."

I began to shake my head and stopped.

"It's all right," I whispered. "I'm sure you had your reasons."

"Maybe," he replied, "but any explanation pales in comparison to the amount of apologies I owe you…"

He looked as if he was ready to say more, his face scrunched up in thought, but he wasn't forthcoming. Instead, he looked away and up. Relief washed over him and a smile softened his features.

"We're almost there."

By the time we arrived at the *k'ynshan,* Elay's palace, an entire crowd had gathered behind us. By then, the fogginess in my brain had turned into a deep aching throb throughout my skull. Even the smallest movement made my vision tilt and my stomach lurch, which was why I kept my eyes closed when Elay stepped off the *camelle* and carried me inside.

"Fetch the healer. Bring hot water. Soap. Everything."

He barked his commands in short order. The patter of feet on the tiled floors indicated people scurrying about.

"Must be great to have people listen to you," I murmured, my voice heavy with sleep. "Wish mi—"

Elay shut me up by placing the softest of kisses on my lips, murmuring against them. "Stop speaking, *amisha*. This is not the time nor the place."

A deep blush coloured my cheeks—at least, I imagined it did because they felt hot even without touching. I gulped and closed my eyes, not wanting to look at him. The only kisses I'd ever shared had been with Tal, and him I'd known. I felt rather than heard the chuckle from Elay, but he made no comment.

"Let's have you looked at first," he said and carefully placed me down on a soft surface.

I cracked one eye open just as it dipped and I found him sitting next to me, worry back on his face.

"I'll send someone to help you undress," he said, rubbing a hand over his short-cropped hair. "The healer should be here soon. Do you mind if I stay?"

"For the undressing?" I managed.

He snorted. "For the healer's assessment."

"No, that's fine."

At that he nodded and rose to his feet. "I'll send Ymahra to help you."

All I could do was nod. Closing my eyes, I listened to his slippers clicking on the floor as he left the room. It served to lull me back to sleep, but just before I did, a hand on my shoulder startled me. My eyes flew open and I stared at the girl from my vision wide-eyed. Startled amber eyes watched me warily, as I expected I did her. Black curly hair, tucked behind long ears, cascaded down her back. Each ear was adorned with at least a dozen small golden hoops,

"I'm sorry," she murmured. "Elay told me to help you..."

I nodded.

Her eyes never quite assumed their normal shape throughout the process of undressing me. The more skin she exposed, the wider they became, until they were as round as the sun. By the time we finished, all I had on me was a short skirt around my waist to keep a sense of decency.

"What happened?" Ymahra whispered, eyes scouring my body.

I shrugged, keeping my mouth shut. Instead, I watched her from under my lashes, inspecting the girl I'd seen in the vision Esahbyen had given me. In a way, she reminded me of Caleena, except that Ymahra seemed less frightened. Shy, I could understand, but she wasn't fearful.

"I'll go get Elay," she said resolutely, squaring her shoulders.

I nodded and closed my eyes again. All I wanted was for this headache to go away, and I honestly wouldn't mind soaking in that pool I knew Elay had. Perhaps, after the healer's inspection, I could ask him to take me there.

As voices entered my room, I opened my eyes, turning my head to watch Elay and an older man come inside. I couldn't tear my gaze away from the latter. Grey hair lay braided across his shoulder, reaching halfway down his chest, but while that was a beautiful asset on his own, it was his skin that kept my eyes on him. It was dark, darker than Elay's copper tone—a rich brown the likes of which I'd never seen before. His ears were his most prominent feature. They were shorter than either mine or Elay's, but still ended in a sharp tip.

"Good afternoon, *amisha,*" the man said. "The *Akynshan's*

asked me to have a look at your injuries and assess the damage your time out in the sun has done."

I nodded, my gaze flicking over to Elay.

He was standing on the other side of the bed, eyes guarded and face neutral, yet from the tension in his jaw, I could tell he was anything but pleased. I stiffened as the healer pulled down the sheets and winced at the sudden movement. Esahbyen had to have bruised my ribs during one of our fights.

"You've got quite the colourful look," the healer said just before he began prodding the bruises on my face.

I yelped.

"Judging by the discolouration on her face," the healer observed, "this happened over a week ago, maybe even more."

A week?

"*Amisha*," the healer began, drawing my attention back. "Could I have a look at your ribs please? You can cover up, of course."

I crossed my arms in front of my chest, tensing as the sheets slid down to my waist. Elay cursed in his musical language. The healer kept on his stoic examination, running his fingers down my ribs, drawing out a groan of pain. He could have done it with a knife, it hurt that much.

"*Amisha*," the healer said, looking worried now. "Do you mind telling what happened?"

I shrugged and winced. "I… I'm not sure."

I doubt they'll believe me if I tell them I've spent time with the God of War.

He nodded but didn't comment. I wasn't sure he believed me, and looking aside, I knew for a fact Elay definitely didn't, but I wouldn't give them the truth. I had to come up with a believable lie and fast. Throughout the healer's examination, my mind worked overtime to come up with a story, but the more he prodded, the more painful everything became, until I could take no more and begged him to stop.

On Elay's command, he did.

"Well," the man said, "I don't think anything's broken, although I'm not sure about her ribs. They could be fractured, but the rest is just bruising. It will fade. Make sure she drinks enough in the next few days, but don't overdo it. You know how it works, *Akynshan.*"

Elay nodded, lips pressed together in a thin line.

"Thank you, *mishan,*" Elay murmured, dropping a pouch into his hand.

It jingled with coins.

The man bowed deeply, murmured something about it being a pleasure, and left the room in haste. I watched Elay as he sat down on the bed next to me, pulling the sheets up to my shoulders.

"I hope," he said, looking at me, "that in due time, you will trust me enough to tell me what happened. For now, you need to heal."

"Can I have something to drink?" I asked in a soft voice. "I need this pounding in my head to stop."

Elay nodded and got up. I watched as he poured two cups of tea and carried them back to the bed. Looking around, I realised we were in his room. With a grunt, I tried to sit up, but I couldn't do it on my own. Before I could ask Elay, he had propped up pillows behind me and helped me sit up against them.

"You're a resilient woman," he said after a while. "I'll give you that."

"I practically grew up on the training fields," I replied. "I'm no stranger to bruises, cracked ribs or even broken bones."

"Or scars," he murmured, his eyes trailing the one going down between my collarbones.

I smiled faintly. "Long story."

"Oh, I have no doubt of that," he said, handing me the cup. "But we have time, if you wish to tell me."

“Maybe someday.”

He smiled at that and took a sip of his cup. “I can live with that.”

The undertone in his voice suggested curiosity more than anything else, but he’d have to wait for that to be satisfied. Steadying my hands around the cup, I took a careful sip, forcing my thoughts in line.

“Now what?” I asked at length.

Elay’s lips quirked up in a one-sided smirk. “Now the game begins.”

CHAPTER 23

TALNOVAR

"What are you doing here?" I repeated, setting the pipe aside.

Ruvaen made himself comfortable in the only chair I kept in my bedroom. Annoyance rolled over me, but instead of hitting him, I sat back, regarding him quietly. His slick black hair was combed back in a ponytail, highlighting elongated ears and a handsome face—so Cehyan had told me many times before in the past. To me, he looked like any other guy in the city. Ruvaen's eyes were on me, accompanied by a scowl on his face.

"You look like crap, Imradien," he said, scrunching up his nose. "What's happened to you?"

I picked up the pipe, casting him a foul look. "That *hehzèh* has."

"Who, Cehy?"

"No, the *Tari*." I all but spat out the last word, my dislike and general disgust towards the woman tangible through that one word.

Ruvaen nodded. "Yeah, I get you…"

"Do you?" I muttered. "Everyone else thinks I'm working with her."

"Nobody in their right mind would do that." Ruvaen ran a hand over his hair, carefully, as not to upset it, his eyes turning dark and brooding. "In the city… you've no idea, Tal. The slums are worse than ever—even the second circle…" He shook his head, clasping his hands between his knees. "That's why I'm here."

I watched him, rapping my fingers on my thigh. "I'm not sure I follow."

"I came to warn you," he said, his voice low. "There will be an assault on the palace."

My hands stilled their progress of filling the pipe, and I almost dropped it to the floor.

I stared at him. "What?"

"You heard me," he murmured. "There'll be an attack, Tal. You have to make sure you're nowhere inside—people will kill you for… for what happened in the streets."

"I was fighting on their side!" I started yelling, thought the better of it, and finished my sentence in an angry hiss. "I was fighting on *your* side, not hers, but she,"—I raked my hands through my hair in anger— "twisted it to benefit her. I never… I would never…"

"I know," Ruvaen replied, one side of his lips pulling up in a wry smile, "but they don't, Tal."

"What about the others?" I asked, breathing in deeply. "What about Evan, Nathaïr, Soren? They're innocent in all this…"

"Don't worry about them," he replied, glancing at the door. "I came to warn *you, mahnèh.* There's more going on than you think, and you're not in a good position right now."

"When?"

"Soon. Watch for the signs," Ruvaen said, rising to his feet. "Make yourself scarce as soon as it begins. I'm sure you know a place."

I merely nodded, contemplating his words. An uncomfortable feeling gnawed at me, but I wasn't sure what it was. Probably the warning Ruvaen had just given me—no more.

"Vaen," I called out as he made to leave.

He stopped, his hand hovering above the doorknob. "Yeah?"

"Be careful."

He flashed me a smile, which never reached his eyes, and slipped out of my room. His warning kept replaying in my mind —there would be an attack on the palace. Soon, everything she was putting me through would be over. Ruvaen had told me, all but ordered me, to stay out of sight—he hadn't even asked me to put up a fight. No, he had been afraid I would get killed.

And what if they do it? At least this misery will be over.

Without a second thought, I picked up the pipe, lit it and put it to my lips. If I was going to be morose, I might as well do it feeling relaxed. I couldn't believe Ruvaen hadn't even asked me to fight on their side, and it occurred to me it had been a courtesy on his part to warn me at all.

Nohro ahrae, what's happening to me? Shal would never have allowed this...she wouldn't have indulged me. Snap out of it, khirr. If she ever finds out about this.

With a shake of my head, I dispelled the thoughts that usually occurred after the what ifs, and instead tried to focus on her face—how her brow creased in concentration, how she bit her lip when she was nervous, or the twinkle in her eyes when she was alive with mischief. I thought of the first kiss we'd shared—a kiss full of pain and need and desire. A kiss unlike any I'd ever shared with a woman.

I swallowed hard as memories flooded my mind.

How often had I not ended up chasing after her during one of our training sessions? I stilled at the faint memory of her pinned underneath me—of sharing a breath, which I'd deemed entirely inappropriate.

Propriety be damned, Tal.

The memories made me cringe and added to the guilt more than they put me at ease, but in a way, they served as a lifeline. They weren't enough to fade out the more recent memories—memories of bloodshed and carnage, of mindless butchering and blackmailing. Just the merest hint at a thought of Azra turned my blood cold and made my skin crawl, eliciting an endless loop of shivers that never quite went away.

Azra.

For some reason, she'd taken a liking to me that went beyond vengeance on my father. She enjoyed hurting me—physically and mentally—entirely too much, but even in that she had dimmed. At least a little. Over the past few weeks, she'd grown less impulsive and more considerate, as if she was planning something rather than being controlled by her emotions. It shouldn't have come as a surprise to me that she was capable of plotting, yet somehow, I was.

She's full of surprises, Imradien. Expect the worst.

THE WORST OF her antics became apparent two days after Ruvaen's visit. The atmosphere in the entire palace had gone from its usual beehive tension to an almost palpable presence heavy enough to choke me. Azra made herself scarce, but if she did move about the palace, people scattered to the four winds lest they find themselves in her way. I'd gone through the whole ordeal in a brain fog of my own creation, and life was much more preferable that way. Not even Ione's tapping into my skin bothered me much.

"Tal," Ione hissed, snapping me from my thoughts.

"What?" I murmured, blinking at her.

"Focus," she muttered. "If you keep nodding off like that, I'll add the *nohro* ink to your forehead."

"Apologies." I rubbed my face and straightened my back, squaring my shoulders. "It won't happen again."

"Uh-huh. That's what you said the last four times. What's gotten into you?"

I waved my hand dismissively, glowering at her enough to watch her snap her mouth shut, a pinched expression on her face. Her tapping turned into a rhythmic staccato and she wasn't holding back. I winced at every rap she made and I could feel my scowl deepening.

"Will you stop that?" I growled at length. "You're doing that on purpose."

"If you stop feeling sorry for yourself."

I stared at her, then looked away. "I have no idea what you're talking about."

"Really?" she huffed, arching a brow. "For the past three days, you've been sulking like a petulant toddler who was denied cookies by his mother. Your mood has gone from passably bearable to utterly unbearable, and you keep passing out. And I'm not even going into how you smell."

I winced as though properly chastised and didn't meet her gaze. A part of me feared Ione would look like her—like Shal, and I couldn't bear the thought of Shal looking at me with pity, or worse…

"Just finish the *nohro Araîth*," I murmured, raking a hand through my hair.

By Esahbyen, I stink.

After Ione finished, I would take a bath…

…and drown myself in it.

The thought didn't come as a shock anymore. These days, that one was foremost on my mind, although I didn't quite have the urge to follow up on it. Besides, if I were to believe Ruvaen, all I had to do was stay in sight and have someone else do it for me. It would save me the trouble.

Coward.

"She couldn't wait to show it to you, you know." Ione's voice cut through my miserable reverie like a sharp knife, and I looked up.

"Saw some of it," I muttered. "Before..." I gulped and looked away, balling my fist, my voice low when I spoke again. "Before that son of a *hehzèh* took her from me."

"I'm sorry," she whispered, returning to her work. "I didn't mean to—"

"It's fine," I interjected, clenching my jaw in an attempt to calm down and not make any sudden moves.

"Almost done."

Ione sounded tense, as if she feared what was going to happen once she finished, and looking up, I found the strain apparent on her face. She quickly hid the fear in her eyes behind a mask of sheer determination.

One thing could be said about Ilvannian women—they never backed down.

Unlike some men.

A low growl escaped my lips at the thought, startling Ione. I mumbled an apology and sunk deeper into thought. Everything was messed up, and I couldn't even remember how or when it had all begun. If Rurin was to be believed, this all started well before any of us were born. All of whom were present then were now dead—all except my father, whose betrayal I was paying for.

My anger flared, but I wasn't sure whether it was directed at Azra, or at him.

AFTERNOON WAS WELL on its way when Ione announced she was ready, and not a moment too soon. Azra entered the room by throwing open the door and storming in, eyes wild and furious, but where I'd expected she'd go for either of us, she did not. Someone—or something—had set her off. Ione stilled beside me, watching Azra like a prey would its predator. She was afraid of Azra, as she had every right to be, but there was more.

I just didn't know what.

Azra's eyes slid over to us, her brows arching in surprise as if she'd only just realised we were there. The thunderous mood she'd come in with disappeared like snow under the sun, making way for something far more dangerous—false cordiality.

"How's it coming along?" she asked, sounding almost curious.

"Finished." I replied in an arctic tone. "Thank be the Gods."

"I'm sure they had nothing to do with it," Azra said with a sneer, moving closer. "Get up, let me see."

I remained seated, much to Azra's displeasure.

"Are we doing this again?"

"Did we ever stop?"

The only positive thing that could be said for her was that Azra's presence livened me up without fail. Around her, I thought of killing her rather than myself, even though I knew I couldn't.

"Get up," she hissed, taking a step towards Ione. "You know what happens otherwise."

"*Hehzèh*," I murmured low under my breath, rising slowly to my feet.

Her indrawn gasp was not what I'd expected, nor the outburst that followed moments later. A loud shriek pierced my ears, and next I knew, her nails were digging into my arm.

"What is this supposed to mean!" she yelled, glaring from me at Ione, and back again.

I frowned, unhooking her talons from my biceps one by one. "The *Araîth* you so desperately wanted me to have."

Her lips curled up into a snarl. "How stupid do you think I am?"

"What are you talking about? It's your *Araîth*!"

"It's not."

My head snapped around to stare at Ione wide-eyed and dumbfounded when she replied. In the brief moment Azra and I had been bickering, she'd steeled her resolve, watching me calmly.

"Ione..." my voice came out strangled, "what have you done?"

"The right thing," she replied, her voice wavering slightly, her eyes never leaving me. "I couldn't live with the idea I'd given you the wrong *Araîth*, but I will die happy knowing I've given you the right one."

Azra howled in anger. I blinked at her, unable to fully comprehend the implications of her words.

"I—"

"Your *Araîth* is the *Tarien's*," Ione said, lifting her chin. "In life and in death you shall be known as her *Anahràn*, Talnovar Imradien. Long live the rightful *Tari*."

Tears were trickling down her cheeks now as the fear she'd tried so hard to push aside surfaced in her eyes. In my peripheral vision, I saw Azra raise her hand and I caught the glimmer of something metallic. I jumped forward, grabbed Ione into an embrace, and growled as a dagger grazed my arm.

"Let me go, Tal," Ione whispered in a tight voice. "Let her have me, but promise me you will fight—fight for *her*, fight for the rest of us."

"I promise."

Another promise I might not be able to keep.

"Goodbye, Talnovar. I'm happy to have met you."

I howled when my arms were forced behind my back. Whatever strength she'd had left the moment guards shackled her wrists together and began hauling her out of the room. She was sobbing, praying, begging—anything to keep herself alive, but we both knew Azra would not let this go.

Ione would pay with her life.

"Bring him to the *Tarien's* chambers and lock him in there," Azra ordered, venom lacing her words. "Let him rot there for all I care."

CHAPTER 24

SHALITHA

Dressed up wasn't quite the right description for what Elay's wives had done to me. If I thought my *Araîth* served as beautiful decoration, it had nothing on the dress and the jewellery they had bedecked me with. Staring at the reflection in the mirror, my gaze couldn't settle on anything for too long—there was so much to take in. I brought a hand up to the silver necklace, tracing my fingers along the blue sapphires adorning it. The earrings matched, as did the headdress Zirscha was pinning into my hair.

And then there was the dress itself.

It was something out of fairy tales but nothing as complicated as the multi-layered Ilvannian dresses. Its colour reminded me of the sky in that moment where dusk turns into night, but it's not quite dark yet—and of the lake at the foot of the Ilvan Mountains in the palace yard as it lay glittering in the sunlight. It was deeper—richer—than the sapphires around my neck but equally as stunning, if not more so. Silver stitching ran along the off-shoulder neckline, plunging down to just below my waist where it split in two, matching the lustrous underskirt underneath.

Zihrin people did nothing half-heartedly, especially not their *Harshâh*—weddings.

My chest tightened at the idea of marrying Elay with the knowledge of Tal being still alive. Interesting times would be ahead if those two ever met.

That's a big if indeed.

And worries for later, I chided myself in silence.

Right now, my focus had to be here—in Zihrin, with Elay, and most importantly, this wedding. When Rhana told me I'd need skills in making tea, she hadn't been joking. The moment Elay announced our marriage to his wives, they all demanded to see this ritual performed. Because of my injuries, Elay had been reluctant to let me go through with it, but I had insisted, arguing I didn't want to be favoured over any of his other wives. He seemed to care a lot less about their opinions, but then he didn't have to navigate through their webs of lies and deceit like I would.

If I'd learned anything at court, it was to have friends in the right places.

Zirscha, his first wife, had been impressed with my skills, although she did have some points of improvements she'd discussed with me afterwards. Most of the wives had gone along with her judgment, except for Maram, Elay's last wife. I remembered her from the party—she was the woman who had stomped up to him that night, and he'd made his apologies to me, for her.

It felt like a lifetime ago.

"Don't scrunch up your face like that." Zirscha admonished me. "It will give you lines."

I huffed. "That's the last thing I'm concerned about."

"Being Elay's wife," she said sternly, "you'll have to be at your best behaviour and look your best."

"Sure," I murmured too low for her to hear.

"What was that?"

"Of course, *amisha*," I said out loud, inclining my head to acknowledge her position as first wife.

My skin crawled every time a pleasantry was expected of me. It boggled my mind realising courtiers at our palace did this every day just to gain favours. If it made me want to vomit on both the receiving and giving end, I didn't want to imagine how they must feel. I knew some of them—like Haerlyon—saw it as a challenge, and they did everything they could to perfect it. I did everything to avoid it, not out of disrespect, but because it was a waste of time.

In my opinion.

My situation here at Elay's court was peculiar. Although I'd be his twenty-seventh wife, my rank—despite it being Ilvannian —was higher than theirs. For some reason, Elay held my status in high regard, and demanded this of his wives and staff too.

I am a royal heir after all.

This was why I appreciated Zirscha's direct approach even more, even if she didn't quite uphold to the standards Elay had made clear to them. I hadn't cared about propriety back home— it was too late to start worrying about it now.

"Do you remember what to do?"

I nodded. "More or less. Shouldn't be too difficult, right?"

Zirscha gave me a pointed stare, thin lips pressed tight. "Do not underestimate this, *Tarien*. If anything doesn't go according to tradition, your marriage to Elay will not be valid, and consider where it leaves you then…"

A shudder went through me at her words and I nodded. I did not want to consider the alternative of not marrying Elay. Zirscha, and Maram even more, had been very clear during their detailed lecture on the *Harshâh*. For the most part, I didn't mind their traditions, except for one. My breath caught in my throat at the thought alone and I started clawing at the necklace, desperate to get it off in an attempt to be able to breathe again.

Zirscha caught my hand.

"Calm down. There's nothing wrong." Her voice was gentle. "Remember what to do?"

I nodded.

"Then do it," she said. "Breathe in deeply, exhale slowly. It's not hard. Nothing's going to happen."

"You call this nothing?" I rocked on the balls of my feet, pointing at myself to highlight the extravagant look on me.

Zirscha smiled. "You'll be fine, Shalitha. You know what to do. You know what's going to happen, and I promise you… Elay is a gentle man."

Not helping.

She patted my hand gingerly, like a mother would a gullible child, before she let go and started fussing over my hair some more.

"It's good they managed to get all the black out of your hair," she muttered. "It didn't look right on you."

I smiled wryly. "Shame there's no blue…"

"Blue?"

With a wave of my hand, I dismissed her question. It was an old life—a childish life, one where I had had the luxury of doing whatever I pleased. For the most part anyway. Looking back now, I couldn't believe my desperate attempts at gaining freedom while I had had it all along.

How naïve I'd been.

"Very well, this just has to do," Zirscha said with a heavy sigh.

It almost sounded like I was a hopeless case—and I probably was, but she didn't have to be so blatantly open about it. Despite trying to shut them off for the day, I still had feelings.

"Remember to smile," Zirscha said. "You're supposed to be happy today, and you're definitely prettier that way."

I sighed. "I'm scared, Zirscha."

"We all were." She offered an encouraging nod. "Ready?"

My eyes almost rolled out of my head from swerving left to right and back again, taking in the amount of people lining the throne room, for want of a better word. From my vantage point at the door, the room seemed to go on forever until it reached Elay. He was a speck in the distance. More than ever I missed the presence of my *Arathrien* behind me. Not until now did I fully realise how reassuring their presence had been, not because they could defend me—I'd been quite capable of doing that myself—but because I hadn't been alone.

I felt incredibly alone now.

Stop feeling sorry for yourself, qira.

A gentle nudge in the back made me take a step forward, and another one, until I was walking down the aisle created for this specific reason. I wasn't entirely alone, but I trusted Zirscha as much as all the other women. For all I knew, she'd put a knife in my back before I took two more steps.

She'd have done that dressing you.

I rolled my eyes at my own thoughts, and would have snorted had I not caught myself in time. With every step I took, I got closer to Elay—with every step I took, my heart picked up speed, and by the time I was almost at the dais, I wanted to bolt. I didn't care where to—I'd go into the desert and take my chances there rather than see this through. Elay must have caught the look on my face, because he skipped down the steps and was with me a second later, taking my hands in his.

The awe on his face made his emerald eyes twinkle and it took my breath away.

I looked away to prevent myself from going down a rabbit hole I wasn't prepared for. Even so, I couldn't help but steal a look in his direction. He wore a silver overcoat with a tunic and trousers underneath that matched my dress. The embellishments on the collar and along the hemlines were the colour of the sapphires around my neck. His coat showed off his athletic physique quite well, and I couldn't help but blush at the thought. Despite the start of these arrangements—the stalking, the teasing, the cajoling—Elay wasn't a hard man to like, and the thought brought back the words he'd spoken that night in the pool.

Falling in love with me.

No, we were miles away from love. If anything, we were closer to a consensual relationship based on compromises and promises rather than anything else. Love had nothing to do with this.

"You look absolutely stunning," Elay whispered, kissing the back of my hands. "Who would've thought…"

I scowled at him.

He chuckled. "Easy, *Mìthri*, I'm joking."

"Apologies," I mumbled. "I am a ball of nerves."

Elay looked quite amused. "There's nothing to getting married. All you have to do is go through the motions and say yes in the end."

My scowl deepened, which had Elay burst out laughing as if I'd told him the funniest joke in the world.

"Come," he whispered. "Let's get this over with."

He escorted me up the steps with both my hands still in his, his eyes never leaving me. As long as I focused on the steps, I was fine. As soon as I'd look up at him, I knew I'd stumble, and making a fool out of myself was the last thing I wanted.

"Ready?" Elay asked softly, his lips tugging up in a one-sided grin.

"Everybody keeps asking me that without actually wanting an answer," I muttered. "If I told you no, would this misery end?"

"Misery? *Mìthri*, am I that horrible?" Elay was fully grinning now.

I elbowed him as we turned back to back, hands fumbling

until we pressed palms against palms, shoulders against shoulders. Despite his easy words, I felt the tension in him, which somehow eased mine. At least a little. This was only the first part of the *Harshâh*. Just like Zirscha had told me, the blindfolds came next. I didn't like my sight taken away, but that was the point of this whole ordeal. It was tradition, of which I assumed the main purpose had long since been forgotten, as it was a test of trust. Two silken cords were placed in our hands and I wrapped mine around them so tight, I dug my nails into my own palms.

We started walking away from each other until the cords were taut between us, and this was where the whole trust part came in. The silks had been knotted and twisted, and it was up to us to unknot and untwist them without speaking to each other. We had to rely on instinct and touch. If we managed to get through this without letting go of the silks, knocking each other over, or getting into an argument, we'd be considered marriage material and the *Harshâh* could continue.

And I was worried about what comes at the end.

This was as much logic as it was trust, and I was glad to find Elay thought in a similar fashion, because soon we were close, our hands touching where the silk was twisted. We were caught in an intricate dance only the two of us understood, moving in ways I'd never thought I was capable of. Heat rose to my cheeks, and I wasn't sure it was because of the exertion alone. Elay's caresses were light and gentle, sending waves of heat blossoming from where we came in contact.

Stop it. Stop it. Stop it.

All too soon, we stood chest to chest, hands to hands, not an inch of silk between us. I could feel the rise and fall of his chest in sync with my own—could feel his warm breath against my face. I stilled, barely breathing, listening to rather than feeling what was going on. The blindfolds slipped away with a soft rustle and the silk cords were taken from our hands. When I opened my eyes, I almost drowned in his, and I had a hard time tearing my gaze from him.

He was staring too.

Elay recovered by clearing his throat and looking away, flashing the throne room a triumphant grin.

"I knew she'd be a good match," he said, his hand brushing mine.

People either clapped or cheered in response. I focused hard on ignoring the fluttering in my stomach, but it was a painful reminder of the person who used to evoke these feelings long before this day. Guilt gnawed its way to my heart knowing that what I was doing would hurt Tal beyond belief. I was so sure he'd be devastated upon hearing I'd gotten married, that I never even considered we might both do everything we could to survive.

Elay squeezed my hands to draw my attention.

"Next part," he whispered. "This one's the easiest."

I bit my lip, nodded and allowed him to position me so that I was more or less facing both him and the officiant on my right. The man silenced the crowd just by beginning to talk, his voice starting loud, but going softer and softer until even I almost strained to hear what he was saying. He was prattling on about the sacred duties of marriage, as well as the sacrilege should either one of us fail those duties, in Zihrin. He spoke so fast, I caught every fourth word or so. By the time he finished, I felt so lost, I glanced at Elay quite helplessly. Amusement flickered in his eyes when he caught my gaze, and he winked, presumably to ease me, but it had quite the opposite effect.

Why does he have an effect on me at all?

I looked down at my feet until Elay grabbed my hands so I could do nothing but face him. The officiant was looking at him.

"Elay è Rehmàh, do you accept Shalitha an Ilvan as your twenty-seventh wife?" he asked, his tone neutral.

Gasps sounded up all around, adding to my overall state of anxiety.

"Yes," Elay replied with a nod of his head. "I do."

"Shalitha an Ilvan," the officiant intoned. "Do you take Elay è Rehmàh as your husband?"

For a second I considered saying no and run—run as fast as my feet could carry me, until I remembered the hike through the desert and how I had almost not survived that. If Elay and his men hadn't found me...

I nodded, my voice coming out in a squeak. "Yes."

"Louder please," the officiant murmured, looking at me with a smile ghosting on his lips.

"Yes," I said firmer. "I do."

Elay was grinning like a madman while I managed no more than the barest of smiles needed to look convincing. Around us, cheers rose in a steady escalation of sound, washing over us like a tidal wave as he pulled me into his embrace and pressed his lips on mine.

"Try to look like you enjoy it," he murmured. "People love a good show."

I was too startled by his action to respond, both in speech and physically, and just stood there like a wooden puppet. Thankfully, Elay was a showman all on his own and made the awkwardness less awkward.

"Now comes the fun part," he whispered, pulling away from me. "We dance."

It wasn't anything like the dances in Ilvanna where it meant standing close or even against one's dancing partner, posture tense and rigid to allow for fluid motions. In Zihrin, dancing was more seductive and sensual, where partners danced facing each other rather than holding each other, following a sequence of intricate moves which made no sense unless you knew them. The result was a fun, uplifting dance that had me smiling bright at the end of it.

Granted, Elay was a magnificent dance partner.

After the first dance, Elay guided me back to the dais—to our thrones and helped me sit down before taking his seat next to me. My gaze swept over the crowd, my chest tightening in its usual response to its size. Maram was watching me from the side lines, hatred contorting her visage into a wicked mask.

Just breathe.

AFTER SEVERAL HOURS of meeting our guests, receiving well-wishes, congratulations and gifts, I was ready to call it a night and leave everyone to their own devices. Unfortunately, there was still one part of the *Harshâh* that needed to be completed in order for us to be properly married, so when we retired to his bedroom, a group of peers followed in our wake. It was a good thing Elay kept my arm hooked through his, or I'd have dropped to my knees.

It felt like drowning all over again.

The pressure on my chest was unimaginable—the throbbing in my head unbearable, and the tremors going through my stiff limbs were painful. Elay was rubbing my hand with his thumb in an effort to calm my nerves, but the closer we got to his room, the worse it became, and I felt sure another panic attack would overwhelm me soon.

"*Mìthri*," Elay whispered. "Look at me."

I did. I looked into those radiant eyes, saw the comforting smile on his lips.

"There's nothing to be afraid of," he said softly, tucking a wayward strand of hair behind my ear, running his finger along the length of it.

The touch sent a jolt through my body and nestled deep inside of me.

"I'm not afraid of you," I murmured, glancing sideways to where people were waiting. "It's them."

Elay chuckled and leaned closer to whisper in my ear. "I was hoping you'd have eyes only for me."

I scowled at him, earning a delighted laugh as he set our entire party into motion. Too soon we arrived in his bedroom—too soon we were facing each other. In the deep silence, I feared my erratic heartbeat could be heard by everyone, announcing my fear like a war drum, but glancing in their direction, I noticed most looked positively bored and anywhere but at us. Swallowing hard, I returned my attention to Elay.

A look of awe had crept back onto his face.

"It's almost a shame to undress you," he said for my ears alone. "You look ravishing."

My lips pulled up in a one-sided smile. "This headdress is anything but comfortable though."

He chuckled softly and took a step closer, running his knuckles along my jaw, his eyes searching my face. A smile lit up his face as he brought his hands up, deftly removing all pins that served to keep the headdress in place from my hair. When he lifted it off my head, a sigh of relief escaped my lips.

"Thank you," I murmured. "This is much better."

He grinned. "Wait until we get to the best part."

I just rolled my eyes.

When he lifted my chin, I stilled. When he pressed his lips on mine, I stiffened, but when he deepened the kiss, my resolve crumbled and I was taken by a sudden feeling of need and comfort the likes of which I'd experienced only once before. All thoughts scattered when his arms circled my waist, pulling me against him, his need as palpable as my own.

"Do you trust me?" he whispered against my lips

"Do I have a choice?" I was breathless from the kiss.

"I would never hurt you, *Mìthri*."

And in that moment, I believed he wouldn't, so I nodded, a

sign to him to move this all forward. I was nervous, but what was more, I had no idea how to go about anything. My sheltered life, a *Tari* for a mother and two overprotective brothers had secured my virtue until now, and although Elay hadn't been my first choice, I could have done a lot worse considering the previous year.

If it had been up to the *Gemsha*, worse would have been an understatement.

Elay's nimble hands undid my top on the back and he helped it slide away from my arms. Instinctively, I hugged myself by way of protection. Instead of taking my arms away, he took a step back and shrugged out of his overcoat. I closed the distance between us, and with trembling hands, undid the buttons of his coat, helping him shrug out of it. Underneath, he wore a simple cotton shirt, which he pulled over his head in one fluid motion.

It was my turn to stare.

Up close, his copper skin appeared to shine in the flickering light of the candles. His body was well-defined, showing he did his work out diligently. My breath caught in my throat and I lowered my gaze, trying to steady myself.

"Look at me," Elay murmured. "Please?"

The moment I looked up, a sudden movement out of the corner of my eye caught my attention, and something flashed in what little light there was. I was about to push Elay aside, certain the attack was aimed at him, when he wrapped his arms around me and twisted himself in front of me.

A grunt escaped his lips, but he held on.

My eyes settled on the attacker behind him—light green eyes in a dark face were peering back at me, hatred suffusing his features.

Then he was gone.

"Elay?"

"I'm fine," he muttered. "Bastard just grazed me."

When he turned his back to me to order his guards to go in

pursuit and to announce the *Harshâh* was finished, I clapped my hands over my mouth to prevent a scream from escaping my lips.

It wasn't just a graze.

"LIE STILL," I growled under my breath, "unless you want an ugly scar on your back."

Elay grunted, fisting the bedsheets as I stuck the needle into his back. The cut wasn't too deep—just quite long, so it took me some time to clean and stitch it, much to Elay's infuriation.

"Thank you," I said at length.

"What for?" he sounded genuinely surprised.

"Saving my life."

He chuckled, grunted, winced and cursed under his breath almost at the same time.

"You're my wife," he said, glancing at me. "Didn't I swear to protect your life with my own earlier this night?"

"Is that what the officiant was rambling on about?" I asked, a smile tugging at my lips.

Elay snorted and shook his head. "You're quite something else."

"So I've been told."

"Where did you learn the healer's trade?" he asked after a while, his voice heavy with fatigue.

"At the palace," I replied. "I spent time with our Master Healer, and he's taught me the basics of it."

"Is there anything you cannot do?"

"Live a normal life?"

His lips twisted into a mischievous grin. "Ah, but *Mìthri*... what fun would there be if life were normal? You and I might never have met—we'd certainly never have gotten married. What's a normal life but shackles to keep the powerless from power, the weak from getting strong, the obedient from turning rebellious? Normal is but a word awarded to others by those who want more, and you *Mìthri*, are certainly destined for more."

"I wish I wasn't."

CHAPTER 25

TALNOVAR

Night and day turned into an endless loop of despair until I no longer knew how much time had passed. Days were a commodity for those sound of mind, and by now, I wasn't sure I was. Pacing up and down Shal's bedroom, hugging myself closely, I tried to ignore the tremors going through my body. I'd been sweating profusely for a while now but had been shivering just as long. I knew exactly what was happening, but I couldn't remember the last time—and the only time—being this bad.

Withdrawals, Imradien. Your own nohro fault.

Although it had been no surprise Azra had finally locked me up, the events preceding it had come as a shock. Knowing the risk she was taking, Ione had gone from placing Azra's *Araîth* while she was still watching, to Shal's design once she was gone. Only two square inches of ink on my hip showed her initial design. This decision had cost Ione her life—Azra had made sure I was there to watch as she was hung from the palace walls, still alive. By now, I assumed she was dead, or at least I hoped she was.

I owed her a debt I could never repay.

"Ruestah mey shareye," I murmured as an afterthought, hoping she would indeed be able to rest in peace.

With a heavy sigh, I crawled back into bed, curling up until my knees were level with my chin, pulling the blankets over my head. All I needed were a few days to get through this. I'd done it before—I could do it again. The worst thing was, I wasn't sure that I wanted to, nor was I sure whether it was the addiction talking or not. While I was grateful for Ione's sacrifice of giving me something that was undeniably Shal's, I still wasn't sure I wanted to continue living under these circumstances.

Azra was deranged in every sense of the word, and I'd much rather she killed me than keep me on a knife's edge, balancing between sane and crazy like an impeccable equilibrist. Any time now, I'd misstep and fall to my death hundreds of feet below. The thought was welcoming—more welcoming than the alternative.

I hated myself for it.

Somewhere out there, Shal was still alive—she needed me, and here I was pitying myself like some lovesick child, waiting for his mother to praise him. I'd been fighting all my life—nothing had changed, yet somehow, Azra had managed to take the worst of the fight out of me. A year ago, I would not have cared much about casualties—I'd have done the job, mourned the dead. and gotten on with things.

Now… now Azra had me by the balls, and it was anything but arousing.

Despite our differences in the past, regardless of whatever he'd done to her, I couldn't let her kill my father for whatever mistake I made. Nor did any of the others deserve to die for them. But that was how Azra operated, and she did it with flair. The fact she couldn't be killed added another problem to the long list of existing problems.

I slipped out of bed, annoyed, restless, unsure what to do

with myself, and it occurred to me that was most likely my main problem.

I was bored, and boredom didn't suit me.

Do something about it, khirr.

Push ups were the first thing I tried, but I barely made it to five without uncontrollable shaking taking me over. Getting down to hands and knees, I tried to get it under control—to no avail. The tremors became worse. Stretching myself, I pressed my forehead to the cold floor, praying for this to stop.

Anything but this. Please, please make it stop.

My heart picked up speed and beat erratically, and for a moment I was afraid it would give out, until I remembered the heart palpitations I had in the past. They always left me short of breath.

"Tal!"

Cehyan skidded to her knees next to me, wrapping her arms around my shoulders and pulling me close. The unexpected touch of comfort sent me into another fit of spasms beyond the point of soreness.

"I know what you need," Cehyan murmured, placing a kiss on my temple. "Let's get you to the bed..."

More by her strength than mine I managed to get into the bed, curling up almost immediately as I did. Cehyan tucked me in before returning to a bag she'd dropped on the floor. I barely took notice as she prepared a *sehvelle* pipe—barely registered when she lit it and the familiar scent wafted my way. The moment I inhaled it, my body roared to life, as if it had momentarily forgotten about its previous state of being. A part of me desperately wanted to decline, but as soon as she handed me the pipe, I put it to my lips and inhaled.

It didn't stop the pain and jitters straight away, but it did put me at ease.

Like before, she made herself comfortable in the bed next to me, snuggling up to my side so we could share the pipe. Over the past few weeks, these had been my favourite moments, if only because they reminded me of a time when life was less complicated, and nobody made any demands of me.

Father had seen fit to stop that.

Anger flared up inside of me at the notion, and it took me all effort of will, or whatever was left of it, not to give in. If it hadn't been for Father's decision to take me away from there and enrol me in the army, I would never have met Shal.

I'd never have fallen in love.

Nor would I have been dragged into this mess called the royal line.

As soon as the thought crossed my mind, I knew it wasn't entirely true. Perhaps I wouldn't have been pulled into Shal's mess, but I'd done quite the job of creating my own. If Father hadn't done what he did, I would most likely be dead by now.

"Do you… ever think about that day?" I asked, glancing at Cehyan taking a drag from the pipe.

"There's not a day that goes by where I don't," she whispered, slowly exhaling.

I watched the tendrils of smoke curling their way up into the air lazily. I took the pipe from her and took another drag from it.

"Perhaps if—," I began, but before I could continue, Cehyan placed her finger on my lips to shush me.

"There's no sense in wondering about the ifs, Tal," she said, sitting up a little to look at me. "We made a mistake that day—a massive mistake, and we've paid for it… we'll be paying for it until the end of our days."

"She was so young," I whispered in a strangled voice. "I should've kept an eye on her, Cehy. She wanted to come to the lake so badly and I"—I swallowed hard and looked away from her—"I know it won't bring her back."

Instead of replying, Cehyan placed a kiss on my lips—soft and gentle first, until I deepened it, pouring all my pain and need into it. Somehow I managed to get the pipe out from between us as she straddled me, dropping it on the bedside cabinet instead, a fleeting thought of hoping nothing would catch fire passing my mind.

She knew exactly what to do to stop my thoughts short altogether.

TO MY DELIGHT AND DISMAY, Cehyan started spending the nights with me again, never explaining why it had taken her days to come and see me at all. When I asked, she was dismissive, mentioning something about having things to arrange, which in turn reminded me of Ruvaen's visit. He'd said Cehyan had warned him I was back on *sehvelle,* and with irritation suffusing my thoughts, I figured she left out that she had provided me with it in the first place.

Not that it mattered—I'd been the one who had taken it.

With the *sehvelle* back in my system, the tremors had mostly ceased. Every now and again, my body twitched, but that was it. My mind did feel heavier than normal though, but I blamed it on the sleepless nights before she had returned. One to two hours a night, and those not even consecutive, wasn't much to go on.

"What are you thinking of?" Cehyan asked softly, trailing her fingers over the lines on my shoulder.

Shivers slithered down my spine.

"Nothing much," I lied, flashing her a smile. "How good this feels."

Cehyan grinned and pushed herself up to her knees. My eyes travelled her body as it was outlined by the candlelight, and a momentary feeling of disgust crept over me when I realised in which room I was.

"Maybe we should go to sleep," I murmured, averting my gaze.

"Really?" she asked in a husky voice, splaying a hand on my abdomen. "Are you sure that's what you want?"

I bit my lip, ignoring the fact my body sprang to life at her touch almost instantly.

"You just need to relax," she whispered, slipping out of bed by crawling over me, drawing a low growl from my throat.

A soft, devious chuckle escaped her lips, and I knew she'd done it on purpose. I grabbed a pillow and stuffed it over my face. Death by suffocation didn't sound half-bad right now. Cehyan was moving around, I could hear her muffled footsteps on the carpet. The sound of glass touching glass echoed through the room, and I was curious enough to remove the pillow from my head to watch.

Unfortunately, Cehyan had her back to me.

I slipped out of bed, a light shiver coursing through me as the cold air touched my skin, and moved over to her. When I slipped my arms around her waist, resting my head on her shoulder, she stilled for a moment.

"What are you doing?"

She grinned up at me. "Fresh *sehvelle*. It's said to be the best batch."

A smile tugged at my lips and I nuzzled her neck. "Let me get the fire going. It's freezing in here."

"We can stay under the furs all night," she purred, watching me with a mischievous grin on her lips.

I chuckled as I set to tending the fire. "You think we can stay under the covers?"

Deep down, I knew all of this was wrong, but Cehyan was a coping mechanism, just like the *sehvelle* and the sex. Whatever feelings I still had for her were part of it—at least, that's what I kept telling myself so the guilt wouldn't gnaw its way through my heart. The sheer fact I was with her, in Shal's room, doing things I'd much rather do with her than with Ceyhan, was ever present in my mind.

She would hate me when she found out. I was sure of it.

Who knows what she has to do to survive.

Once I had a good fire roaring in the fireplace, I walked over to the bed where Cehyan was already waiting in one of the most seductive poses I'd seen her yet.

Nohro.

Back then, she'd been the only one who had been capable of keeping up with me, and even now, she seemed to know exactly what I needed. I got onto the bed and prowled over to her, claiming her lips with mine. The taste of them was invigorating, sending little sparks through my mouth. It felt almost numbing, but at the same time exciting.

I'd never noticed it before.

"Here," she whispered against my lips and when I pulled back, found her offering the *sehvelle* pipe. "Let's do this properly..."

I wasn't sure how to do it improperly at this point, but I wasn't going to argue. After I took a drag from the pipe, I handed it to her. It was heady—headier than what I was used to, sending my body to a level of awareness I'd never experienced before. For the first time in weeks, I felt alive, and I wanted to act on it in every possible way. Cehyan was looking at me, eyes dark and full of lust.

THE FIRST EXPERIENCE was something else, as if she and I had never shared a bed like this before. Every touch was more arousing than the one before, as if my skin had become overly sensitive. I felt every kiss, every breath, everything deep in my core, and I wanted more—more of whatever this was.

"This is..." I whispered.

"...mind-blowing?" Cehyan gasped in awe, arching her back under my touch as my hand travelled along her side.

"Better," I murmured, claiming her mouth.

When our bodies met, a moan of pure delight escaped her lips, and I lost myself in her. All my thoughts, all my feelings, dissipated into nothing. My mind was heavy with desire, and it was all I could act upon. The last thought to flee my mind was how this had never happened before, and then I didn't care anymore.

This was good. Life was good.

It was all that mattered.

Our breaks were brief and few, mostly to share the pipe or a glass of *ithri* before we continued. The strange taste lingered on her lips—clearly present one moment, less so the next, but every time, I felt more relaxed than before. Somewhere in the back of my mind, hidden by lust, a voice screamed danger at me, but I ignored it.

When Cehyan pulled away from me, I almost pouted, until she pushed me back on the bed, leaning over me.

"Remember this," she murmured in my ear as she brought my arms above my head. "You used to enjoy it."

I growled low under my breath, nipping at her neck.

"For old times' sake?"

Again, there was the feeling of something being off, but it was so faint, I paid no mind to it, and allowed her to tie my arms above my head. When she kissed me, all thoughts scattered and I closed my eyes, just enjoying our time. If what Ruvaen had said was true, someday soon I'd meet my end anyway.

I might as well enjoy my last few hours.

"Keep them closed," Cehyan whispered, her breath warm in my neck. "Let me surprise you."

And surprise me she did, until I was no longer sure what left or right, or up and down was. My body was heavy, languorous, and by now I'd expected I'd be spent, but after another gulp of *ithri*—another taste of *sehvelle,* and Cehyan had me ready within no time.

Something changed the moment she sat on top of me, and I knew with every fibre of my being it wasn't her. My eyes flew open, but my sight was clouded. Somewhere along the lines, Cehyan had placed something over my eyes.

"What the..."

Whoever had taken over—and I didn't need to guess who—continued where Cehyan had left off, and like the traitor my body was, it responded to every single touch.

"Please," I whispered. "Stop... please."

I fought the lust that was building up inside of me—fought the urge to move along. Nails raked across my chest, eliciting goosebumps, making me gasp.

"Cehy? Where are you?"

She didn't respond, but I could hear her breathing nearby.

"Cehy, please, respond..."

There was no reply, but I knew she was still there. Lips were pressed on mine, but I kept my mouth shut tight.

"What is it, *shareye*?" Azra whispered in my ear, then nipped the tip of it with her teeth before drawing her tongue down my neck. "Don't you like it?"

"Not with you, *hehzèh*," I hissed, but my body didn't seem to agree.

Azra was clearly as skilled in bed as Cehyan was, and perhaps even more so. She found places to touch that drew moans from me I didn't want to let her hear. I didn't want to give her the idea I enjoyed it.

She drew the blindfold from my face so that I had to look at her—look at her as she took my body as if she owned it. In an attempt to get her off, I bucked, but it only served as enjoyment for her—I could see it in the delighted look on her face.

"I knew you'd be worth the wait," she purred. "If only you would have done this voluntarily. Such fun we could have had."

I clenched my jaw and made myself lie as still as possible, but it was hard, so hard. My body, for whatever reason, began to feel heavy, as if I no longer had any control over it. Warning prickled in the back of my neck, but I didn't know how to fix it. There was no way to amend this.

"Why?" I whispered, my voice strained. "Why me?"

Azra leaned forward without breaking her pace, moving her hands up my chest as she did so. When she started placing kisses on my collarbone and on my neck, I stilled and closed my eyes. Her tongue licked over my lips, but I clamped them shut.

"You really want to know why, *shareye?*" she gasped in my ear, followed by a soft moan. "I will tell you why..."

She nuzzled my neck, bit the tip of my ear, and trailed her tongue down to my earlobe. A deep shiver ran through me, and I jolted involuntary, drawing out an even deeper moan from her.

Azra was doing this on purpose.

"Had I known you were this... good," she murmured. "I'd have instructed Cehyan to drug you with *oukourou* weeks ago."

"You did what?"

My voice was barely a whisper when I spoke, filled with anger and something else I couldn't quite place. I looked around for Cehyan, and found her sitting in one of the chairs, knees drawn up, hugging herself. I wasn't sure, but I thought there were tears on her cheeks.

"Oh, by Nava," Azra gasped, pushing herself up on my chest, throwing her head back.

Having to watch her enjoy this was even worse than having to feel it. When she looked at me, a devious grin spread across her lips, but her eyes were dark with lust. She closed them, picking up her pace, grinding and gyrating until both of us were close—so close.

I felt her tense around me and that was all that was needed.

A grunt escaped my lips. Azra let out a pure moan of delight, but where I had expected her to stop… she didn't. She lay down on top of me, pressing her lips to mine once again.

"I know she's still alive," she whispered, placing kisses on my jaw. "Killing you would be easiest… and I still might. But knowing that I had you before she did is the best part of all of this. You may bear her *Araîth,* but your body was mine first, and I'll make sure you will hate yourself enough to want to end it by the time I'm finished."

I breathed in deeply, waiting for the anger to rise, but it didn't come. Azra did exactly as she said. Somehow, she managed to get me over the edge several more times, and with each time, I felt more spent—more tired. In between, I was given something to drink, and knowing now that Cehyan had been drugging me, I noticed the different taste of the *ithri.* Where I thought it had been the *sehvelle,* it had been the *oukourou*—whatever that was.

SOUNDS from outside the door jolted me back to awareness. I wasn't sure if I'd been asleep or blacked out. Azra was lying next to me, leg curled around mine, one hand still stroking me, even though my body had quite given up by now. The effects of the drugs, whichever of the two it was, seemed to be wearing off, but Azra didn't seem worried. Glancing to my left, I noticed Cehyan was gone. She'd most likely left sometime during this whole ordeal.

I'd completely lost count of how many times Azra had succeeded.

The door banged open all of a sudden, and the sound of screaming entered the room along with the scent of smoke—the rebellion had started. I jolted up, but my arms were still tied above my head and they were numb. With a yelp of pain, I fell back, gasping at the fierce ache in my shoulders. Azra sat up slowly with a wicked smile playing on her lips, not even bothering with pulling the sheets around her.

She was expecting this.

"Hello, Cerindil," she purred.

My gaze snapped to the door, watching my father approach with wide eyes. His look was guarded—yet unsurprised—but from the way he moved, I could tell he was angry. He moved stiffly, and his face hadn't quite healed yet either, but he looked better than the last time I'd seen him.

"Let my son go, Azra," he said, his voice deadly calm. "You've had your fun. It's over now…"

Azra slid her hand under the pillow next to my head and pulled a dagger in sight. She settled herself on her side next to me, trailing the tip of the blade from my jaw down to that sweet spot between my collarbones.

"You know it's only just begun, Imradien," she said, watching my father. "None of you will get out of the palace alive."

He stiffened, but other than that, there was no indication of his worry.

"As usual, you underestimate me," he replied. "Let my son go, and let's settle this between us once and for all."

"Ah," she cooed, "but you're forgetting one thing, Cerindil…"

I closed my eyes, an indrawn gasp escaping my lips as she pushed the dagger into my skin. My heart rate picked up speed.

"I'm tired of your games, Azra," my father said with a heavy sigh. "Let Talnovar go, and you can have me in his stead."

Azra snorted, almost as if she were offended at the offer. "No offense, Cerindil, but if I have to choose, I'd choose him over you any day. Now… speaking of choices…"

She sat up and placed the dagger just above my left hip. If she did it well, she could kill me straight away, or let me bleed to death.

"You can either save your son," she said, and slowly pushed

the dagger into me, drawing out an elongated grunt, "or go after me. Choose. Fast."

Pain, much like the time Yllinar had me run through with a sword, spread through me, drawing out a deep, feral growl. It was strange how it registered so slowly.

"Tal!"

Father was at my side in an instant, eyes wide in worry, raking my body to see the damage that had been done. He cursed. Father never cursed. His hands fumbled with the ties around my wrists, but it seemed to take forever.

"F… Father," I whispered. "G… go after her. S… stop her."

"I'm not going to let you die," he hissed. "I've already lost a child, my wife… I'm not losing my only son as well."

"She cannot win," I groaned, surprised at how difficult it was to string those words together.

My brain was foggy and thoughts became hard to grasp. The pain was there, it registered, but somehow not in its full capacity. In the distance, I heard my father yelling, but his words turned into mumbles by the time they reached me. Even his face became a blur in the distance. I wasn't sure what damage Azra had done, or if this was because of the *oukourou*, but I felt lighter than ever.

I felt free.

CHAPTER 26

SHALITHA

The air was crisp when I stepped outside into the garden, but there was a hint of warmth to it—a promise of a good day. Soon, I'd be warm enough not to be bothered by the cold anyway. After stretching my legs and arms, I started running, focusing on my bare feet slapping the dirt rhythmically and on my breath coming out in short, hard puffs. I had to focus or I'd start thinking, and that was the last thing I wanted.

Ever since the attack during the *Harshâh*, I'd been sleeping poorly, waking up from a nightmare I could never quite grasp. Elay's injury caused him to be restless too, and I'd soon learned my new husband didn't sleep well on either his side or his stomach. I'd never heard a man complain so much in my life. So each morning, I went for a run to clear my mind, followed up by training to keep my physique, my strength, and my stamina.

Something told me I'd be needing it.

"You're up early." Elay's voice sounded from the doorway to his—*our*—bedroom.

I looked up from my push-ups with a wry smile. "Couldn't sleep."

"Again?"

With a soft nod, I returned to my training, determined to reach twenty-five more push ups. A few times, my shoulder locked up, so I had to lower myself and try again, but it became increasingly more difficult.

"What happened?" Elay asked at length. "With your shoulder?"

I pushed myself to my knees and looked at him, knitting my brows together. He was seated in the doorway now, hugging a cup of tea to his bare chest—he'd only bothered with trousers and an overcoat this morning.

"It's a long story," I said with a sigh, rising to my feet. "And you'll be frozen by the time I've finished."

"It won't be that bad," he said, rising to his feet too, putting the cup aside. "How about you tell me while we train together?"

I tilted my head, pursing my lips. "Are you sure? Your back still hasn't quite healed properly. The healer told you to take your rest."

He snorted. "This coming from the woman who was out of bed two days after I found her on the brink of death?"

"I never said I was a good example."

"We can start slowly," Elay offered. "And I can teach you some of the Zihrin fighting style... if you're interested?"

A grin spread across my face. "Why didn't you say so?"

Elay laughed and shook his head. "Out of all my wives, *Mìthri*, you surely are the most intriguing."

I shrugged. "We'll see how long you'll admire that."

"Much longer than you'll expect, *Tarien*," he replied with a roguish grin.

It was weird hearing my title on his lips, mostly because he refrained from using it when other people were around, and he seemed to prefer *Mìthri* over anything else. Still, it was nice to hear it from time to time in a place where I was nothing more than a twenty-seventh wife, even if I was married to the *Akynshan*.

"Are you ready?" he asked, shrugging off his overcoat.

His copper skin shimmered in the rays of the rising sun, and although I knew it was a trick of the light, it highlighted all the right features. I shook my head to dispel the thoughts and returned my focus to Elay, who was watching me in amusement.

"Like what you see?"

"No," I replied too fast.

He chuckled and took a step closer, running his knuckles along my cheek. "We never did finish what we started that night…"

I outright stared at him, lips pressed into a thin line. Instead of replying, I made to grapple with him, but he stepped out of the way.

Elay laughed. "Is that a yes after all?"

I gave him a firm enough push to force him to step back, but he only laughed harder. It was difficult to upset Elay, let alone anger him. The only time I'd seen him in all his glorious fury was the night of the attack, and I felt that wasn't even half of what he was capable of.

He'd be the wrong person to be on the wrong side of—that much was clear.

"Well then," he said, looking at me mischievously. "Shall we get on with it?"

ALTHOUGH FIGHTING WAS A UNIVERSAL PRINCIPLE, countries had developed their own styles over the centuries. They had the same fundamentals, but the moves Elay guided me through were much more fluid—almost like a dance, if you will—than what I'd been taught. It was also a lot harder than I thought it would be, because the idea was to not hit each other, as opposed to the full contact sparring I was used to.

"I'm confused." I stood gasping for breath when Elay allowed for a break. "How is this in anyway related to fighting?"

Elay chuckled. "I suppose it's as much fighting as it is dancing, but it requires an infinite amount of control and self-restraint to make the moves as fluidly as possible. On top of that, it's great exercise in many ways."

I scowled at him. "I'm already sore all over..."

"Next time," he said, grinning, "duck when I'm about to kick you."

I grunted and rubbed the spot where his foot had connected with my head. I'd teetered, and he had to grab my arms to steady me. I wouldn't hear of stopping though. Both Tal and Esahbyen had been quite clear in that regard—my enemy wouldn't stop, either.

"Come, have a seat." Elay patted the bench next to him. "You can do with some rest from the looks of you."

For the sake of peace, I flopped down next to him, stretching my legs. With a grimace, I leaned forward to rub my calf. My balance on that foot was still off—I doubted it would ever get better.

"Care to tell me what happened?" he asked, inviting me to place my legs on his lap.

I frowned but complied. As nimble hands began massaging my calf, alleviating the tension with practised ease, a sigh of relief escaped my lips and I leaned my head against the wall, closing my eyes.

"I was kidnapped." My voice was strained, and my chest tightened at the memory. "By a delusional Ilvannian nobleman. He had this insane notion we belonged together and tried to make me see the truth of this."

Elay listened quietly, his hands not stopping their work.

"He had a temper on him," I continued, swallowing hard, "and I had the uncanny ability to set him off every single time."

A soft snort escaped his lips. "Why am I not surprised, *Mìthri*?"

I glowered at him. "Anyway, that's where most of my scars come from. In order to make me compliant he… used a cane on me, and I suppose, after a while, it worked."

Elay's hands stilled momentarily and I felt him tense. One side of my lips quirked up in a faint smile, touched by this small sentiment. He hadn't even known me then.

"He managed to keep me hidden for over a moon, and then one day, my brother and Talnovar showed up. He dragged me down to the dungeon, kept me quiet with a knife at my throat, and… he didn't like the way I responded to hearing Tal's voice…"

A shudder went through me at the memory of that fight, and more so at the thought of the aftermath. I'd been sure he would let me die down there.

"How did you respond?" Elay asked, curiosity lacing his voice.

"He said I loved him," I replied, swallowing hard. "And then we fought."

Elay stilled again, his voice deeper when he spoke. "Loved who?"

For some reason, the question didn't surprise me, but coming from a man with a plethora of wives, it came across fairly hypocritical. I clenched my jaw, scowling at him.

"Tal, of course," I replied as casually as I could. "He's my *Anahràn*."

"Your what?"

"Captain," I explained, "of my personal guard."

Elay whistled, his lips curling up into a smile. "I see. Did he give you these injuries?"

"What?" I asked with a frown. "No, of course not! Eamryel did!"

His lips pulled down into a deep scowl, the look on his face one I couldn't place. When he looked at me, he narrowed his eyes.

"Please," he said, flexing his fingers. "Continue."

His sudden change of demeanour, other than pretending to be the overprotective husband, made no sense, but I did as he asked, telling him the story of how Eamryel had left me to die first, then changed his mind and sent me off, only to hunt me.

"He shot an arrow into my shoulder first, and my leg second," I said, devoid of emotions. "Strangely enough, he warned me not to trust anyone the day I left for *Hanyarah*."

I sighed deeply and rubbed my temples where a headache had started to form. Elay had stopped the massage altogether, staring dead ahead, biting his lip in thought. It was so uncharacteristically him that it worried me.

"What's wrong?" I asked, laying my hand on his biceps.

He tensed beneath my touch. "Nothing. Nothing's wrong." He flashed me a roguish smile. "I was just thinking."

"About what?"

"How you seem to attract so much misfortune, *Mìthri*," he said, taking my hands in his and placing a kiss on them. "I've never met a person as unlucky as you."

I heard the lie in his voice, but decided it wasn't worth the trouble. I bore no illusions that either of us was completely honest with the other, and it suited me fine—for now.

"Tal said something similar," I replied with a shrug. "I guess it came with the title."

Elay smiled, patting my legs before placing them on the ground while rising to his feet. "Come on. It's market day and we need to get some things before we leave."

"Leave? Leave where?"

He grinned. "Off to fair Kyrintha, *Mìthri*. I have business there, and after what happened at the *Harshâh*, I am not leaving you behind."

Kyrintha. Maybe I can find a ship there that will take me to Ilvanna.

I managed to fake a bright smile, following his example. "That sounds wonderful. When are we leaving?"

"In a few days," Elay replied. "There are some things I need to arrange before we leave, and you may need some extra clothes for the journey."

"How long will we be on the road?"

"At least three weeks," he replied. "If all goes well and there are no sandstorms."

"Sandstorms?"

Elay chuckled. "You might be in for somewhat of a culture shock, *Tarien*. We have no snow—we have sand."

Before, market days meant I'd go out and rob the rich of their riches. Now, I was regarded as the rich person—not that I had anything of value on me—and my eyes kept scanning the area for anyone trying to rob Elay, who did have everything on him. With his lazy grin and careless manner, he appeared an easy target.

I knew first hand he wasn't.

"How nice it is to know I won't be robbed today," Elay murmured, flashing me a mischievous grin.

"Really? And what makes you say that? I've spotted at least three thieves eyeing your pouch hungrily. One behind you, one on your left..."

"And number three?"

"On your right," I replied with a cheeky grin, tossing the pouch in my hand to make it jingle. "Quite easy too when I manage to distract you."

Elay awarded me a flat stare, snatching the pouch from my upheld hand. Mischief twinkled in his eyes as he leaned forward, speaking in a voice meant only for me.

"I really should punish you for that," he murmured, taking my hand gently in his. "Thieving is punishable by chopping this off"—he kissed my knuckles gingerly—"which, if you ask me, would be a terrible shame indeed."

I rolled my eyes at him. "You're enjoying this way too much."

"I've always enjoyed our banter, *Mìthri*," he said with a smile. "Most of my wives either ignore me, yell at me, or are so completely subservient they'll do anything I ask of them. But you"—he pushed a strand of hair out of my face—"you've never tried to be anyone but yourself."

My brows shot up in surprise. "Except for the months I lived with the *Gemsha*."

"Hush." He placed a finger on my lips. "That's not a conversation for outdoors."

I pressed my lips together and shot him a look. Elay continued forward unperturbed, his ever-ready smile back on his face. People greeted him as he passed—stallholders offered him goods to try, food to taste, wine to drink, and he did, but all in moderation. He purchased herbs and spices at one stall, cloth for dresses in another—furs, shoes, and gloves as well. Anything he thought we would need for our journey, he bought. Clearly, money wasn't the issue—many families would eat well that night.

"You're not at all like what people make you out to be," I mused out loud on our way home.

Elay looked amused. "Really, and what do they make me out to be?"

"A monster," I replied. "The kind who'll kill you for looking at him the wrong way."

"Interesting..." He flashed me a wide smile. "I wonder why they think that?"

"I'm sure you have no idea..."

His laughter echoed off the walls as we entered the *k'ynshan* where a rather nervous looking Zirscha was awaiting us. Elay's mood shifted immediately.

"What's wrong?"

Zirscha paled. "I... you'd better come have a look..."

Curious to what was going on, I trailed behind Elay and his first wife through the corridors and up a flight of stairs. When we halted in front of the *harem*, the coppery scent of blood reached us, and unease settled in my body. The last time I'd smelled it this bad had been at *Hanyarah*. The massacre had filled the air with a mix of odours I would never be able to erase from my memory—this smelled exactly the same.

Zirscha looked rather pale.

Elay's features had turned dark and foreboding. My senses went on high alert, my eyes scanning the corridors for anything unusual, but everything appeared normal. I couldn't shake the feeling something was wrong though, so when Elay moved to step inside, I grabbed his hand to stop him.

"Don't," I murmured, looking at him.

"I have to look for myself," he said, taking my hand from his. "They're my wives."

I hadn't even looked inside, so when he nodded in the general direction of the room, I did. Blood coloured the tiled floor a dark crimson, and it was enough to tell me more than one person had died. Steeling my resolve, I stepped past Elay, drew the dagger from his belt and slipped quietly inside the room. My skin prickled with the sensation of being watched—my hair stood on end, and when I turned to look in the direction it came from, I was barely in time to dodge a knife flying my way.

In the next moment, a body barrelled into me, and we went down in a tangle of limbs. My head slammed on the floor, sending stars into my vision, but at least it didn't knock me out straight away. I dodged a punch aimed for my jaw and reciprocated by head-butting my assailant on the nose. There was a sickening crunch and a loud howl. I had a small window of opportunity. I drew up my knees into the place where it hurt and was met with a groan, but something felt off.

A woman!

Before I fully comprehended what was happening, she'd drawn a dagger to my throat in the second my assumptions betrayed me.

"Stop the antics," she hissed, drawing the hood from her face. "Or we'll kill your husband."

My heart stopped.

"Rhana?" I whispered, my eyes widening.

Her lips quirked up in a mischievous grin. "Surprise... *Tarien.*"

Swallowing hard, I glanced at Elay, only to find him on his knees with a sword against his throat, murder written all over his features. His hands had been tied behind his back, and a gag kept him from speaking coherently, but the moment our eyes locked, he started to scream and curse into it. Rhana turned my head back by placing the blade against my jaw and applying pressure to it. I balled my fists as I laid them on the ground.

"What do you want?" I growled.

"You," she replied matter-of-factly, "and him. This pay will be outrageous!"

"What?" I looked at her in confusion.

She rose to her feet with a chuckle, instructing two men to haul me to my feet and tie me up like Elay. Instead of responding to me, she walked over to him, taking his chin between her fingers.

"You've grown cocky, Elay," she said and patted his cheek, "but I am glad you still enjoy your women entirely too much. You have no idea how *thrilled* I was when you brought me the

Ilvannian heiress, although"—she turned to me, eyes narrowing—"I was less than impressed with your sudden disappearance."

I frowned, but kept my mouth wisely shut.

"No matter." She shrugged. "We'll have a few weeks on the road. There's enough time to share stories. Take them outside… it's time we start moving. I want to be well on our way before night falls."

Darkness descended upon me as a hood was placed over my face, but it was thankfully not thick enough to block out everything. I could still see the darker outlines of people, but the confinement did nothing to ease my nerves. In that moment, I wanted nothing more than to touch Elay and feel assured—secure.

It was anyone's guess where they were taking us.

CHAPTER 27

TALNOVAR

All I could remember was pain and the vague sensation of being on the move, if the gentle sway underneath me was any indication. My dreams were vivid and frightful in their intensity, dragging me to the recesses of my brain I'd kept shut for years, and in turn became full-fledged nightmares I had no way of escaping from. I was tied to this imaginary pit of anguish of my own creation.

It made me want to die even more.

To make matters worse, I was aware of the tremors, of the sick feeling wreaking havoc on my body, but above all, of the complete and utter state of weakness I was in. In my subconscious state, I was aware, too, of the voices over my head, of their concern in them. They were familiar and yet, I could not place them. But they were friendly, that much I knew.

"Drink." A cup was placed against my lips.

No more than a few sips. I knew the drill by heart because it had been happening for a while now. Not that I was aware just how long, or the numerous occasions I'd been told to drink, but it was an indication of time passing.

"How is he doing?" This voice belonged to my father. I'd

know it anywhere, but as desperate as I was to tell him I was not all right, no sound escaped my lips. I felt like a spectator to my own life, except that I was kept in the dark and could only listen to it. Whoever responded sounded muffled and I knew I was taken under again while my body was fighting for—something.

Fighting to live.

A sudden thought washed over me like a wave, but rather than it upsetting me, it calmed me as I drifted further away on the sea of unconsciousness. At some point, I would go under the surface to the one nightmare I was so desperate to escape from. Around me, darkness swirled into a room barely lit by candlelight, but before its edges could sharpen, the image dissolved, and I was standing at a lake instead.

Gods, please, no. Anything but this, please.

My chest tightened as my eyes drew to the water. It was peacefully calm, as it always was during the summer. A light breeze tickled my skin, and it felt so real that for a moment I believed I was transported elsewhere rather than dreaming. A clear laugh drew my attention, and when I looked in the direction it had come from, my breath caught in my throat.

A young girl not yet in her teens ran across the field, white hair trailing behind her like a banner of surrender. Her face lit up with joy, and another laugh rolled my way as she passed. I staggered backwards before dropping to my knees, watching the girl wide-eyed. She hadn't noticed me yet.

"Varayna," I whispered. "But... how?"

My little sister stopped and turned to me slowly, and when she finally laid eyes on me, they lit up, her smile as bright as I remembered it to be.

"Tal! You're here!"

Bare feet sped through the grass, carrying her to me. A second later, she flung her arms around my neck, and I hugged her tight to my chest. She felt so real.

"You're real," I whispered. "Vara... I..."

My voice fell away when I remembered what had happened to her and I buried my face into her hair, silent sobs racking my body. She patted my back.

"I forgive you," she whispered in my ear, placing a kiss on my cheek. "You're here now. Will you play with me? It's been ever so long!"

She began wriggling out of my embrace so I let her go, rising to my feet like a drunk man, staggering backwards until I'd regained my footing. I watched as Vara hopped from one leg to two, and back to one again. *Pehrîn*. She'd loved the game with that fierce intensity only children had.

I started towards her and stopped.

"This can't be real," I murmured. "What's happening?"

"It's as real as you make it, *shareye*," a woman's voice—a voice I'd longed to hear for so long now—came from next to me.

I wanted to look, but I was afraid that when I did, she'd be there too.

"Mother?" my voice came out feeble, and I turned at last.

She looked exactly like I remembered her—dark hair swept back in a messy bun, sable eyes as kind as ever, a small, soft smile on her lips. Her overall demeanour was one of sadness, and I was the one to blame. Tears stung behind my eyes, and I had a hard time keeping it together. But when she cupped my face in her hands and stepped into my arms, I broke down. She rested her cheek against my chest, wrapping her arms around my waist.

I'd forgotten how small she was.

"I'm so sorry," I whispered over and over again until my voice was hoarse and barely audible.

She just held me.

"I should've been paying attention to her," I whispered. "It's all my fault. All of it..."

"Hush, *shareye*," mother began, her voice soft. "Calm down... you have to calm down."

Her words had the opposite effect, and instead of calming down my temper flared. I pushed her away from me. Pacing up and down in front of her, I regained a semblance of control, balling my fists at my side.

"You don't understand," I hissed. "She died because of me. She died, because I didn't pay attention. She died, because I was having my way with Cehyan, too high to know better. You should never have trusted me with her. Never!"

Something was wrong.

The angrier I became, the harder it was to breathe. I dropped to my knees, hands around my throat as if I were choking. Mother knelt in front of me, taking my face in her hands.

"It's not my forgiveness you seek," she said. "Or Vara's, or your father's. You must forgive yourself, Talnovar, or it will consume you."

Tears rolled down my cheeks unbidden while I sat gasping for air.

"Go back, *shareye*," she murmured, placing a kiss on my forehead. "You do not belong here. Go back…"

Other voices were drifting in—worried voices, angry voices, voices I knew I should know but could not place. Somebody was calling me from faraway and I thought it was Vara, but when I looked up she was gone, as was mother. There was a persistent tug in my chest, as if my body was reminding me to do something—something vital.

Breathe!

My lungs were aching fiercely, and my heart was hammering in my chest. I saw the outlines of people in my vision, but the sudden light blinded me. I tried to focus, but for some reason, my sight remained double. The voices that had sounded faraway before were now close by and seemed less worried.

"Tal?"

"Soren…" I murmured.

I brought up my hand—or tried to anyway—to rub my face, when I realised it didn't cooperate. It felt heavy to say the least.

"Welcome back," Soren replied, apprehension in his voice. "I thought I'd lost you."

"I was right here."

Pushing out the words was hard—harder than it should have been, and my voice was soft and faint, croaking on every syllable. My sight still hadn't returned properly, but outlines were becoming faces at least.

"I'm glad your humour's still intact."

I wanted to say his wasn't, but speaking appeared to be the hardest task due to the fog in my brain. My eyes were heavy and I was unable to fight it. Voices drifted in and out as I went under.

"How long before we're there?"

"Three days at this speed."

"How long does he have?"

"Less than that."

A deep, guttural growl was the last thing I registered before I slipped into oblivion.

INSTEAD OF GETTING BETTER, it felt like I was getting worse. I cried out in pain more than I was silent, and my delirium had taken an interesting turn of events. Reality intertwined with dreams in such a way I wasn't sure which was what, but the voices kept telling me it was bad—really bad. They'd saved me once.

They weren't sure my body could handle a second time.

"I won't lose him too," one voice said eerily distorted.

"We need to break his fever," a second voice, equally disjointed, responded. "We need to cool him down somehow."

"There's a stream nearby," a third one said. "It'll be cold enough."

"The sudden cold might kill him…"

"…this fever most definitely will…"

On and on it went until their voices turned into a maelstrom of sounds. Trying to focus on it was too exhausting, so I let it go, sinking back into my own world of misery. The uncontrollable tremors made it hard to actually doze, so I spent my time in that halfway state of wakefulness and sleep.

A sudden cold bit into my skin, stealing my breath from me.

I gasped and my eyes flew open. Cold, azure eyes were staring down at me, but they held no malice. I closed my eyes, convinced my mind had conjured another fever dream, but when I opened them again, those eyes were still there.

"W… what are you doing here?" I asked, grinding my teeth at the cold.

Eamryel's lips twisted up in a wry smile. "Saving your ass from the looks of it."

"That's enough," Soren's voice spoke up from somewhere above and behind me.

I hissed when arms pulled me out of the cold water and an even colder breeze bit my skin. A splash of water indicated Eamryel was getting out too and when I looked up, I found him wrapped in a cloak, just as they were wrapping me up. My teeth were chattering so badly I felt certain they would rattle out of my mouth, but at least I knew I wasn't shivering from the fever now.

"Will this help?" my father asked from close by.

Soren answered. "Time will tell. We need to stay here for the night. It will be easier to monitor him."

"Staying will put us at risk more than we can afford." Father didn't sound pleased, and fear laced his voice.

Fear of what, I didn't know.

"Travelling now will put your son at risk," Soren replied stoically. "The choice is yours."

"I'll track back," Eamryel offered. "See if I can find out how far behind they are. I'll see you here in the morning."

There was a rustling, the whinny of a horse and the clatter of hooves disappearing into the night. I turned my head, finding that was all I could move, and narrowed my eyes at the brightness of the campfire—they still needed adjusting to any kind of light. As I pushed myself to my elbows, a sharp pain lanced through my abdomen and I fell back, stifling the scream at the tip of my tongue.

"Lie still," Soren instructed. "You sustained quite the injury."

"What happened?" I croaked.

My throat was parched, despite my submergence into the cold water. Soren was at my side a moment later and helped me up just a little so I could take a sip from the cup he was holding. The scent was oddly familiar, and as soon as the liquid came in contact with my tongue, I knew he was drugging me.

"*Grissin,*" I muttered.

I felt my head loll and my eyes roll back before I slipped back into darkness.

I CAME AROUND to different voices—softer, gentler, without stress or worry in them. The worst of the pain had subsided, and the fever seemed to have broken. Not that I knew for sure, but I felt a good deal less miserable than the past days. Or was it weeks? I had no recollection of how much time had passed. When I cracked one eye open, I was relieved to find the lights were dim. When I tried to move, I found that I could, although my stomach still lurched at the effort.

"Easy, *mahnèh*," Evan's tired voice sounded from my side. "You've been quite beaten up."

"What happened?" I asked, trying to sit up.

Putting any strain on my muscles turned out to be a bad idea. My arms gave way almost immediately, and I banged my head against the headboard. Evan snorted, then set out to help me by adding extra pillows behind my back.

"Soren instructed me to keep you in bed," Evan said, looking at me. "So be a good boy, and behave?"

I grunted. "And why would I listen to you?"

"Because you're a smart man, *Anahràn*," Soren's voice came from my other side. "And I assume that despite your intake of—herbs—you still know what it's like to make the right decision."

I scowled at him. "So, why this son of a h—"

Before I could finish the sentence, I stopped myself short, realising I would insult *Tari* Arayda, and I wasn't going to start that.

"Why is *he* here?" I growled, then turned to face Evan. "I thought you believed I was working for… for… *her*."

I spat the last word with venom, my skin crawling at the memory of what she had done to me—what Cehyan had done to me. My stomach clenched painfully, and if it hadn't been for Soren's fast response, I'd have thrown up all over him. The sudden movement made him grimace and jerk, bringing his other hand to just above his hip—the same location as my injury—as if something hurt him. When I blinked, his hand was gone and there was a hint of a smile on his face.

"Get some rest, Tal," Soren said with a heavy sigh. "The journey's been rough, and you need to recuperate. Please, for once, listen to advice."

I grimaced. "Let me rest alone then."

Without complaint, Evan rose to his feet. It was hard to tell in the dim light, but he looked almost guilty. I looked away while he plucked the pillows from behind my back. Before he left, Soren checked my heart rate and my pupils.

"Soren?"

He turned around to face me. "Yes?"

"Where are we?"

His lips turned up in a wry smile. "Welcome to *Denahryn*."

CHAPTER 28

SHALITHA

Never in my wildest dreams of travelling other countries, meeting new people, and having adventures of my own did I consider the option of all three at the same time while sitting tied up in the back of a wagon with my husband. The incessant screech and lurch of its wheels had gotten on my nerves miles ago, doing nothing favourable for my mood, and even Elay, whose usual cheerful disposition and abundance of energy exhausted me, appeared downright depressed by our situation.

At least it didn't rain here.

I shuffled around to make myself more comfortable, but my legs had started aching a while ago, and I wasn't sure my spine was still properly aligned.

"That scowl doesn't make you any prettier," Elay commented, a wry smile on his face.

"I wasn't going for pretty today," I muttered. "Happy isn't in the cards either."

Elay's lips curled up on one side in an attempt at amusement. I knew this had to be as hard on him as it was on me.

"Thankfully your sarcasm knows no bounds."

I huffed. "I'm surprised you haven't tried your charming personality yet. It works on every other woman."

Elay chuckled. "Are you saying you fell for my charms, *Tarien?*"

"No," I replied, swifter than intended. "And that's not the point either. How are we going to get out of this situation?"

Elay burst out laughing, eyes twinkling as he regarded me. "Sometimes, there's no way out of things."

I grunted and slumped back against the side of the wagon, glowering at him while mulling over his words. If we managed to escape, where would we go? We were in the middle of a massive desert, with nothing but sand in every direction. I'd learned first-hand what happened if you went out unprepared.

"I really don't feel like getting sold—again," I grumbled. "I'm not a piece of meat one can buy at the butcher's."

"Really?" Elay smirked, wiggling his eyebrows suggestively.

"Is that all you can think about?" My voice rose in indignation. "You're disgusting."

"Calm down, *Mìthri.*" He held up his hands in a placating manner—as far as the rope allowed him to. "I'm not trying to antagonise you. In case you hadn't noticed, I'm pretty much in the same situation, and I'm just trying to make the best of it."

I scrunched my nose but didn't comment, looking off into the distance instead. He was right, of course, but he was the only one I could lash out at.

"Apologies," I said with a heavy sigh. "All of this..."

"I know," he replied in a soft voice. "It puts me on edge too. Come"—he patted the side next to him—"sit with me. Please?"

Elay never said please if he wanted something.

I relented with a heavy sigh and scooted over to his side. The wagon tilted a little, but not enough to topple over. If he could have, he would have wrapped an arm around my shoulder, but as it was all he could do was take my hands in his and place a kiss on my knuckles. It was a sign of respect I wasn't sure I deserved right now.

"I'm scared," I whispered after a while. "What if"—I gulped, fighting back the tears—"I never get to return home?"

"I won't allow that," he replied with more confidence than I thought he had. "We'll get through this, *Mìthri*. You will get through this. You're strong."

He managed to caress my cheek, and not for the first time I found myself leaning into his touch, closing my eyes. Despite our arrangement—despite me denying the truth, Elay was having an effect on me, and it was intoxicating. It was just the moment—the entire situation. Nothing more.

There is nothing between us.

But while these thoughts circled through my mind, Elay placed a gentle kiss on my lips, and I found myself answering it. Had he been able to, his hand would have slid to the back of my neck to pull me close, but our movements were awkward due to our restraints, and the kiss was all the comfort he could give me.

"Get some rest, *Mìthri*," he murmured, resting his forehead against mine. "There's enough time to worry and make plans. You look like you can do with some sleep."

The bumpy ride and uncomfortable sleeping arrangements made for short nights and longs days, so when Elay offered for me to rest my head in his lap, I didn't object. It was a lot more comfortable than the floorboards of the wagon.

THE WAGON LURCHED TO A HALT, waking me up in the middle of a dream that left me gasping and groggy once the shock of being awake settled. I'd been back at the palace—Xaresh and Elara were still alive, and everything was the way it was supposed to be, except for one thing. Tal had been there too, I was sure of it, but somehow always on the edge, as if he'd been watching rather than participating. He'd been a blur, as if I somehow couldn't remember him correctly.

"Are we there yet?" I mumbled, making to rub my face when I remembered the ropes around my wrists.

A grunt of annoyance escaped my lips.

"No," Elay replied, his voice husky. "I think we're stopping for the night."

"Good, I'd like to stretch my legs."

Before I'd even finished my sentence, our captors hauled us out of the wagon. Pins and needles started in my feet and gradually travelled up to the rest of my legs until my face contorted in a grimace while stomping my feet on the ground to make it pass quicker.

"Interesting dance," Elay observed drily. "Ilvannian?"

I scowled at him. "Shut up, *grissin.*"

He sniggered but made no further comments. Despite having spent Gods know how much time cramped up in that wagon, he didn't seem too badly off.

"Get moving," my guard grunted, pushing me after Elay. "The captain wants to see you."

Captain?

It should have been obvious Rhana was the captain, but somehow my mind failed to connect the dots until we were ushered into the tent and she was the only one inside. I scowled at her.

"Don't look at me like that," she chided. "I'd expected more of a *Tarien*."

"I expected more of you too," I replied with a shrug. "Look how that turned out."

Rhana pulled up her lips in a snarl and stepped closer to me with a growl, raising a dagger against my chin.

"I can add more scars to that pretty face of yours," she hissed. "See if your husband still likes you then."

I pressed my lips into a thin line, eyes blazing furiously as I watched her.

"Rhana..." Elay sounded tired. "For old times' sake, can we not do this?"

She glared at me a little longer before she turned away with a derisive snort, but not before cutting the rope from our wrists.

"Get some rest," she muttered. "We'll be hunkering down due to sandstorms."

"What does that even mean?"

Elay smiled at me as he sat down, patting the pillow beside him. "Sit down, *Mìthri*. I'll explain."

He sounded as if he was talking to a child, which annoyed me, so I lay down next to him instead, pushing down my temper. I couldn't let it rule me—I had to rule it. Elay watched me with a soft smile, tucking some hair behind my ear.

Why was he so calm under all of this?

"What will happen when the sandstorm comes close," he began, "is that we'll take the tent-pole down, cover our faces, and pray to all the Gods and Goddesses that we'll live through it."

I frowned. "Pray? That's your solution?"

"There is nothing else we can do," he replied with a heavy sigh, rubbing his face. "Trust me, if there was, we'd be doing it."

"I suppose," I replied, and shrugged. "So, what happens when the tent blows away?"

"Then our lives are in the hands of *Fayra*," Rhana commented. "Pray you'll live through it."

"That's reassuring."

"What do you do in snowstorms?" Elay asked, his eyes alight with curiosity.

I wondered why he'd ask something like that when I realised he may never have seen snow, let alone a snowstorm.

Like I've never gone through a sandstorm.

"We stay indoors and try not to get kidnapped," I said

smugly, awarding Rhana an arched stare, "and definitely wouldn't take them through the mountains if we did. That's suicide."

"As you can see," Rhana spat back. "There isn't any other option than desert."

"You could have *not* kidnapped us," I retorted. "Problem solved."

"*Mìthri,*" Elay growled under his breath. "Calm down. Your snide comments aren't helping our case."

A scowl pulled my lips down and I turned on my side. "Fine. Wake me up, if this *nohro* sandstorm doesn't kill us first."

Elay laid a hand on my shoulder, but I shrugged it off. I had no mind to be nice to him—or to anyone for that matter. Honestly, I just wanted this nightmare to be over. Biting the inside of my cheek, I did my best not to fall apart, but silent tears trickled down my face regardless. Elay had offered me a different life—a chance of survival and a possibility to go home someday, but now all of that was made undone by a greedy *hehzèh*. Bile rose in my throat at the thought, and I had to fight the urge to throw up. Instead, I crawled into a ball and laid my arm over my eyes.

"THE SPECTACLE at the *k'ynshan* was quite unnecessary if you ask me," Rhana said. "How long do you plan on keeping this up?"

I didn't move, afraid their conversation would stop as soon as they noticed I was awake. I kept my breathing deep and slow as if I were asleep, but my body was strung tight as a bow.

Elay sighed heavily. "I don't want to keep anything up, Rhana. I have to tell her…"

"She might not forgive you if you do."

"That's what I fear."

They were silent for a little, the tension in the tent deepening with every passing moment. There was a rustle right next to me and the sound of someone walking around. A part of me wanted to turn around and look who it was, but that would surely give me away.

"I should have told her from the start," he said, sounding contrite. "She's not stupid, and she would have gone along."

"Are you sure?" Rhana asked. "Her temper tends to get the best of her in stressful situations."

"I know."

"What will happen if you don't tell her?"

"She'll slit my throat one night for not trusting her, I'm sure."

They had to be talking about me, but their words hardly made sense. What was Elay keeping up and what hadn't he told me?

"Does she know who you really are yet?" Rhana asked at length. "I planted the idea, just like you asked."

"She's not mentioned it," Elay replied, and I could feel him sit down next to me again.

In the next moment, I felt him brush my hair out of my face, so I quickly closed my eyes.

"Shalitha's been through so much already." He sighed. "And yet, I am putting her through this, for what?"

"Because you need her?"

He scoffed. "You and I are as much a warrior as she is. We could have done it."

"Maybe," Rhana replied, slower this time. "But I've never seen you this—happy. Relaxed even. She's doing something to you, *mishan,* whether you like it or not."

"That's exactly what I'm afraid of."

They fell silent again, and I wasn't sure I wanted to hear any more. My blood was boiling, and it took me all effort of will not to jump up and demand answers straightaway. I stretched lazily, attempting to appear to be waking up. Blinking, I turned on my back and looked straight into dark emerald eyes.

"You sleep like the dead," Elay murmured, leaning over to place a kiss on my lips.

I stiffened and turned my head away. After what I'd heard, I didn't want to kiss him. My response surprised him, because since our marriage, I'd never denied him one. I swallowed hard and sat up, rubbing my eyes.

"Did that sandstorm pass yet?"

"No," they replied simultaneously.

"Good."

Without saying anything, I rose to my feet and stalked out of the tent, arms wrapped around myself. The wind had picked up speed, sending sand dervishes to race each other across the wasteland. It bit my skin, but I didn't care. From the way they'd spoken I assumed this whole kidnapping wasn't what it appeared to be. There was no other explanation to it otherwise.

"Shal, wait!" Elay's voice sounded behind me, but it came from faraway.

No Mìthri now?

I stubbornly trudged on, shielding my eyes with my arm against the whirling sand, gritting my teeth against the sharp bites on my skin wherever it brushed past.

"*Mìthri*, come back! It's not safe out here!" His voice was muffled by the upcoming storm.

Even so, I kept moving forward, although it became harder and harder to go against the wind. Somehow, in this storm, Elay managed to catch up to me and grab my arm, making me turn around. His eyes were watering, and small lacerations appeared on his cheeks where grains of sand cut him.

"Please, come back inside," he all but shouted over the wind. "We'll die out here!"

"So what?" I shouted back, wrapping my arms tighter about me. "You don't trust me anyway, so why not just leave me here? Go back inside...save your own ass. I don't care!"

He stilled despite the storm.

"*Mìthri*, please! Let me explain!"

"No," I snarled. "You explained enough to Rhana. You're afraid of what I'm doing to you anyway… and just for the record, I would *never* slit your throat in the night. Ever."

I turned away from him.

Next thing I knew, he was on top of me and we went down into the sand. A howl of pain escaped my lips as my shoulder landed on something hard, sending sparks into my fingers. A moment later, something flew over our head, landing behind us with a loud crash.

"Please, Shal," he said, his voice close to my ear. "Please come back inside and let me explain."

Between the two of us, we managed to get back into the tent, and as soon as we did, Rhana pulled down the pole.

"Lie down," she instructed. "Cover your nose with your shirt and keep your eyes closed."

"And pray," I murmured.

By the Gods, don't let me die here.

CHAPTER 29

TALNOVAR

Between my father and Soren, I managed to get to my feet, taking a few steps before my legs gave way and I hung between them. A frustrated growl escaped my lips, and if I could have, I would have pushed both of them away. It was bad enough I had had to rely on them for the past week for even the most basic of needs, and now this? Gritting my teeth, I pushed myself to a standing position and locked my knees so I wouldn't sink through them again.

"Baby steps," Soren said. "Don't try to take giant leaps just yet."

"Easy for you to say," I muttered. "You don't have to."

"Reminds me of a time when he was much younger," Father said, his lips turned up in a mischievous grin. "He tried to run before he could take proper steps."

"Father," I groaned. "I'm sure Soren doesn't need to hear about my baby years."

"On the contrary," Soren mused. "It would be interesting to find out what makes you tick, *Anahràn*."

I growled at both of them, earning laughter from either side. With a derisive snort, I placed one foot in front of the other.

Baby steps. That's what Azra had reduced me to—what I had allowed her to reduce me to. A sudden wave of nausea hit me, and I had to make a conscious effort not to throw up. Whenever I thought of her, a deep hatred rose within me, and I wanted nothing more than to go back and rip her head off.

No, she deserves a slow, painful death.

I grimaced as pain rippled through my abdomen, cursing her in my mind with fervour. Father and Soren noticed and halted our progress.

"Tal? Everything all right?" Father asked.

I shook my head, biting down the pain. "No. Please, get me back."

They managed to get me to the bed and tucked me in before it got any worse.

"Mind if I have a look?" Soren asked.

Father excused himself on account of having business elsewhere, and left us looking a little squeamish. One would think the *Ohzheràn* of an army could deal with blood.

"Have at it," I replied, lying back with a groan. "I'm not sure I could stop you."

"Probably not."

A hiss escaped my lips when he pulled up my shirt and unwrapped the bandage around my waist. Despite myself, I looked at the still healing injury no wider than the blade of a dagger. According to Soren, I'd been a lucky man—half an inch either way and she would have damaged more than he could have healed.

I didn't believe him.

Despite my delirious dreams, I remembered the night I almost died quite vividly. I'd seen Varayna, my sister, and my mother, but there had been a feeling in the background I hadn't been able to place. I was sure I had died, or had been so close nothing could have gotten me back. For a moment, that feeling of pain, cold and despair had made way for warmth, light and confidence, much like an embrace.

Like life pouring back into me.

But that made no sense whatsoever.

My focus returned to Soren when he began prodding the flesh around the injury, and I hissed.

"By Esah," I grouched. "I did not miss this."

"I would hope not." Soren chuckled, eyes twinkling. "I'd be concerned if you actually enjoyed this."

I awarded him a deadpan stare. "What's the verdict?"

"Nothing to be concerned about. The injury is still healing, although I wouldn't be surprised that it's still sensitive on the inside too. No training anytime soon."

I grunted. "Not what I wanted to hear."

"You need to take it easy, Tal," Soren said, suddenly serious. "This injury is healing, but I have no idea the mental or physical damage the drugs have done"—he rubbed his jaw, adding much more softly—"or her abuse for that matter."

"I don't want to talk about it."

"I know." He smiled at me. "Nobody blames you for that."

"So you've finally come around to my side of the story?" I muttered. "All of you?"

He arched a brow. "Nobody ever took another side, Tal. We saw what she was doing to you—what you were doing to yourself because of it."

"Yet none of you intervened," I snarled. "None of you came to see how I was doing after..." I swallowed hard. "Please, leave."

Soren left the room without arguing, and I slumped back into the pillows, rubbing my temples. A bout of self-loathing rose to the surface and started dragging me down into its depths. A howl of fury escaped my lips, like it did several times a day, and I banged the mattress with my fists, letting rage consume me until I was spent and drifted off to sleep almost immediately.

SOME TIME HAD PASSED since our arrival at Denahryn, which for me had been measured in constant pain and agony, but after what felt like forever, Soren gave me permission to pick up training. I hadn't wasted any time. Sweat ran in little rivulets between my shoulder blades, down my back, sending cold shivers down my body whenever a lick of wind kissed it. My arms were trembling under the effort of going through the calm set of motions called *iñaeique* that we used to regain our focus. It was both the easiest and the hardest part of training as it required being both calm and in control.

I felt neither.

I moved so shakily it frustrated me, and Evan's orders to keep my arms up, twist my body farther, and mind my feet didn't make it any better either. It reminded me of a time when I was giving these orders, perfecting positioning, showing them through the moves. All of these, I knew by heart, or should have known by heart.

It was as if a lifetime had passed and I struggled to remember.

"Focus." Evan's voice cut through my reverie. "You're slacking."

"I'm trying," I growled in response.

"Try harder."

He looked as happy to be here as I was. We hadn't spoken since our first night at *Denahryn,* nor had we resolved any of the issues between us. I was still mad at him for believing that *hehzèh* and thinking I was on her side, even though he did follow up on my information. The memory of that day stopped me short and a wave of nausea hit me. I staggered back a few steps, inhaling deeply to make the feeling go away.

It didn't.

When Chazelle's face came to mind, all I could see was the

vacant expression in her eyes and feel the warm blood on my hands as I relived the memory of killing her. I turned away, adding the contents of my stomach to the grass. When I dropped to my knees, Evan was there in an instant.

"Are you all right, *mahnèh*?" he asked worriedly.

"Why do you care?" I muttered, carefully sitting down with my knees drawn up, head between them.

"Because," Evan began, his voice strained. "Despite everything that happened... you're still my friend, Tal."

I huffed. "I could have used one when that *hehzèh* was making my life miserable."

Evan was silent for a while. He settled himself next to me, stretching his legs out in front of him.

"I know," he said at length. "And I tried in the beginning, but"—he dragged a hand through his hair, pushing himself up to sit cross-legged—"She was doing it to everyone, you know? Maybe not as bad as to you… She really seemed to have it in for you, but our steps were watched, our decisions controlled. It was hard enough as it was and I… I had Nath and the baby to think of."

I nodded mutely.

"These moons have been rough on all of us, Tal," he continued in a soft voice. "And you—you changed. Soren's been to visit you on several occasions, but he was turned away every time by Cehyan. Ever since you hooked up with her…"

I growled under my breath at the mention of her name, then stopped short when my mind caught up with something else he'd said. "Moons? What do you mean, moons?"

Evan glanced at me, confusion written on his face. "It's been six moons since Mother's death, *mahnèh*."

I blinked stupidly. "When was the... when did we… how long ago when she…"

While I struggled to find the words, make sense of the questions in my mind, Evan's face took up a look of compassion.

"It's been almost three moons ago," he answered, clearly knowing what I was referring to. "Between the injury and withdrawals, you've been out of it for more than a moon, including the journey here."

I rubbed my face, trying to process all the information.

"A lot has happened," Evan continued, a faint smile on his lips. "But the telling of it will have to wait until you've regained more of your strength. Ready for some actual training?"

He laughed when I scowled at him, then helped me to my feet.

"Listen, Tal. I'm truly sorry for what happened and… I hope you can forgive me. Maybe not yet, but… later."

"We all make mistakes," I replied with a shake of my head. "I might have done the same had I been in your situation."

His lips quirked up in a faint smile. "Don't judge until you've heard everything."

The tone of his voice was laden with guilt and something I couldn't quite place, but I couldn't argue his assessment I needed my strength back. With Azra out of my life, at least for now, I could finally focus on the promise I had made the *Tari* so long ago, except that I had no idea where to begin looking.

"Ready?" Evan asked.

"THE GOOD NEWS," Soren said falsely cheerfully. "It's not broken. The bad news is that it will be sore for a while."

Evan grunted, holding a cloth against his nose.

"Had I known you could still throw a punch," he muttered, glaring at me, "I'd have been more careful."

I smirked. "Rule number one, *mahnèh*. Never underestimate your enemy, no matter how injured he is. He's got nothing left to lose."

He grunted again. "Duly noted."

"As for you," Soren turned to me, eyes narrowing. "I thought I told you not to overdo it. Lie down."

I gave him a deadpan stare which he returned with more enthusiasm than I felt, so I lay down as instructed, grimacing as the stitches pulled at my flesh. Soren smirked at me.

"Is everyone at *Denahryn* like you?" I asked.

"Like what?"

"A sadist," Evan commented drily.

Soren laughed softly. "For a pair of strong men like yourselves, you sure complain a lot. The *Tarien* has more balls than you."

I started up.

Has. He doesn't believe it either?

"You mean had?" I ventured carefully.

Soren awarded me a close-lipped smile. "Yes, of course, had. Apologies, I still find it hard to believe at times…"

The blatant lie fell off his lips too smoothly. The look in his eyes was one of warning, and when he glanced at Evan, I understood why.

Evan rose to his feet with a heavy sigh. "I'm going to check in on Nath. Same time tomorrow, Tal."

I nodded, anxiously waiting for Evan to leave so I could interrogate Soren, but the moment he was gone and I turned on the healer, he pressed his fingers to his mouth.

"Not here," he murmured. "The walls have ears. Come with me."

DENAHRYN LOOKED SIMILAR TO *HANYARAH*, the sisterhood where I'd lost Shal, in many ways, yet the difference was that it wasn't just men here, there were women too—women dressed in the attire of *haniya.*

"Is this where the sisters went after *Hanyarah*?" I asked softly.

"Those who survived, yes."

I shuddered at the memories. Despite Rurin's warnings, we'd been late—almost too late. The Sisterhood had been burning, and many women had been slaughtered. Haerlyon, Shal and their men had fought with everything they'd been worth, and although we'd won that fight, we'd lost the battle. So many men and women had died that day, and all because of the ambitions of one woman in particular.

We lost almost everything that day.

I clenched and unclenched my fists, keeping my temper in check.

"*Denahryn* has always been home to those who had none," Soren said. "For many centuries, people have come here to rest, to study, to live. As many have gone away again, ventured elsewhere, taken up different lives. Some stayed to follow the path and become a *Dena*, a brother."

"Like you?"

Soren smiled softly. "Yes, it was the only place for me to go."

"Why?"

Sadness crossed his features, but it was gone as quickly as it'd come, but his voice was soft and heavy when next he spoke.

"My mother worked hard to earn a living for the both of us, but we lived near a small town in the mountains, and although she knew her craft well and many people sought out her expertise, it was always hard," he said. "So I did what I had to do and went to fend for myself."

"What about your father?"

He shrugged. "I've never known him. He died before I was born."

"I'm sorry to hear that."

"Don't be."

We continued our way in silence. In the late afternoon sun, *Denahryn* looked a picture. Surrounded by snow-capped mountains, I imagined being back at the palace, on the training fields, and for a brief moment, I was happy. The only difference I could discern was the thinner air.

That explains a lot.

It also explained the heavy garments the *Dena* wore, as well as the cold air I'd felt the few times I'd been outside. For the most part, I'd spent my time under blankets and fur in a hut where a fire was kept going all day and all night. Training had happened in a secluded garden, and my surroundings hadn't exactly been my focus. Today was the first time I had a good look at the place.

The huts were built in clusters of fours and fives, dotted throughout what I assumed to be a valley of sorts, creating the image of a peaceful mountain village. Tall pine trees seemed to sprout haphazardly around the premises, whereas the outskirts blended with a forest. Not only was *Denahryn* protected by the mountains, but by the trees as well. From where I stood, I could see no clear entrance—or exit for that matter.

Like Hanyarah, and yet, we'd found it.

"Where is *Denahryn* exactly?" I asked.

Soren looked up. "We're in the mountains of Naehr."

I blinked. "But that's at least three weeks of travelling..."

"More than four when you carry around deadweight," he replied, looking amused. "But yes."

"What about... *her*?" I asked, swallowing hard. "Does she know where we are?"

"No," Soren replied, eyes turning steely. "Unless someone on the inside is working with her, but I highly doubt that."

"Why?"

"Because the *Dena* know what she's done to *Hanyarah*." A female voice, one I thought I'd never hear again, answered.

"Mehrean?" I whispered in shock, my gaze snapping towards her. "Y... you're alive?"

"Hello, Tal," she said with a soft smile.

CHAPTER 30

SHALITHA

The sandstorm had been relentless in its passing. Most of the *camelles* hadn't survived, nor had the wagon, and we were missing one of the guards. Thankfully, the water and food supply had been in Rhana's tent, but our mode of transportation was gone, which had left us trudging through the desert for almost a fortnight now. Our progress was slow, not just because of the sand, but because Rhana had decreed that the tent should be brought, because between here and wherever we were going, there was hardly any shelter. It was too cold to stay outside during the nights, and too hot to travel when the sun was highest, so we walked in the morning and the late afternoons, until the weather made us stop.

I hadn't spoken to Elay since the night of the sandstorm.

Not because of the lack of effort on his part, but because I felt betrayed. Again. Sure, our arrangements were completely insane to begin with, but I had promised my help with whatever problem he had, and that alone warranted some trust, in my opinion. Normally, I wouldn't have cared about him not trusting me, yet somehow, it had hurt.

Deeply.

He'd given up trying after three days.

His misery was palpable and obvious in the way he hunched his shoulders or snapped at the people around him. Although Rhana was Captain, it was clear he was in charge now. The restraints hadn't come back on, but that was probably on account of me not being stupid enough to flee into nowhere.

As if he would care.

One night, I'd overheard them talking of finding a town for new supplies, even if it meant veering off the path and adding days, if not a week, to the travelling schedule. My interest had been piqued when they mentioned it was a coastal town. Perhaps, if I played my cards right, I could find passage to Therondia, maybe even to Ilvanna, and figure out my next move from there. The thought of leaving Elay just like that after him saving my life—more than once—made me feel sick though.

But he didn't trust you. He could have told you—should have told you.

I scowled at my inner voice, reminding it that he wanted to explain, but I wasn't letting him. Whatever his reasons, they were already moot. Aggravated by my own thoughts, I stomped along, tired of seeing and feeling sand *everywhere*. All of a sudden, sand rustled beneath me and I lost my footing, sending me crashing down whatever hill we'd been on.

"Elay!"

At least I had the presence of mind to keep my eyes closed and press my arms to my body. My momentum kept me moving forward and forward until I landed at the bottom, hitting my head on the ground.

"*Mìthri*!" Elay's voice sounded from above and distant.

The world was a myriad of shapes and colours.

"Shal, talk to me." He was close now.

He brushed hair and sand from my face, and helped me sit up. My head spun and a wicked headache was spreading fast, but other than that and sand everywhere in my clothing, I appeared to be fine.

"Are you all right?" Elay asked, fussing over me.

"I guess," I muttered, "but I'm quite done with the desert now."

He smiled faintly. "We're only a few miles out of a city, according to one of the scouts. We'll resupply and change clothes there."

I'd never been happier with those words.

After Elay helped me to my feet, we waited for the rest to catch up to us as they half-slid, half-walked down the slope I had rolled down from. It looked so easy for them. Meanwhile, I was trying to get sand out of the most uncomfortable places and failing miserably at the attempt. Elay's smug smile only infuriated me more.

"What are you smiling about?" I grumped.

"You're talking to me again."

I scowled. "Don't get used to it. I still haven't forgiven you."

"*Mìthri*," he said with a heavy sigh. "Please, just let me explain."

"No," I said, turning away from him so I could wipe the sand from under my breasts without giving him any ideas.

"You are one stubborn woman," he said, annoyance in his voice. "Why can't we talk this over?"

"Because!" I yelled, turning to him so fast he took a step back, my voice low when next I spoke. "Because you betrayed me, Elay, and I've been betrayed enough to last me a lifetime. Two lifetimes, in fact."

"*Mìthri*, I..." He fell silent, a despondent look on his face. "I'm sorry. I didn't mean to—"

"But you did."

When I turned away from him, I could feel him step closer, and I stilled. I expected him to place a hand on my shoulder, or wrap his hands around my waist, but there was none of it.

"Ready to go?" Rhana's voice cut in. "We can make it to the city before nightfall."

"Yes, we are," Elay replied steadily.

I watched him as he sidestepped me, watched as he glanced back, pain suffusing his features. I wrapped my arms around myself and started after them, trying not to feel like the worst *hehzèh* in this world.

He'll forgive you, but you may have to forgive him too.

I hated my inner voice, especially when it was right. I just didn't want to talk to him with Rhana around or any of the others for that matter. If I talked to him, it would be on my terms and in my time. I felt deplorable at that reasoning, but Elay needed to learn that not everyone danced to his tunes. A cry of happiness caught my attention and when I looked up, a city the size of Y'zdrah was in full view.

Thank be the Gods.

THE CITY WAS a lot like Y'zdrah in its setup and there were people everywhere. The main road, which began as soon as we entered through the gate, had stalls lined up left and right, and vendors were selling their wares by shouting at the crowd. My eyes swept every which way, trying to take it all in when Elay suddenly stepped in front of me.

"Put this over your hair," he murmured, placing a shawl on top of my head. "Portasâhn is a trader's city with ships coming in from every direction. If someone recognises you…"

I nodded and began tucking my hair underneath the shawl, keeping my eyes downcast. Elay hooked my arm through his, resting his hand on mine.

"What are you doing?" I asked through my teeth. "I'm still mad at you."

"Be mad all you like," he replied in kind, "but I promised to keep you safe when I married you, and that's exactly what I'm doing."

I snorted but didn't respond.

"Things are different over here, *Mìthri*, and you may not like it, but in my world, women usually don't go about alone," he whispered. "Respectable women are always accompanied by a male family member, or their husband."

I stiffened. "Why wasn't that the case in Y'zdrah?"

"Because my city was built from scratch and became home to those who were outcasts. Such rules were unnecessary."

"Except for your wives?"

Elay shook his head. "My wives were a target because they married me. What kind of husband would I be if I didn't protect them?"

"I'm not like your other wives," I muttered. "I do not scheme, and I can perfectly well fend for myself."

His lips quirked up at the corners, but the amusement never reached his eyes. "That may very well be true, but you're also in a country you know little about, and who you are makes you a target for anyone who has any idea of what's going on outside their little world."

"Fine." I snapped my mouth shut.

"Come." He sounded resigned. "Let's go find a place for the night. You look like you can do with some proper sleep tonight."

I was of half a mind to decline, but the headache had only gotten worse throughout the day, and if I was being completely honest with myself, Elay was right. I needed more than some soldier's shuteye.

After instructing her men, Rhana guided us to the harbour side of Portasâhn with an easy swagger inviting anyone with ill intentions to give it a try. My hand hovered above where my sword was supposed to be, only for me to realise I wasn't carrying one. A disgruntled sound escaped my lips, catching Elay's attention.

"What's wrong?" he asked under his breath, staying close to my side.

"Nothing of importance."

Nevertheless, my eyes swivelled left to right, fast enough to increase the headache tenfold. I wouldn't be caught off guard though. Not now—not ever. The back of my neck prickled as if I was being watched, but casting a furtive look over my shoulder revealed nothing.

"Relax, *Mìthri*," Elay murmured. "We're almost there."

I glared at him, lips pressed together.

We halted in front of a decent enough stone building tucked away between two derelict looking places on the water's edge. Paint was peeling off the window sills, and the door looked about ready to rot from its hinges, but if I'd learned anything in the past weeks, it was that looks could be deceiving. When Rhana pushed the door open, we were welcomed by music and song the likes of which I'd never heard before.

The inside of the waterfront inn was a far cry from its outward appearance, in the positive sense of the word. A mish-mash of tapestries lined the floor from front to back, left to right, cushioning our footsteps to a dull thud as we stepped inside. The walls appeared as if they'd recently seen new paint, and the furniture was polished until it gleamed in the candlelight.

A man the size of Xaresh in both height and width walked towards us with surprising grace, flashing a set of pearly white teeth in night dark skin. The sides of his head were shaven and decorated, but it was too dark to tell whether it was his version of an *Araîth,* or something else.

"*Mishan,* welcome to the *Scarlet Queen*," the man said in a pleasant enough voice. "How may I help you?"

His blatant disregard for both Rhana and myself didn't go by unnoticed. Her hand inched upwards, ready to take the quarterstaff from her back, but one scorching look from Elay halted her progress. He turned to the man with a bright smile.

"I'd like two rooms, if you have them."

Two. Not after your betrayal, grissin.

"Of course, *Mishan.* Right this way."

Before either of us could protest, Elay guided us up the stairs after the innkeeper, the look on his face warning us to curb our annoyance. His earlier words about women not going alone came to mind, and I realised it was probably the reason behind the man's dismissal of us. To him, we were non-existent—commodities brought in by Elay, our master in some way. The thought turned me cold from the inside out.

As if Ilvanna is much better.

By all accounts, Ilvanna was the same with its ridiculous laws about men not being allowed to ascend the throne and all that nonsense. But it was custom—tradition. It had been done like this forever.

As is this, most likely.

It reduced my annoyance about the man's behaviour at least, but it came back with a vengeance as soon as he showed us two rooms next to each other. One for Rhana, one for Elay and myself. At least, that's what I assumed. Indignation towards Elay's careless assumptions rose within me, but I managed to constrain myself and listened with eyes cast down, a demure smile on my lips.

Two rooms. Keep dreaming.

The innkeeper's words passed me in a haze, and as soon as he was gone, I made a beeline for the closest room, shutting and locking the door behind me. As expected, a knock sounded on the door.

"*Mìthri?*" Elay asked, confused. "Why did you close the door?"

"You know why, Elay. And if you don't, you've got an entire night to figure it out!"

"But I—," he began.

"Sweet dreams, Elay."

Ignoring the rest of his protests, I stripped down to my underclothing and flopped down on the bed, barely able to pull the blanket on top of me before drifting off into a deep sleep.

NEXT MORNING ARRIVED with a persistent knocking on the door that wouldn't go away even after I told it to stop. At first I thought it was in my dream, but opening the door hadn't helped. With a few choice curse words in whoever-was-banging-my-door-down's direction, I slipped out of bed and pulled the blanket along, wrapping it around me as I made my way over to answer. After unlocking it, I cracked it open, only to find Elay standing there, holding a plate of breakfast.

"Good morning."

I grunted and contemplated slamming the door in his face for the simple fact that his style of waking me up was barbaric, but he did bring me food, and my stomach was protesting quite fitfully. With a heavy sigh, I pulled the door open and shuffled back to the bed, crawling back in it.

"I've never seen you this groggy in the morning," Elay observed, placing the tray on the bedside cabinet. "Is everything all right?"

"I'm fine."

He lifted an eyebrow and cocked his head as if to ask if the lie convinced me.

I glowered at him. "Don't look at me like that."

A snort escaped his lips, and with a shake of his head, he sat down on the bed, offering me a cup of something I couldn't quite place. The scent was deep and earthy, almost as if something had burnt. A frown creased my brow as I took the cup from him, inhaling deeply.

"What's this?"

"*Keffah*," Elay replied, smiling brightly. "The best brew in the world for those mornings where you're not sure whether you're alive or dead."

I smirked. "Like this morning?"

"If you say so."

His eyes were alight with joy as he took a sip of his drink. I sniffed it as if it were poison before taking a careful sip. A bitter taste immediately washed through my mouth, and I shuddered, pulling a face. Elay burst out laughing.

"Not a *keffah* lover, I see."

"This stuff is vile!" I retorted, resisting the urge to clean my tongue with the back of my hand.

I knew it would be futile, but I needed something to take away the ashy taste. My eyes fell on the breakfast tray, and leaning over, I took a slice of bread from it, wolfing it down as if it were the last piece in the world.

"Hungry too? I should've brought more."

"In my defence," I began, "we haven't had a proper night's rest, or proper food in some days."

"I know." He sighed, a dark look in his eyes. "Rhana's already out to buy supplies. She told me to take it easy today, catch up on sleep, but there's something I'd like to show you."

I raised a brow in question. "What would that be?"

"A *sa'aneh*," he answered. "Or bathhouse, in the common tongue. You can freshen up and relax some. It's the least I can do after…"

Anger rose inside of me at where his words were going, and whatever he saw on my face stopped him short. We still hadn't spoken about what I learned during the night of the storm, and I still wasn't quite sure I could forgive him for not trusting me. By all accounts, I was being a *hehzèh* about it, but I didn't want him to think he could get away with everything.

I wasn't like his other wives.

At all.

If the *sa'aneh* was anything like the pool at his palace, or the hot spring at *Hanyarah,* I was in for a treat. Regarding him with my head slightly tilted, I watched him squirm underneath my gaze, but only a little.

"Very well."

His shoulders sagged in relief, and a smile hinted on his lips. "I'll let you dress and meet you downstairs."

I scowled at the idea of having to put on the dirty, sand-riddled garments and made a face. "I don't suppose we can pick up anything clean to wear?"

Surprise stole over his features. "Why not?"

"Good. Let's do that first then. Going to this… *Sa'aneh* will be pointless if I don't have anything not containing sand to dress in."

"That bad?"

"You have no idea."

Elay left me to my dressing with a chuckle. As the door closed behind him, I gathered my garments from the floor and shook the worst of the sand from them. I wrinkled my nose at the smell as I pulled them on, thanking Elay in my mind for agreeing to get something new. It wasn't that I despised the smell, but sand had the nasty habit of getting everywhere, and my skin was already raw in uncomfortable places. After making sure I had all my possessions, however few they were, I left the room, wrapping the shawl over my hair.

TRUE TO HIS WORD, Elay bought me a new set of undergarments and clothing before heading to the *Sa'aneh,* which was situated in the upper class part of the city. Here, people regarded us curiously as we passed, eyes on the flamboyant Zihrin noble with his easy smile and exotic woman on his arm. If I were to believe their own words, it was unheard of for our races to mingle. Elay wasn't perturbed, if he had heard them at all. As for me, I couldn't care either way what they thought of us.

Not this time.

When we halted in front of a grand mansion close to what appeared to be the outskirts of the city, Elay turned to me with a gentle smile.

"Welcome to Portasâhn's most famous *Sa'aneh*."

"Thank you?" I replied somewhat hesitant. "I think."

The bathhouse was quite something else. High arched windows were spaced evenly throughout the walls, and all of them were dark as if they held solid black rock instead of windows. Elay guided me through a vaulted doorway into an open space with a single desk. A stout man stood behind it, hunched over something in front of him. On a gentle cough of Elay, he looked up, his features transforming with the bright grin he awarded us.

"*Mishan. Amisha.* Welcome. What can I do for you?"

"How busy is it today?" Elay asked, his voice taking on a tone of business.

I took a step back, tilting my head slightly.

"Business is slow, *Mishan.* People can no longer afford it."

I perked up at his words. "How come?"

The words left my mouth quicker than I'd formed them, which was met with a stunned look from the *Sa'aneh's* proprietor, and a bemused look from Elay.

"Forgive my wife," he said. "She's still learning our customs."

"It's quite all right, *Mishan.* Taxes have gone up, and people earn less and less ever since trade with Kyrintha stopped after the borders were closed. Although we're a trader's port, goods and foods are in short supply. Kyrintha was our biggest trade partner."

Elay tensed. I could tell from the way his shoulders straightened as a familiar tic started in his jaw. If the man's words had triggered the response, I wasn't sure about the reason, but I doubted he would want to talk about it.

After enough haggling and several gold pieces passing hands, the *sa'aneh* was emptied from the few occupants present so that Elay and I had it for ourselves—something I was fairly certain wasn't up to normal standards judging by the frown on the proprietor's face as we entered.

Past the desk was a hallway lit by candles, their flames dancing in the light draft wafting through an endless tunnel. At its end was another open space where we could undress. Despite having been married to Elay for a little while now, I'd never seen him fully naked, and the thought was somewhat disconcerting.

"Here." He handed me a thin towel. "You can wrap it around yourself if you want."

"Thank you."

We both undressed separately from each other, and after having wrapped myself in the sizeable cloth, I stepped out of the room into the next one. My breath caught in my throat in surprise. The rectangular space was enormous, its ceiling at least three storeys up, but the most striking feature of all was the way the light, streaming in from small windows at the top, played on millions of little tiles in hues of green, black and gold.

"Beautiful, isn't it?" Elay asked from my side.

I nodded.

"We'll have a proper bath first," he continued without looking at me. "I've arranged for a massage after."

"A massage?"

He looked at me curiously, his head tilted. "You sound as if you have no idea what I'm talking about."

"I know what it is." I sounded exasperated, a little annoyed even. "But why a massage?

"Because you look like you could do with one."

Breathing in deeply, I watched tendrils of steam rise lazily from the warm water and exhaled in a loud puff, turning to him.

"Perhaps you're right."

I'm tired enough not to want to fight him.

As if reading my thoughts, Elay guided me to one of the hot baths, and while he dropped the towel, I slid into the water with mine still wrapped around me. Even though he was my husband, and even though he'd seen me half-naked before, full naked even, I didn't feel comfortable this time.

After what had happened, he felt more like a stranger than ever.

"Do you have siblings?"

I touched my throat, lifting an eyebrow. "Two brothers, why?"

"I have a younger sister, Naïda," he said, sadness coating his words. "I haven't seen her in a very long time. Two brothers, Jehleal and Nahram, and a half-brother too, but Kehran and I never got along well."

"Why not?"

He flashed me a lopsided grin. "Sibling rivalry."

I smiled at that. "I understand."

"Do you ever fight with your brothers?"

"Literally or figuratively?"

Elay snorted. "I should've expected an answer like that."

"My brothers, Evanyan and Haerlyon, are both *Zheràn* in the Ilvannian army. We've trained in the past, but Haer and I… We used to pull pranks on each other, one worse than the other, until Mother would step in and make us stop. We usually did, for about a week or so." A smile tugged at my lips. "Haer and I. We understand each other on a level most people don't."

"It was the same between my middle brother, Nahram, and me too."

"Was?"

"He died when I was young." His lips quirked up in a faint smile. "An accident."

"I'm sorry."

We were silent for a long time after, both of us drawn into our own complicated worlds of emotions. If I'd learned anything about Elay, it was that he guarded his well. What he did show was what he felt comfortable with, but it was easy to see it was a ruse he held in place for those who didn't know how to observe.

A gentle cough startled us both from our reverie and looking up, a young man and a young woman stood waiting off to the side.

"It's time for your massages, *mishan, amisha,*" the young man said. "If you could please come with us."

I glanced at Elay and my heart started to race. He inclined his head and rose to his feet, stepping out of the tub careless of who would see him in his naked glory. Torn between watching him and looking away, I opted for the latter as I got out, keeping the heavy wet towel around me.

"Go with the young woman, *Mìthri,*" Elay said softly, looking at me. I'll see you after."

I tensed. "Where will you be?"

"Close. Don't worry."

Before I could ask what he meant, the young woman ushered me into another room. Elay's deep tenor rumbled towards me from another room, but I couldn't make out the words. Hearing it took away the edge of my discomfort, so I looked around, gazing at my new surroundings. A tiled table stood in the middle, and the scent of a flowery soap hung in the air.

"Please, take off the towel," the young woman said gently, "and lie down on the table."

My moves were awkward when I let the towel drop to the ground, trying to cover up everything with only two hands, but when I looked, the young woman had her back to me. As I got onto the table I found, much to my surprise and delight, that it was warm, and wetter than I expected, so I nearly slithered off the other end. With my heart racing in my chest, I carefully settled down, holding the edges as if my life depended on it.

A hiss escaped my lips when a warm cloth was placed over my hips first, and shoulders next, only to settle into a sigh of relief as some of the tension left my body. The young woman took my arms and placed them gently along my sides.

"Relax, *amisha,*" she murmured. "Just let this happen."

Even if I'd wanted to fight against relaxation, between the warmth suffusing my muscles, her deft hands massaging my body, and the scent of lavender in the air, I soon found myself drifting off to a state where I was neither asleep nor awake. I heard her move around, kept feeling her hands on my skin, but I was too far away to respond properly.

All too soon, she finished.

"You are done, *amisha,*" the young woman murmured. "I hope you enjoyed it."

I nodded, a pleased smile spreading across my lips.

Unfortunately, the peace and quiet was short-lived when Elay came barrelling into the room, holding a package in his hands.

"Get dressed."

"What? Why?" I asked as I slipped off the table, taking the offered parcel.

"*Mìthri,* now is not the time for questions."

The urgency in his voice had me hopping around on one foot as I struggled into the right pants leg. As soon as I had my shirt over my head and my feet in my shoes, Elay grabbed my wrist and started pulling me along.

"Elay, what's going on?" I hissed, stumbling after him. "You're hurting me."

We stood in a small courtyard when I heard it—loud,

demanding voices coming from inside. A sudden fight and flight reaction kicked in, preparing my body to flee.

A loud groan escaped my lips. "Not again."

Elay grinned mischievously. "Hope you haven't lost your touch."

I glanced at him and followed his steps without conscious effort. One step back, two steps back, until our backs were against the wall.

"Can you make it?"

I grinned at him. "Can you?"

He counted down on his fingers. Five. Four. Three. Two. One.

"Go!"

CHAPTER 31

TALNOVAR

Flames danced in the light draft seeping through the hut while the fire crackled in the hearth on my right. Goosebumps rippled across my arms, so I hugged the mug of tea tighter to my chest. I'd have preferred something stronger, but with my recent past, neither my father, nor Soren, nor Mehrean allowed me any *ithri*.

I couldn't blame them.

Pinching the bridge of my nose, I looked at Mehr. "So, you're saying you've been planning this since before Arayda's death?"

She nodded, her face calm and unapologetic.

"Why didn't you tell me?" I asked, hurt I'd been left out of their plans.

"Because you, Evan and Haerlyon were her primary targets," Mehrean explained. "If we had told you, our plans would have failed..."

"And they haven't now?"

She grimaced and looked away. Although the rebels had managed to enter the palace and do damage, Azra had known they were coming, and her men had been waiting for them.

"We still don't know who tipped her off," Father said with a heavy sigh, rubbing his cheek. "We've been very selective with people, and only a handful knew the full plan."

Something jogged my memory. "Who?"

Father began ticking off a list of people from the top of his head and I listened attentively. When Ruvaen's name fell, I stopped him.

"What happened to Vaen?" I asked, tightening the hold on the cup in my hands.

"He was killed almost straight away," Father said. "It was almost as if they were expecting him."

"They were," I growled, looking up at him. "Has Cehyan been found?"

"Cehyan?" Mehrean and Soren sounded surprised.

Father just sighed and shook his head. "No, I haven't seen her at all except for a few times at the palace, but during the night of the rebellion, I didn't see her."

I stilled. "Oh, she was there all right… and she must have told Azra."

"How do you know?" Mehrean tilted her head.

"I just do," I said clipped, refusing to look at her.

I couldn't tell her what had happened. I had the vague idea Soren knew—Father most definitely did, and those were already more people than I thought was necessary. Taking a swig from my cup, I stared into the fire, my voice soft when I spoke.

"I have reasons to believe she's been playing both sides," I said. "If Cehyan is one thing, it's an opportunist. She'll have done everything to save her own ass."

"You seem to know her quite well?" Mehrean tilted her head.

"And it's none of your business," I snapped. "Stop asking."

"I never did."

Downing the cup of tea, I put it aside and rose to my feet, pacing up and down the small space in front of the hearth. The injury was more than a nuisance, but I bit back the pain and continued anyway.

Soren could have a go at me later.

"Now what?" I asked, turning to face all three of them. "We're outlaws, exiles… one step in Ilvanna and they'll come after us with pitchforks and fire."

Mehrean's lips twitched up in a faint smile. "Now we go find the *Tarien*."

I stared at her, then glanced at Soren and my father. "So, you all believe she's still alive?"

"We… know she is," Father said almost hesitantly.

"How?"

"Because I've seen her." Eamryel stepped out of another room.

I lunged at him straight away but was caught by my father before I could do any real damage. In hindsight, I might have done more damage to myself than to him had I been fast enough.

"Sit. Down," Father growled, pushing me back into the chair. "And don't you dare get your ass out of it."

I scowled at him, folding my arms in front of my chest.

"You don't know what he's done," I hissed.

"As a matter of fact," Father said darkly, "I do, and while I may not forgive him for his past transgressions, we need him."

"Because he's *seen* her?" I quipped. "She could be miles away from where she was when he saw her."

"It's better than nothing at all," Eamryel said.

I narrowed my eyes at him. "Because of your father, *nothing* is all we have."

"At least I came back to do something about it rather than resort to *sehvelle* and the Gods know what else you took."

"You came back for your own gain," I spat. "Who's to say you're not secretly spying for that *hehzèh*, hm?"

He stilled, eyes flashing furiously. I could tell from the way he stood he was ready to pounce on me, and it took all of my self-control not to invite him to do it.

"That's enough," Mehrean said with a finality in her voice that stopped us both short. "You"—she pointed at Eamryel—"sit down and shut up. And you"—she pointed at me, raising herself to her full height—"dim down on that temper or I'll make you regret it till the end of your days."

Eamryel slunk into his seat, face devoid of emotions while I backpedalled fast, not eager to find out what she meant by that threat. Father and Soren took a seat as well, both looking exhausted and much the worse for wear. Mehrean sat down too, folding her hands in her lap.

I wouldn't ever mistake her for weak again.

"Now," she said, her voice calm and calculated. "It's time we start planning."

NIGHT WAS WELL underway by the time Soren and Father escorted me back to the infirmary, our heads filled with ideas, our moods darkened by the upcoming tasks Mehrean had assigned each of us. I hadn't been wrong in saying we were outlaws—she confirmed it almost straight away by saying we were high on Azra's wanted list, and that she didn't care whether they'd bring us in dead or alive. The bounty on our heads was enough to make people desperate enough to attempt it.

"I can't believe she's making me travel with Eamryel," I grumbled. "I'd rather be chased with pitchforks and fire."

Father snorted. "He came here of his own choice, Tal. He could have gone straight to Azra with the news, but he didn't."

I stopped and stared at him with a frown. "Now that you mention it... that makes no sense. Besides, Azra knows Shal's alive."

Father went completely still, brows furrowed in thought. "How?"

"Maybe Eamryel did tell her before he came here," I offered, unable to help the smirk on my face. "It doesn't make any sense for him to come here."

"Doesn't it?" Soren asked with a tight-lipped smile. "You know how infatuated he was with the *Tarien*."

I scowled at him. "Don't remind me."

"Be reasonable, Tal," Father said with a heavy sigh, rubbing his temples as if to ward off a headache. "What he did... I agree he still deserves punishment for it, but it's been over one and a half years, and right now, he's the only one who can help you get her back."

"Why doesn't *he* get her then," I growled, by now thoroughly annoyed with the discussion.

Soren chuckled softly. "Really, *Anahràn*? You have to ask?"

He only called me by my title when he was making fun of me, and thinking about it, I supposed he was right.

"She'd never go with him," I said, rubbing the back of my neck. "By Esah, I should have gone when the *Tari* made me promise to go."

"You couldn't have," Soren replied with a shake of his head. "Azra had everything under lockdown almost immediately after the *Tari's* death. We didn't realise straightaway, but she moved fast—faster than any of us suspected."

"Plus, we never counted on Haerlyon switching sides," Father said. "No matter what you might say or think of him, Haerlyon's a lot more cunning than anyone gives him credit for. He would have figured out your plan sooner or later anyway."

I clenched my fists. "I still can't believe he did that."

"Grief does strange things to a man." Soren was looking at me now, and I wasn't sure whether he was still talking about Haerlyon.

With a heavy sigh, I started walking again.

"Why then did he save Mehr's life?"

They both went tense beside me.

"Who says he did?" Father asked.

"Ione told me," I replied with a shrug. "During one of our sessions. I asked her about Mehr, and she told me what happened. She said Haerlyon was covered with blood when he returned."

"That makes no sense." Father frowned. "Haerlyon's not gone against any of Azra's instructions since he took her side."

I shrugged. "It's what I heard."

There was something they weren't telling me, but I decided to let it go. Between training and staying up most of the night to plan our next moves, I was exhausted, and I wanted nothing more than to lie down and sleep. From the sounds of it, I'd be busy in the time leading up to our departure, which wasn't scheduled for at least another six weeks. If it had been up to Mehrean, I'd have left tomorrow, but both Soren and Eamryel had argued I was nowhere near fit enough to walk a few miles, let alone ride.

So it was decided I'd spend that time training.

A part of me was excited about it—the other part frustrated, because I knew how far I'd have to go to get even close to where I came from. I knew I was out of shape, and it would take me months of rigorous training to get me to where I was before Yllinar had someone run a sword through me.

That was another reason for hating Eamryel's guts.

It had been his courtesy.

Only a few candles were still alight when we entered the infirmary, and after making sure the injury was looking well enough, Soren took his leave on account of almost toppling over. Father sat down on the bed next to me, resting his face in his hands.

"What's wrong?" I asked, turning to look at him.

"This is all my fault," he whispered. "Our fault."

I went completely still. "Why?"

A heavy sigh escaped his lips when he looked up, his eyes reflecting the light of the candle on the bedside cabinet. Resting his elbows on his knees, he leaned forward.

"This all began many years ago, when I was your age and just a *Svèran* in the army," he began, his voice soft. "We were sworn not to tell anyone. If we did... *Tari* Xeramaer wasn't the forgiving kind."

"Rurin had mentioned something about it," I mumbled. "Just after Arayda had passed away. He said Azra killed her own twin-sister?"

Father nodded. "She did. There were no witnesses, of course, but it was too much of a coincidence considering the injury she'd sustained."

"Rurin said something about Gaervin having taught her?"

"Not quite," he replied. "From what I gathered, he had a scar in almost the exact same place as Shaleira did, except he didn't bleed to death—she did. Azra had seen it, and he had told her what happened. The moment he saw the injury he knew it had to be her."

"But that's proof, isn't it?"

Father's lips quirked up. "Not quite, and that's where I come in."

"You tricked her?"

"I'm surprised Rurin hasn't told you the entire story."

I huffed. "The man was fraught with grief. I was surprised he could string a coherent sentence together."

"He'd always been a strong man," Father said with a faint smile. "Not unlike yourself."

I looked away. "Azra said she wanted to take vengeance on you. She hated you with a passion."

Father was silent for a while, running his hands through his hair.

"During the trials, she kept denying the truth which was right in front of us." Father's voice was soft and distant, as if he was reliving the moment. "It was only a few of us—the *Tari*, Arayda, Rurin, myself, some of the council, and Gaervin—but Azra kept denying she had killed her sister, so I did the only thing I could think of and tricked her. I told the *Tari* the weapon had been found, even though we both knew we never would, knowing Azra. She mercifully played along, and the more we spoke of it, the more paranoid Azra became, until she finally admitted her guilt."

I remained silent, watching Father struggle through this.

"When she did, she must have realised I'd baited her," he continued, clenching his fists, "and she went absolutely insane. If you think she is crazy now… you should have seen her then. Now, she's become more calculating and with it even more dangerous."

I inhaled deeply, trying to settle my nerves, while forming the question in my mind without sounding accusatory. "What happened next?"

"Tari Xeramaer sentenced her to death," he replied, "but she had escaped come morning. Somebody had to have helped her."

"Who?"

Father shook his head. "That is a mystery nobody ever solved, although I have my suspicions."

I arched a brow at him, and he looked away.

"This is mere speculation, son," he said with a heavy sigh, "and I do not wish to anger the dead, but"—he fell silent and slumped a little farther—"I think her mother let her go…"

"*Tari* Xeramaer?" I asked surprised. "Why would she do that?"

He shrugged. "Your guess is as good as mine, Tal. Maybe she had a change of heart, or maybe she didn't want to lose another child. I don't know."

"She's condemned us all." I rubbed the back of my neck. "All over sentiment."

"Losing a child is the hardest thing for a parent to come to terms with."

I winced at those words. There was no hint of accusation in his voice, just sorrow and pain. He'd lost a child.

Because of me.

"What happened after she fled?" I asked at length. "Surely she had to have gone somewhere."

"The *Tari* exiled her," Father replied, sitting up. "So I assume Azra went overseas somewhere. She was brave, not stupid—she wouldn't have stuck close to Ilvanna. She'd have gone elsewhere to hatch a plan..."

"How come she was able to come back then?" My frown deepened.

"Law," Father said in a low growl. "The moment Arayda ascended, Azra's exile was lifted."

I rubbed my jaw. "Why didn't Arayda reinstate her exile?"

Father flashed me a faint smile. "Because the law didn't work that way back then, Tal. For some reason, *Tari* Xeramaer chose not to change the laws of exile while she was still in power. Arayda did as soon as she could, but since she wasn't the one who exiled her sister, there wasn't much she could do. To exile her again, Azra would have had to commit another serious crime, but as she came back only occasionally and showed no sign of trouble, Arayda didn't have much to go on. Trust me, I offered to make it look like an accident more than once, but she wouldn't have it, arguing we wouldn't stoop to her level."

I stared at him slack-jawed. "You'd have killed her?"

"Without a second thought."

"It wouldn't have mattered," I said under my breath, averting my gaze. "She can't die."

"What was that?"

Inhaling deeply, wringing my hands, I risked a glance at my father, momentarily unsure whether I should repeat myself. I didn't want him to laugh at me—think I'd lost my mind after smoking too much *sehvelle*, but as much as I had tried to pass it off as a drug induced dream, I'd been clean then, and my eyes hadn't deceived me.

"I tried to kill her," I said in a strained voice. "A knife to her jugular. She didn't die. She just looked at me, pulled out the knife and laughed."

Father paled. "How's that possible?"

"I don't know." I balled my hands into fists to keep them from trembling. "For the longest time I thought I'd dreamt it, or that it had been a drug induced memory, but when I did it—when I tried, I was still sober."

He gave me a curt nod. I watched his facial expressions change as his mind worked to make sense of what I'd just told him, and regarded him warily, still afraid he'd burst out laughing.

"You should have told us sooner."

"I know."

Father shook his head. "There are things in this world none of us will ever understand. Maybe there's a trick, maybe there's more. Your information is invaluable to our cause."

I merely nodded and looked down at my hands, unsure of what to reply to that. Instead, my mind returned to the task at hand—finding Shal.

"What if I don't succeed?" I asked after a while. "What if Eamryel is wrong and… what if she…"

Father placed a hand on my shoulder, lips curled up in a one-sided smile. "Believe in the *Tarien*, son. She's a warrior and she won't go down without a fight. Believe in her like you always did..."

"I miss her."

Not once had I uttered those words out loud. I'd kept them hidden deep down inside, but for the first time in many moons, I felt I could let my guard down at least a little.

"I should've listened to you," I said, raking my hands through my hair.

"Listen to what exactly?" Father asked, slightly amused.

"I never should've fallen in love with her."

Father was silent for a while, then lifted my chin so I had no choice but to look at him. The expression on his face was solemn and without reproach.

"We do not choose who we fall in love with," he said, a soft smile playing on his lips. "And if you truly do love her, then you know what you must do."

I frowned, not feeling certain at all.

"You must forgive yourself, Tal," Father said, urgency in his voice. "Nobody else can do it for you... if you don't—"

"Have you forgiven me?" I asked, my voice barely above a whisper.

Pain contorted his features, but only for a moment before he nodded. "I have, Tal... because it was never your fault to begin with."

CHAPTER 32

SHALITHA

People yelled obscenities at our backs as we scrambled through the narrow alleys, barely avoiding collisions as we went. Elay, to my surprise, was nimbler than I thought he'd be, and much more skilled at scaling walls, traversing stairs and jumping rooftops than me. Not that I'd mastered it, but I'd almost always managed to escape. It explained why he had had no trouble following me back in Y'zdrah.

"This way," he yelled over his shoulder, checking if I was still following him.

The chase was strangely exhilarating, transporting me back to a time when my guards pursued me through the streets of Ilvanna, yelling at me to stop.

"*Mìthri*, watch out!"

Elay yanked me out of the way of an oncoming wagon and pulled me close to him, pressing his back against the wall as it passed. His chest rose and fell with rapid breaths, which I could feel brush my hair while standing in his embrace. My heart picked up speed, and not just because we'd been running, as heat rose to my cheeks.

"I know you like holding me," I said, my lips pulling up in a grin, "but I thought we were trying to lose them?"

I jerked my thumb in the direction the wagon was trundling and our pursuers had appeared.

Elay smirked. "Ever perceptive, come on."

As he took my hand in his, we started running, veering off to the right into another alley, left into a new one, and right again, until even I was lost. We slowed down to a brisk walk, and while I glanced over our shoulder, Elay was looking for something else.

"Up there," he murmured. "We can rest for a bit…"

After he lifted me on the ledge, he pulled himself up, and we navigated our way over small rickety stairs to the rooftops where we settled down low so we couldn't be seen from the streets. Closing my eyes, I stretched my arms over my head and inhaled deeply, opening up my lungs to get air back in. When I opened my eyes, I found Elay's face inches from mine, a roguish grin playing on his lips.

"Don't tell me that wasn't fun," he said, placing a kiss on my forehead before flopping on his back, lying down spread-eagled.

"Your definition of fun is quite a stretch," I replied, turning my head to look at him. "But I have to admit I enjoyed myself. Let's not do this regularly though."

Elay chuckled softly. "Sounds fair."

"So," I ventured, turning on my side, "who are they?"

His lips pressed into a thin line as he sat up, his back towards me. "Those men were sell-swords, mercenaries… in it for the money."

I frowned. "And why would they come after us?"

Elay fell silent and stiffened. When next he spoke, his voice was tense.

"I thought you didn't want to know?"

I stilled before pushing myself up to a sitting position, brows knitting together as I regarded him.

"You're throwing it back at me now?" I asked snidely. "This has been your mess from the beginning, Elay, and I won't let you blame me for your mistakes. I came to you for help, we made an agreement, and I would have fully seen it through as long as you would keep your side of the deal. I meant what I said that night—I have nothing left to lose."

I made to rise to my feet, but Elay grabbed my wrist, keeping me on my knees. Breathing in deeply, I turned to him, surprised at the contrite look on his face.

"You're right," he said with a heavy sigh. "I keep forgetting you're not like my other wives."

"What's that supposed to mean?"

"You won't put a knife in my back when it suits you," he said, scratching his chin. "Will you please let me explain now?"

I glanced over his shoulder.

"Not now," I said, and when he made to protest, I pointed ahead of me. "They're here."

Elay cursed, and we scrambled to our feet. It was a mercy that the Zihrin people loved to build their houses with flat roofs —in Ilvanna, we'd have been sliding off of them due to their slanted angles. Shouts arose from behind us, and it served to propel us forward even faster. We weren't holding hands now— we needed them to navigate the higher edges, or to pull ourselves up, or lower ourselves to other rooftops.

"We can't keep this up!" I shouted. "We'll never outrun them!"

"I know," Elay replied. "Which is why we need to get to the gates."

I frowned at him, dodged a low hanging pole and vaulted over another ledge while Elay did the same. Risking a glance backwards, I saw the mercenaries were still on our tail, but farther behind than I'd expected. We stopped, and I looked around. The gates were on the other side of the city from the looks of it and traversing the roofs to get there was impossible.

We needed to get back down.

"What's at the gates?" I stood catching my breath, hands on my hips.

"Rhana," he said with an easy grin. "She should be ready with *camelles* and supplies."

"Good," I said, surveying the area we were in. "Now to get down."

The shouts were suddenly close by, and looking over my shoulder, there were only two rooftops between us and our pursuers.

"*Nohro ahrae,* let's move!"

I didn't need to tell Elay twice, and so we started running again. My arms were aching, and my right calf was cramping up. If we didn't manage to find a spot to get to the streets soon, I wasn't sure I could keep outrunning them.

"Over here!" Elay called, and when I got close, there were stairs running halfway down the building.

It was more than we could have hoped for.

We skipped down the steps and halted on the platform. Our choice was to either climb down or go inside the building, which was most likely somebody's home.

"We need to jump," I said, less than pleased at the notion, knowing full well my bad leg might give out.

"I'll go first," Elay said, climbing over the edge. "Lower yourself, I'll catch you."

I kept glancing over my shoulder as he scampered down the wall, my heart racing in my chest. Just when he yelled my name, the mercenaries appeared at the top of the stairs. My throat tightened, my chest constricted, and I fumbled getting over the railing. The closer they got, the harder it became to make my body follow my commands.

Get over it. NOW!

I was about to let go of the railing to lower myself when a hand clamped around my wrist, and I found myself staring into dark eyes and an even darker face. He looked positively happy with his catch—I did not. In his short moment of pride, I twisted my arm out of his grip and punched him. He reeled back with a howl. I scrambled down, but in my haste to do so, I lost my footing.

And my grip.

I'd experienced feeling weightless before—back at home, and in the sea. Both times, I was dying.

This—this was different.

Air whistled past me. A scream tore from my lips. My arms and legs were flailing, desperate to get a hold of something. When I landed, a fierce pain shot through my right leg—my injured leg—and a loud crashing noise enveloped me. My vision blurred and it took me a moment or two to find my bearings. A grunt sounded from behind me, and opening one eye as I turned to look, I found Elay there, a painful grimace suffusing his handsome features.

"That's one way to go down," he grunted. "Due warning would have been welcome."

"I'm sorry," I mumbled, getting to my feet.

Looking up, the mercenaries were no longer there. We had to get moving now if we didn't want them to catch up.

"Get up," I hissed to Elay. "They'll be here soon."

"I'd love to," he muttered, "but I don't think I can."

"What do you m—" I stopped short when my eyes fell on the piece of wood protruding from his lower leg.

Judging by the look of things, he must have caught me and fallen back into a stack of crates, which had shattered underneath our weight. I knelt next to him, hissing as pain flared through my leg.

"This is going to hurt," I said, looking at him.

"No more than it already does, I'm sure."

I flashed him a wry smile and without warning, pulled the shard from his leg. In this light, I couldn't tell how bad it was, but I doubted the alternative would be any better. Relying on what Soren had taught me, I tore a strip of fabric from my shirt and wound it tight around the injury. A hiss of pain escaped his lips, but that was all the indication he gave of feeling it. When I helped him to his feet, it was clear he couldn't properly stand on it, so I wrapped my arm around his waist, and placed his across my shoulders.

A wicked grin played across my lips.

"What are you so happy about?" he muttered.

"Now we do this my way," I said, sounding a little too cheerful.

His brows knit together in confusion. "I thought we were doing this your way?"

"Well," I began, chewing my lip. "Yes and no. We'll do it the other way."

Elay looked positively confused at my statement, but I didn't elaborate. To be honest, the cheerfulness with which I announced my idea was at odds with the turmoil going on inside. My other way meant we had to stick to the shadows and move annoyingly slow. But Elay couldn't run, and I didn't fancy being captured again.

"If it's too much," I said softly, "tell me. We can rest."

Elay glanced at me, a faint smile on his lips. "I'm fine."

"I used to say that too, even when I wasn't."

We ducked into another alley just before the sound of our pursuers reached us, and I pulled a piece of cloth from a nearby line. There was nowhere for us to hide, so in plain sight it was. I quickly wrapped the cloth over my hair to hide it, letting the ends cascade over my shoulders and back. When I pushed Elay against the wall, he began protesting until I pressed my lips against his.

"What are you doing?" he murmured.

"Hiding," I replied, keeping an eye on the alley we'd come from.

Sure enough, the mercenaries passed by swiftly without so much as casting a glance in our direction. I listened and counted like I used to back in Ilvanna when my guards had passed me and I needed to estimate the time between myself and them. When I was certain the coast was clear, I wrapped my arm around Elay's waist and returned to the alley, proceeding in the opposite direction of our pursuers.

We went through the city this way, sticking to alleys as much as possible. Sometimes, the mercenaries seemed to gain on us, but every time we managed to hide. I'd learned a long time ago that people never looked where they didn't expect you to be—right in front of their eyes.

"C… can we stop?" Elay gasped.

He'd turned several shades paler, and sweat beaded his brow. We weren't far away from the gates now, but I could tell he'd collapse in a dead faint if we didn't rest soon. Up ahead was an alley hidden behind a row of stalls. The only downside was that we'd have to cross the busiest street of the city, and we'd be in full sight doing so.

"Can you hold on a little longer?" I asked, casting furtive glances left and right.

There was no sight of our pursuers, but it didn't mean they weren't there.

"If I have to…" he said through gritted teeth.

I flashed him a faint smile and nodded. "All right, here's the deal. Do you see that alley over there, behind the stalls?"

He nodded.

"You'll have to get there on your own."

He grimaced. "I'm not sure—"

"You have to," I interjected, "so that I can create a diversion. They'll catch us if we go together."

Elay looked troubled. "What if they catch you?"

"Then I hope you'll come and save me," I said with an easy grin I didn't feel at all.

I untied the cloth from my hair, turned it inside out, and draped it over Elay's head and shoulders.

"This should provide you with enough cover," I murmured. "Stay in the shadows as far as possible. Don't go until they're after me. I'll come find you."

"*Mìthri.*" Elay grabbed my wrist and turned me back to face him.

My brows shot up in surprise, but before I could ask what was wrong, he pressed his lips firmly to mine, his hand snaking behind my neck, pulling me closer. My heart rate spiked, and butterflies fluttered in my stomach while a strange sensation nestled itself deep inside of me.

"Be safe," he murmured. "Don't get caught."

I grinned at him. "Have a little faith, *shareye*. This isn't my first time."

And hopefully not my last.

Before I could change my mind, I stepped out of our hiding place onto the busy street, away from the direction Elay had to go in, flaunting my white hair like a banner. If I didn't stand out like this, I wasn't sure what would. Sure enough, as soon as I was in sight of everyone at the plaza, shouts sounded behind me. A grin spread across my lips as I glanced over my shoulder, watching them come closer.

Behind them, Elay hobbled into the street, keeping his head down.

Come and catch me, if you can.

Having spent time on the rooftops, I'd gotten a pretty good idea of the layout of the city, and knew I had to stick to the districts on the left. The main road divided two sides of the city —on my left was the merchant's and upper class district where we'd been crossing rooftops for what felt like days. On my right were the wharfs. I remembered from the night before how intricate the layout of the streets was there. It should be easy to shake off my pursuers in that mess.

Weaving my way across the plaza and the main street, I dodged carts, *camelles* and people with practised ease. Behind me, curses and grunts told me the men hunting me were less lucky. My heart picked up a steady beat, and my breathing came hard. My body protested against the abuse I was putting it through, but if I played my cards right, this was the last time it had to obey me to this extent.

At least the last time today.

Ducking past a stall, I stole another shawl, much to the vendor's displeasure, but I was out of the way faster than he could catch me. I doubted he wanted to leave his wares alone.

"Apologies! I need it!"

All that followed me were curses slung at my persona, but I could live with that. While navigating my way through the alleys, listening for my pursuers, I tied the shawl over my head to hide my white hair.

"There she is!"

The voice came from a different direction than I expected. Two men emerged from behind at the same time as two men approached me from the front, closing me in. I cursed under my breath and surveyed the area. The buildings were sleek on either side, but there were beams nestled between them. I glanced over my shoulder, found the two men there were close —looked ahead, and found the others were even closer.

One chance, Tarien. Better make it work.

I stopped and breathed in deeply, willing my racing heart to calm down. As soon as they were with me, I held up my hands in defeat, keeping an eye on all four of them as best I could.

"I think this is a misunderstanding, *mishan*," I said, looking from one to the other.

"You're coming with us," one of them growled around a split lip.

I recognised him from the platform and was glad to see my punch caused him discomfort.

"Now see, that's the misunderstanding," I replied sweetly. "I'm not going anywhere with you."

"Grab her!"

I used the momentum of the man grabbing me to kick off against the one in front. The one holding my arms staggered backwards, losing his grip. I went in for a sweep kick and swept him off his feet. A loud thud sounded in the alley as he hit his head against the wall, and I looked to see him crumple.

He wouldn't be getting up for a while.

If at all.

Two men charged me at the same time. At the last moment, I pressed myself back against the wall and stuck out my foot so one of them would stumble into the other. The momentary confusion bought me time to run in the direction I'd been going. They were in pursuit soon after, cursing me in Kyrinthan.

Isn't that interesting?

I veered off into an alley on my right, barrelled into one on the left, and took another turn to the right. The alley was a dead-end street and there was no way up either. I could hear my pursuers getting closer, their ruckus alarming everyone on the street. Now would be a great time to learn how to actually disappear.

"Psst."

I glanced up and around to see where the sound had come from, only to find two eyes peering at me from behind a giant plant. Moments later, a small girl crawled out from behind it.

"Down here," she whispered, pointing somewhere behind her.

Her state of dress was deplorable at best, her face dirty as if she hadn't seen a bath in many moons. But her eyes were bright and held a certain mischief I could appreciate, and although I was a little apprehensive, she was my only option. 'Down here' was a hole in the wall hidden behind the plant, and it was barely big enough for me to crawl in.

The girl started singing in Zihrin and twirling around without a care in the world.

"Hey you!" a gruff voice said. "Have you seen a woman here?"

The girl tilted her head at him as if he had spoken in a foreign language, then shrugged and continued her nonsensical game. He tried again, this time by grabbing her shoulder and shaking her, but the girl didn't seem perturbed. That notion bothered me. I moved forward, ready to get the girl out of trouble, disturbing a patch of dust or sand which settled uncomfortably in my nose. I tried not to sneeze…

...and failed

"What was that?" The man growled as the girl sneezed. "Where is she?"

"I don't know who you are talking about, *mishan*," she said, looking up at him. "I am here alone."

She sneezed again.

Although I couldn't see the man, I could hear his displeasure in the derisive snort—saw it in the way he let go of the little girl. She staggered back but didn't fall, and instead watched the men curiously for a little longer, before she went back to her singing and dancing.

"Keep looking," the man growled in Kyrinthan. "She can't have gone far."

"What about her mate?" the other responded in kind.

"We don't need him."

My heart picked up speed at the mention of Elay, and I realised I needed to get to him as soon as possible, but I didn't dare come out of my hiding place. To make matters worse, the girl disappeared from sight too. I rested my forehead against the cool ground, counting to ten in Ilvannian to calm myself.

Way to go, qira.

"You can come out now," the girl said, peeking around the plants. "They be gone."

I crawled out of my hideout on my elbows, upsetting even more dust as I went. The girl watched me curiously.

"You're not from around here."

It was a statement rather than a question.

"I'm not," I replied, dusting off my clothes and face. "And I really need to get out of here fast."

"Those are bad men," the girl said, scrunching up her nose. "They often come and steal children—those without a home. Sometimes women too. Nobody ever sees them again."

I hunkered down in front of her so I was at eye level. "What's your name?"

"Prisha," the girl said, looking proud.

"Thank you, Prisha. For saving me." I bit my lip and glanced at the alley behind her. "Where do you live?"

"Everywhere."

She said it so casually, I almost missed the implication of her words.

"That's a really big place to live," I replied with a nod, worrying at my lip. "I was wondering if you could do something for me, Prisha. I will pay you for it."

The girl perked up. "Anything, *amisha.*"

"I need to find my friend," I said. "Without the bad men finding me."

She grinned back and thumped her chest and nodded. "I can do that."

I smiled at her, and when she took my hand, I followed. We weaved through narrow alleys, through backyards, and places hardly wide enough for a child to move through, let alone an adult. When she asked me where this friend was, I gave her a description and she almost ran off without me. Not much later, she guided me into the alley where Elay was supposed to be. A shadow disengaged itself from the wall, and I was about to get ready to pounce when it turned out to be Elay staggering forward. I caught him just before he fell flat on his face.

Even in the dim light I could tell he wasn't doing well.

"Prisha?"

"Yes, *amisha*."

"I have one more thing to ask of you," I said, wrapping my arm around Elay's waist. "Can you help us to the gates, discreetly?"

"Will you pay?"

The words sounded harsh coming from the mouth of a child, but her life was hard enough as it was. I'd rob Elay of his money if I had to, just to pay this girl for saving our lives.

"Of course I'll pay."

A wide grin spread across her dirty face, showing crooked and missing teeth.

Poor thing.

"Who's your friend?" Elay asked softly, a grimace of pain hardening his features.

"Let's get you out of here first," I murmured. "That injury needs looking at."

As promised, Prisha guided us through several back alleys and out of the gate without our pursuers noticing us. I bore no illusions we'd seen the last of them, especially after what I'd heard them say. Like Elay had said, Rhana was waiting outside the gates with *camelles,* and a new cart with supplies.

Good. Elay won't be able to sit on one of those beasts.

After bringing Elay to Rhana and giving her the abbreviated version of what had happened, I went back to Prisha who stood waiting at the gate, rocking back and forth on her heels.

"Here you go," I said, giving her three silver pieces. "Hide them well."

Prisha tucked them away in a pouch she kept around her middle and smiled at me. My eyes swept over the little girl in front of me. Out in the light, she looked different. Big, light eyes complimented a rich, dark skin, and a mop of unruly black curls, from which pointed ears peeked out in defiance to her hair, shaped an oval face. She was a pretty girl, and a shudder went through me.

"Promise me you will stay away from the evil men?"

She nodded. "You too, *amisha*. I heard them say they won't stop looking for you."

I smiled. "They won't catch me that easily."

"But I won't be there to help you."

"I know," I replied, "and it's a brave thing you did. Now, you'd best return, before they catch you out here with us."

She looked at me a moment longer, then grinned and skipped back inside the city, humming the tune she'd been singing before. I returned to our posse, squatting down next to where Elay was sitting.

He wrinkled his nose. "You smell, *Mìthri*. What have you been doing?"

"Saving your ass. Come on, let's have a look at that injury."

CHAPTER 33

TALNOVAR

"Is that all you've got?" Father frowned, a smirk on his lips. "I taught you better than that."

I attacked again without any of the finesse or skill I used to have. I was a raging ball of fury, annoyed at the lack of strength I had to get in a proper blow. Whatever Father's reasons were, he let me get on with it, adding snide comments which only served to infuriate me more. At one point, I charged him head on, planting my shoulder into his ribcage and taking him down. With my knee on his chest, I kept him down.

My fist stopped a bare inch from his face as it hit home what I was doing.

I sat back on my ass, gasping for air, trying to regain my self-control while watching him.

"Got it out of your system?" he asked gruffly, rubbing his chest. "Or should we go another round?"

I scowled at him.

"You used to fight better," Eamryel said from behind me, mockery in his voice. "It's not even worth throwing down with you now."

Fury built up in moments, and before my mind caught up

with my body, I lunged at Eamryel. He side-stepped as if he'd expected it and kicked me for good measure. A howl of anger escaped my lips as I turned and went for him again. He blocked my blow, came in with his own, and hit me in the ribs before my elbow came down on his upper arm. He hissed, pulled back, and took up a fighting stance. I mirrored him, getting my head back into the game.

"If you want a fight," I hissed. "I'll give you one... but I'm not holding back."

"Good." Eamryel grinned. "Because I'll skin you alive if you do."

My threats were as good as my promises—empty. I stepped in, threw a punch, was blocked, side-stepped, kicked, but I barely made an impact. Eamryel fought controlled, calculated, weighing every step, every punch, as if this was some kind of problem to be solved. All I wanted was to get this rage out of my system, but he wouldn't take the bait.

"Really, Tal?" he sneered. "I thought you weren't going to hold back?"

His words sent me over the edge and I charged him. Eamryel took the punch in good stride, and I noticed he was giving in to his emotions too. Gone was the calculated look in his eyes. He was a man on a mission, as was I. I put all my anger in my punches, all my hurt in the kicks—I gave this brawl everything that I was.

Eamryel paid me in kind.

By the time my father pulled us apart, we were both bleeding from several cuts, and I could feel a bruise coming up under my left eye. I doubled over, spit blood out of my mouth and wiped my lips with the back of my hand. A large red smear adorned it when I pulled it back. Glancing up, I saw Eamryel didn't look much better, but he had the biggest grin on his face.

"That's what I'm talking about," he said.

Father stood watching us, face impassive, arms folded across his chest. I wasn't sure what he was waiting for, but it was clear he was waiting for something.

"Look," Eamryel said. "About Shal—"

"Don't you dare speak her name," I hissed, stepping within his personal space, my face a mere inch from his. "You have no right whatsoever."

He stiffened, eyes flashing momentarily, but he backed off, holding up his hands to show he meant no harm. I noticed Father starting forward.

"I know you hate my guts," he continued, "and I suppose you have every right to, but I wanted to let you know I mean her no harm."

My lips curled up in a snarl, and I would have pounced on him again had Father not stepped between us, turning to him.

"Thank you, Eamryel," he said calmly. "I think you'd best see one of the *dena* for those injuries."

Wiping the blood from his nose, he saluted Father and left, walking away with a swagger. I let out a shuddering breath and glanced up at my father.

"Feeling better?"

I shook my head. "Not really. I'm just so… angry."

"I understand." He patted my shoulder. "But you will have to learn to control it before it consumes you."

"How?" I asked with a heavy sigh. "We've been trying for days and there's no difference whatsoever."

"This isn't your first time, Tal. You know how to do this… just remember what—who—you are doing this for."

I nodded and wiped my nose again.

"I guess I'd best go see Soren," I muttered. "He'll love another opportunity to berate me, I'm sure."

"Come back when you're done," Father said. "We've got little time and a lot of training to catch up on. Once your strength returns, you'll find your fighting will follow."

I nodded mutely and waved as I made my way to Soren.

Something about what had just happened bugged me, but I couldn't quite place my finger on it. It wasn't something that had been said, but rather something I'd noticed in Eamryel's eyes. Remorse. When I stepped inside the infirmary, Soren took one long look at me and sighed.

"Really, *Anahràn?*"

OVER THE COURSE OF WEEKS, training intensified to five times a day, varying between physical exercise and mental exercise—the last one assigned after my struggles to keep my temper under control. Every day, my strength returned step by step. Both the *sehvelle* and the *oukourou* were well out of my system now, and the injury Azra had given me had healed quite nicely on the inside, but the outside was a different matter entirely. The scar was a thick line of hardened skin.

Soren had informed me it had been the only way.

I didn't mind much, except that the waistband of my trousers snatched on it during practise, causing discomfort and rubbing it raw, often leading to it bleeding, despite the bandage I'd taken up wrapping around it. Gritting my teeth, I pulled the bandage free from my waist, discarding it into a basket next to my bed. I dipped a piece of cloth in the water bowl on the nightstand and carefully dabbed the edges clean. Every warrior knew the basic principles of dealing with minor injuries—how to clean them and bandage them so you might live to tell the tale to a healer. Not that I had any of the extensive knowledge Soren seemed to have, who—so I'd learned here at *Denahryn*—was quite a marvel unto himself to begin with. His knowledge far superseded that of other *Dena*.

Why he wasn't their leader was beyond me.

A knock on the door startled me, but before I could go to

open it, somebody stepped inside. I quickly wrapped a bandage around my waist and pulled up my trousers.

"*Anahràn?*" a tentative voice asked.

I frowned and while pulling a shirt over my head, walked out of the bedroom, stopping short when I saw who stood there.

"Samehya?" I asked surprised. "I didn't know you were here."

She turned to me, and before I knew what was happening, she wrapped her arms around my waist and hugged me.

"You *are* alive!" she said in shock.

Too stunned to speak, I watched her as she suddenly seemed to realise what she was doing. Her cheeks flushed red, and she took a few careful steps backwards, looking anywhere but at me.

"I… I'm sorry," she whispered, fumbling with her hands. "I just arrived, and they said… they said you were here and I… I needed to see if it was true."

With a shake of my head, I dispelled the stupor. "If what was true?"

"That you survived," she whispered. "Rumour at the palace is that you died."

Her words brought me up short. "Wait, you came from the palace?"

"Yes," she replied softly. "I managed to escape along with some others."

I narrowed my eyes, looking at her. "What others?"

During my time training her, I'd never seen her this nervous or scared. Her eyes kept slipping to the door, almost as if she expected someone to step in any minute, and she wouldn't stop wringing her hands.

"Samehya?" she looked at me when I said her name, eyes wide. "How did you know where we were? Who came with you?"

She swallowed hard. "I just followed a large group of people who left in the middle of the night. I don't think they even noticed I was there."

A pounding in my ears started. "How many of them?"

"I'm not sure," she answered, slightly panicked. "Twoscore? Maybe more?"

A string of expletives left my lips in rapid succession. Without wasting time, I pulled on my boots, grabbed a coat, and propelled Samehya out the door.

"Where are they?" I hissed.

"I don't know," she whispered. "We were taken to the infirmary, but I left as soon as Soren told me where you were."

I cursed again and stopped her. "Samehya. I need to know..."

"Know what, *Anahràn*?" She tilted her head.

"Whose side are you on?"

She frowned at me as if I were asking the most stupid question in the world. "Yours, of course, why?"

"I need you to find Soren," I said softly. "Tell him to get the infirmary ready, but don't alert anyone."

"Why?"

"Because I think it's a trap."

Without waiting for her to do as I told her, I barrelled down the path to find Father and Mehrean. On my way there, a familiar voice coming my way caught my attention.

Cehyan.

I slipped behind a building and waited for her and her companion, a *Dena* I didn't know, to pass. By some miracle, I managed to keep myself from jumping her and strangling her. Once they were out of sight, I continued my way at a brisk pace. Thankfully, Mehrean and Father were together at her cottage, poring over maps of Ilvanna and Therondia. They looked up when I barged in.

"Tal?" Father asked in surprise. "What's wrong? I thought you were training with Soren?"

"It's *Denahryn*," I said. "There's an attack coming. We need to prepare."

"How do you know?" Mehrean asked, rising to her feet. "The scouts would have come and told us."

I shook my head. "No, they wouldn't, because all they've seen is a group of refugees coming to seek shelter."

Father stilled. Mehrean frowned, tapping pursed lips in thought.

"Do they know we know?" she asked.

"I don't think so."

"What makes you think we're under attack?" Father asked. "If there's just a group of refugees coming."

"Because Cehyan's here, Father," I hissed. "And that *hehzèh's* been on Azra's side from the moment she crawled back into my bed. It's no coincidence."

His brows shot up in surprise at my confirmation. It had no doubt been common knowledge at the palace, but I'd never admitted it.

"She gave me the *oukourou* on Azra's orders, so that Azra could—"

Swallowing hard, I ran my hands through my hair, stepping back and forth like a caged animal while trying to process my emotions and not give in to them. Cehyan had been Azra's puppet all along. She'd played me right to the very end, and disappeared before Father entered the room. She'd always been an ambitious woman, but I never thought she'd go this far. I didn't have any proof of her misdeeds, but I just knew in my gut her appearance here was no accident.

"She betrayed the rebellion," I said in a strained voice. "I cannot prove it, but I just know it, and whatever she knows, Azra knows. Those twoscore refugees? I bet they're all carrying weapons. You have to believe me."

"I believe you," Mehr replied, looking straight at me. "This is

Hanyarah all over again, except Azra must have known that bringing an army here would be her downfall."

"I thought nobody knew where this place was?" I asked with a frown.

"People know," Mehrean said, "but usually only come here if they have nothing left to lose, or if they want to learn, considering the fact it's up in the mountains."

I sighed and started pacing again, rubbing my jaw. "And being of the royal house, I assume Azra would know where places like these are situated?"

Mehrean nodded.

"As do the higher in command in the army," Father replied, a wry smile on his lips. "I might have been the only *Ohzheràn*, but Evan and Haerlyon were but two *Zheràn* amongst a dozen. Even if Azra didn't know, one of them would."

"All right. What are we going to do now?"

"Let them think we have no clue," Mehrean replied with a smile. "Cerindil?"

He inclined his head and left the hut without the need for further instructions. I massaged my temples, glancing at Mehrean from under my lashes.

"Looks like you've got everything well under control?" It came out harsher than intended.

Mehrean nodded, a faint smile on her lips. "It's like a game of *Sihnmihràn*, Tal. You have to think steps ahead if you want to defeat your opponent."

"Except that we will never defeat ours," I replied gloomily.

"Not now," she said, a mysterious smile on her lips when she looked at me. "Which is why it's so important that you find the *Tarien*. She's the key to solving this puzzle."

"Why?"

"The prophecy," Mehrean replied. "The lines we know are just a fragment. I've been trying to figure it out ever since I heard them."

"Is that why you requested to stay at the palace? Close to the *Tarien.*"

Mehrean awarded me a tight-lipped smile. "Amongst other things, yes."

"What about the rest of that prophecy then?"

She shook her head, walking around the table littered with maps, moving them around to find a sheet of parchment that had clearly seen better days.

"A sister once of us, now she is no more, a Goddess aeons past, an ancient Queen of yore."

A ripple of unease went through me. "What's that supposed to mean?"

"I'm not sure," Mehr replied, dropping the parchment on the table. "But I think it's connected somehow, and I think it's linked to Shal. All we—you—have to do is find her."

"Provided she's still alive."

"You used to have more faith in her," she observed, tilting her head. "What changed?"

Her question came unexpectedly, and I shook my head, unsure of what the answer to it was. Deep down inside I knew and it had nothing to do with Shal whatsoever. It wasn't that I didn't believe in her—I no longer believed in myself.

"How do you think we should go about this?" Mehrean said, waving her hand towards the window to encompass *Denahryn*, and what I assumed was the situation we were in. "Should we attack? Should we wait?"

I looked at her with a frown.

What are you doing?

"I would let them believe they have the element of surprise," I said, looking at her. "Welcome them with open arms, make them feel at home… and turn the tables on them."

"Good," she replied. "You're in charge."

"I thought Father was?"

She chuckled softly. "No, your Father has gone to warn

Evan and Nathaïr. If what you say is true, Cehyan or her men cannot find out where Nathaïr is. She's due very soon, and the baby is still a possible threat to Azra. I wouldn't put it past the woman."

A cold shiver slithered down my spine. "Nor me."

When she walked over to me, it struck me again how small she was, which was at complete odds with the power she wielded. Without prior warning, she embraced me.

"We need you back, Tal," she said softly. "I cannot imagine what she's done to you, but the realm needs you—Shal needs you."

I placed my arms around her shoulders awkwardly, surprised by the fact this was the second woman to hug me today.

Since when do I look huggable?

The thought both amused and terrified me, but Mehr's embrace felt safe—like my mother's had that night when my delirium had been at its peak. I rested my chin on her head and closed my eyes.

"Will these nightmares ever go away?"

"Someday, maybe."

I exhaled deeply and nodded. "Stay safe, Mehr."

"You too, *Anahràn*."

With my mind in turmoil, I left her hut and made my way over to the infirmary where I assumed Soren would be. On my way there, I was waylaid by no other than Eamryel, who looked everything but pleased.

"What do you want?" I asked in a low growl. "I've got stuff to do."

"Let me help," he said, walking along.

"Why would I?"

In my peripheral vision, I saw him clamp down on his temper. "Because I owe you that much."

Today was full of surprises.

"You owe me a lot more than your help," I commented drily. "What did you have in mind?"

"Let's not discuss that out here," he murmured, glancing around. "We don't want to be seen making plans, do we?"

"I guess not."

CHAPTER 34

SHALITHA

"For the love of everything holy, will you stay down?" I growled, pushing Elay back into a lying position.

He growled in return, emerald eyes flashing in annoyance. Putting my hands on my hips, I scowled at him, begging him with my eyes to try that again. I would tie him to the wagon if I had to, and judging by the fact he stayed down, he knew I would.

"Good," I muttered. "You finally got some sense into that thick skull of yours."

"I'm fine," he complained, pushing himself up to his elbows. "I can walk."

"You've been spiking a fever for almost a fortnight," I replied, staring him down. "If I let you walk now, you'll undo all my handiwork."

His scowl deepened as he lay down again. "This wagon isn't the most comfortable."

"Would you have preferred being dragged behind a *camelle*?" I looked at him amused.

He rolled his eyes. "When did you turn so mean?"

"About two hundred and seventy-eight years ago."

"Huh," he mused, lips quirking up in a mischievous grin, "no wonder you can be so immature."

I put light pressure on his ankle, drawing out a grunt. "What was that?"

"Kohpè!"

With a snigger, I returned to the injury on his ankle, inspecting the stitches just like Soren had taught me. I wasn't as meticulous, or skilled, as he was, but I'd managed to save Elay's foot. The skin around the stitches looked good, and there was no nasty smell coming from it. A few more days and he would be able to take his first steps again.

If we have that many.

I glanced over my shoulder across the endless plain of nothingness, watched and waited for what I knew had to happen sooner or later—the arrival of our enemies on the horizon. They'd been following us since we left Portasâhn, keeping their distance—for now. My nerves had frayed beyond repair, and mouthing off to Elay was the only way I knew how to deal with it.

He deserved at least part of it.

"Thank you."

The sincerity in his voice rattled me out of my thoughts, and my brow knit together in confusion. "What for?"

"Risking your life to save mine," he said. "I never even thanked you for that."

I shrugged. "Wouldn't you have done the same?"

"Maybe," he said, sounding thoughtful, "but I doubt it would have been in the way you did."

"Yes, well." I flashed him a wry smile. "That was more a desperate attempt than anything else."

"Still, you did it."

Admiration shone in his eyes and I could swear my heart did a backflip at the smile he gave me. When he took my hand in his and placed a kiss on it, I looked away, inhaling deeply to settle my erratic heart.

"Lie down, *Mìthri*," he said softly, tugging me towards him. "You've been on the lookout almost all the time, you need some rest."

"I'm fine," I replied, pulling up my knees, resting my back against the side of the wagon as it rattled on towards the sunset.

"I did what I did," Elay said after a while, "because I couldn't just disappear. If I made it look like a kidnapping, less questions would be asked."

I glanced at him but said nothing. I folded my hands on my knees and rested my chin on them, deciding quietly that I might as well hear him out.

"I should have told you," he continued quietly, "but I was afraid that if I did, you'd become a target for my last wife, Maram."

I curled my fingers. "Maram doesn't scare me, and you know that..."

He sighed, pinching the bridge of his nose. "Fine... I was afraid you wouldn't agree with it."

"It makes sense," I said, "but I am still mad at you for it."

He pushed himself up on his elbows, a deep frown creasing his brow. "Why, *Mìthri*? I am telling you the truth!"

"You didn't trust me, Elay." I turned to him, my voice level. "You didn't trust me with this knowledge because you were afraid I'd run. You're afraid that if I find out who you are, and what you did, I won't hold up my end of the bargain."

Elay stiffened and looked away, his voice barely above a whisper when next he spoke. "Wouldn't you have done the same had you been in my position?"

"No."

He slumped back against his makeshift pillow and rubbed his face, staring up at the darkening sky.

"You're right," he said at length without looking at me. "If life has taught me anything, it's to trust no one."

"Yet you trust Rhana."

"Rhana is…" He stopped, looking forward. "Rhana has been my friend for as long as I can remember, and the only one who has never judged me. She's my—what did you call it, *Anahràn*—and has had my back all this time." He turned to me, taking my hand in his. "You, *Mìthri*. You've intrigued me from the beginning, and to this day, I'm still not sure what makes you tick, but I stand by what I said in Portasâhn—you're not like any of my other wives."

I pressed my lips together.

"What I'm trying to say," he continued quickly, "especially after what you did for me back there—I do trust you, *Tarien*."

"You do now," I replied softly, looking at him. "So now that you do, care to share where we're going exactly?"

"Kyrintha," he said, "and there's something you need to know…"

I watched him from under my lashes as he struggled to find the words for what he was about to say next, and I had to do my best not to burst out laughing.

"Know what?" I tried, biting the inside of my cheek.

He ran both his hands through his hair, glancing at Rhana who was currently riding behind us. Not that she was paying attention to our conversation, occupied by scanning the horizon as she was, but it gave him comfort.

"That I…"

"I know you're the Kyrinthan prince," I said, sounding as if it was the most common knowledge in the world.

"How did you know?" he asked surprised.

I smirked. "Putting two and two together."

It hadn't been hard to sort the puzzle after Rhana's allusions back in the cave, and the hints she'd dropped while I was fighting to get his fever down with the limited resources I had had at my disposal.

"What I don't know," I continued, looking at him, "is what you need me for?"

Elay opened his mouth to respond when something caught his attention behind me. When I followed his gaze, I noticed riders in the distance.

"Rhana!" Elay shouted, but she was already on it.

"You two get on a *camelle* and ride!" she yelled back. "We'll lead them astray."

After I helped Elay off the wagon and onto a *camelle,* I climbed in front of him, knowing my abilities to ride one of these things was limited. Elay wrapped an arm around my waist, took the reins, and urged the animal to something that resembled a gallop. I held on as tight as I could, glancing over our shoulders to estimate the distance between Rhana and our pursuers.

"Will she be able to lead them away?" I asked, worry lacing every word.

"If anyone can do it," Elay said, his voice strained, "she can."

I just nodded, trying to hold it together as we rode off into the night. It was getting colder by the minute, and I cursed myself for not bringing one of the blankets.

"We'll figure this out," Elay murmured. "I won't let them get you."

It occurred to me I had never told him what I had found out in the city while I was hiding from the mercenaries in the gutter.

"Elay," I murmured through chattering teeth. "Did you know they're Kyrinthan?"

He pulled me close. "Who are, *Mìthri?*"

"The ones pursuing us. You said they were sell-swords and mercenaries. Did you know they were Kyrinthan?"

He stilled before he replied. "I had my guesses. You just confirmed it."

"What does that mean?"

"The King knows we're coming."

RHANA CAUGHT up with us well after midnight, worry etched in fine lines around her eyes. None of the guards returned. Elay decided we needed a short rest before we'd continue, desperate to put as many miles between us and our enemies. By now, I was well on the verge of collapsing into a dead-faint if I didn't get rest and food soon. I wrapped a blanket around myself, and crawled into the wagon, curling up in the faint hope of fighting the shivers running rampant through my body. I was cold to the bone, which made it hard to warm up even with the blanket, but we couldn't make camp tonight.

"How much time do you reckon we have?" Elay asked, his voice strained.

"A couple of hours at the most," Rhana said with a heavy sigh. "I did what I could, but they won't be fooled for long. They'll always be faster as long as we keep the wagon and the tents."

I tensed upon hearing those words. It didn't sound promising.

"What if we would leave them?"

"We'd be faster, but we'd also be more vulnerable during the night."

Elay was quiet for a while. The only sound I heard was the buzzing in my ears and the sighing of the wind.

"How far out are we from the mountains?"

"Are you insane?" Rhana hissed. "The mountains are dangerous, you know that!"

"Perhaps," he muttered, "but it's a good deal better than being caught by the King's men, don't you think?"

She huffed. "The King's men? I thought you said they were mercenaries?"

"That's what I thought, until Shal mentioned them being Kyrinthan," Elay replied with a deep sigh. "You and I both know the King would not hire mercenaries for this—he'd send his *Vahîrin*."

"What are those?" I asked, leaning over the side of the wagon.

"They're an elite guard," Elay said. "Much like your —*Arathrien*, was it—but deadlier."

"My *Arathrien* were deadly too," I scowled, offended he would think so low of them without even knowing them.

"These men, and sometimes women," Elay went on unperturbed, "are trained to kill."

"Then why didn't they kill us in Portasâhn?"

"That, *Mìthri*," he said with a sigh, "is the question of the century. I don't know. I assume because they want either one of us or both alive."

"It also means we need to rethink our strategy," Rhana commented. "Sooner rather than later. The *Vahîrin* are bloodhounds and will not stop until they have what they want, and we cannot stay here to discuss the details."

"What's wrong with the mountains?" I asked.

"They're treacherous at night," Rhana muttered. "Not to mention the mountain people who live there."

"What about them?"

"They'll sooner kill us than let us stay there," Elay said. "But it's our only choice."

Rhana let out a sound of disgust and threw up her hands, shaking her head while mumbling something in Zihrin.

"I guess I have to get up on a *camelle* again?" I lamented, dragging myself out of the wagon.

Elay lifted me, wincing as he did so.

"How's your ankle?" I asked softly, worry gnawing at me.

"Sore," he replied with a faint smile. "Also something that cannot be helped now, but you may want to take the medical pack with you."

I grabbed the small leather bag from the wagon and slung it over my shoulder while stomping after Elay, drawing the blanket farther over my shoulders. After he had mounted his *camelle*, he helped me sit in front of him.

"Mind sharing that blanket?"

A soft grumble escaped my lips, but I helped him wrap it around his shoulders, and then around me anyway. I knew sharing body warmth would work much better than trying to do it on my own.

"How far are these mountains?" I asked, stifling a yawn.

"If I judge correctly, less than two days from here."

A deep groan escaped my lips. "I'm not sure I can stay awake for two days."

"Then don't," he whispered, placing a soft kiss on my cheek while wrapping an arm around my shoulder. "Rest against me, I'll keep you up. You'll find *camelles* are more comfortable than a horse."

"Except when they run," I mumbled, settling myself against him. "It feels like being jostled around like a sack of grain."

"How do you know what a sack of grain feels like?"

I harrumphed, too tired to argue his point or even go into a discussion. I would get to that once I woke up.

WHAT ELAY and Rhana called mountains, I called hills. Sure enough, they had the makings of mountains, but they were few and far between and barely rose into the sky. I snorted upon catching sight of them, earning an amused look from Elay.

"What's wrong?"

"Those are hardly mountains," I said. "Ilvanna has mountains —these are anthills."

Elay harrumphed. "Really? Sounds like someone got spoiled."

I thumped him against the chest, earning a clear laugh I hadn't heard in weeks, and much to my horror, it sent my heart fluttering.

"We'll be safe there for a while," he said softly. "We can rest, hopefully stock up, and make new plans."

"New plans?"

His lips quirked up in a smile. "Now that the King knows we're coming we'd better make it spectacular."

"You make no sense whatsoever."

"Are you two lovebirds quite done?" Rhana called. "We have to hu—"

All of a sudden, she slumped over and fell from her *camelle*, an arrow protruding from her throat. Elay howled in agony, and I could feel him get ready to slip off the *camelle.* Steeling my resolve, I grabbed his arm to stop him.

"Don't."

"I have to help her," he replied, hurt lacing his words. "I cannot leave her alone."

"You'll have to if you want the both of us to survive," I countered. "I don't care if you have a death wish, but I'm not staying to find out how lethal these *Vahîrin* are exactly."

Elay growled under his breath, but remained seated on the *camelle.* His arms slipped around me to grab the reins tight, circling me in the safety of his arms.

"Hold on tight," he muttered. "This is not going to be a pleasant ride."

Unpleasant didn't begin to describe how awful it was, nor did my comparison to a jostled sack of grain come anywhere close. With Rhana dead, we had no protection whatsoever, and all Elay could do to dodge arrows was to direct the *camelle* from left to right in a zigzag pattern.

Seasickness was nothing compared to this.

The world suddenly lurched and spun as the *camelle* came to a sudden halt, throwing us both off. A sharp pain shot through my shoulder when I landed in the sand, wincing at the screeching of the beast. Judging by the sound, it was dying, so I scrambled over to Elay.

"Come on, get up," I hissed. "We cannot stay here."

If we'd run, we could make it to the mountains, but we had to go—now.

"Get up, Elay," I said, wrapping my arm around his waist. "We can make it if we go now."

He grunted as I helped him to his feet, a pained grimace contorting his features into a hideous mask.

"I can't, *Mìthri,*" he gasped. "I can't run."

"Then we'll hobble," I replied, worry gnawing on the inside. "We'll crawl if we have to, but we have to move."

A faint smile ghosted his lips as he laid his arm across my shoulder. My words amused him but didn't quite convince him.

"You should run," he said in a soft voice. "Save yourself, get back to Ilvanna. There's nothing holding you here."

"Of course there is."

Without elaborating, I set us in motion, placing one foot in front of the other. I knew our chances of actually getting out of here without a fight were slim to none, but I'd be cursed if I didn't try. Elay suddenly stopped, jerking me backwards. Over his shoulder, I could see that the *Vahîrin* were gaining on us, even though they appeared to be holding back.

As if they're toying with us.

A low growl escaped my lips as I turned to Elay.

"What in Esahbyen's name, Elay!" I yelled. "We have to move, or we *will* be caught."

"Maybe we should let them."

"Over my cold, dead body," I hissed. "I did not survive getting shot at, a shipwreck, and a night in a freezing desert just to die in the middle of nowhere!"

"Then leave!" he snapped. "I told you, there's nothing holding you here! The *Harshâh* was never finished—never consummated. You are not beholden to me in any way. Leave me here and run. I'm serious!"

"Do you think I care about that?" I balled my fists and took a step closer to him. "If you think I am staying here just because we're married, you're a stupid *khirr*."

"*Mìthri*," Elay said with a heavy sigh, holding up his hands in surrender. "I don't want you to die."

I awarded him a deadpan stare, breathing out in a hard puff to expel some of the anger rising within me. If the idiot believed his life meant so little to me, he was more stupid than I'd given him credit for. *Harshâh* or not, I cared about him—a lot. Swallowing hard, I looked away from him, catching movement in my peripheral vision. Adrenaline spiked within me. In the same motion of pushing Elay aside, I slipped the dagger from his belt. An arrow whistled between us. I took the dagger by the hilt, pulled back, turned and threw it.

One of the *Vahîrin* toppled from his *camelle.*

He lay grunting in the sand, but wasn't dead yet.

"Get to the mountain ridge," I told Elay, casting a furtive glance in his direction. "Now!"

Whatever he saw on my face made him scramble to his feet and hobble out of the way. I turned my attention to our attackers. The archer lay moaning in the sand, but there were eight more closing in on me, all of them carrying weapons.

I had none.

I'm not going down without a fight.

Taking up a defensive position, my mind briefly returned to the sparring sessions I used to have with my *Arathrien*. One in the middle, the rest on the outside. This would be just like practise.

Except this is real.

I felt a wicked smile spread across my lips.

"Come on then, *grissin*," I whispered in Ilvannian.

They attacked almost simultaneously, giving me very little time to recuperate or catch myself, but somehow, I managed. A quarterstaff landed on my shoulder just as I dodged a sword aimed for my head, drawing out a hiss of pain, sending me to one knee. After I kicked backwards, I landed on all fours, grimacing at the pain lancing through my bad leg. I dodged an attack by rolling out of the way barely in time and staggered to my feet. Although by no means gracious, I swung a crescent kick at another, glad to find it hit something.

A cursory glance told me Elay had hobbled well out of the way of the fight. If what I'd heard in Portasâhn was true, they didn't care about him, although it didn't explain why they weren't going after him to kill him.

He's an easy target. They'll get to him once they have me.

A loud howl followed by ululations rising up in a fierce culmination of voices came from the mountain ridge, and when I risked a glance, I saw a dust cloud rising to meet us. It soon swallowed Elay, and then myself and the *Vahîrin*. Hands grabbed my upper arms and I was hauled along. I started to fight, kicking and screaming and screeching.

"*Taleh. Taleh.* Calm."

The words were spoken in Kyrinth, which only served to annoy me further, and I started flailing around me, desperate to hit something. A stabbing pain shot through my head and my limbs went numb beneath me. I had a habit of passing out lately.

This is it. They caught me.

CHAPTER 35

TALNOVAR

My breathing came in short, ragged gasps, and blood was running from a gash above my eyebrow. With a smirk, I wiped the blood from my face and gripped the hilt of my sword firmly in my hand. It felt good holding one again. Evan's lips twisted up in a mischievous smile before he attacked. The sound of steel ringing against steel echoed through *Denahryn*, making it appear as if a battle was going on.

Those of us who knew the truth were on edge.

I saw it in Evan's cursory glances towards his hut, in my father's constant vigilance, in Eamryel's foul moods, in Mehrean's endless gazes. The only person who seemed entirely unperturbed by it was Soren, who went about his business as if it were just any other day. The other *Dena* didn't appear too worried either, which worried me even more.

"Why are they not taking this seriously?" I muttered to Evan when we sat down for a break, glancing around at the brothers going about their daily chores.

My eyes caught Cehyan standing off to the side, her eyes on me. I felt my pulse quicken as my muscles strained against my skin. The moment she realised I was looking at her, she walked away, hugging herself. Evan was watching me with a raised eyebrow, but he didn't ask and instead took a swig of his flask before handing it to me, lifting his shoulders in a careless shrug.

"No idea, *mahnèh,*" he replied, keeping his voice low. "I wonder what's taking them so long."

I shook my head. "They're waiting for something."

"Or getting a lay of the land." Evan looked around, sitting back while stretching his legs, seemingly unconcerned.

He was anything but.

"It's what I would do," he continued. "See how things work around here, figure out the routines. Strike when people least expect it."

"I'd have killed them in their sleep," I replied darkly, dabbing my sleeve against the gash just above my eyebrow.

The bleeding was worse than the injury, no doubt. Evan had gotten lucky with a blow, and I wasn't thanking him for it. It hurt like a *hehzèh.*

"It won't be long now," Evan said, glancing in the direction of his hut.

I wasn't sure if he was talking about Nathaïr giving birth, or the refugees attacking the camp, so I just nodded. To my annoyance, I kept wiping away blood from my eyes, and my sleeve had turned a deep shade of rusty red rather than it being the regular off-white it was supposed to be.

"I'd best go see Soren," I said, pushing myself to my feet with a grunt. "The bleeding won't stop."

"I'll walk you there," Evan offered. "I want to check in on—well, you know."

I nodded. "Thanks, *mahnèh.*"

Him walking along was as much for his benefit as it was for mine. A perpetual brooding look took up his demeanour whenever he wasn't otherwise occupied, etching deep lines into his face. I clapped him on the shoulder.

"Everything will work out," I said, going for a reassurance I wasn't quite feeling. "One way or another."

Evan nodded slowly, awarding me a wry smile. "I know. I'm just… nervous, I guess. I mean, I…" He dropped his voice to a whisper, raking his hand through his hair. "I'll be a father soon, Tal. I have no clue about being a father! Mine died so long ago, he's a vague memory. I don't know what to do."

I chuckled. "Not that I have any idea, *mahnèh*, but I doubt any father knows what to do when their child is born."

For a man whose strength lay in rationale and logic, this had to be frightening. I couldn't even begin to imagine how he was really feeling.

A wan smile adorned his features.

"There are stories," he whispered, turning even paler than normal, "about women who… who do not survive childbirth. I couldn't raise a child on my own, Tal."

"You won't have to," I replied. "You've got us."

"Evan!"

We both turned to the voice yelling his name. Eamryel came striding down the path, face expressionless, lips drawn tight. He acknowledged us with a slight nod of his head and glanced around.

"It's begun," he said in a low voice.

"The attack?" I ventured carefully.

He shook his head. "Nath's in labour. Mehrean sent me to fetch Evan and Soren. We need to keep it quiet, in case…"

Evan looked even more frightened than before.

"Go with Eamryel," I said. "I'll get Soren."

They both nodded, and I watched them turn into the direction Eamryel had come from. I had no idea why, but an ominous feeling settled in my stomach, as if something was about to go horribly wrong. When I stepped inside the infirmary, heat assaulted me from every direction, and the hair on the back of my neck stood on end. They'd always kept it insanely hot in here, but this was too much.

The eerie silence promised nothing good either.

I slid my sword out of its scabbard and moved forward tentatively, keeping my breathing slow and steady not to give myself away. The infirmary was an h-shaped building, with a central room in the middle. One of the side buildings comprised of beds—the other building was where the actual healing happened. Smoke was coming out of that side of the building.

"*Nohro!* Soren!"

There was no response.

After wiping blood and sweat from my face, I buried my nose and mouth in the crook of my arm and stepped inside, keeping low. If what I feared was true, the building was on fire, and there was no doubt in my mind people were still in there. I knew there had been only two other patients in the infirmary with me, and they'd been sent away before I was. Soren would have been here though.

"Soren!"

Still no response.

My heart picked up speed. Heat assaulted my skin, and despite covering my face, smoke seeped through it into my lungs.

"Anyone in here?"

I coughed, cursing myself in my mind. Nobody responded, and I was about to turn back when I saw something out of the corner of my eye. Moving closer, I realised it wasn't a something but a someone.

Soren.

Without thinking twice, I sheathed my sword as I knelt next to him, quickly checking him for a pulse. He was breathing but laboriously, and in the thick of the smoke, I couldn't tell if it was because of an injury or something else. With difficulty, I lifted him onto my shoulders. A grunt escaped his lips.

That's a good sign.

I made my way out of the infirmary as quickly as I could, not bothering with checking if anyone was waiting for me. Only someone stupid or suicidal would have stayed inside the building.

So how come I found you out cold, mahnèh.

Shouting assaulted me the moment I stepped outside. Screams bounced off of the mountains, bringing me back to a different time, a different place—back to a moment where I believed I'd lost the woman I loved, only to find her on her knees at the end of a sword, blood staining her left side. Her fearlessness—her blessing, my curse—had screamed defiance in silver eyes turned dark. As it mingled with the scent of blood, other memories resurfaced—other eyes resurfaced, and all I could see was Chazelle's hardened gaze as she gave me permission to end her life.

I pushed the thought away and stumbled, barely able to keep a hold of Soren.

"*Anahràn*? Are you all right?" Samehya asked.

I looked up, finding her crouching in front of me.

"Fine. What's going on?"

"The fight has started," she said, glancing over her shoulder. "The *Dena* are holding their own under your father's command. He's waiting for you."

"I need to get Soren to Mehrean," I replied, my throat aching with the effort of talking.

Samehya just nodded and without me giving her any orders, she helped me get him to his feet, lifting him with one arm around his waist. I got up to support his other side, and between the two of us we managed to carry him away from the burning infirmary. After only a few feet, he began to regain consciousness, taking in deep shuddering breaths that ended in coughing.

"Welcome back, *mahnèh*," I muttered.

"Tal?" he croaked.

"At your service."

"What happened?" he asked, his voice raspy.

"I was going to ask you the same," I said, glancing at him. "Found you out cold in the infirmary. Good thing I got there when I did."

"Why?"

"Because there won't be any of it left after the fire's out," I said with a heavy sigh. "Come on, Mehr needs you."

Soren made us stop, carefully trying out gravity to see if he could stand on his own feet. He was a little unsteady but managed to stay up.

"Why does Mehr need me?"

"Nath's in labour," I murmured for his ears alone. "I guess she wants a healer at her side. Besides, you'll be safer there too. The fight's begun as well."

Soren narrowed his eyes. "That can't be a coincidence."

"I agree."

We started walking and picked up speed, all while still supporting Soren between us, until we were all but running to Nathaïr's hut. Halfway there, two enemies stepped into our path, but before I could even respond, Samehya charged them, two short swords in her hands.

Where did those come from?

"I've got this!" she yelled.

Surprised by the little feminine whirlwind, one of the men went down, a sword protruding from his abdomen, the look on his face one of disbelief. I whistled low under my breath in appreciation, and flashed her a grin before moving on with Soren. Someone had taught her well.

"*Nohro*," Soren muttered, stopping short. "They're fighting in front of the hut."

Sure enough, Eamryel, Evan and two *Dena* were holding off at least a dozen men, neither of the groups gaining the upper hand. I motioned Soren to find cover while slipping my sword out of its scabbard.

"Don't come out until I whistle," I whispered. "And when I do, get inside, lock the door, and wait for one of us to come get you."

"Provided we're done," he muttered. "Go, what are you waiting around for?"

With the element of surprise on my side, I snuck up behind the enemy and had two of them down before the rest realised I was there. Their attention divided, their coordinated attack soon crumbled, and at least another five of them found their deaths at the end of our weapons before the rest scrambled and scattered.

Following my whistle, Soren appeared from his hideout looking pale and drawn, but determined.

"Ev, go with Soren," I instructed. "Bolt the door."

"I can fight," Evan objected. "You will need every available sword you can find. Word has it more have arrived."

"Then one more sword won't matter. Be with Nathaïr. Protect your family. Let us handle the rest."

Judging by the look on his face, he wasn't happy with these arrangements at all. Either that, or he wasn't happy being bossed around by me. In that moment, I didn't care. Aside from the fact he should be there when his child was born, it made sense to have someone on the inside who could wield a weapon. After seeing the *Dena* fight, it occurred to me Soren would probably know how to fight too, but he'd be busy.

"The three of you stay here," I ordered. "For whatever reason, they targeted this hut specifically. I'll send more people this way."

"What about you?" Eamryel asked grimly, wiping his sword on his leg.

My lips pulled up in a smirk. "I'm going to put an end to this, one way or the other."

Eamryel's eyes twinkled in mischief, the Arolvyen sneer returning to his face. This time, it didn't hold the menace it usually did.

"Don't die," he remarked, switching from sword to bow and arrow. "We have another mission to go on."

I inclined my head and turned to leave when Eamryel called my name. He was about to say something more, shook his head and waved me off.

"Go on, move," he growled. "Let's not turn this into another massacre."

EAMRYEL'S WORDS were still ringing in my ears when I found my father back-to-back with a *Dena*, fighting a group of enemies that came at them from every direction. The twoscore people Samehya had warned us about had doubled, if not tripled, but unlike *Hanyarah*, *Denahryn* was nowhere close to being overrun. For the first time, I witnessed the true power of the *Dena* as they fought, their prowess with weapons unparalleled. Never in my life had I witnessed skill like that, and I felt momentarily envious. I'd always prided myself on being a good warrior.

Compared to them, I was a toddler playing at being a fighter.

"Tal! Behind you!"

I swung around fast enough to parry the sword aimed for my back, but was too late to prevent it from cutting my shoulder. The pain barely registered as instinct took over and I swung my sword from left to right to gut my opponent. He wasn't fast enough and went down with his intestines spilling out. The stench of blood filled my nostrils, and I staggered at the sudden impact. Never before had it bothered me, but after Azra… I pushed the thought aside and went for the next enemy.

The next kill.

The idea bothered me, and I had to fight not to give in to it, to keep focusing on what was ahead, yet my mind kept playing tricks on me, showing images of the throne room, of the rebellion in the main street, of killing Chazelle. I swallowed hard, pressing the heel of my palm against my forehead.

"Tal. Tal. Tal!"

Someone shaking me returned me to my senses. Looking up, I found Samehya hanging onto my shirt, a concerned frown creasing her brow.

"Snap out of it," she ordered. "There's a battle going on, and you cannot break down now. Your father's been taken to the healers." A grimace pulled her lips down. "You need to fight. You need to take control. Are you with me?"

I looked momentarily confused, but nodded. She let go of my shirt and took a step backwards, stumbled, and went down to one knee, clutching her side. My eyes travelled down, only then noticing the dark stain on her shirt.

"You need to see a healer too," I growled, helping her up. "Come on."

Around us, the *Dena* were fighting fiercely, and I was glad to find most of the dead and dying didn't wear their robes. We could not afford a repetition of *Hanyarah.*

I can't afford a repetition of Hanyarah.

Samehya was struggling at my side, sinking to her knees more and more often. I sheathed my sword and picked her up in my arms, cradling her close. When she rested her head against my shoulder, I gulped away the lump in my throat, if only because this was almost exactly like *Hanyarah.*

"If you die on me," I said, "Xaresh will come and haunt me, and trust me when I tell you that's the last thing I want."

Her lips quirked up. "I know. I won't."

I left her with the healers. Mercifully, the injury wasn't lethal, but she'd lost a lot of blood already. Gratitude coursed through me, and after ordering her to stay down, I went for a quick check on Father. He was conscious but in the foulest mood I'd ever seen him.

"When are you going to set that plan of yours in motion?" He scowled at me. "It's long overdue."

I grunted. "Good to see you're still alive, Father."

"Go," he hissed. "Don't come back until you've won."

"Yes, *Ohzheràn*."

Although the plan had focused on about forty men rather than three times that amount, by now, their undercover force had been diminished to a few stragglers—the sizeable part of their army was still waiting outside the gates according to our scouts. It could still work. Once I reached the main body of our little army, I was glad to find they'd taken care of the remainder of the so-called refugees. I instructed the *Dena* to follow the plan. More than half of them disappeared from the field, leaving me with slightly more than two dozen men at my side.

It was a risk, but one I was willing to take.

"You know what to do," I said.

Disgusted by my next step, I smeared myself with blood from one of the fallen before I lay down on the ground between the bodies of our enemies. In my peripheral vision, I saw the *Dena* follow my lead. My sword lay where it had fallen, but it was still within reach. Knowing Azra, she would have instructed her men to leave nobody alive. Massacres had become her trademark, and this would be no exception. Whatever Cehyan was here for, and I had my suspicions, she would not leave without it, unless I had a say in it.

Cehyan was a smart woman, ambitious, but overconfident when it came to her abilities. Azra may have sent her for something, but she was no *Zheràn*, and even if she had been one, I wasn't convinced these men would listen to a woman like herself. She was strong, yes, but she wasn't the merciless killer Azra was. These men would obey her because of Azra, their loyalty bound to the *Blood Tari*, but no more. My plan hinged on the assumption Cehyan would overplay her hand.

I just needed to make sure not to go off the deep end.

Releasing the breath I was holding, I closed my eyes, counting to the steady beat of my heart while straining to listen. A whistle in the distance was our cue. The rest of the enemy was moving inside *Denahryn*. The two whistles following shortly after meant they were in sight of our second group—the one hiding from view. Three whistles were unnecessary. They'd be upon us by that time.

Footsteps on the gravelly path alerted me, most likely the others too, and I prayed to the Gods everybody would stick to the plan. It was as strong as the weakest link. Voices laced with uncertainty reached me, settling the nerves inside me somewhat. A few more breaths until I sucked it in and opened my eyes.

Pretending to be dead was a lot harder than I imagined.

No sooner had I opened my eyes than Cehyan came into view. Dressed in armour, she looked every bit the warrior, but the way she carried herself was a clear indication she was everything but. Insecurity flashed in her eyes, and the moment she saw me, a gasp escaped her lips. I had to give it to her—she pulled herself together fast. Squaring her shoulders, she turned to a man who looked more impressive than she did, and ordered him to do something. Her words were too low for me to hear what it was, but it soon became clear as her men spread out between us and their fallen comrades.

My lungs were burning something fierce by then, and if I didn't make a move soon, I'd be the one to blow our cover.

Come on, Cehy, step closer. You know you want to.

Sure enough, after her men had dispersed, she knelt down next to me, placing a hand on my cheek. In the same moment as her eyes widened in realisation, I grabbed her, placing one hand over her mouth as I pinned her beneath me, dagger at her throat. From the corner of my eyes, I saw the *Dena* move too, diminishing their force by two dozen men in a heartbeat. More followed when our unseen forces joined the fray.

"Tell your men to stop," I hissed, "or I swear on Esahbyen's name, I will end you."

Cehyan's eyes widened briefly before she became furious. She tried to kick, but after the first time she did, I pinned her legs with my own and added extra pressure to the dagger against her throat.

"I'm not fooling around," I said icily. "Tell your men to stand down, or every single one of you dies. Nod if you'll comply."

She didn't.

"Azra will find you," she hissed, "and kill you. She'll tear you limb from limb and enjoy it while doing so."

"Wrong answer."

Fighting my scruples to hit an unarmed woman, I punched her hard enough to knock her out cold.

CHAPTER 36

SHALITHA

A fierce throbbing throughout my head was the first sensation when I came around, followed by the feeling of having swallowed half the desert. Smacking my lips, I opened my eyes, peering into the semi-darkness I found myself in. That was a blessing at least. Bright light would surely have set off the headache further.

"You're awake," Elay croaked from my left.

Turning my head to the side, a sudden wave of nausea hit me, and I closed my eyes again in an attempt to steady my vision and my stomach. When I opened them, I found Elay sitting next to me on the bed, looking far less horrible than I expected him to look.

"Where are we?"

"Safe," he replied, stroking a lock of hair out of my face. "We're with the mountain people."

"I thought you said they were dangerous?" I frowned, trying to make sense of the situation. "Why are we here?"

"They saved us from the *Vahîrin*." he said, looking rather bashful.

"What aren't you telling me?"

"One of the mountain people hit you over the head," he replied, a faint smile tugging at his lips, "because you started fighting them. He had no other choice."

A grunt escaped my lips, and I scowled at him. "Then he'd better have something for this massive headache, or I'll return the favour."

He snorted. "I'll go fetch their healer. I'll be back in a few."

While Elay was gone, it gave me time to look around the hut we were in, only to realise it wasn't a hut but a large round tent. In the middle, they'd built a round fireplace, right under a sizeable hole in the ceiling, so the smoke was drawn out of the tent. The floor was covered in rugs and carpets while the walls were decorated with cloth in varying shades of red. Bright red doors marked the entrance. The bed I was in appeared to be made of sturdy wood and was big enough to accommodate a family of four. Pelts served to stave off the worst of the cold, while the cotton sheets made it feel comfortable.

Only then did it occur to me I wasn't wearing much.

"Son of a—," I muttered as I sat up and swung my legs out of the bed.

As soon as cold air hit my skin, I scooted back under the covers, waiting until the onslaught of cold shivers disappeared as warmth seeped back into me. The cold had never bothered me this much. Pulling the blankets up, I settled myself cross-legged underneath them, waiting for Elay to return and the headache to subside. I perked up at voices coming to the tent and watched the entrance warily as the doors swung open and Elay walked in, followed by an elderly woman.

A wizened old face peered out from under a curtain of small braids. Her hair, as stark white as my own, was in contrast with copper skin—similar to Elay's. Kind eyes regarded me curiously as she shuffled over to the bed, supported at one arm by Elay who bore nothing but awe on his face as he watched her.

My brows quirked up in question when our eyes met.

"You must be Shalitha," the old crone croaked gently. "Would you mind coming a little closer, *amisha*? I'm afraid these old bones aren't as supple as they used to be."

A faint smile tugged at my lips as I moved closer, glancing at Elay curiously. He lifted his shoulders in a half-hearted shrug and took a step back, letting the old lady do what had to be done.

"My name is Fahira," she said, and turned to Elay. "Be a dear and stoke up the fire, *mishan*."

Elay inclined his head and tended to the fire while Fahira turned her attention to me. She stooped over and peered into my eyes intently, brows knitting together until they formed one line.

"How's your head?" she asked.

"As if something's trying to make its way out."

Without warning, she cupped my face in her hands. I stiffened underneath her touch as a sudden wave of panic washed over me. She cooed at me, as if I were a frightened animal, or a little child, in a tongue I did not understand, but the effect would have been the same in any language. I calmed down and let her do what she needed to. Her hands moved from my jaw to my neck, from my neck to my shoulders, and from my shoulders down my arms to my hands. She repeated the process several times, and the longer she continued, the less my head ached.

A shiver ran down my spine.

"How is your head now?" she asked, a secretive smile on her lips.

I blinked stupidly. "The headache—it's gone. How?"

She cackled. "Ah, *amisha,* some secrets must be kept to preserve the mystery. Now, if you could lay down on your side, please. I'd like to check your back."

Confusion marred my expression. "My back, what for?"

"You had an ugly bruise on your shoulder when they brought you in," Fahira explained. "Didn't you feel it?"

I shook my head and lay down, wondering how I had not noticed it. Turning my back to her, I stilled when she lifted the nightgown I was apparently wearing. She prodded the skin around my shoulder blade, but there was nothing more than a dull ache and some discomfort as she did so. She clucked and tutted to herself before tugging my nightshift into place.

"Everything looks well, *amisha*," she declared, patting my good shoulder. "There are clothes on the chest at the foot of your bed. If you feel well enough, feel free to look around the village."

She turned to leave, stopped mid-movement and looked at me, a frown on her face. "The Chief will want a word with the both of you before the day ends. Don't go wandering off."

With those words, she shuffled out of the tent, the door banging shut behind her an ominous sound in the quiet of our place. Elay sat down on the side of the bed, several emotions crossing his face before it settled on relief.

"Do you need anything?" he asked tentatively.

Judging by the way his mouth kept working, it wasn't the first question that came to his mind, but he was obviously trying to come to terms with something.

"Clothes, please," I replied, sitting up. "We need to get out of here."

Elay halted upon my words and turned to look. "You do realise we're safe here, right?"

I scowled at him. "I know, but you said we needed to get to Kyrintha, and my journey home is starting to get long overdue."

He clenched his jaw, running a hand over his short cropped hair. "I'm aware of that…"

I narrowed my eyes. "But?"

"It's nothing," he said with a shake of his head, handing me my clothes with a smile. "But let's wait for what the Chief has to say before we start making plans, all right? There's no point in running headlong into our enemies' hands. It would be poor payment to these people."

There was more to what he was saying, I could tell from the guarded look in his eyes, but I decided not to pry. We'd been fighting for long enough, and I was tired of it. In one thing he was right—we were safe and right now, that was all that mattered. The bundle of clothes Elay brought me was quite a pile, and as I sorted through it, it became apparent there was at least one under layer and two or three over layers. I snorted.

"What's wrong?" Elay asked, looking up.

I smiled softly. "Nothing. This just reminds me of home."

"How so?" He looked at me curiously.

While slipping my legs into the tight fitting material, I glanced at him. "The dresses they made me wear at court were always multi-layered affairs too. The more layers it had, the more regal the gown was considered to be."

"You never struck me as a dress kind of person," Elay mused, lips curving into that mischievous smile. "Although you wear them well."

He added it as an afterthought, almost, but the twinkle in his eyes and happy look on his face was one of memory, and I didn't have to guess hard which one that was.

"I'm not. I hated them with a passion, but now..."

My ribs grew tight, restricting my breath while I tried to fight the lump in my throat as I thought of home. With a heavy sigh, I dropped my arms in an attempt to struggle the shirt over my head as tears began to trickle down my cheeks. Elay sat down next to me and gently pulled me into his embrace.

"Cry it out," he murmured into my hair. "You've been strong long enough."

"*Grissin*," I cursed him half-heartedly as heavy tears rolled down my face, turning into full-fledged sobs moments later.

Elay guided us down on the bed and held me in his arms,

rubbing my back slowly while I cried against his shoulder. It was the first time in a very long time I allowed my grief to take over. Sobs turned into screams of pain, which in turn became fury, and I ended up thumping Elay's chest in pure frustration, although I was as weak as a mewling kitten by then. Through it all, Elay held me, or allowed me some room when I wanted it, but always, always, he pulled me close when I needed it.

He placed a soft kiss on my head when the sobbing subsided into sniffling, a loving smile ghosting his lips. When he placed a kiss on the bridge of my nose, I closed my eyes and released a shuddering breath. Inhaling deeply, I tried to stop the uncontrollable trembling that came with the aftermath of crying, only to end up trembling even more.

"Hush," Elay whispered against my forehead. "I'm here, *Mìthri.*"

I swallowed the lump in my throat and closed my eyes, allowing myself to feel the comfort of his arms around me, the steady beat of his heart against my cheek, his warm body close to mine. I let out another shuddering breath and tilted my head up, opening my eyes to look at him. Emerald eyes bore into mine. Without conscious thought, I pressed my lips against his —soft first, but more demanding with every breath we shared. I pulled myself against him, ignoring the erratic beating of my heart and the buzzing in my ears.

To my surprise, Elay released me from the kiss and pulled back.

"Not like this," he whispered, running his hand gently through my hair. "It wouldn't feel right."

His rejection hurt more than I ever thought it would and I sat up with a start, pushing myself out of his embrace. Without replying, I slipped into my clothing, pulled on my new fur-lined boots and stomped out of the tent. Heat rose to my cheeks and tears threatened to spill again. People looked up curiously as I passed, but I ignored every single one of them.

"Shal, wait!" Elay called after me.

I picked up a brisker pace, wrapping my arms around myself while ignoring his pleas for me to stop. Soon enough, he caught up to me, halting me by taking my elbow and stepping around me.

"*Mìthri*, what's wrong?" he asked, honestly confused.

"What's wrong?" Indignation rose in my voice. "You have to ask me what's wrong?"

He frowned at me. "Apparently, I do."

Annoyance sounded through in his voice, but on the outside, he remained calm. I, however, did not, and when I spoke, it rather resembled a banshee's shriek than anything else.

"You've been trying to get me into your bed since before we got married," I yelled, "and now that I make a move towards you, you reject me?! You're a *grissin*, Elay. Son of a *hehzèh*!"

He folded his arms in front of him, face impassive while I continued my shrieking tirade, clearly unconcerned.

"How can you do that? Is the thought of me suddenly repulsive? Have you laid eyes on another girl to make your wife while I was out?"

Elay opened his mouth to reply.

I wasn't done yet.

"I finally plucked up the courage to do what I did," I said, desperation lacing my words, "and you rejected me."

He let out a heavy sigh and dropped his arms along his sides, watching me with compassion. "Are you finished?"

I scowled at him in response. He carefully took my hands in his, placing kisses on my knuckles by way of respect. He'd done that from the beginning and never stopped doing it, but this time it served to deflate my anger. Taking in deep, ragged breaths, I watched him.

"I didn't reject you because I do not want you, *Mìthri*," he said softly. "I rejected you, because I don't want you to make a decision like this based on grief."

Chewing my bottom lip, I listened quietly, feeling how shame crept its way to my face in a fiery sensation. Elay cupped my cheek with one hand, lifting my chin.

"Trust me when I tell you I would want nothing more than that, but I won't allow you to do it out of pain and hurt. If you choose it, I want you to be sound of mind and heart."

I looked anywhere but at him. Mulling over his words, something else he'd said in anger came to mind, and I frowned at him.

"You'd have willingly done it at the *Harshâh,*" I scolded, pulling my hands from him. "You didn't even let me make a decision then."

He breathed in deeply, and judging by the look on his face, he was searching for words.

"Because I couldn't," he replied. "Zihrin, Kyrintha—these countries are so steeped in their beliefs, their superstitions and traditions, that I had no choice but to continue that way."

"And you would have enjoyed it too," I replied, my voice venomous.

Why was I lashing out to him? His reasoning made perfect sense. Was I mad at him for rejecting me, or was I mad at myself for offering in a less than perfect moment?

"Of course I would have." He sighed in exasperation. "Any sane, normal man and woman would enjoy consummating their marriage, *Mìthri,* but I couldn't do it… not to you."

I frowned in confusion. "I'm no—"

He placed a finger on my lips and stepped closer, his eyes searching mine with something I couldn't quite place. There was a hunger, sure enough, lust, possibly, but it was more than that.

Love?

"I arranged for the attack to happen," he whispered, meeting my gaze steadily, "so the *Harshâh* would be disrupted. I ordered Zirscha to arrange the rest, so people wouldn't start inquiring."

He swallowed hard. "You were so opposed to the idea, and after your time with the *Gemsha,* I couldn't put you through that. I'm sorry I didn't tell you before."

I gawped at him, blinking a few times before my brain took up its function and started processing what he'd just told me.

"I..." I fell silent, brows furrowed in thought. "I made you a promise in exchange for you keeping me safe. That was part of the deal. I..."

He smiled softly. "I'd rather it happens because you want it than because you are forced to. I care about you, *Mìthri.* A lot. But y—"

His sentence was cut off by a high voice yelling *mishan ì amisha* repeatedly, and when we looked, a young boy was running in our direction, waving his hand. He was winded when he arrived, doubling over to catch his breath.

"Stand up," I said. "You'll be able to fill your lungs faster."

He blinked at me.

"What's the matter?" Elay asked, stepping around me, circling my waist with his arm.

The boy stared at him, eyes wide in wonder. "The Chief wants to talk to you. Please, follow me."

CHAPTER 37

TALNOVAR

With Father out of commission and Mehrean still with Nathaïr, I was left to deal with the aftermath of battle. One side of the infirmary had completely burnt to the ground, the stone building in the middle the only reason the left wing hadn't burnt too. It was a small mercy. Now it housed those who had gotten injured during the battle, which were luckily just a few. There had been casualties amongst the *Dena*, but no more than fifteen, which was negligible compared to how many were still alive and how many enemies had found their end at the hands of the Brotherhood.

After the battle, I'd gone to check in with Soren, but Nathaïr was still in labour. Evan's nerves were frayed all around, and even Eamryel had looked all doom and gloom. Since Nathaïr was no more than an acquaintance to me, I was happy enough staying outside. Although vaguely, I remembered my sister's birth—more so the endless amount of bloodied cloth the midwives had carried out of the room.

I'd seen enough blood to last me a lifetime.

Massaging my temples, I sat back in my chair, regarding Cehyan quietly from across the room. Her *Inzheràn*—lieutenant

—had been killed in the last altercation, an arrow to the heart his undoing. It made her the only person in charge. Her men had known nothing but to attack *Denahryn* and follow orders, so the only way to get information was by talking to her. I had enough ideas about what I wanted to do to her—none of them involved talking nor were any of them positive.

Her betrayal hurt worse than anything Azra had done to me.

"Like what you see?" she asked, snapping my attention back to her.

"Not in the slightest."

"You used to," she said, a playful smile on her lips. "You used to love to play with me, take your time with me, have your way with me... again, and again, and again."

I was surprised at how little her words did for me.

"And I am more than grateful that's all in the past," I replied icily. "Why are you here, Cehyan? Why did that *Hehzèh* send you?"

"What?" she pouted. "No foreplay?"

I gave her an arched stare. "I'm not playing around, Cehyan. Tell me why you're here, and you'll live."

She snorted. "Do you think I'm afraid to die?"

"No." I rose to my feet and walked over to her, placed my hands on the armrest and leaned in to whisper in her ear. "But I know you are terrified of pain, and trust me when I tell you I'm not beyond torturing you at this point."

"But..." Her lips began to tremble. "What about our child?"

"What are you talking about?"

"I'm with child, Tal," she said in a husky voice.

I stiffened and went still, my voice dangerously low when I spoke. "What did you say?"

A deep blush was on her cheeks, and she was wetting her lips as if her mouth had suddenly gone dry. Cehyan never blushed, and I remembered Father telling me some tell-tale signs of lying once.

My lips pulled up in a smirk. "You used to lie better."

"I'm telling you the truth."

While facing her, I bared my teeth, shaking my head. "Don't mistake me for a fool, Cehyan. You never were good at covering your tracks. Drugged I may have been, but I've seen the *Tahrash* in your bag. I've seen you making the concoction many times in the past. Do you think I've forgotten?"

She paled underneath my scrutiny, her pupils dilating as she watched me. "Please, Tal. Don't do this. I'm begging you."

"You should've considered your options more carefully." I straightened, my gaze never leaving her. "You get one more choice. Either you tell me what I want to know, or I'll get it out of you, and you won't like it this time."

"You can't do this to me," she whimpered.

"Try me."

"*Grissin*!" she shrieked. "As if I'd want your child anyway!"

I smirked and stepped away from her, folding my arms in front of my chest.

"You've chosen your side, Cehy," I said, "and now you have to face the consequences of that choice. Either you tell me why you are here, and I'll spare you the pain, or you don't, and I'll make you wish for a swift death. Think about it. I expect an answer when I return."

Her pleas fell on deaf ears as I made my way out of the hut, instructing the two *Dena* outside to keep watch inside, while ordering four more men to guard the hut.

I wasn't taking any chances this time.

Releasing a shuddering breath, I made my way to Evan's hut, eager for some fresh air and news. Night had settled over *Denahryn* like a cold blanket, and torches had been lit to light the paths. Aside from the occasional owl hooting, it was quiet, which was a blessing considering the mayhem earlier. If it hadn't been for Samehya warning us, we might not have known at all.

We owed her.

I need to ask Father to give her a place amongst Shal's Arathrien. She deserves it.

Eamryel was pacing up and down in front of the hut, arms folded in front of him to stave off the cold, which I'd come to learn only worked with a proper woollen cloak and something warm in your hands. I hadn't thought of bringing either of those items. His head snapped up the moment my foot crunched on the path towards the hut, hand on the pommel of his sword.

"Oh, it's you."

"I'd be disappointed too," I replied, flashing him a wry smile. "How's it going?"

He shrugged. "It's been quiet for a while, but there's no baby yet. Last I heard, there are some issues, but Evan didn't elaborate."

I nodded slowly, folding my arms across my chest in a similar fashion to his. I really should have brought something warmer.

"Did you find out why they came here?" Eamryel asked at length, stuffing the toe of his boot into the pebbled path.

I shook my head. "No, that *hehzèh* won't talk, but I know how to make her."

Eamryel stopped mid-movement of another aimless kick at the pebbles and looked up. "Really? And how is that?"

"Torture."

He stared at me as if I'd gone insane, only to burst out laughing a moment later, slapping his thighs.

"You?" he howled. "Torture?"

I glared at him. "You have no idea what I'm capable of."

In a sudden bout of anger, he grabbed my shirt and slammed me against the wall of the hut, a dagger at my throat.

"I know perfectly well what you are capable of, *Anahràn*," he hissed, narrowing his eyes. "You will kill if it's your duty, and you will lament their loss. You will feel guilty, but not overly so because again, it's duty, but trust me when I tell you… you do not have what it takes to torture someone, especially *not* someone you used to screw around with."

I shoved him away. "You. Know. Nothing."

He was at my throat again just as fast, trailing the dagger across my cheek. "Then tell me, *Anahràn*… how *would* you go about torturing a woman?"

I opened my mouth to reply, but the words lodged in my throat, and with horror I realised he was right. No matter what I threatened, I would never be able to put her through the pain I promised her. No matter how tough I thought I could be, the thought alone made my insides twist and turn. I could kill in the line of duty—I could not maim for sport. He snickered when this realisation dawned on me and let me go, putting his dagger back in place.

"That's what I thought," he mused, cracking his knuckles. "Fortunately for you, I do not have those qualms at all."

I stared at him in shock, which was followed by contempt first and anger second. Before either of us knew what was happening, I slammed him into the wall, arm at his throat with enough pressure to be painful.

"Don't think for a moment I've forgotten what you did to the *Tarien*," I hissed. "For that alone, I will never forgive you."

He grunted. "And I regret doing that to this very day, but if you want answers from that woman, I'm your only option."

Again he was right, and I hated that even more than the fact he was about to torture the woman I used to care about a long time ago—a woman I had contemplated marrying one day. The worst of it was the hollow feeling inside when he offered it. Cehyan had burnt what little there had been left between us. I had meant what I said when I told her she'd made her choice, and now she would have to live with the consequences. With a growl, I let go of Eamryel.

"Fine."

CEHYAN'S SCREAMS still echoed through my mind hours after Eamryel had finished. Despite not having the balls to do it, I had forced myself to stay in the room and watch. While he administered the pain, I asked the questions, and while she wasn't forthcoming at first, after enough incentive, she was only too eager to give us the information we wanted.

It was worse than I'd thought.

Not only had Cehyan divulged why she'd been sent here, she'd also told us about Azra's plans of going to war with Therondia. Ilvanna had never had the numbers to invade our neighbouring country, and every war that had come to pass between the two monarchies had ended in bloodshed alone. The silver lining was that it was one of Azra's long-term plans. According to Cehyan, she was still waiting for something. As for Cehyan being here, the reason was what I had thought it would be—abducting Nathaïr and Evan's baby, but only if it were a girl.

"It makes no sense," I murmured, more to myself than to anyone else.

"What doesn't?" Eamryel asked too calmly.

I still didn't trust him fully, even though he'd just done what I couldn't.

"Why she'd only want the baby if it were a girl," I replied. "Aside from the obvious with her being a possible heir to the throne."

"There's your answer."

I glowered at him. "Why not kill it then? Be done with it? Wouldn't that be much faster than abducting it?"

Eamryel offered a nonchalant shrug at my question. "Azra's taken leave of her senses many years ago as far as I can tell. Her reasons are anyone's guess."

A heavy sigh escaped my lips. "Well, at least we prevented that from happening."

"This time."

I glanced at him and nodded. "This time."

I closed my eyes and rested my head against the outside wall of the cabin, enjoying the cold air on my hot skin. It had been disconcerting to watch how easy it was for Eamryel to administer pain, but the joy I had expected to see on him had not been there. To him, it had been a job, no more, but I had noticed the tremor starting in his hand and the twitch in the corner of his mouth.

We all had our demons.

I still didn't forgive him for what he'd done to Shal. Maybe one day, but that day wasn't today, nor—as far as I was concerned—any day in the foreseeable future. Looking aside, I watched Eamryel rub sand on his hands until they were almost raw. The more he rubbed, the more blood came off, but he didn't seem bothered by it.

"Where did you learn all of that?" I asked at length.

He glanced at me. "Learn what?"

"Torture…"

"My father," he replied after a while, a tic in his jaw starting. "He rules his household with an iron fist."

I was about to ask more when quick footsteps on gravel alerted both of us. We shot to our feet in time to find a *haniya* rushing in our direction, eyes wide.

"*Iràn* Arolvyen," she said, inclining her head. "Soren requires your presence."

With a stiff nod, he followed her to Evan's hut. Although I hadn't been summoned, curiosity won over. Add to that the fact Evan was my friend, and I had reason enough to be there. If something was wrong, he could do with one. Besides, it wasn't as if Cehyan was going anywhere. Ordering the *Dena* to stand guard with the promise of being back soon, I hastened after Eamryel and the *haniya.* By the time I arrived, everybody had gone inside, and I didn't have the heart to knock on the door.

I would wait it out.

After sitting down, I closed my eyes and focused on the sounds around me—on the wind rustling the trees, on water lapping against rocks a little farther off, to nightjars singing their churring song somewhere high above in their nest. Inhaling deeply, I was transported to another time, another memory where I enjoyed these sounds with Shal agonisingly close, talking about things that had happened and might still come. I'd wanted to kiss her again and again, until her body melded to mine, and we became two parts of a whole, but the timing had been inappropriate, and I'd only kissed her. She'd asked me, in so many words, to run, and I had laughed it away.

If only we had run away that night.

A LOUD WAIL from the hut woke me with a start, and I knew without seeing Nathaïr hadn't survived. I stilled and listened, straining to hear the sound of a baby's cry, but there was nothing. Swallowing hard, I rose to my feet, and just as I was about to knock on the door, it was opened and Eamryel stepped out, face ashen, tears brimming his eyes. Had I been a better man, I would have tried to comfort him, but as it was, I stepped out of his way and let him go. Instead, I ducked inside the hut, the scent of blood and death immediately overwhelming.

Evan was seated in a chair, holding a little bundle in his arms. Soren was tending to Nathaïr, which was to say, covering her with a sheet. Even in the dim light, I could see the dark stains beneath her.

Poor woman. She didn't deserve this.

"*Ruesta mey shareye*," I whispered. "May the Gods and Goddesses favour you."

Evan looked up at my words, eyes filled with tears, but it was hard to tell if it was from sadness or joy.

"It's a girl," he croaked.

It was neither sadness nor joy I decided, but pure undiluted wonder. Swallowing hard, I moved towards him, apprehension settling heavy in my bones. The little girl in his arms still looked a little wrinkled, but her eyes were wide open, and she was listening attentively, as if trying to understand the world around her.

"Here," Evan murmured. "Will you hold her, please?"

"I... I do—"

"Please," he interjected, sounding tired. "I want to say my goodbyes to Nath."

I swallowed the lump in my throat and nodded, feeling awkward when he placed the little girl in my arms. She was so small—so fragile. Soren laid a hand on my shoulder and nodded in the direction of the door, indicating we should leave Ev alone for a bit. I didn't need a second reason to leave the stifling hot hut.

Outside, I breathed in deeply, cradling the girl in my arms, pulling the blanket farther over her little face so she wouldn't catch a cold. She appeared to be watching me curiously.

"She's a fighter," Soren said, sounding exhausted. "Like our *Tarien*."

My lips curled up in a one-sided smile as I watched her.

"We can only hope she doesn't turn out the same," I replied.

Soren gave a derisive snort. "She'll be Evan's death if that happens."

"No doubt," I replied, a faint smile tugging at my lips.

Returning my attention to the little bundle in my arms, I

understood at once why Evan had marvelled at her. She began smacking her lips and turned her head to nuzzle my chest.

"I'm sorry little one," I murmured. "Not going to happen."

Soren snorted. "I'll go see if there's a wet-nurse ready."

Just as he left, Evan stepped out of the hut, looking wan, tired and utterly lost. His usually immaculate hair stood on end, and there were large, dark circles under his eyes. Before handing the girl to her father, I hugged her.

"I'll protect you, *shareye,*" I whispered. "Until my very last breath. I promise."

Evan's lips twitched as he took her in his arms, holding her as if his life depended on it.

"What will you name her?" I asked.

"I don't know," he whispered. "I'm open for suggestions."

CHAPTER 38

SHALITHA

The Chief had greeted us amiably the moment we entered his tent, inviting us to sit with him and have a drink. Soon after he'd poured us our tea, he went straight into why he'd asked us to come, and the atmosphere in the tent had gone from calm and pleasant to tense and irritable in a matter of moments. Elay was pacing up and down in front of us, raking his hands through his hair until it stood on end. The Chief, who had introduced himself as Dûshan, was watching him with sadness and compassion, almost as if he felt guilty for bringing him the news that his father had been overthrown and a usurper had now been crowned King. As for me, I knew exactly how he had to be feeling. I watched as desperation flickered into anger, trying to come up with something to say to comfort him.

I came up empty.

"What happened to everyone?" Elay asked, his voice strained.

"Those who remained loyal to your father were either killed, enslaved, or sent to the arena, *Akynshan*," the Chief replied.

I stilled. "To what end?"

"Excuse me?" Dûshan frowned, heavy brows knitting together.

"Why would they be sent to an arena?" I ventured.

"For entertainment." Elay turned to me, expression guarded. "Kehran's always had a wicked soul."

I nodded, pressing trembling hands between my knees so they wouldn't notice. What was happening at Elay's home was too close to what had happened in Ilvanna, and I doubted it was a coincidence.

"He's sent Jahleal there," Dûshan said softly, looking anywhere but at him, "as well as Naïda."

Elay stiffened, turning so pale his skin took up a yellow hue. He grabbed the chair for support, holding on to it so tight his knuckles turned lighter. When he brought his other hand to the chair, his face went from pale to flushed fast, and I jumped to my feet, placing one knee on the chair, my hands on his to stop him from throwing it.

I'd never seen him this angry before.

"That son of a... I'll kill him."

"Do not make any hasty decisions, *Akynshan*." Dûshan's words carried authority and warning. "He has managed to win the people to his side, as well as most of the army. Why do you think the *Vahîrin* were after you?" He looked at me then, gaze heavy with unspoken words. "Both of you."

"He wants Elay dead," I whispered, glancing at Dûshan, "but what do I have to do with it?"

"You, Princess," he said, chuckling darkly, "are the price he has to pay for the crown on his head."

Elay let out a low growl under his breath and pulled his hands away from mine, resuming his pacing. I turned to watch the Chief, my thoughts trying to catch up with what he was telling us.

"The only one who would want that price is—" I cursed as realisation hit me, suddenly remembering what Rhana had told me back at *Vas Ihn*. "He's Azra's illegitimate son, isn't he?"

The sound coming from Elay at that moment was nothing

short of animalistic. Dûshan merely nodded, a deeper sadness crossing his face. I let out a trembling breath, running my hands through my hair, nodding as pieces of the puzzle clicked together in my mind.

"She's been a *Tari*—Queen—here, there, if I'm not mistaken?"

Dûshan looked from me to Elay, who did his best not to look back, shaking his head from side to side slowly, reminding me of the large *sallelles* on the Ilvannian coast.

"That she has been indeed," he replied, rising to his feet, "but it's not my story to tell, *amisha*."

He clapped Elay on the shoulder and leaned in close, whispering something in his ear. Elay's head drooped, and he gave a short inclination of his head before Dûshan left us to our own devices. Staying in the Chief's tent was awkward, but I figured there was a purpose behind it. For a long time, the only sound was the crackling of the fire and Elay's muffled footsteps as he continued pacing up and down. Caught in my own thoughts, I didn't notice straight away when he knelt in front of me and took my hands in his, placing kisses on my knuckles.

Looking through my lashes, I noticed the pain and humiliation in his eyes.

I cupped his cheek. "You're allowed to have your past, Elay. It doesn't matter."

"It does to me," he murmured. "I've kept enough secrets from you, *Mìthri*, and I'm afraid that"—he looked away, licking his lips—"if I do not tell you everything, you will get hurt because of it."

"Let them try," I replied, awarding him a wicked grin. "So far, I've survived the odds. I don't think your past will make much of a difference."

"You don't understand," he growled, pulling away from me. "Kehran will stop at nothing. He will hurt you. Humiliate you. Anything to ruffle my feathers, and I cannot let that happen."

I clenched my jaw, forcing my temper down. "Again, Elay. Let him try. He'll soon find it won't be that easy."

He turned to me so fast I jerked back. "You don't get it, do you? He's murdered half of my family already! My brother will die in the arena, no matter how skilled he is. My sister—oh Gods, Naïda... Do you have any idea what they might do to her down there?"

"As a matter of fact," I said in a quiet voice, my mouth going dry. "I do."

He stared at me, cursed under his breath and slammed his fist into the small table we'd been sitting at. The look on his face was one of anger, and it was clear it reigned supreme in his mind. I could talk to him all I wanted, but none of it would go through. I understood every word he said, every emotion he felt, but he wouldn't believe me.

Not until he calmed down.

"We'll talk when you get over yourself," I said, and made my way out the door before he had a chance to call me back.

Once outside, I inhaled deeply, enjoying the fresh air on my skin. It reminded me of the mountains back home—of training early in the morning when the air was still crisp and heavy with morning dew, when the birds were slowly waking up, singing their songs of welcome to anyone who would listen. Folding my arms across my chest to keep my hands from freezing, I started walking in no particular direction. Although I had managed to clamp down on my anger, it didn't mean it wasn't there, and I needed a way to get rid of it.

On the outskirts of the village, I found a place that would keep me sheltered from the worst of the wind while providing me with a view across the desert. Pulling my knees up, I wrapped my coat around them, tucking my hands under my arms. Far off in the distance, beyond the sands, beyond the seas, was Ilvanna where my brothers and Tal, Mehrean, and Soren, and others were under the rule of a woman whose plans were as dark as the night and as deep as the sea.

Over one and a half years later, and I still hadn't figured out her motives, other than it being her birthright. What was it Esahbyen had said about a dead sister? My thoughts returned to Elay, and the unknown Naïda caught in a web of lies and deceit which were not of her creation. Elay had looked close to falling apart, and I felt momentarily bad about leaving him, but he wouldn't listen to reason.

Not now.

Let's hope he calms down soon.

My gaze drifted off to the horizon as my thoughts returned to my friends and family. I knew I had to go home soon, but my gut told me it wasn't yet time. There was something else I needed to do, and while I sat there, contemplating my old life, I realised what it was.

ELAY DIDN'T SPEAK to me for two days. In fact, he didn't speak to anyone at all, and preferred staying inside our hut over going outside. It was so unlike him, it had me worried, but every time I tried to make contact, he turned away from me.

"Well, I don't know about you," I said, adjusting the dress I'd been given, "but I'm going to enjoy myself tonight."

The mountain people were having a celebration in honour of Derana, the Goddess of the hunt, and Leyalleh, Goddess of Love, and they'd invited us as their guests of honour. Elay's clothing lay untouched on the bed.

"Are you coming?" I tried.

He gave no response, and instead turned on his side on the bed, his back to me. I shrugged.

"Suit yourself." I wiggled into a warm overcoat. "I'll see you tonight, I guess."

It was difficult to leave him behind like this, but I was tired of him sulking and moping around. We had plans to make, a trip to prepare, and he was being everything but helpful. It suddenly occurred to me he might not even want to save his country, although I couldn't believe for a single moment he'd leave his brother and sister to their fate.

If Kehran was as bad as Elay claimed him to be, he'd want something done about it. I know I did, if only to get back at Azra for selling me to a slave-trader. Had she asked nicely—and not been such a scheming *hehzèh*—I would have given her the throne, no questions asked. Yet even as I thought about it, I knew I never would have. While I had no idea what was going on in Ilvanna, my instincts told me it wasn't anything good.

Not just for Elay's people did we have to hurry up—for mine too.

"Thank you for coming," Dûshan said when I arrived at the main area where everyone had gathered. "Will Elay be here?"

I shrugged. "Your guess is as good as mine, *mishan*. He's not spoken to me either."

"He'll come around," he said with a gentle smile, patting my hand. "Come, we're about to start."

During the ritual to honour the Goddess, I wasn't allowed to participate, but I was allowed to watch. Dûshan had set me off to the side, so I could watch the procession of light appear on the mountain path, and in the darkness, it was a spectacular view. While the mountain people weren't many, the line of lights was still an impressive sight to behold. One by one, they placed their lanterns at the foot of the statue in the middle of the square, if one could call it that, sending up their prayers in silence. Without exception, every single one of them placed their hands together, followed by touching their brow and their lips, and then a deep bow.

When all the lights were gathered around the statue, a new procession arrived. These were the young women of the tribe, dressed all in white, carrying bowls of scented water, so Dûshan had explained earlier that day. I watched in awe as they splattered the statue once, then added their offering to the sea of lights, murmuring prayers. Last but not least, the young men of the tribe arrived, carrying platters of food. When they got closer, I realised they were dressed for hunting, and I wondered if it was ceremonial, or if they'd actually just caught the animals. On second thought, I wondered where they possibly could have. During my sojourns to the outskirts of the village and into the mountains, I'd barely come across rodents, let alone the kind of prey these young men were carrying.

Their offering was much simpler, more animalistic, but nothing short of inspiring to watch. With moonlight illuminating their movements, it was easy to follow as they circled the statue, war cries in high-pitched voices streaming through the night. Their slow, steady cadence of their depiction of a hunt enraptured me, allowing me to let my thoughts wander to another time, another place, one in which I'd been like the statue and six *Arathrien* circled me.

By some unseen command, the young men and women formed a circle around the statue and out of nowhere, the tunes of a pipe floated through the night, accompanied by drums and instruments I couldn't place. Regardless, they made for a haunting, mysterious tune. My eyes followed the young people as they danced—alone, together, in pairs, reminding me of the intricate steps I'd had to learn for the *Harshâh.* A momentary pang of sadness overwhelmed me when I realised the object of that day wasn't here with me, but soon the beatings of the drum reverberated deep inside me, carrying me somewhere higher as I was swept up in the revelry.

"You looked stunning that night," Elay said from my side, sounding bashful. "I had a hard time not staring."

I glanced up. "Finally decided I'm worth talking to?"

He knelt in front of me, taking my hands in his. "I'm sorry, *Mìthri*. I've done you wrong these past two days. I just—"

"Didn't know what to make of it? Felt as if your entire world was crumbling apart, turning to sand in your hands?" I offered, a sad smile on my lips. "Yes, I know."

Elay sighed heavily. "I didn't mean to shut you out."

"It's fine, Elay," I replied, looking at him. "I understand where you are coming from. I was just waiting for you to figure that out for yourself."

A faint smile tugged at his lips, but it didn't dispel the sadness in his eyes. "Naïda, she will not survive that place."

"I told you," I whispered, forcing myself to smile at him. "We will figure this out. Let's enjoy tonight and start making plans to conquer the world tomorrow."

A short bark of a laugh was his answer, and for a moment, the old Elay resurfaced, mischievous twinkles and all. As he rose to his feet unsteadily, he helped me up.

"Dance with me," he said in a husky voice.

"I don't know this one."

His lips quirked up. "I do."

Resting his hand on the small of my back, he pulled me close against him, and I put my left arm on his right biceps. Placing a kiss on my forehead, he set us into motion, his movements somewhat ungainly due to his injured ankle. The dance was slow and intimate, perfectly in sync with the deliberate, steady drums and the high, almost eerie tunes of the flute. Glancing sideways, I noticed almost everyone was caught up in their own bubble, swaying together in perfect synchronisation.

As were we.

Elay nuzzled my hair and planted a soft kiss on my temple. I closed my eyes and swallowed, my thoughts drifting to where our bodies connected, to the gentle sway of our hips—to the rumble of the drums deep inside my core. The scent of fresh air and earth mingled with his unique blend of masculinity made for a heady combination, and soon I found myself adrift, with Elay being my anchor to the world.

I wasn't sure how much time we spent dancing like that, but at some point I took his right hand in mine and guided him back to our tent. I wasn't the only one with something else on her mind. My heart was still beating to the steady beat of the drum in the background, my senses still overwhelmed, but my mind was made up.

Only a few candles were lit around our hut, and the fire was nothing more than a burning pile of embers. As Elay set to tending it, his back towards me, I slipped out of the warm coat and dress, taking off everything until I was fully naked. Goose-bumps rippled across my skin as I stood waiting for him to turn around, trying to keep my breathing under control. I took a tentative step closer, my heart picking up speed.

What if he rejects me again?

The moment he turned around, I pressed my lips on his. A low growl rose from his throat and he returned the kiss with much more fervour than I'd expected. Twisting one hand into my hair while placing the other on the small of my back, he pulled me closer, only to still completely against me.

A shuddering breath escaped his lips.

"*Mìthri*, are you sure?" he whispered against my lips.

"Never more so."

He pulled his lips from mine and watched me with adoration, his eyes searching my face for a trace of doubt, I was sure. I snaked my hand around his neck and pulled him to me, my lips crushing against his. He grunted as he lifted me in his arms, and I wrapped my legs around his waist.

His breath hitched.

Mine quickened.

The furs tickled my overly sensitive skin when he placed me on the bed, eliciting a sound that was halfway a moan and halfway a gasp. His lips quirked up in a roguish grin, his eyes taking up their mischievous twinkle. I swallowed hard and watched as he shrugged out of his coat and overcoat, discarding them on the floor in a mindless gesture. His eyes never left mine, and the intense longing in them made me squirm beneath his gaze.

He was clearly enjoying this.

His shirt followed in rapid succession to his coats, leaving him bare-chested. Copper skin gleamed in the firelight and my eyes raked his body as he leaned onto the bed. Soft lips brushed my ankle and his warm breath left goosebumps in its wake as he moved up my leg, kiss by arousing kiss.

The moment his lips touched the skin about two inches under my navel, all thoughts ceased immediately, and I arched my back in response.

A dark chuckle escaped his lips as he continued his sojourn across my skin, prowling closer with every kiss. His body remained close to mine as he moved, allowing me to feel the effect it was having on him. Not only did it excite me, it was also deeply humbling. A low moan escaped my lips by the time he reached my neck, earning a satisfying growl from him as he pressed his lips to mine, deepening the kiss until I was liquid in his arms.

"You're absolutely sure?" he whispered in between kisses.

"Yes," I replied in a thick voice I barely recognised as my own. "Don't you dare stop now."

He laughed and kissed me again, allowing his hands to wander my body in slow caresses, adding to the extreme sensitivity I was already experiencing. When he rolled away to take off his trousers, I trailed my fingers along the outlines of his chest and down to his abs, drawing out a soft moan from his side.

"You're killing me, *Mìthri*," he growled under his breath, and moved back on top, never quite putting his full weight on me, but enough to clarify who was in charge.

Inexperienced as I was, I didn't mind.

ELAY'S LOVEMAKING WAS as gentle as Zirscha had promised and better than anything I'd ever conjured in my imagination. He'd known exactly which places to touch and when to draw out the best responses, and he'd seemed to enjoy every moment of it. I wasn't sure if it was because he was in control of something, because he finally got what he wanted, or both, but in the aftermath of our throes, he looked utterly pleased with himself.

I snuggled up against him, my body languorous and spent.

"No remorse?" he asked, his voice husky.

"Not at all," I replied softly. "It was quite enjoyable."

He chuckled. "Quite enjoyable? It sounded a lot more than 'quite enjoyable'."

I poked him in the ribs, drawing out an *oomph* and a chuckle. He nuzzled my hair and placed a kiss on my forehead, his fingers trailing lazily across my upper arm. A shiver rolled down my spine, and I snuggled closer against him. The feeling of bare skin to bare skin was quite extraordinary, and I was surprised at how much I enjoyed it. The comfortable warmth he exuded made me drowsier than I already was.

"I'm glad it was as good for you as it was for me," he murmured. "Thank you, *Mìthri*."

"For what?"

"Your trust in me."

I smiled at him, placing a kiss on his jaw. "I'm glad it was you, and not somebody the *Gemsha* would have sold me to."

He stiffened beneath me, but only for a moment. His lips found mine once more, but it was gentle and sweet, nothing like the hot scorching kisses from before.

"I won't ever let that happen to you," he whispered, nuzzling my hair. "I promise."

I nodded, my mind returning to the task at hand.

"Elay?"

"Yes?" He turned a little to look at me.

The satisfied smile vanished upon seeing my face, and I knew I had his attention. "*Mìthri,* what's wrong?"

"I have a plan."

CHAPTER 39

TALNOVAR

Snow lay heavy on the mountaintops by the time Eamryel and I departed from *Denahryn*, both with heavy hearts for various reasons. We had waited until after Nathaïr's burial, which had been a small, solemn affair. Evan had pulled himself together better than could have been expected from someone who had just lost his wife. Eamryel had gone through it stoically, but I'd caught the glimpse of a tear when the pyre was lit.

Who knew he was capable of such feelings?

As for myself, I'd managed to get through it feeling very little, shutting down everything before it had a chance to bubble into existence. I'd seen enough pyres, massacres and battles to last me two lifetimes, yet something told me I hadn't even seen the worst yet. With a heavy sigh, I turned to the road ahead, allowing my horse to pick its own pace and footing. Out here, the mountain roads were treacherous, and I didn't feel like meeting an untimely death at the bottom of a ravine.

I glanced at Eamryel riding a little ahead, his cloak all but swallowing him up whole. The proud man I'd seen so many times before had turned into a mean, hunchbacked ogre, snarling whenever I opened my mouth to strike up a conversation. Not that it happened a lot—usually only when I tired of arguing with myself.

"Thank you," I said.

Eamryel perked up, glancing over his shoulder through narrowed eyes. "What for?"

"Your help with Cehyan."

He shrugged. "I'm a mean, sadistic *grissin*, am I not? It was right up my alley."

I clenched my jaw and tightened my grip on the reins, causing my horse to start up briefly. Patting its neck, I shushed it until it was calm enough to continue my way and respond to Eamryel.

"I won't say the thought didn't cross my mind," I replied. "Especially considering what you did to the *Tarien*, but"—I swallowed my pride and shook my head—"you were right in saying I couldn't have done it."

Although his lips pulled up in a sneer, undoubtedly to mock me, the troubled look on his face didn't ease. Squaring his shoulders, he rolled his head left to right, the deep sigh he released turning into a puff of mist.

"I wish I could undo it," he said after a long time, jerking his hand through his hair.

I looked up in surprise, barely managing to keep my face composed and my voice level. "Why?"

"Because she didn't deserve any of it."

Breathing in deeply, I willed my temper down.

"That is true. What made you realise that?" I couldn't help the venom dripping from my voice when I said those words, and the scowl he gave me was proof enough it hit home.

"If it hadn't been for *you*," he spat, his normal temper flaring, "she wouldn't have almost died, and I wouldn't have had to hunt her!"

"You're blaming me?" Indignity at his accusation rose within me, and if we hadn't been on horseback, chances were I'd have pushed him up against something.

Your temper is as bad as his, Imradien.

I scowled.

"You made the decision to injure her," I said through clenched teeth, fighting hard not to give in to my anger. "You decided to hunt her like prey. That was not on me."

"But she loved *you*," he snarled. "She was supposed to love *me*!"

His words were those of a maniac, a deranged person, but the look on his face was one I knew only too well—a face of a man broken and lost. He inhaled deeply and slumped forward, burying his face in his hands. To my surprise, I felt sorry for him.

"You see," he said, his voice barely loud enough for me to hear. "Ever since we were little, I've loved her, but... I never dared speak to her so, she didn't know. When we grew up, being Nathaïr's brother, or my father's son, didn't do me any favours."

The snort that bubbled up froze halfway and I nodded, deciding that hearing him out wouldn't hurt me—too much.

"And my father," Eamryel sat up again, his body tensing. "You know what kind of a sadistic *grissin* he is."

"But he didn't make you do what you did," I commented, doing my best to keep the cynicism from my voice, "so why *did* you do it?"

Eamryel was silent for such a long time I was sure he decided not answering was the best move. He looked even more tense than before with his back ramrod straight, and jaw clenched as if he were fighting some unwanted emotions.

"It's how I was raised," he said after a while. "Father had clear ideas on how women should be treated—he'd made a fine example of Mother before he, before she..." His voice trailed off and he slowed his horse to a stop. "After she died, he didn't stop. Whenever something displeased him, which was quite often, he took it out on Nathaïr. There have been times where I'd take the beating for her, because she could no longer bear it. That was until Father made me do the beatings. I was young, full of anger and hatred. Anger at my mother for having left us—hatred for the father who did this to us, but even more so hatred for the woman who let him go on with it, and allowed him inside her court. The beatings, the humiliation, everything became a means to an end—a way to cope."

He breathed out deeply, refusing to look at me. My hands were tight on the reins, but I kept my temper in check, understanding well enough the feelings of anger and hatred.

"After many years, I guess I didn't know any better," he continued, his voice distant and full of pain. "I never meant to kidnap her… my threats were idle and in vain. I knew you'd be there to protect her wherever she went. But add to that alcohol and *sehvelle…* When I found her there, on her own… I don't know. Something inside of me snapped."

"You *hunted* her." I couldn't help the growl escaping my throat. "Do you expect me to believe all of this crap?"

"Isn't it enough that I regret it?" he snapped back.

"No!" I yelled. "Of course it's not. Whatever your reasons were, Eamryel, they were messed up, and you know it. You won't ever be able to set it right."

He went deathly quiet.

"I know," he said, "but now that I know what it must have been like for her, I have to do everything I can to get her home."

I frowned at his words, but the look on his face warned me not to pursue the issue any further, so I let it go, despite the million questions crowding my mind. The fact he had opened up so much already was more than I'd ever expected from him. Not that his words eased me in any way, but I did believe he felt some remorse for what he'd done, although his reasons for doing it were too wild to make any sense of. In the time he'd been gone, something had clearly happened that had changed him—broken him.

I knew that feeling only too well.

I'd never harmed anyone though.

No, you just killed your own sister.

Father's words sprung to memory. It hadn't been my fault, according to him, but I hadn't been paying attention to her at the lake's edge. If I had… I inhaled deeply, the crispness of the air burning my nose, and I focused on Eamryel's back. I had to get out of my own head and fast.

"How long till we reach the border?" I called out to Eamryel.

"A few days," he replied. "If the weather holds. There isn't much room for delay. The ship will sail in a fortnight, with or without us."

THE WEATHER DIDN'T HOLD. Before long, clouds heavy with snow turned the sky almost as dark as the night, looming over us with its treacherous promise. Pulling the scarf farther across my face, I adjusted my grip on the reins, and huddled in on myself, grateful for what little warmth my cloak offered. Up ahead, Eamryel had done the same as I. He was hugging himself and had drawn his hood far over his face.

For all I knew, he was asleep.

"Eamryel," I called out. "Are you all right there?"

"Yeah." His voice took a moment to reach me. "I'm just not very fond of the cold."

"That makes two of us."

Snow began to fall steadily until we could barely see three feet in front of us. Eamryel halted his horse so I could close in. If we lost each other in this, we'd be dead.

"We need to find shelter!"

"I'm aware of that," he yelled back, "but I'm about as knowledgeable about these parts as you are."

I glowered at him but didn't reply at first.

"I think we passed a cavern about a mile back." I pulled the hood over my face. "Maybe we should turn around and see if we can find it!"

"Better walk the horses," Eamryel returned, sounding everything but pleased.

Doubling back was not the best idea, but it was the only thing we could do short of risking freezing to death. In an unspoken agreement, we dismounted and guided our horses along the path. If it had been treacherous without a snowstorm, it had become downright dangerous now. We'd picked a poor time to travel, but it had been our only opportunity. A ship had been arranged for this time of year weeks ago and finding another one that would carry us across the sea without questions asked would be hard. According to Father's spies, Azra controlled all ports in Ilvanna and some across the border in Therondia. On top of that, we were considered wanted criminals, so walking into Ilvanna could mean an arrow in our backs, no questions asked.

A mile was a long way to go when you could barely see a hand in front of your face. By now, the storm had kicked up in intensity and speed, making it almost impossible to navigate anywhere. My face was beginning to go numb from cold, as were my fingers, and not even staying close to my horse made it any better. Glancing over my shoulder, I realised I could barely make out Eamryel.

"Tal!" he called.

"Still here."

We continued our way in silence until we came upon the small cavern I'd spotted. It wasn't much, but it was big enough for the two of us and our horses to shelter without catching the worst of the storm. After coaxing my horse inside, I stroked its neck and hummed low under my breath to keep it calm. The last thing I wanted was for it to spook and gallop off.

That would delay us beyond our arranged meeting.

"Let's hope this passes soon," Eamryel muttered, trying to keep his horse under control too. "We should have left sooner."

There was no accusation in his voice, just remorse and grief. He had nobody left aside from his father, and he wasn't exactly the paragon of fatherhood. I'd never considered Eamryel to have a full range of emotions like the rest of us.

"Get some sleep. I'll keep watch." I almost had to shout to get over the howling of the wind.

Eamryel nodded and pulled his cloak tight about him, curling up in a corner. I couldn't imagine him being comfortable, but then, no part of this trip had been so far, and I doubted it would be anytime soon. While I detested the snowstorm, I didn't look forward to going on a ship either.

I preferred keeping both feet on the ground as much as possible.

Anything to get her back.

THE SNOWSTORM LASTED ALMOST a day and the delay it caused had put Eamryel in the foulest of moods I'd ever seen him. We had to let the horses pick their own footing due to the amount of snow that had fallen, slowing down our progress. We'd gotten to one of the passes where the mountains still protected us on the left side but sloped down on the right. One wrong step and we'd tumble down a good forty feet, if not more.

As if the Gods were listening, misfortune followed on the heels of my thoughts.

Eamryel's horse spooked, and he barely managed to stay on, until it reared and threw him off its back. Before I'd registered what happened, Eamryel slithered over the edge, a scream piercing the sky as he fell.

"Eamryel!" I bellowed, feeling my horse prance beneath me.

I dismounted as fast as I could and scrambled over to the edge, my heart racing in my chest. Without him, this whole mission was lost.

"What are you looking at?" he grunted, holding onto a protruding piece of rock that looked like it wouldn't hold him much longer.

"By Esah." I let out a sigh of relief.

"I'm sure he's got nothing to do with this," Eamryel growled, showing his usual bad temper. "Are you waiting for me to drop to my death, because I'm about to."

I held out my hand, but as I did, I began to slide forward, so I quickly scrambled back before I'd drop to my death first.

"Hold on!" I called. "Need to get some rope."

My heart was thundering in my chest by now as I fumbled for the rope in my pack, cursing the storm for my cold fingers.

"Any time now," Eamryel yelled. "I'm not enjoying the view."

"Hold your horses!"

"How apt…"

I growled under my breath just as I pulled the rope out. As fast as my frozen fingers allowed, I knotted the rope around the pommel of my horse's saddle and threw it over the edge next to Eamryel.

"Hold on to that!"

"And risk falling? Are you insane?"

"I'm saving you, so I must be," I muttered under my breath for my ears alone and continued louder for him. "It's either that or an attempt at flying!"

He cursed me in the old tongue. I smirked at his words but decided not to reply and instead focused on the rope. The moment it drew taut, I clicked my tongue and carefully guided my horse to pull Eamryel up. It whinnied, clearly not happy with the extra weight I'd put on him, but as much as I hated Eamryel's guts, I needed him. Once he was visible above the ledge, I moved closer, sat down and kicked my heels into the snow until I found enough purchase to help Eamryel over without both of us sliding down. My foot slipped once.

He yelped.

I cursed.

With a deep grunt, I hauled him up and fell back, gasping for air.

"You should consider skipping meals," I gasped, enjoying the cool snow on my back for a second or two before sitting up.

"You must be the life of the party," Eamryel scowled, looking as if he was hugging the snow for comfort.

"You have no idea."

He snorted before pushing himself to his feet. Only then did I notice how much he was trembling, and I doubted it was from the cold.

"Are you all right?" I ventured, glancing at him as I started untying the rope from the pommel of my saddle.

"Nothing a stiff drink won't fix," he replied, moving carefully over to his horse, coaxing it to come closer.

"I didn't bring any."

"I did."

"Cheers to you then," I commented drily before swinging myself into the saddle.

We'd lost precious time enough as it was, and I was itching to be on the road and out of these *nohro* mountains as soon as possible. Thankfully, Eamryel had made it into the saddle as well, nursing a flask that made the look on his face relax and the trembling cease. It wasn't every day you stared death in the face at the end of a cliff. A deep shudder ran through me and once I was sure Eamryel was ready to go, I nudged my horse to move, allowing it once again to find its own footing.

"Tal," Eamryel called from behind.

"Yeah?"

"Careful with the dark patches," he said. "They're slippery. It spooked my horse, and I really don't feel like dragging your ass out of a ravine right about now."

"You're welcome."

He huffed in response.

AFTER EAMRYEL'S INCIDENT, we made good time in the mountains and reached the border of Therondia almost two days later. By then, Eamryel looked dead on his feet, and I wasn't feeling much better. Lack of sleep was taking its toll, our conversations had turned clipped, and they were conducted in snarls rather than words.

"We need to cross the border as soon as night falls," Eamryel muttered, stretching his legs, "and put as many miles between us and the border as possible."

I nodded. "How much time do we have left?"

"Less than a week."

Pinching the bridge of my nose, I considered his words carefully, estimating the time it would take us to travel to the shore, and the time we actually had.

"It'll be close."

Eamryel exhaled deeply. "That's why we have to travel as much as we can at night."

"Pushing the horses might kill them."

"Do you have a better idea?" He looked unimpressed.

"Find replacements close to the border," I said. "Surely not everyone is on Azra's side."

"Maybe," he replied, sitting up, "but the people are scared of her. You've seen how she retaliates."

I grunted. "Don't remind me."

"Like it or not," Eamryel remarked, "we're outlaws. We will risk everything if we do what you are proposing."

"And what if we try in Therondia? There are enough farms between here and there to give it a try."

"They're vassals to various lords, some—if not most—of whom have sworn allegiance to that *hehzèh*." Eamryel settled against a tree, folding his arms over his stomach and closing his eyes. "Wake me when I need to stand guard. You need to catch up on some sleep too."

A non-committal grunt was all the response I gave him as I watched him get comfortable. He was right though. I did need some sleep before we left. Making myself relatively comfortable on a nearby rock, I focused on our surroundings. Overhead, birds were chirping their happy songs and underneath, rodents scurried in the undergrowth. The wind rustled through the treetops, as if it had not almost blown us off the mountain two days before. With everything so at ease, I fought to keep my eyes open, until they no longer obeyed my command and shut of their own accord.

CHAPTER 40

SHALITHA

Dawn had barely made its presence known when we shouldered our packs and thanked Dûshan for the thousandth time for saving our lives and providing us with safety these past weeks. Now, he sent us on our way with warm and sturdy clothing, enough provisions to last through the rest of our journey, and well-wishes for our health, and safe travels.

My heart was heavy when we went on our way.

Elay, confident in the plan we'd polished to perfection, walked a little ahead, whistling as he went. I took it harder, much more reluctant to be leaving the mountain people and the safety of their home. In truth, I'd loved the serenity and the peace with which they'd gone through life. They all had a role to play, and everybody seemed to have known their worth within the tribe.

Even the children had known their place and future.

The thought of going into the hubbub of a palace again, one that was unfamiliar territory at that, frightened me, and if I could have turned back, I would have. But I'd made Elay a promise long ago, and I was intent on keeping it. I would do what was necessary to help him, and in return, he would help me.

Provided we get out of this alive.

"Planning to take over the world?"

"Hm?" I looked up to find Elay waiting for me, an amused expression setting his eyes to sparkle.

I smiled softly. "Just thinking."

"About?"

"What's to come," I replied, shifting my pack. "I never thought Ilvanna wouldn't be the first court I'd return to after my abduction."

His lips quirked up, but his eyes hardened. "I've no idea what will be awaiting us, *Mìthri,* but I do know I'm grateful we're in this together."

"I'm hardly the proper court type though," I said with a careless shrug. "Mother often complained about that."

He chuckled and took my hand. "I'm sure you'll do magnificently."

"We'll see about that."

I didn't want to consider the options when I wouldn't be magnificent. According to both Elay and Dûshan, Kehran was manipulative and sadistic with a penchant for punishments that went beyond sanity. Little did I know he'd inherited that from his mother.

"I'm scared too," Elay said at length, his voice soft. "I haven't been at court for years while playing at having my own, and the *k'ynshan* didn't even come close to the real deal."

"You appeared perfectly comfortable running it," I remarked dryly, glancing at him sideways.

Delight marked his features. "And I was, but there I was the *Akynshan,* the fearless leader, the Prince of thieves and cutthroats. One mistake and I'd have your head."

I snorted. "Is that why mine's still attached?"

"Oh, but *Mìthri*"—he slipped one arm around my waist and

pulled me close, running his thumb along my jawline to rest on my lips—"don't I have your head?" He brushed my lips with his own, sending shivers down my spine and warmth to nestle deep below my navel.

I growled softly against his lips.

He laughed as he released his grip, stepping away from me. "Your head. Your heart. Your body."

Before I could aim a well-placed kick, he stepped in and kissed me, snaking his hand into my hair while gently pulling me close.

"I'm joking, *Mìthri,*" he whispered against my lips. "I would never diminish the gift you gave me that night. I will cherish it —forever."

His words dissipated my anger and letting out a shuddering breath, I stepped away and readjusted my pack. The bands were cutting into my shoulders. At least we had bedrolls to sleep in this time. Dûshan had advised us to stay in the mountains for as long as we could. There would be enough caves to offer us shelter during the night, but we both knew we had to go back into the desert at some point, and when we did…

My skin crawled at the thought of the *Vahîrin,* knowing they would be there—waiting.

I'd been surprised they hadn't come to find us in the mountains, until I resolved to ask Dûshan one day and he told me they had, but all of them had met with an unfortunate accident. He didn't need to tell me those unfortunate accidents had been orchestrated by him and executed by the tribe.

They knew the mountains better than anyone.

"How long till we reach the capital?" I asked, more to drive away the deafening silence than anything else.

"At least a week or two on foot," Elay responded, looking at me curiously. "Why?"

I shrugged. "I like to be prepared."

He arched a brow but didn't comment on it. Instead, he took

my hand in his, and like that, we continued our way through the mountains. In the east, the sun rose steadily to its zenith, and once it was high up in the sky, perspiration trickled down my back underneath my warm coat.

"Do you think we can take a break?"

Elay nodded, wiping his brow. "Sounds like a terrific plan."

We found a place in the shade and dropped our packs. Elay rummaged around in his for some bread and goat cheese, while I put a flask of water to my lips and took a few sips, mindful not to take too much in case we didn't get to one of the streams on time.

"Here." He offered me some bread and cheese while settling himself cross-legged on the ground, his back resting against a rock.

I settled down beside him and took the offered food. I'd not been fond of the goat cheese back at the tribe either, but it was one of the few things they could produce and would remain edible for a long time. It was the smell as much as it was the taste, but it was better than nothing.

Dry bread would only be tasty for so long.

"What is the Ilvannian palace like?" Elay asked between a bite of bread and cheese.

"Is or was?"

He flashed me a wry smile. "Was, I guess."

"A beehive." I shook my head. "It always reminded me of a beehive. The only time it was really quiet was close to dawn."

"How come?"

"Most courtiers had gone to bed by then, too tired of their scheming and dallying, and mostly too drunk to know better. It used to be a great time for larks like myself."

Elay chuckled. "I've been wondering about that."

"Talnovar or Xaresh used to get me up for training at the crack of dawn. I suppose after years of that, I've gotten used to it."

"You did sleep in a few times." He grinned, looking me up and down in a suggestive manner.

I rolled my eyes and threw a small rock at him, hitting him on his arm, drawing out a yelp. He made to throw one back when a sound close by alerted me. I brought a finger to my lips and motioned Elay to stay down while I crawled in the direction the sound had come from, drawing a dagger from my belt. Elay perked up, tilting his head. I shook my head, then mimed to him to keep on talking, hoping he understood what I meant.

He did.

The one sided monologue he kept up was too suggestive to my taste—too detailed, but it would serve its purpose.

Staying low, I listened carefully for the sound, only to hear it again—pebbles shifting as something, or someone, moved. I crept closer, until I heard the sound come from behind a rock, followed by a muffled gasp. Without waiting, I jumped from behind my side of the boulder, dagger at the ready as I dropped into a crouch.

Wide hazel eyes regarded me in fear, and the girl in front of me pushed herself back against the stone structure, holding up her hands in surrender.

"I mean no harm," she stammered, her voice high. "Please."

I narrowed my eyes at her. "What are you doing here? Dûshan will be extremely upset if he finds you missing."

She was his daughter.

"I left papa a note," she whimpered, her voice small. "Please, don't send me back."

I folded my arms across my chest, my eyes darting to the side as my heart picked up speed when I heard someone approach.

It was just Elay, a dark look on his face.

"What's going on here?" he asked, looking past me to the girl.

"I was about to ask the same thing," I replied, glancing at him. "She doesn't want to be sent back."

"Really now?"

The girl, Sahar I remembered, looked at us with eyes round in shock, and began fumbling with the ties of her coat.

"I hate my life in the tribe," she murmured. "Everything's the same every day. I'm bored out of my mind. Father won't let me hunt, won't let me fish. He won't even let me go out of the village."

"So you thought following us was a good idea?" Elay's look darkened even further.

She cringed beneath his gaze, and I couldn't help but feel at least a little sorry for her. I knew that look, and it didn't promise anything good.

"I just want to see the world," she whispered, tears glistening in her eyes.

The sad part of it all was that I understood full well where she was coming from—it had been my dream for so many years. With a heavy sigh, I squatted in front of her so we were at eye level.

"Can you fight?"

She shook her head.

"Can you defend yourself?"

"No." Her voice came out in a squeak.

"What can you do?" Elay asked, foregoing the kindness he'd shown me months before.

Sahar's lower lip trembled, but where I thought she'd crumble into tears, she straightened her shoulders and looked at him with defiance.

"I cannot do any of those things," she said, "but I learn fast, and I'm willing to learn anything you can teach me."

I risked a glance at Elay, trying not to look amused.

He scowled at me.

"It will be very dangerous where we're going." He crossed his arms, turning his scowl on her. "You could get killed."

"I know," she replied, "but anything's better than being

married off to one of those stupid boys back at the tribe who thinks he's quite something. I don't want a man who thinks he's better than me by default."

I had a hard time keeping my face in check, so I rose to my feet and turned away under the pretence of having to stretch my legs, going for a grimace instead. Elay rolled his eyes at me, seeing through the ruse with ease.

"How do you think your father will respond when he finds out you're gone?" Elay was adamant and unrelenting.

"But I left him a note," she countered vehemently. "He knows where I am."

He grunted, pinching the bridge of his nose and rolling his eyes heavenward as if to ask the Gods to witness his predicament.

I snorted.

"What's wrong, Elay? Having a hard time?"

His scowl deepened. "You just wait."

I grinned. "For what?"

He threw up his arms in defeat and turned away, shaking his head as he returned into the direction he had come from. Sahar perked up while looking at me, eyes wide with delight.

"Does this mean I can come?"

"No."

She stared at me as if I'd slapped her in the face. Hard. With a heavy sigh, I sat down across from her, rubbing my jaw.

"Listen," I began. "I understand like no other the need to go out and explore the world. I used to be exactly like you, but trust me when I say it's not as fantastic as the stories make it out to be, especially not when there's danger involved."

"But I—" I held up my hand to stop her, glaring at her.

"You're going to go home," I said. "Right after this conversation, because I do not want you to get stranded in the mountains after nightfall. Then, if Elay and I survive our journey and succeed, we will come back for you."

Her eyes flashed furiously when I spoke, but at my promise to her, she just exhaled deeply, resentful of my words.

"I thought you'd understand," she said, glancing up at me.

"And I do," I replied, "but I am not taking you, or anyone other than Elay, on a mission this dangerous. It's not romantic, it's not incredible. It's more than terrifying, and neither Elay nor I can spare our focus on another person, especially not one who cannot defend herself."

"But I can learn!" she protested. "You can teach me!"

"Teach you what?" I managed to remain calm. "How to fight like us? Do you have any idea how much time we spent training to do what we do?"

She must have seen our sparring sessions back at the village then.

She shrugged.

"We've been training every day for years. We cannot teach you what we know in a few days and hope you manage to pick it up fast enough." I rubbed my face and sighed heavily. "Promise me something. When you go back, train to become stronger. Start running, lift heavy things—anything to build up strength and stamina. Then, when we come back for you, I promise we'll teach you. Deal?"

Sahar stared at me, contemplating my words while biting her lower lip. In the end, she relented with a sigh and a nod.

"Very well."

"Go on then," I said, rising to my feet. "Run home. It'll be good practise."

At first, she looked hesitant, but then she did as I instructed, and started back in the direction we'd come from at a steady jog. I watched her disappear before returning to Elay, who had made himself comfortable against one of the rocks, his eyes closed, hands folded behind his head.

"I could stab you and you wouldn't even know it," I remarked drily, stuffing the flask back in the pack.

He opened one eye. "I welcome you to try at any given time, *Mìthri*. Let's see if you can indeed."

"We need to get moving."

Without arguing, he rose to his feet and slung his pack on his back. We continued our way in silence, and I couldn't help glance over my shoulder in the hopes Sahar wasn't still trailing us.

"What did you promise her?"

I tilted my head. "What made you think I did?"

"Because she's not here."

A soft smile played around my lips. "If we survive this, we'll pick her up and teach her what she wants to know."

Elay gave a derisive snort. "*If* we survive this?"

"There's never a one hundred percent guarantee, *shareye.*"

He grunted. "I hate your logic."

OUR JOURNEY through the mountains was more than uneventful after our run in with Sahar. We managed to find enough caves before nightfall to spend the night in safety, but it was far from comfortable, even though Elay went out of his way to look after my well-being. It was kind on his part, but unnecessary in my opinion. Every time I voiced these thoughts, however, he waved them away as if they didn't matter and still did it, so I gave up trying.

A few days in, we arrived at the desert, and that was when my heart began to take up uncomfortable bouts of erratic behaviour. My throat tended to squeeze shut, or my hands would turn clammy. Thankfully, never at the same time. If Zihrin, or being with the *Gemsha*, or with Elay had done me one favour, it was diminishing—if not taking away—my panic attacks, and for that alone, I'd be forever grateful. Even so, I felt ill at ease as we started crossing the sands. Dûshan had assured us there was a small town less than a day's travel from the mountain ridge, and we would be able to find shelter there.

If we made it.

He'd also assured us the *Vahîrin* were close, so we had to be careful. With that threat hanging over us, the journey became more tense, and neither of us spoke much, keeping our hands close to our weapons and our ears and eyes peeled for the sound of anyone approaching. If the look on Elay's face was any indication, he liked our chances as much as I did.

"We'll get there," he assured me at some point. "They don't know when we left the mountains."

"You don't know that," I muttered. "For all we know, they've been keeping watch ever since the mountain people took us. You heard Dûshan—they killed some."

Elay rubbed his face and shook his head. "I have to believe we can make it to the village. Once there, we can get *camelles*."

I nodded, but his words did nothing to ease my fear.

The sun made its slow decline through the sky until dusk was upon us. In the distance, torches flared to life, but from our vantage point I couldn't see if it was the village or a camp.

"Almost there," Elay said.

A ululation rose in the darkening sky, alerting us to the presence of others. Neither of us needed to guess who. I dropped my pack and drew my sword, noticing Elay doing the same. Heroic as he was, he stepped in front of me—I turned around, standing back to back with him. I sought his hand with mine, and when I found it, pressed my palm against his, for once glad his right hand wasn't his sword-hand. It reminded me of the *Harshâh*, and of the silken cords, of the trust we'd shown each other then. If we could get through that, we could get through this. I inhaled deeply to steady my nerves.

"Elay?"

"*Mìthri?*"

"Don't die on me."

"I was about to ask you the same thing."

I felt the tension in his body as he took up a defensive stance and heard his breathing rise in his throat.

"Calm down," I muttered. "You'll be out of air before you begin."

He grunted. "I'm trying."

"Think of something that relaxes you."

"Like spending the night with you?" he asked, turning in for a quick kiss. "Promise me we'll have another one when this is done?"

I smirked. "Depends on whether I have to save your ass or you mine."

"How so?"

"If you save my ass," I replied. "You can have your night."

He all but whooped in delight.

And then it began. Out of the darkness, shapes stalked towards us, metal gleaming in the moonlight. Two against many would be hard enough, but fighting them in the darkness even more so. Despite what little vision I had, they were outlines against a darkening sky, and if they were as good as Dûshan and Elay had told me, anticipating their moves would be impossible.

The first attack came somewhat expected, but I had barely time to parry. My attackers turned into a blur, and I'd lost contact with Elay soon into the fight. A hiss escaped my lips when a sharp pain stung my leg, and I realised one of the attackers must have cut me. I swung around but caught nothing. Another sharp pain—my other leg this time. I growled, biting back a scream. Attack after attack landed on my sword, and sometimes on me, but I kept going. My trousers and shirt stuck to me where I'd been cut, but by that time I'd lost count where the injuries were exactly.

"Elay?" My voice was tentative, strained.

Fearful.

When he didn't respond, my heart skipped a beat and my

breathing hitched. For all I knew, he was bleeding on the sand, drawing his last breath.

"Elay?" I called out louder this time.

My attacks were getting slower, each blow jarring my sword-arm in the most agonising way. When a quarter staff caught me square on the wrist, I dropped my sword, and sunk to one knee, my breathing coming in ragged gasps. A blade was placed against my neck—one slice and I'd be gone.

I lifted my chin to face my killer.

All air was sucked from my lungs and I sank to my other knee. My throat constricted painfully, and my chest tightened as my eyes settled on the person holding the sword to my throat.

"Elay?" I whispered in disbelief.

"I'm sorry, *Mìthri*," he replied. "Their offer was too good to pass up."

Hot tears trickled down my cheeks as I fixed my gaze on my husband's hard eyes, watched his lips quirk up in the mischievous grin I'd come to love so much. A fierce pain settled itself in my chest, and I barely registered when my arms were tied behind my back, or when I was pulled to my feet.

"Keep her alive," Elay ordered, voice devoid of all emotions. "The King will want to have a good look at her."

Before they dragged me off, he knelt in front of me, gripping my chin between his fingers. I tried to jerk my head free, but he was too strong.

"I did love our nights," he whispered, then grinned. "You still owe me one."

All fight left me after those words, and I crumpled into a sad, miserable mess. Although I should have expected it, his betrayal cut worse than Eamryel's knives had—worse than Yllinar breaking his promise.

Worse than Azra sitting on my throne.

In that moment, I wished they'd killed me.

CHAPTER 41

TALNOVAR

A shake to the shoulder woke me up with a start and I was on my feet in three heartbeats, looking around bewildered. Obviously, I'd fallen asleep and slept long enough to watch the sun go down beyond the trees. I grunted and rubbed my eyes, glaring at a highly amused Eamryel.

"Good nap?" he asked, sounding much too cheerful.

"It was all right."

"More than all right from the sounds of it." He sniggered. "Sounded like you were having a good time."

I growled at him, stepping forward. "None of your *nohro* business."

"Easy, *mahnèh*," he muttered, holding up his hands. "You slept like the dead."

Growling even deeper, I pushed him out of the way and stalked over to my horse. Of all the things he could have made fun of, that one was the least bit funny. Muttering under my breath, I sorted through my pack for a quick bite to eat and a swig of water before we'd be on the road.

I could only assume that was why Eamryel had woken me up.

“Tell me something.” I frowned as the idea suddenly struck me. “Why go through all this trouble of coming with me, when you could just have told me where she is and save yourself this journey?”

Eamryel smirked. “How good is your Zihrin?”

“Fairly non-existent.”

“There’s your answer.”

Too tired to even scowl at him, I stuffed everything back in my saddlebags and snapped them shut with more ferocity than intended. My horse sidestepped and snorted, looking at me with big, baleful eyes.

“Sorry,” I mumbled and patted its neck before gathering the reins in my hands.

Hoisting myself in the saddle, I waited till Eamryel had done the same. When we set off, we glanced at each other. This was it. The last leg of the journey, and we’d better make it count, or our chances of finding Shalitha and reinstating a proper *Tari* to the throne would be gone.

“Let’s go.”

We nudged our horses on and navigated the forest at a steady trot. Although we followed small paths to ease the horses’ passage, we sometimes had to go off-road in order to cut a more or less straight line to where we’d be crossing the border. We expected troops to be patrolling them, but in the dead of night, chances were there would be sentries, no more.

Who would be insane enough to cross the borders?

Then again, they could very well be on the lookout for us and have everyone there. It was anyone’s guess.

“In case you die,” I remarked at some point. “Where do I go?”

Eamryel snorted. “You sound awfully happy about that prospect.”

“Hardly, I’m just being pragmatic.”

“It’s the beach just outside Fayrehnear,” he said. “There’ll be a rowboat waiting that will take us out to sea.”

"Terrific," I muttered. "I hope I still have some strength left by then."

"If not," Eamryel replied cheerfully, "I'm sure Azra would love to have you back."

I scowled at his back but didn't respond, knowing full well he had the right of it, and the last thing I wanted was to be returned to Azra, so I swallowed my reservations and focused on the road ahead instead. It wouldn't be long before we'd clear the forest. My heart rate spiked, taking on the steady yet rapid *thump-thump* it always did when I was about to enter a fight, whether it be mock or real. I felt the surge of energy go through me, preparing my body for fight or flight, whichever came first.

"Tal?"

"What?"

"Don't get killed."

We'd come to the edge of the forest.

I rode up next to Eamryel and halted my horse, surveying the area from left to right. Sure enough, extra guards had been posted here judging by the camp sprawled on our right, but that wasn't the worst of it. The sound of a saw easing its way through wood reached us from up ahead. Closer by, I heard someone give instructions in a tone of voice reserved for workers, and at the border, barely visible in the firelight, people were milling about a construction.

"What in Esah's name?" I muttered.

Eamryel cursed low under his breath. "That son of a *hehzèh*. He finally got what he wanted."

"He?"

"Father," he replied, turning to me with a deep scowl on his face. "He's closing the borders—literally. Anyone who wants to come in or go out has to identify themselves and state their business in Ilvanna."

I clenched my jaw and tightened the grip on the reins. I'd heard the rumours before, when Arayda was still alive, and Shal still at the palace. More than once, Yllinar had tried to push this through, and more than once, Arayda had put a stop to his madness.

Clearly, Azra didn't share her sister's sentiment.

"This complicates matters," I said, relaxing my vice-like grip when I noticed my horse dancing beneath me.

The last thing I wanted was for it to bolt.

"That's quite the understatement, *mahnèh,*" Eamryel commented drily. "We have to get through tonight."

"I know."

"I'm open for suggestions."

I smirked. "I thought you were the scheming kind?"

He glowered at me before snapping his attention back to the problems ahead of us. Dismounting, I handed the reins to Eamryel.

"Stay here."

"Where are you going?"

"Up."

He frowned at me until I walked to one of the trees and jumped up to a low-hanging branch and swung myself onto it. Climbing trees had been something I'd done as a kid, but it had been a while, and on several occasions, I was barely able to catch myself in time. I managed to get about halfway before the branches became too thin to support my weight, but it was high enough to get a good view of what was going on down below. Even though most of the activities were obscured by darkness, patches of light every few feet illuminated just enough to see the wall, which was indeed what they were building, stretching to the west. It appeared they were about to finish it. There was a gap of about thirty feet they still needed to close.

It was all we had, and all we needed.

Before I climbed back down, I looked for the best way to get to the opening, and realised we had to get close and circumvent the camp to get a clear passage. It was either that, or straight through the camp. When I returned and related what I'd seen, Eamryel's scowl deepened, but his eyes took up that calculated look he got whenever he was considering all our options.

"If we go around the camp," I said, taking the reins from him, "we risk ourselves much more."

"But riding through that camp is a sure-fire way to get noticed," he remarked.

"But faster."

He nodded, tapping pursed lips with his finger. "We need to divert their attention."

"And how do you propose we do that?"

He grinned at me. "Riding and yelling."

"Yelling? Are you out of your *nohro* mind?"

"Perhaps." He shrugged. "But I don't see you coming up with anything better."

Rubbing my jaw, I regarded him quietly. "And what do you want us to yell?"

We arrived at the camp at breakneck speed, staying low to our horses while yelling something about having messages from the *Tari*. People jumped out of our way as we hurtled past, cursing us in either Ilvannian or Therondian. Up ahead, the wall was getting closer with every hoof beat, the opening in it our only chance. Our arrival had been noticed, obviously, and guards were getting ready to close the gap by creating a line in front of it, weapons at the ready.

Messengers would stop.

We spurred our horses on, keeping the reins short while hovering just above our saddles, moving along with their fast, rhythmic pace. I could hear my horse's breathing coming in hard and heavy, but he continued steadily, fearless of the living wall just up ahead.

"We've got to jump!" Eamryel shouted.

I nodded, preparing myself so the horse wouldn't toss me off and watched as Eamryel scaled the guards first, landing behind them with well-practised ease. Although I'd spent my time on horseback ever since I was a small boy, jumping had always been one of those things I found uncomfortable—scary even.

Trust your horse to know what to do and do not restrain it.

Father's voice whispered in my mind and I followed its suggestion. I kept tension in my body, leaned forward out of the saddle and allowed the horse to follow its own path. When it jumped and soared over a man's head, I closed my eyes, only opening them when I felt my horse's hooves hit the ground and continued pounding a steady rhythm. Looking over my shoulder, guards scrambling around to go in pursuit drew my attention.

"Ride!" Eamryel yelled at the top of his lungs.

So we rode as if Esahbyen himself was chasing us with his horde of immortal warriors, glancing back only to estimate the distance between the enemy and ourselves. No more than a dozen men had gone in pursuit, confident in their endeavour from the looks of it. Beneath me, my horse was slowing down, and up ahead I saw Eamryel's mount was struggling too.

If we didn't find a place to hide soon, they might actually succeed.

"Eam!" I called out, urgency in my voice.

"I know!" he yelled back.

My eyes scanned the area, but other than small houses strewn haphazardly across the countryside, there was no hiding place that caught my eye. Judging by the way Eamryel was looking around, I surmised he was doing the same, most likely coming to the same conclusions.

I glanced over my shoulder, judging the distance between myself and our enemy. They were closing in on us—not surprising after the journey our horses had already had—and it occurred to me there was another option, one I'd rather not resort to, but it looked like we had no choice. Grabbing the reins in one hand, I unsheathed my sword and turned my horse around, preparing myself for a desperate man's attempt. I had to find the *Tarien*, whatever it took, even if it meant the lives of men who only did what they were ordered.

Azra had started a war.

Shalitha would have to finish it.

Inhaling deeply, I steeled my resolve, focusing my gaze on the quarry ahead. This had to be done, for the sake of our future. I didn't have the luxury to consider these men, so I banished all thoughts and emotions. I ignored the aches in my body, the stiffness in my legs, the heaviness in my arms. I exhaled, and with it obtained the mindset I'd been training for most of my life.

I spurred my horse to a gallop.

A war cry would have been apt, releasing all of my pent up frustration, but it would also alert them. They'd have seen me turn around, but I still hoped to have some element of surprise, if only because they didn't expect either of us to double-back with them so close behind.

After all, who was insane enough to risk it all for a small chance of survival?

I was upon them fast, and it barely registered when my sword sliced through soft flesh, severing tendons and arteries. In passing, I saw the man I'd attacked first tumble off his horse, and soon, I was upon another one. Leaning to the side, I came in with a wide arc, cutting the second man across the chest as if it was nothing. The impact jarred my arm, sending a tingling sensation down to my fingers, and I almost lost hold of my sword.

The distraction nearly cost me my life too, but the man intent on plunging his sword into my side went down with an arrow through his eye. Glancing over my shoulder, Eamryel came barrelling our way, a second arrow nocked to his bow. A moment later, he released it with immaculate precision straight into a man's chest.

No wonder he'd been able to shoot Shal so easily.

The man was more than a little skilled in archery.

Pushing the thought aside, I veered off to the left to go after an enemy who was doubling back to the border. Spurring my horse on, I clutched the saddle tight with my knees, and when I reached the man, I swept my sword along his neck. His sudden jolt at the impact nearly jerked the weapon from my hand.

A second time. Pay attention, Imradien!

By then, my arms and legs were trembling, and my breath came in puffs and gasps. Turning my horse around, I caught the remainder of the guards from the back, hamstringing one of them as I rode past at the same time as one of them passed me. Unable to defend myself on the other side, I caught the sword on my right arm. Although the blade skidded off the bracer I wore, I felt the sting as it cut from the middle of my lower arm to my biceps.

A second later, the man slumped over his horse's neck with an arrow protruding from his back.

Gritting my teeth, I quickly estimated the damage as I rode in Eamryel's direction, trying to keep breathing in through my nose, out through my mouth. By Esah, that hurt. Before the pain became overwhelming, I managed to take down another one, as did Eamryel, and turning around, only two were still in the saddle and they looked reluctant to fight. Their comrades—those who were still alive—lay squirming and moaning on the ground, their horses long gone.

"Cease your pursuit," I yelled, "and gather your fallen! Tell the *Tari*, Imradien sends his regards!"

The two men, barely out of their teens from the looks of them, glanced at each other and dismounted. I cast a furtive look at Eamryel, who was staring back at me with the trademark Arolvyen sneer on his face.

"You couldn't have warned me?"

"And risk warning them too?"

He rolled his eyes. "You're a death wish on legs."

"It was either this," I replied, "or be run down. The horses are about to collapse, and neither of us is faring much better."

My lower back was a knot of pain and discomfort from being in the saddle for too long, my left arm was sore from the misuse of my sword, and my right arm was such an aching mess I was convinced it would fall off soon.

"We need to rest," I said after a while, grimacing at the flares of pain my body was sending as a warning. "And I may need some bandages."

"There's a farm up ahead," Eamryel replied, glancing in my direction with contempt masking his worry. "We can try there."

"What if they're allies to Azra?"

His lips pulled up in a smirk. "I have sufficient funds to make them reconsider their choice."

I nodded, too tired and in too much pain to argue such trivialities. While I stayed on horseback, barely able to stay upright in the saddle, Eamryel knocked on the door, ready to flee from the looks of him. With light at their backs, it was hard to make out who answered the door, but from the way Eamryel seemed to converse, I assumed it was a man. As I waited, I felt the heaviness of sleep settle behind my eyes, chasing all coherent thoughts into a jumble, making it feel as if I was wading through mud to get to them. I had a hard time keeping my eyes open, and I wasn't sure if it was because of the exhaustion, the pain or blood loss in general.

"Papa!" a woman's voice called out from right below me. "This man is injured."

I looked down to find a young woman at my right side, barely outlined by the light coming from the cottage.

"Take him in then, don't dawdle," the man replied a tad too eagerly. "We cannot let our guests bleed to death."

Risking a look in Eamryel's direction, I found him being ushered inside by another woman—the mother I assumed, so I turned back to the girl at my feet, a grimace pulling my lips down in a snarl.

"Well," she said, hands on her hips. "You heard the man. Get off so I can take your horse down to the stables."

My brows shot up at the bossy attitude as I grabbed the pommel and swung my leg around to dismount. Due to the injury, I couldn't use my other arm to hold on to the saddle, so my landing was a bit off and I staggered backwards, only to find myself steadied by a pair of strong hands.

"Come in, son," the man I'd heard called papa said from behind me. "My wife will have a look at that arm while you get some warm food into you. You look like you need it."

I inclined my head, my lips pressed together in a thin line. Despite Eamryel's words about money not being an issue, I didn't trust the situation at all—call it a gut feeling—but we had no choice. We needed to rest—our horses needed to rest, and my arm definitely needed tending to if I wanted to keep it.

Where's Soren when you need him?

CHAPTER 42

SHALITHA

The fierce ache in my chest gradually subsided to something less painful—to something infinitely colder than what it used to be. It felt as if all emotions had left me, and I was staring into a deep dark abyss, weighing the pros and cons of stepping into it. A part of me wanted to take a step forward and plunge down, finding my death at its end. The other part—the part that was furiously mad at Elay and ready to fight—kept me from going there.

His betrayal had stung, but it shouldn't have come as a surprise.

After all, he'd had a hidden agenda ever since I met him, and I doubted any of that had changed during our time together. What was most painful, however, was to have to admit to myself that he had been right all those months ago.

It had been easy to fall in love with him.

Too easy.

And I'd given him exactly what he wanted.

The one thing I couldn't figure out though, was why he had orchestrated the attack at the *Harshâh* if all he wanted was to have me. The thought of sleeping with him brought on a wild array of emotions I had a hard time placing. The memories still made me weak in the knees, and made me believe that perhaps he was playing a different game while simultaneously filling me with a deep feeling of disgust and self-loathing, so that all I could think of was murder—either his or my own.

A growl escaped my lips, and I began to kick around the cart, slamming my feet flat against the side until my captors halted and came to check what the ruckus was about. I'd managed to wriggle onto my back, and as soon as one of them peered over the side, I clipped him under the jaw with my feet, sending him reeling back with a loud howl. I grinned in satisfaction. The feeling lasted until somebody grabbed my ankles and hauled me out of the cart. The world spun for a moment before it straightened itself out, and I found myself staring into Elay's emerald eyes.

I swear my heart stopped. For only a beat or two.

Rage built up inside of me steadily, beginning somewhere deep in my stomach until it flared everywhere, and I launched myself at him. Elay had clearly expected it, because he caught me with ease, and instead of going down, he just twirled me around and placed me back on my feet. He did rub his chest where my shoulder had connected with his ribcage.

"Keep up the fight." He grinned. "The King will love it."

I launched myself at him again, and this time he wasn't quick enough to keep himself from falling flat on his ass. My lips pulled up in a satisfied smirk, but the feeling didn't last long as two of the *Vahîrin* grabbed my arms and dumped me back into the cart unceremoniously. I hissed at the pain it sent through the injuries on my legs. Although one of the *Vahîrin* had tended to them, he'd not been a healer. I'd been lucky the cuts had only been superficial—a warning to cease my fighting.

Rather than riding a *camelle*, Elay opted to stay in the cart with me, one side of his lips quirked up in a perpetual grin. I rolled my eyes and turned my back to him, grimacing as the wood dug into my shoulder and hip.

Comfort was not in the cards.

"Giving me the cold shoulder, *Mìthri?*" He gave a dark chuckle. "Not that I mind, your backside's quite the view."

I kicked out but hit only empty air.

Elay sniggered. "You know I love to watch you fight and struggle, don't you? It's what drew me in the first time."

I clenched my jaw and closed my eyes, trying to ignore his words, but he just wouldn't shut up.

"I'll be here for the rest of the ride," he remarked drily. "So we can either make this pleasant or unpleasant. Your choice."

"I'll go for unpleasant," I growled, still not looking at him.

"You know I like that." His hot breath tickled the skin of my neck, his voice deep and husky.

"Get off of me." I jerked away, pressing my cheek against the floorboards of the cart so my hair fell across the other side of my face.

I did my best to ignore the weight of his hand on my hip. He didn't even have to move it to melt my insides. Closing my eyes, I began to recite an Ilvannian nursery rhyme I hadn't thought of in many years—the one Mother used to sing for me when I was still a young girl and got frightened of the monsters in the dark.

Hush, my child, and take my hand, off we go, to a faraway land, where monsters are fair, and dreams come true, and let me show, what you can do. When brave and bold, with nothing to fear, I will love you, I will be here.

It was a nonsense rhyme, come to think of it, but it calmed my frazzled nerves and settled my fear of what was to come. The fact I had no idea what it would be now that Elay had switched sides was unsettling at best, and positively terrifying at worst. Albeit difficult, I managed to pull my knees up to my chest, curling in on myself until the world ceased to exist.

At least for a bit.

I NEVER NOTICED how the irregular jolt of the cart turned into an even rattle, nor how we passed from the desert into a city. The entire journey there, Elay made good on his promise to stay in the cart, which made it so much more uncomfortable that I'd resorted to staying quiet and asleep for as long as I could. Not that I felt rested—not by a long shot. My shoulders were stiff, and no amount of rolling them helped. My hips felt as if they were on fire from lying on my side so much, but anything was better than looking at him.

"*Mìthri*," Elay said, his voice taking on a gentle tone. "We're here. Look."

Despite my reservations towards him, curiosity won over, and with a bit of help from his side, I managed to sit up.

Akhyr was a city unlike anything I'd ever seen, despite its similarities to Portasâhn or even Y'zdrah. White houses lined a wide cobbled street in eerie perfection, no house crooked or out of place. Small wooden balconies overlooked the street, all of which looked exactly the same. Windowsills were painted a daffodil yellow, giving it an overall welcoming feeling, even though I felt anything but welcome. Surveying the area, my eyes swept from left to right, trying to take it all in for future reference. I didn't know when the information would prove useful.

Something wasn't right though.

Looking again, it occurred to me the streets were eerily quiet, and the shutters of the houses we passed were closed. I frowned and almost made to ask Elay when I realised his explanation was the last thing I wanted. Although he had negotiated on his own behalf with the *Vahîrin*, these men were dangerous and fierce warriors in their own right—maybe more so than Dûshan had led me to believe.

Perhaps people were afraid.

"Welcome to Akhyr," Elay whispered, a sad undertone in his voice.

Risking a glance in his direction, I realised the sadness wasn't just in his voice—it was in his eyes too.

I quickly returned my gaze back to the streets, unable to deal with him. It wasn't as if I didn't remember why we had decided to come here—half his family had been murdered, and his brother and sister were at the mercy of a tyrant. We'd come here to save them, but that was before Elay chose for the King.

Your family is in the wrong hands too, qira.

With a heavy sigh, I lay back down, suddenly uninterested with the rest of the view. It wasn't as if it was important anyway. I listened to the cart trundle along the cobbled street, ignoring the jarring sensation in my bones. Closing my eyes, I started counting the turns we took, regardless of whether they were left or right, counted the times we stopped, or when I heard a voice —anything to keep my mind busy, really, because if I didn't, there was no telling how much I would freak out between now and then.

"Almost there," Elay stated.

I wasn't sure if it was to ease me or himself, and I suddenly realised he was nervous too. He may have negotiated his way out of a fight with the *Vahîrin*, but he now had the King to contend with—a king who was as likely to spill his blood as he was mine. No wonder he sounded anxious.

He made his own bed, and now he must lie in it.

Perhaps if I tried really hard, I could feel sorry for him on account of what we'd been through together, but I found I had a hard time doing so. He wasn't the only one with issues, his life on the line, or that of his family's. By Esah, he could actually go and figure it out, while I had a *nohro* sea between myself and my family.

I'd not been able to say goodbye to my dying mother either.

A sob caught in my throat, squeezing it shut until I managed to calm myself down, reminding myself of Tal's breathing exercises, of Esahbyen's training, of Xaresh's calming words, and Elara's motivational speeches. I was doing this for them—all of them. One step at a time.

When the cart suddenly lurched to a halt, Elay fell on top of me as if he hadn't noticed it coming. A grin spread across his lips when he realised they were close to mine. I turned my head away.

"Don't even think about it."

Instead of kissing me, he tucked a lock of hair behind my ear, eyes searching mine.

"I wish things had gone differently," he whispered, his voice full of remorse before he slipped out of the cart.

"*Grissin*," I yelled at his retreating back moments before strong hands wrestled me out of the cart.

I kicked and screamed and put up a fight until one of them hit me in the back of my knees with something hard and I buckled underneath their grasp. When they pulled my head back, forcing my head up, I realised why.

The King had deemed us interesting enough to greet us in the courtyard.

If I had had any doubt about Kehran being Azra's son before, there was none of it left now. His skin wasn't quite the copper of his father's people, but it definitely wasn't the white of an Ilvannian either. In fact, here and there it was splotched with both. Although hidden by a high collar, I could just make out the traces of very light skin underneath. The one plain thing marking his Ilvannian heritage were the elongated ears—longer than the Kyrinthan's were, even if the difference was less than an inch.

Azra's experiment hadn't quite turned out well.

A derisive snort escaped me, earning me a backhand from one of the men standing next to me. The King's eyes were immediately drawn to me.

"And who is this?" King Kehran asked in a lazy drawl.

I looked up defiantly but didn't reply.

"I've brought you *Tarien* Shalitha an Ilvan, daughter of *Tari* Arayda an Ilvan. Your cousin, your majesty," Elay said in his best courtly voice, bowing deeply.

Kehran awarded him with a hard, cold stare, then turned to the Captain of his men. "Why is he not in chains?"

"Because he exchanged her life," the captain began, looking from Elay to me, "for his."

The King's brows shot up in surprise. "Really?"

When he turned to his half-brother, he did so with newly kindled interest, although his light blue eyes remained frosty.

"And how did you figure your life is worth as much as hers?"

Elay smiled and bowed again. "Is it not true the *Tari* of Ilvanna seeks her niece's death? Imagine getting into your Mother's good graces, your majesty, for catching the one person she desires most."

Kehran turned to me, curiosity lighting up his youthful features. "And I thank you for that, but why should I keep you alive?"

Elay hesitated for a brief moment. "Because I can give you all the information you desire, your majesty."

With a quick glance, Kehran observed his half-brother, tilting his head like a demented little owl. He said nothing before turning back to me, taking a step closer.

"Get her to her feet."

The *Vahîrin* weren't gentle about it.

"Is it true?" he asked curiously, glancing at Elay rather than me. "About their tattoo?"

Elay's lips curled into a one-sided grin, eyes twinkling. "True and more, your majesty."

"I want to see it." It wasn't a question.

"Out here, your majesty?" Elay asked, worry lacing the first two syllables before he caught himself.

I narrowed my eyes at him, clenching my jaw before turning to speak to the King. "I am not a puppet on display."

"You dare speak?" he asked incredulously.

"I dare kick your ass given the chance," I growled, jumping forward.

Only the firm hold on my restraints kept me from getting into his face, but he took a step back all the same. I felt my lips pull up in a feral snarl.

"Take her inside," Kehran ordered. "And my brother too."

All the way inside, I kicked and screamed and fought against the men holding me, until they tired of my antics and one of them threw me over his shoulder, clamping down on my legs so I couldn't kick him in the face. My howls of frustration pierced the air, which were cut short when the *Vahîrin* fighter dropped me back on my feet and released me, so I had no choice but to fall back on my ass.

A grunt escaped my lips.

"Undress her."

The King's orders sounded nonchalant. My gaze flew up and settled on Elay, but only briefly as our contact was broken by the sheer bulk of one of the *Vahîrin.* He grabbed me by the scruff of the neck and hauled me to my feet. As soon as he let go of me, I planted my shoulder between his ribs.

He just stared at me.

Kehran chuckled. "I like her spirit."

"You should see her fight," Elay offered. "She could join your *Vahîrin...* and best them, given an equal chance."

"Nobody bests the *Vahîrin,*" Kehran grumbled.

"She would."

In order to take off my clothing, one guard unbound my hands. I would have attacked then had I not caught the slight shake of Elay's head. A low growl escaped my lips as another guard tore off my coat, and I snapped at him much like a prey would at its predator moments before it would die. In my desperate attempt to fight this guard, I lost not only my coat, but my shirt too, and I quickly covered my chest with my arms. It mercifully showed off all of my *Araîth.*

Kehran whistled under his breath and walked closer, his eyes moving slowly from my waist up till my neck and back again.

"How far does it go?"

"All the way down." Elay sounded entirely too pleased with himself.

"All the way?"

Although frustrated at what was going on, I kept my peace, biding my time, fully aware of the *Vahîrin's* presence in the room. I was desperate, but not that desperate. At least not until the King ordered to have me stripped naked, so he could admire the rest of the view.

Something snapped and blind fury tore through me.

I elbowed the first guard in his face—the one I'd kicked before after I'd woken up in the cart, and he howled in pain, grabbing his nose.

In that moment, I didn't care about propriety.

The *Vahîrin* charged on their King's orders. Elay had taken a step back, watching me with his face perfectly composed, giving me no inclination as to how he was feeling. The King's eyes, on the other hand, were flashing furiously.

"What are you waiting for, grab her!"

With a downward kick, I incapacitated one of the men by dislocating his kneecap, and in another swift move, I clipped one under the jaw, sending him sprawling to the floor for a nap. A third managed to get a hold of me from behind, drawing out a grunt. I struck my elbow into his abdomen, causing his grip around me to weaken, and in the next move planted my heel on his foot as hard as I could. He grunted, momentarily confused and in that moment, I brought the bottom of my clenched fist down on his nose, for once happy with my height. He released his grip on me, I turned and kicked him where it hurt most.

When he crumpled to the floor, I turned and broke his nose for good measure.

Four *Vahîrin*, if they were that, jumped me then and wrestled me to the ground, pinning my arms painfully behind my back.

"You see, your majesty," Elay remarked in the smoothest voice I'd heard him use yet. "She's a remarkable fighter."

Kehran lifted his chin, the look in his eyes full of contempt.

"She took down four of my men," he said icily, pacing up and down the room. "I've killed men for less than that."

"Ah, but you see, your highness," Elay continued, pressing his palms together in a half-bow, "you could make great money off of her."

I jerked against my restraints, which only caused the vice-like grip to tighten.

"Go on," Kehran said with a wave of his hand, his eyes never leaving me.

I stared back in defiance.

"Throw her into the arena as one of your prized fighters," he suggested, lips pulled up into a devious smile, eyes alight with a plan I could only guess at. "She will fight for everything she's worth to get out of there."

"How can you be so sure?" Kehran asked, scrunching his nose as if he smelled something foul. "Once a spirit is broken, it cannot be restored. She looks as if she's about to crack."

Elay chuckled darkly. In that moment, I hated him with everything that I was, and began contemplating ways to murder him in his sleep, despite the promise that I never would. Perhaps when he came for that one last night.

Not that he'd saved me.

"Trust me, your majesty. This woman is far from broken."

Kehran raised his brows, lips slightly parted. "How can you be so sure?"

"One only needs to look into those eyes to see the truth of it, my King," he replied simply. "A broken spirit would not regard you with such disdain—such hatred."

The King appeared to consider his words before turning to him. "Give me one good reason not to throw you in there with her?"

Elay bowed deeply. "I have no desire to be King. I wasn't born one, nor raised one. I am content with a place at court, and on my honour, I promise not to betray your cause."

"My cause?" Kehran narrowed his eyes. "What is that supposed to mean."

"Why, you yourself of course, your majesty! What other cause could I possibly be talking about?"

Kehran grunted. Of the many things Elay was, a swindler was absolutely one of them, and for a brief moment I didn't feel so bad about falling so hard for his charms. He'd clearly had enough time to practise them.

"Good money, huh?" The King rubbed his chin, looking thoughtful. "I'm not sure whether I should believe you or not, *brother*. You've always been the conniving kind."

"Let her fight your best warrior," Elay offered, "and see the truth for yourself. If she wins, you will see I am right. If she loses—"

"You will take her place," the King finished, glaring at Elay. "Until then, make yourself at home, brother."

Elay bowed so deeply, his forehead almost touched the ground. Our eyes locked when he got back up, a thousand unspoken questions and insults flashing between us. One day, I would be his death.

I swear it on my life.

Kehran dug his fingers into my jaw to make me look up. I merely stared at him, hoping to appear completely unaffected.

"Mother would love to have your head," he murmured, "or perhaps even whole, I don't know. She's entirely insane if you ask me, but before I do that, I'll have my fun with you."

My blood ran cold at his words.

In response, I spat him in the face, which earned me a backhand so hard I reeled, my ears ringing painfully.

"Take her to the dungeons," he said, voice devoid of emotions. "Let's see how willing she is to fight for her life."

CHAPTER 43

TALNOVAR

The cottage was no more than a living room with one door to the left, and one to the right, behind which I assumed were bedrooms. From the fireplace, the smell of warm food wafted our way, and my stomach growled in response. Eamryel looked as hungry as I felt, but kept a decent composure with a gentle smile on his lips. A grimace of pain contorted my features while I tried to assess the damage to my arm. The cut was about five inches long, and thankfully superficial from the looks of it.

The worst of the bleeding had stopped.

I allowed myself to have a good look around, inspecting our hosts more covertly. The woman was small of stature and curvy, dressed in simple farmer's clothing. Elongated ears—not as long as my own—peeked from under a mop of chestnut curls. Kind green eyes were set in a soft pink face. She was Therondian through and through. Her husband on the other hand—I assumed he was her husband—clearly had some Ilvannian heritage along the line. His hair was dark grey and his skin neither the Therondian soft pink nor the Ilvannian ivory white.

"Here you go," she said, placing a bowl in front of each of us on the table. "There's more if you want."

We both set to the warm food with alacrity, our progress followed with amusement by our host. He was a tall man—taller than his wife and clearly used to being the one in control. I watched him sit down at the head of the table, folding his arms on top while regarding us with open interest. As the woman returned from another room carrying a chest, the door to the cottage opened and the girl I saw outside slipped in, stomping her feet and blowing into her hands.

"There's a storm coming," she said, sounding way too cheerful for that kind of news. "I made sure the horses have enough water and food, and everything is locked securely, as you asked, Papa."

The man grunted in response, nodding at his daughter.

She was the spitting image of her mother in everything but her height and complexion, looking more Ilvannian than Therondian. As she moved over to the fire, there was something about her that struck me as familiar, only to realise it was in the way she bore herself—proud and confident.

"What brings you to these parts of Therondia in such troubling times?" the man asked, regarding us with a humourless smile.

In the meantime, the mother had started on cleaning the cut on my arm, and I hissed when she touched a particularly painful spot. She apologised under her breath.

"Here, mama." The girl had come to my side. "Let me."

The woman appeared only too happy to relinquish the task to her daughter, who sat down on the bench next to me, her back to her father. The lines etched into his face deepened as he watched her, before turning his attention back to us.

"We are messengers from the *Tari*," Eamryel lied smoothly, watching the man unblinking. "The rebels found us and gave chase, hurting my friend."

The man glanced in my direction, and I could have sworn something akin to recognition flickered behind his eyes.

"I see," he replied, rubbing his jaw. "As the *Tari's* men, you are welcome to sleep in the stables for tonight, but you must be gone before the break of dawn. You understand I do not want these… rebels burning down my house."

"Of course, *Irìn…*" Eamryel inclined his head, a question hanging unspoken between them.

"Hareldhean," the man replied. "Most people call me Eldhean."

"A pleasure to meet you." Eamryel flashed him a smile. "We accept your offer, and will be gone before dawn, troubling you no further."

Eldhean squinted and gave him a hard smile.

What are you not telling us…

My attention was drawn to the girl sitting next to me, tending to my arm in a meticulous fashion. She was neither Soren nor a *Dena,* but she clearly knew what she was doing.

"Lurah, see the men to the stables when they've finished their food," the man said, "and come straight back inside. As you said, we're in for a wild night."

"How do you know there's a storm coming?" I asked, feeling slightly stupid for asking.

"You learn to notice the signs in the weather." Lurah cut off her father's reply. "Out here, close to the shore, you learn to do so if you know what's best for you."

I inclined my head.

"Well, good night," the man said, placing his hands on his wife's shoulder. "I hope your rest is peaceful."

The moment the door to their bedroom closed behind them, I glanced at Eamryel, opening my mouth to say something. He shook his head, nodding in the girl's direction.

"You're quite skilled at tending injuries," I commented, watching as she bandaged my arm.

"I have some experience with them," Lurah replied without glancing up. "I'm rather... clumsy."

Somehow, I had a hard time believing that, but I wasn't going to pry any further, not in the least because I couldn't afford to do so. We just needed a few hours' sleep before we'd continue on our way.

"Come," Lurah said softly, rising to her feet. "I'll show you where you can sleep."

THE BARN WAS MUCH LARGER than the cottage, housing not only horses from the smell and sounds of it, but other animals as well. Lurah, carrying two lanterns, showed us to a corner at the back of the barn where two blankets were placed on top of a pile of straw. After she handed me the second lantern, she turned to go. In the dim light, she appeared to look troubled, but when she turned back to us, she smiled.

"Try to rest. I'll wake you up when it's time to go."

"Thank you," I said, awarding her a light bow.

It was the least I could do. Yet as she left, an ominous feeling settled itself in my stomach. Something was off, but I couldn't place my finger on what it was. When I voiced my concerns to Eamryel, he waved them away.

"I've paid them enough to last the rest of the year," he said. "Money's always a good reason. For everyone."

I ground my teeth as I lay down, drawing the blanket over me. From the smell I could tell it was a horse-blanket, but I didn't care—it was actually quite comforting in a way.

"I don't know," I said, staring up into the darkness. "Something's not right."

"Maybe," Eamryel murmured sleepily. "Maybe not. But rest while you can, *mahnèh*. You heard the girl, she'll wake us up when it's time to go."

He turned on his side, and before long, he was snoring in a slow, rhythmic cadence. I folded one arm behind my head and closed my eyes, trying to push the feeling of danger to the background. Perhaps it was because of my training, or perhaps it was having spent time as Azra's play-toy, but my sleep was restless. In the background, as the wind began to howl around the barn, I could hear Eamryel's snoring, as well as the shuffle of a horse in its stable, and the snort of a pig on the other side of the building.

At least my body was resting, even if my mind wasn't.

I WAS awoken by the sound of the barn door opening and had my fingers wrapped around the hilt of my sword before whoever came in was upon us. Lurah stood before us, a lantern in her hand, hair dishevelled and wet, and eyes wide. The howling had ceased.

"You need to leave," she hissed. "My father turned you in. He left shortly after you went to sleep."

Eamryel had barely woken up by the time I was already on my feet, looking groggy and tousled with straw sticking from his hair.

"What's going on?" he murmured, rubbing his face.

"They're coming," I growled. "Your money clearly wasn't enough."

That woke him up. Lurah took a hesitant step back at the ferocious growl that left Eamryel's lips, before turning to me, shivering uncontrollably.

"Take our horses," she said, not unkindly. "Yours look like they're about to fall over on the spot. Don't worry, I'll look after them."

I clenched my jaw and nodded, gathering a saddle and my saddlebags as she led me to another stall. A beautiful chestnut thoroughbred was watching me with lambent eyes, ears pricking up when he realised something was about to happen. I'd expected him to sidestep and cause a ruckus, but he waited patiently. The girl was rubbing his nose, murmuring soft endearments in Therondian.

"Thank you," I said softly, adjusting the saddle and straps where necessary.

"It's nothing," the girl replied, looking around the horse's head. "I'd flee from your Queen too if I could."

Remorse spiked her voice, and her lips set in a thin line as memories crossed her delicate features.

"Lurah, was it?"

She looked up at me with a faint smile. "Liyelurah."

"Thank you," I said again, finishing strapping on the head-gear. "I will never forget your kindness."

She inclined her head and stepped out of the stall, allowing me to guide the horse out.

"His name's Magavin," she offered. "Mag for short. He'll listen to it."

Eamryel stood scowling next to his horse, arms folded across his chest.

"We don't have forever," he muttered.

"Give her some money," I ordered.

"I paid her father more than enough," he commented snidely.

"And look what he did."

With a heavy eye roll, he dug deep into his pouch and offered the girl three gold coins and some silver. Her eyes widened as she caught them, staring at the prize in her hands.

"Go, now," she said. "I'll stall them for as long as I can."

Rain came pelting down from the heavens as we guided our horses outside. When we stopped to mount, I glanced over my shoulder once towards the barn doors where Liyelurah stood watching us. She inclined her head and raised her hand in farewell. I copied her move and mounted. Without looking back, I nudged Magavin into a trot and followed Eamryel into the night. It was early enough for the sun to not having made its appearance yet, which meant we'd only gotten a few hours of sleep—much less than what we'd hoped for.

At least we had fresh mounts.

As soon as we cleared the premises, we nudged the horses on to a gallop, wanting to put as much distance between ourselves and the farm in case half of an Ilvannian army came knocking.

As the morning progressed, the rain let up, and unease became a constant companion. I glanced over my shoulder more and more often. Eamryel had been quiet all this time, the look on his face warning me not to engage him in conversation. It suited me fine—I had nothing to tell him I hadn't said already. Although grateful for the food and what little rest we had had, our stop had gotten us into much more danger.

"How long before we get there?" I asked eventually, riding up next to Eamryel.

"I expect us to arrive close to sunset," he replied, glancing over his shoulder. "Provided nothing happens."

I nodded, raking a hand through my wet hair. "Perhaps we should ride a little faster for a bit."

"To what end?" He looked up curiously. "There's nothing on the horizon."

"Yet."

He shook his head and shrugged, allowing silence to stretch out between us. I fell back a little, returning to my own thoughts and fears. This was our last day—our last chance, and the thought was more unsettling than ever. If Azra found out about our plan, I was sure she would do anything in her power to stop us. Although Ilvanna didn't have much of a fleet due to the high rise of the land and the cliffs, she had some ships at her disposal. If rumours were true, and she indeed had Therondian lords to do her bidding, she might even have more than a few.

She'd make sure we wouldn't be able to find a captain crazy enough to allow us passage on his ship.

It had to be tonight, and as that realisation dawned on me, my chest tightened uncomfortably. I couldn't allow fear to get the best of me, but it was a good motivator for sure.

"Tal! Look out!"

Eamryel's voice startled me out of my reverie just in time to see an arrow whistle past, lodging itself into the ground a few feet away. I didn't need to look to know they had found us. Without the need for speech, we urged our horses into a gallop. Magavin was fast—faster than I had expected, and I had to find his rhythm before I could ease up a little and go along with his movements.

Another arrow flew past, closer this time.

We were out on the Therondian flatlands by now, with no place to hide anywhere in sight. The sea glistened in the distance, and I could almost make out the outlines of a ship—or it was my imagination playing tricks on me. Either way, we were close, and it would be a *nohro* shame if we didn't get to it now.

A sharp pain lanced through my right shoulder as an arrow lodged itself there, eliciting a cry of anguish. I urged Magavin on, surprised to find there was even more in him. I reached over my shoulder for the arrow, but my fingers only brushed past it. There was no way I could snap it off myself. A curse escaped my lips.

"We need to get rid of them!" I yelled.

Eamryel glanced over his shoulder, his eyes moving from me to the enemy coming from behind. Despite the speed of our horses, they were gaining on us, and it wouldn't be long before they caught up.

"There's twoscore of them!" Eamryel returned. "At the very least. What chance do we stand?"

"A very small one," I growled, "but I have no ambitions to sit back and turn into a porcupine!"

He frowned at me, and only then seemed to notice the arrow. A steady string of curses left his lips, and he glanced over his shoulder again. An arrow grazed his cheek, drawing blood as it sped by. Wiping his cheek, his lips curled up into a sneer.

"They're getting bolder."

"No," I muttered. "They're getting close enough to actually hit a target."

He scowled at me. "No matter."

I looked over my shoulder again, finding half a dozen riders coming our way at high speed. Without a second thought, I began to unsheathe my sword, only to find I could barely keep my fingers curled around the hilt. Hissing under my breath, I pulled my weapon out of its sheath anyway and managed to hold it with my left hand, my off-hand.

This will be interesting.

Our chances were dwindling rapidly.

Eamryel was no longer riding by my side, and turning my horse around, I saw he had stopped completely and sat with an arrow nocked to his bow, waiting, watching. When he released it, one man slumped over a few heartbeats later, and in that time, he'd let fly another arrow. The remaining four were closing in on him however—he'd not be fast enough.

I kicked Magavin in his flanks and he responded by jumping forward.

This time, I didn't care about staying silent. This time, I yelled at the top of my lungs, letting out a war cry as I sped towards them, brandishing my sword in my left hand. Eamryel managed to shoot a third before he resorted to his sword. He parried an attack on the left, but missed another coming from the right, catching the sword in his side.

"Eamryel!" I roared.

A loud buzzing started in my ears as a feeling of pure serenity stole over me. My eyes were on the enemy, ready to strike a deathly blow to Eamryel's back. All thoughts ceased to exist, and before the man knew what had happened, my sword pierced his chest. His weapon fell to the ground harmlessly—as did he, dragging my sword with him.

Four down, more to go.

"We need to ride," I told Eamryel.

He nodded, a painful grimace stretching his features into an ugly mask of contempt. With one arm around his ribs, he grabbed the reins and nudged his horse to a trot first, then a gallop. From the way he was swaying in the saddle, I could tell he wouldn't be able to keep this on for long, so I rode up next to him.

"Ride with me," I offered, making a grab at his reins to stop both horses. "You can't ride on like that."

Eamryel looked up at me, pain suffusing his eyes, mouth set in a grim line. With trembling hands, he picked up his bow and nocked an arrow.

I frowned. "What are you doing?"

"Giving you time."

"For what?"

His lips pulled up into a sneer. "You can be such a dimwit at times, Imradien. Get to the ship. Don't look back."

"What about you?"

"I'll hold them off as long as I can," he said, hissing through his teeth.

"I won't let you do this on your own," I snarled, leaning over to grab his sword.

Before I could reach it, he pointed an arrow at my chest. From this close, it would be lethal.

"You'll do no such thing," Eamryel said, his voice deadly calm. "Get to the ship. Tell the Captain you're my plus one and sail for Zihrin. Once there, go to Y'zdrah, find the man they call Elay, and you'll find her."

I frowned. "That sounds almost too easy."

"Don't let his appearance fool you," he replied. "He's not to be trusted."

Before I could ask anything else, he turned around and nudged his horse into the direction of our enemy.

"Ride, Tal! Find her!" he yelled. "For Ilvanna!

His last words came out as a battle-cry and I couldn't help but respond in kind, exhilaration coursing through my body as I nudged Magavin into a gallop. I looked over my shoulder to find Eamryel shooting arrow after arrow as the enemy bore down upon him. Soon, he would have no arrows left, and with his injury, he'd barely be able to wield a sword. A heavy pressure settled on my chest when it occurred to me fully what he was doing.

The grissin's sacrificing himself. For me. For her.

Clenching my jaw, I urged Mag to go even faster, only occasionally glancing over my shoulder to see how many were in pursuit. Eamryel was no longer in sight by then, and I had no way of knowing if he had at all survived. What I did know was that a sizeable portion of the twoscore men following us were now pursuing me, although they were mere specks in the distance.

Zihrin. Y'zdrah. Elay.

I repeated the words over and over in my mind, in part because I was afraid I would forget them, in part to keep my mind off the pain blossoming in my shoulder to something that was close to unbearable.

Breathe in. Breathe out. Repeat.

In the distance, the sea was turning orange as the setting sun slowly sunk on the horizon. I could barely make out the beach, but it was there. Risking a glance over my shoulder, I saw the enemy was gaining on me, but they were still far enough away to not be a threat—yet.

"Come on, Mag," I whispered. "Last push."

Sure enough, the thoroughbred stallion picked up speed as if it was nothing. Its hooves drummed the ground rhythmically, and for a brief moment, I felt like I was flying. For a brief moment, I could taste freedom.

By the time Mag and I arrived at the beach, the sun cast a deep red glow over the sea, setting it alight as if it were on fire. I would have to make my way to the ship in the dark, but at this distance, its lights made it hard to miss. After I dismounted, I undid the straps of the bridle, and took it off, followed by the saddle. Resting my head against Magavin's neck, I stroked its nose.

"Thank you, *mahnèh*, for getting me this far. It's time to go home now."

I whacked him on his rump and watched as he took off at a trot, whinnying into the evening air. Slinging my saddlebags over my non-injured shoulder, I stumbled the last few feet onto the beach, my eyes surveying the area. Just like Eamryel had promised, there was a rowboat waiting for us—for me, I corrected myself. All I had to do was turn it over, push it into the water, and row over to the ship in the distance.

Let's hope the Captain won't turn me in then.

I'd barely gotten the boat onto its good side, ready to push it into the sea, when footsteps crunching in the sand behind me alerted me. Without looking back, I tossed my saddlebags into the boat, but not before I slipped the dagger from where I'd stashed it, and pushed the boat until it was just loose from the sand.

I maybe had a minute—two if the sea was doing me any favours.

"In the name of *Tari* Azra an Ilvan," a man whose voice I knew only too well sounded from behind me. "Talnovar Imradien, you are hereby arrested."

I turned slowly. "Why did it have to be you, *verathràh?*"

"If you come without putting up a fight," Haerlyon said, "the *Tari* will grant you your life."

"Please," I said with a heavy sigh. "Kill me then. I'm done playing her *nohro* deranged games."

Haerlyon stilled at those words, caught off guard by my answer most likely, and looked momentarily confused.

A moment was all I needed.

With the last bit of strength I had left, I jumped him. Surprise settled on his face, but only momentarily, and he recovered himself quickly. He caught me and snapped the arrow protruding from my back by accident. A howl of pain escaped my lips and the sudden flare of pain dizzied me. It was all the time he needed to wrap his arm around my neck firmly, but not enough to choke me. His closeness pushed the remainder of the arrow through the other side. Grinding my teeth kept me from screaming like a wounded animal.

"Your temper never has been your best asset." Haerlyon said snidely. "And I never thought you'd stoop this low, but I suppose you were bound to go back where you came from one day."

"It was a setup and you know it," I hissed.

All I needed was a moment for him to be caught off guard to get out of this. The knife in my hand felt heavy, but I kept it flat against my wrist. It would be my only chance.

"Traps only work if the prey is oblivious to everything around him, its focus solely on what it desires most. You were easy prey, Imradien."

His grip relaxed, but only slightly.

The dagger slid into my hand and I drove it into his side

without thinking twice. Haerlyon's hold around my neck released and he staggered back, clutching the protruding blade. I watched blood seep through his fingers for only a second, before turning around and dashing for the skiff bobbing forlornly towards the ship in the distance. Cold water wrapped its icy tendrils around me in a successful attempt to steal my breath. My body tensed and for a moment I wasn't sure I'd be able to make it.

Keep going. Almost there. You must get there.

Somehow, I managed to reach the skiff, hauled myself over the side, wrapped my hands around the oars and started pulling with every bit of power I still had, trying my best to ignore the uncontrollable shivers wracking my body. Some men had followed me into the water, but their armour was too heavy to continue their pursuit.

"You will never be able to return, Talnovar!" Haerlyon howled. "You are hereby exiled from Ilvanna, as decreed by the *Tari*."

My lips quirked up in a wicked grin, my voice audible only for me. "We shall see, *verathràh*. We shall see."

Once I was far enough out of reach, I pulled at the oars, biting back the intense pain consuming me. I had to continue. The ship was close enough, its lights a beacon of hope in the distance. Voices in song accompanied by an upbeat tune travelled across the silent waters in invitation to its merriment. All I had to do was grab the oars, pull, and keep on pulling until I reached that floating death trap. The thought alone made me nauseous, and it was then I realised I was already on a boat out at sea. With a grimace, I grabbed the oars, hissing at the pain in my shoulder, and rowed as if my life depended on it.

Maybe it does.

Glancing over my shoulder, the ship grew on the horizon and as it did, trepidation coursed through me. What if I didn't make it? That ship was my only way to finding Shal. If I'd miss it, if it would sail off without me… Gathering my wits, ignoring the pain, I continued dragging the oars through the water, listening to the words of the song as they drifted towards me, a steady rhythm driving me to my goal.

So close.

By then, the pain in my shoulder was pure agony, and I wasn't sure how much longer I could keep going. My hold on the right oar was slipping more and more often, and I cursed.

Last chance, Imradien.

A sudden spell of dizziness overwhelmed me, and the last thing I remembered before everything went black was hitting my head on the side of the boat followed by a blinding pain and a vaguely familiar voice in my mind.

Rest, child. You're safe now.

EPILOGUE

HAERLYON

"You've done an outstanding job, *shareye*," Azra said, watching me while lounging on the throne.

Mother's throne.

Straightening my shoulders, I inclined my head, awarding her my easy grin—the one that didn't come as easy as it used to. I watched as she deliberately cleaned each nail with the small knife she'd once gifted my sister.

"But I cannot forgive you for letting Talnovar go." In one rapid movement, she turned and sent the knife flying in my direction.

I dodged it with ease, but judging by the grunt behind me, one of the guards standing there had been too slow.

That's what you get for dozing on the job, khirr.

"He outsmarted us, *Tari*," I replied, inclining my head in a gesture of apology without taking my eyes off of her. "Not to mention the fact he had help."

She perked up at that, eyes narrowed. "Help?"

With a flick of my wrist, I motioned for my men to bring forward our captive. He'd barely made it out alive, and only because I had refused to let my men kill him. He had answers—

answers we wanted, answers that *I* wanted. If it had been up to me, I wouldn't have brought him here at all, but after losing Talnovar, I had to appease her somehow, and he just happened to be the next best thing. Besides, Azra's men knew about him, so if I hadn't brought the captive in, they would have.

Leaning forward on her throne, she watched as the guards dumped the captive in front of her feet, but when I pulled the hood off his face, the response wasn't what I expected.

"You!" she hissed, laying eyes on Eamryel, who still looked the worse for wear despite having seen a healer. "How *dare* you return!"

His lips pulled up in a weak smile, eyes blazing. "My exile was lifted the moment Arayda died, much like yours was after your mother died. Or had you forgotten?"

Disdain marked her features upon hearing his words, but the expression was gone as quickly as it had appeared. She composed her features rapidly, instead watching him with a radiant smile as she rose to her feet.

"Of course I hadn't forgotten," she purred. "Honestly, I'm glad to have you returned to the palace."

The tone of her voice sent chills down my spine, and judging by the look on Eamryel's face, down his too. This woman had no scruples whatsoever, and her mood was as changeable as the weather. One moment, she was a calm breeze with a hint of warmth as if predicting summer, the next she was a full-blown storm ready to tear apart anything in her way.

Right now, it was anyone's guess which way she'd go.

I stood back, hand hovering on the hilt of my sword in case things turned nasty. Eamryel's eyes rested on mine, and it took me all of my willpower to remain impassive, staring back without remorse.

"Glad, are you?" Eamryel asked, lips quirking up. "Such a nice sentiment, *Mother.*"

Azra stilled beside me, paling beyond the point of ivory to

something more translucent. My gaze snapped to Eamryel, who was watching her with his tell-tale smirk on his face.

"Cat got your tongue, *Mother*?"

She looked ready to lunge at him, but managed to compose herself and stay exactly where she was.

"I have no idea what you're talking about."

He laughed at that—a loud laugh reverberating through the throne room. If I didn't know any better, I'd have called it maniacal.

"Stop the charades," Eamryel said with a derisive snort. "We both know the truth, and there's no point in beating around the bush. I'm here. You're here. Now what?"

Her posture and the lethal look on her face suggested Azra was getting ready to pounce on him, and I wouldn't be able to stop her if she did, so instead I stepped forward and back-handed Eamryel.

"You do *not* speak to the *Tari* that way," I growled. "Next time, I'll have your tongue."

Eamryel smirked. "Kitten got claws, huh?"

I glared at him. He returned the look unfazed. Azra began pacing in front of him, making a steeple of her fingers. I didn't need to look at her to know she was trying to come up with a way to deal with him.

"Take him to a cell," she ordered. "He and I will talk later."

From the way she hesitated on the word talk, I knew she meant something else. With a stiff nod, I hauled Eamryel to his feet, drawing out a grunt of pain.

"I'll personally see to it, *Tari*."

She awarded me a dazzling smile. "Do come back when you are finished with him? We have business to discuss."

"As you wish, *Tari*."

With my hand on his shoulder, I propelled Eamryel out of the throne room none too gently. Only when I was sure we weren't being followed did I yank him into another direction.

"You weren't supposed to be back yet." It took everything I had not to yell at him.

Despite being hidden well away in one of the towers, far enough from prying eyes and curious ears, I couldn't risk it. Not now.

"Yeah well," Eamryel grumbled, rubbing his unshackled wrists. "I hadn't planned on coming here either, but your men were quite persistent."

I scowled.

Eamryel leaned back against the wall, a grimace on his face as he folded his arms across his chest. Pacing up and down, I rubbed the back of my neck, hissing at the sharp pain in my side. The injury Talnovar had left me as a parting gift hadn't been lethal, but it was *nohro* uncomfortable.

"Please tell me you were successful?"

"Not entirely," he began, continuing quickly as I opened my mouth to snap at him, "but I've been able to set things in motion, at least."

I released a sigh I hadn't realised I was holding, closing my eyes for a brief moment as if it would make it all go away. Opening them, I found Eamryel looking out the single window of the tower, his eyes distant, his mind clearly processing something. A part of me wasn't sure I wanted to know what was going on inside his head.

They called me a schemer, but I could learn a thing or two from him.

As I went to stand beside him, staring out the window to the training fields below, my mind began to take a leap into the abyss of memories. I quickly turned away and shut that part of my mind where I stored them. Eamryel was looking at me with his head slightly tilted, curiosity in his eyes.

"What do you reckon our odds are?" I asked, putting every ounce of authority I felt into my voice so it wouldn't wobble.

"Depends on how good that *Anahràn* is in following instructions," he replied. "I'd say it's a throw of the dice."

I grimaced.

"Does she know?" Eamryel asked at length.

"Not that I know of."

He nodded. "What about my father?"

"Haven't seen him around much," I replied. "He comes and goes. Where to is anyone's guess."

"Best bring me to that prison cell, *Zheràn*," he said, glancing out the window. "Before it's all been for naught."

"She'll hurt you."

"Nothing I can't handle," he replied with a smirk, although the wobble in his voice betrayed he didn't quite believe it himself.

I inclined my head and returned the shackles to his wrists.

Without knowing the rules, shareye, we're all pawns in a game. Learn them, and you'll beat the player.

More of Shalitha and Talnovar in book 3 of the Ilvannian Chronicles.

ILVANNIAN CHARACTERS

TARI ARAYDA AN ILVAN, Queen of Ilvanna.
TARIEN SHALITHA AN ILVAN, daughter of Arayda. Princess of Ilvanna.
ZHERÀN EVANYAN AN ILVAN, first born son of Arayda. General in the army.
HAERLYON AN ILVAN, second son of Arayda. General in the army.
AZRA AN ILVAN, sister of Arayda. Queen of Ilvanna.
GAERVIN AN ILVAN, husband of Arayda. *Deceased.*

OHZHERÀN CERINDIL IMRADIEN, General of the army. Father of Talnovar.
ANAHRÀN TALNOVAR IMRADIEN, Captain of the Arathrien. Son of Cerindil.
LEYANDRA IMRADIEN, mother of Talnovar and Varayna. *Deceased.*
VARAYNA IMRADIEN, sister of Talnovar. *Deceased.*

YLLINAR AROLVYEN, noble. Father of Eamryel, Nathaïr and Caleena.
EAMRYEL AROLVYEN, noble. Son of Yllinar.
NATHAÏR AROLVYEN, noble. Daughter of Yllinar. Betrothed to Evanyan an Ilvan.
CALEENA AROLVYEN, Daughter of Yllinar. Half-sister to Nathaïr and Eamryel. *Deceased.*

FEHREAN LAHRYEN, noble. *Anahràn* in the army. Father of Amaris.
SYLLAHRYN LAHRYEN, noble. Wife of Fehrean. Mother to Amaris.
AMARIS LAHYREN, noble. Son of Fehrean.

CHAZELLE SERATHYR, noble. Leader of the Ilvannian Council.
NYA ZETRU, noble. Member of the Ilvannian Council.

ANHANYAH LAELLE, former leader of *Hanyarah* (sisterhood). *Deceased.*
ANHANYAH MEHREAN, leader of *Hanyarah.*
IONE AN HANYA, sister at *Hanyarah.* Araîtiste.

SOREN AN DENA, master healer at the palace.

DAHRYEN AN DENA, master healer. Retired.

ELARA SEHLYN, noble. *Arathrien. Deceased.*
QUERAN PAHLEANAN, noble. Arathrien. *Deceased.*
RURIN TRIQUELLEAN, noble. *Arathri.*
CAERLEYAN VIRS, noble. Arathrien.

XARESH NEHMREAN, commoner. Arathrien. Deceased.
SAMEHYA NEHMREAN, commoner. Sister of Xaresh.
KALYANI NEHMREAN, commoner. Mother of Xaresh.
TYNSERAH NEHMREAN, commoner. Sister of Xaresh.
GRAYDEN VERITHRIEN, commoner. *Àn* in the Ilvannian Army.
CEHYAN NE HIRAEN, commoner.

OTHER CHARACTERS

Therondian Characters

HARELDHEAN, Therondian farmer.
LIYELURAH, daughter of Hareldhean.

Zihrin Characters

Y'zdrah

KHAZMIRA, Shalitha's friend.
ELAY È REHMÀH /ELAY IHN GAHR, Akynshan of Y'zdrah.
Prince of Kyrintha.
MARAM È REHMÀH, Elay's twenty-sixth wife.
ZIRSCHA È REHMÀH, Elay's first wife.
YMAHRA È REHMÀH, Elay's seventeenth wife.
THE GEMSHA, Master of the whorehouse. Shalitha's Master.
RHANA, Elay's Captain.
VANYA, herb seller in Y'zdrah.

Portasâhn

PRISHA, homeless girl.

Mountain people

DÛSHAN, leader of the mountain people.
SAHAR, daughter of Dûshan.

Kyrintha

KEHRAN IHN GAHR, King of Kyrintha. Half-brother of Elay.
NAÏDA IHN GAHR, sister of Elay.
JEHLEAL IHN GAHR, brother of Elay.
NAHRAM IHN GAHR, brother of Elay.

ILVANNIAN PANTHEON

AESON, God of music, arts, and medicine.
ARRAN, God of fire, inventions and crafts.
ESAHBYEN, God of war, violence and bloodshed.
ESLANDAH, Goddess of wisdom, knowledge and reason.
NAVA, Goddess of love and passion, pleasure and beauty.
RAWEND, God of travel, communication and diplomacy.
SAVEA, Goddess of harvest, nature and seasons.
SEYDEH, God of water and seas.
VEHDA, Goddess of hunt, protection, and the moon.
XANTHIER, God of law, order, and justice.
XIOMARA, Goddess of life, marriage, women, and childbirth.
XARALA, Goddess of death, darkness and loneliness.
ZORAY, Goddess of hearth and home, and family.

ZIHRIN/KYRINTHAN PANTHEON

ALEYA, Goddess of harvest, nature and seasons.
BEAHDEH, God of music, arts, and medicine.
DERANA, Goddess of hunt, protection, and the moon.
FAYRA, Goddess of life, marriage, women, and childbirth.
GHAYETH, God of water and seas.
HEZA, Goddess of death, darkness and loneliness.
KEHMARI, Goddess of hearth and home, and family.
LAROS, God of war, violence and bloodshed.
LEYALLEH, Goddess of love and passion, pleasure and beauty.
MEDHA, Goddess of wisdom, knowledge and reason.
RESHAD, God of travel, communication and diplomacy.
SAQIB, God of fire, inventions and crafts.
YDRES, God of law, order, and justice.

ILVANNIAN GLOSSARY

Royal terms

TARI, Queen
TARIEN, princess
ARATHRI, Queen's guard
ARATHRIEN, Princess' guard

Military terms

OHZHERÀN, General of the army
ZHERÀN, General
INZHERÀN, Lieutenant-general
IMHRÀN, Colonel
INIMHRÀN, Lieutenant-colonel
MAHRÀN, Major
ANAHRÀN, Captain
SVERÀN, Lieutenant
ÀN, Men-at-arms

Sisterhood

HANYARAH, sisterhood
ANHANYAH, leader of the sisterhood
HANIYA, sister

Brotherhood

DENAHRYN, brotherhood
DENA, brother

General

ARAÎTH, tattoo; the size depends on what class someone is born into
ARAÎTIN, feast held in honour of the one receiving their full Araîth
DIRESH, porridge
DOCHTAER, daughter
IÑAEIQUE, a sense of tranquillity obtained through specific moves
INÀN, a pawn in Sihnmihràn
IRÌN, lord(s)
IRÀ, lady(ies)
ITHRI, an alcoholic beverage of vanilla, often drunk with oranges and ice
KHIRR, idiot (m)
LYADRIN, beggar

MAHNÈH, my friend
MEY, my
OUKOUROU, heavy, hallucinating drugs
PEHRÎN, hopscotch
QIRA, idiot (f)
RUESTA, rest
SALLELLES, seals
SEHVELLE, drugs similar to weed
SEVAETHTAER, projections of the Gods.
SHAREYE, my dear/my love
SIHNMIHRÀN, a strategic board game similar to chess
SIHRA, miss
TAHRASH, an herb used as anti-conception
VERATHRÀH, traitor
CIRTAE, Deja vu

Expletives

GRISSIN, bastard
HEHZÈH, bitch
NOHRO AHRAE, damnit!

ZIHRIN GLOSSARY

Royal terms

AKYNSHAN, prince

General

AMISHA, my lady. Miss
CAMELLE, camel
CH'ITI, porridge
GEMSHA, whoremaster
HARSHÂH, wedding
Ì, and
KEFFAH, coffee
K'YNSHAN, palace
MISHAN, my lord. Sir
MITHRI, my dear. My love
SA'ANEH, spa
TALEH, calm

HIJRATH, a garment worn by women to cover their hair
YGR'ETH, feast
ZRAYETH, whore

Expletives

KOHPÈ, fuck

Places

VAS IHN, safe place where women are trained as spies, assassins etc.

FROM KARA

Dear Reader,

I would like to thank you for taking time to read Dance of Despair, the second installment of The Ilvannian Chronicles. I hope you enjoyed reading it as much as I enjoyed writing it, even though it did give me a headache at times. There have been moments where I seriously doubted myself, and the story, but I'm glad I persisted and got to share it with you. After all, you, my readers, are what I'm doing this for.

As of yet, I do not yet know when book three will be out. I have vague ideas. But I won't leave you hanging! If you follow me on Instagram and Facebook, you will be kept up-to-date on my daily activities. If you sign up for my newsletter on my website www.karasweaver.com, not only can you download the prequel to Crown of Conspiracy and Dance of Despair for free, you will also receive a snippet of a story each month, and you'll be the first to know about upcoming releases, cover reveals and all that.

Before you go, I'd like to ask you one more thing. If you enjoyed Dance of Despair, please consider leaving a review on Amazon and/or Goodreads. As an Indie author, your review is invaluable to me. Thank you in advance for taking the time.

Until next time, and happy reading.

Love,

Kara

ACKNOWLEDGMENTS

Oh boy, where do I start. I suppose that would be with Natalie, my kick-ass drill-sergeant of a friend, cover artist and formatter. How often I haven't yelled and cried in her inbox because something didn't work out, or because I was freaking out over something trivial. Thank you so much for being my critique-partner, my soundboard, and my lifeline in this author world. Thank you most of all, for being my friend.

Dance of Despair would not have been where it was without Jodie and Cassidy who have read my snippets over and over again to fine tune it. I couldn't have asked for better beta readers. Thank you for reading everything I throw at you, for yelling at me, calling me evil, for loving my characters, for cheering me on, and for being there when self-doubt rears its ugly head. Thank you for being my friends.

Jeroen, thank you for the endless amount of pictures showing the mistakes I've made. Always nice to wake up to a tonne of WhatsApp messages. Thank you for pointing them out, and for discussing things at the start of the book which absolutely needed some adjusting!

Ciara. You were probably one of my very first fans, and for

that alone I cannot thank you enough. In this case, however, I want to thank you for being an invaluable beta reader, for providing me with insights I desperately needed, and for making me laugh at your comments as I went through my edits.

Michelle, for your help and insight on marketing. I hate that side of things with a passion! Andre and Courtney, thank you for betareading.

Then there is Douglas. Thank you for going through a pretty much last-minute round of edits/advice. I really do think you helped tighten the story. Thank you so much for your invaluable insight and your help.

Last but not least, to Saskia and Anita, for going to the spa with me whenever we feel like it. Loads of ideas for Dance of Despair were born there!

P.S. My husband and kids are obviously the best of all for allowing me to pursue this dream.

ALSO BY KARA S. WEAVER

The Ilvannian Chronicles

In reading order

Song of Shadows (available for subscribers)

Crown of Conspiracy

Dance of Despair

ABOUT THE AUTHOR

Kara S. Weaver currently lives in the Netherlands with her husband, two children, and Kita the cat. English teacher by day, and aspiring author by night, Kara has always loved creating fantasy worlds and characters. Not all of them have found their way on paper yet.

When not teaching or writing, Kara is well versed in the mysterious ways of binge-watching Netflix, and speed-reading books. Occasionally, she whips out her DSLR camera to take pictures, but those days are far and few between.

If you would like to share your thoughts, ideas, or comments on Crown of Conspiracy, Song of Shadows, or Dance of Despair feel free to contact Kara S. Weaver at: weaver.kara.s@gmail.com .

facebook.com/authorkarasweaver

instagram.com/kara_s_weaver

Printed in Great Britain
by Amazon

64143626R00298